8/05 5.99

COMANCHE RAIDERS

Once again the Comanche warriors slid behind their racing ponies making themselves difficult targets. This time one of their muskets barked from under the neck of a stampeding horse, and the bullet slapped David's wagon. David ducked, his heart racing, and slid deeper into his hole, scarcely daring to peer over the edge of the box.

For the second time the warriors had ridden close to the caravan without drawing a shot and had raced back to safety. Now the whole war party, encouraged by the lack of resistance, shouted and whooped and nerved itself for the coup de grace.

A teamster near David's wagon yelled, "I don't care what anyone says! This time I'm gonna shoot!"

How could anyone not shoot? David rested his piece on the box, snugged the butt to his shoulder, and prepared to die.

BOOK YOUR PLACE ON OUR WEBSITE AND MAKE THE READING CONNECTION!

We've created a customized website just for our very special readers, where you can get the inside scoop on everything that's going on with Zebra, Pinnacle and Kensington books.

When you come online, you'll have the exciting opportunity to:

- View covers of upcoming books
- Read sample chapters
- Learn about our future publishing schedule (listed by publication month *and author*)
- Find out when your favorite authors will be visiting a city near you
- Search for and order backlist books from our online catalog
- Check out author bios and background information
- Send e-mail to your favorite authors
- Meet the Kensington staff online
- Join us in weekly chats with authors, readers and other guests
- Get writing guidelines
- AND MUCH MORE!

**Visit our website at
http://www.kensingtonbooks.com**

THE ROCKY MOUNTAIN COMPANY:

FORT DANCE

RICHARD S. WHEELER

PINNACLE BOOKS
Kensington Publishing Corp.
http://www.kensingtonbooks.com

PINNACLE BOOKS are published by

Kensington Publishing Corp.
850 Third Avenue
New York, NY 10022

All Kensington Titles, Imprints, and Distributed Lines are available at special quantity discounts for bulk purchases for sales promotions, premiums, fund-raising, educational or institutional use. Special book excerpts or customized printings can also be created to fit specific needs. For details, write or phone the office of the Kensington special sales manager: Kensington Publishing Corp., 850 Third Avenue, New York, NY 10022, attn: Special Sales Department. Phone: 1-800-221-2647.

Pinnacle and the P logo Reg. U.S. Pat. & TM Off.

First Printing: September 2002
10 9 8 7 6 5 4 3 2 1

Printed in the United States of America

CHAPTER 1

May, 1842

Guy Straus couldn't sleep. The moist night air of St. Louis glued his nightshirt to him. He surrendered at last, and rolled out of the fourposter, taking care not to disturb Yvonne. Her arm flopped into the place where his thickening body had been, probed the hot sheet, and withdrew.

He dressed quietly in the dark, knowing where to find everything. He didn't bother with his waistcoat or a frock coat, not on a steaming spring night. He padded gently down the creaking stair, taking care not to awaken Clothilde or the slaves, and let himself out the front door and onto Chestnut Street, where the hum of crickets assaulted him. He walked quietly next door to the red brick offices of Straus et Fils, and climbed the four iron steps.

He entered, bolted the polished door behind him, and padded through the silent salon toward his office at the west side of the building, past beeswaxed chairs and tables and desks so familiar that he could have negotiated the obstacles blind. Within his office, he settled into his quilted leather chair. He always came to his office when he was troubled, and always found solace there, some mystical continuity with his father, who had sat in the same chair for most of a lifetime and built an empire.

More than a damp nightshirt and steamy air had driven him here at some small hour of the night. He had a momentous decision to make, and could delay no longer. It had been a grinding worry as mean as a toothache. Sometime in the next two months he'd *know. Maybe.* In this business the news came in fragments, miserable bits and pieces, and sometimes it never came at all. If all went well, his partners would arrive in June for the first annual meeting of Dance, Fitzhugh, and Straus—and then he'd know. They'd made a profit in buffalo robes, or they hadn't. Even now, he supposed, the wagon train from Fort Dance was on its way—with or without buffalo robes.

He sank deep into the plush leather, finding the murky office reassuring even though little was in the strongbox. Oh, he had had a few bits of news. He'd gotten a couple of letters from his younger boy Maxim, up there on the Yellowstone at the new post run by Brokenleg Fitzhugh. And more news from that splendid man, Joe LaBarge, the master of the packet that had toiled its way clear up into that wild northland. And still more tidbits from his rival, old Pierre Chouteau, Pierre *le cadet,* who plotted the destruction of Guy's new robe-trading company from his grimy lair down on the levee.

They'd made a terrible miscalculation last spring, supposing they could commandeer the abandoned Fort Cass on the Yellowstone and begin a trade with the Crows there. Chouteau had somehow gotten wind of it and reoccupied the post, forcing Brokenleg Fitzhugh to build one of his own, with a handful of men, in the worst circumstances.

Guy sighed. The Yellowstone half of the enterprise would be a loss. Old Pierre had whipped him. Whatever had inspired him to get into a trading battle with a giant company like that? Doubts swarmed through him; doubts about the competence of Brokenleg, who drank too much. And doubts about the conduct of his Cheyenne wife, Little Whirlwind, who despised the Crows, along with most other tribes not her own. How did he ever get himself involved with a rough mountain trapper and a mean-tongued woman like that? Why did he ever abandon the safe, conservative arbitrage and brokering business his father had built in frontier St. Louis? Straus et Fils had earned the family a comfortable income for two generations, exchanging gold and silver and Spanish reals and dollars and pesos and bank notes for whatever was of value where money and credit were scarce. He sighed, remembering how he had gotten involved with a pair of rough mountain men the year before.

Jamie Dance. Guy smiled in spite of himself. It was up to his other partner out there on the Arkansas River to bail out the company—Jamie Dance, whose wife, Teresa María, was the daughter of the alcalde of Taos. Jamie Dance, comic and sociable, not a bit like solemn Brokenleg Fitzhugh. Jamie never stood up if he could find a wall or post to slouch against. And he was a born trader. He didn't work hard, but then, he had native abilities that enabled him to slide through life without a lot of toil. Jamie had ridden out the Santa Fe Trail, along with Guy's older son David and a gaggle of teamsters driving a long line of ox-drawn wagons filled with tradegoods, to build a new trading post. From it, Jamie was competing with the other fur-trading giant, Bent, St. Vrain, and Company, and doing it within a few miles of Bent's Fort on the Arkansas River.

Guy had gotten a few notes from David, brought by travelers on the trail, and the news coming from the edge of Mexico hadn't been quite so devastating as the news drifting from the Yellowstone Country. But it was bad enough. They didn't expect to trade robes with the Southern Cheyenne, not with the Bent family intermarried with them. No, but there remained the more dangerous trade with the Comanche and Kiowa, and the Jicarilla Apaches too. Maybe, just maybe, lanky lazy Jamie would return with the giant freight wagons laden with bales of good robes that would sell in the East for carriage and sleigh robes, or be sewn into greatcoats. But Guy knew he wouldn't. The Mexicans were always unpredictable. Guy frowned. There'd been bad trouble out in New Mexico.

For reasons he couldn't fathom, he liked Jamie more than Brokenleg. Maybe it was nothing more than Jamie's good humor. But Guy saw something beyond that. Jamie managed people brilliantly, traded brilliantly, forged alliances. And if it came to that, the lanky mountaineer could fight

7

with the best of them. He'd be one to laugh in a brawl — and win the brawl while he enjoyed it.

Guy slid into melancholia again, acutely aware of how much he had invested in this wild enterprise. More capital than Straus et Fils could safely raise and borrow. His boys, too. He feared for them daily, knowing the acute dangers around trading posts and on the long trails. He had a special worry about David: whenever the Mexican governor, Manuel Armijo, wanted to milk Yankee traders or punish them, he marched them into the bowels of a Mexican prison in Durango or Ciudad Méjico, where they rotted their lives away. The thought sent a chill through Guy. David, his bright David, rattling the bars of a miserable *cárcel*.

In the quiet of the night he turned at last to the thing he had come to do. He had a decision to make. Why had he formed the Rocky Mountain Company, keeping two-thirds and giving a sixth each to Dance and Fitzhugh? Yvonne had asked him the same thing over and over, and he hadn't much of an answer. Often, in midnight moments like these, he came here to sit in this important chair and commune with his father; indeed, with his grandfather as, well. They'd established a different business. A familiar one, a safe one for his forebears. Slowly, carefully, they'd become the financial lifeblood of St. Louis, profiting from making markets and exchanging one form of wealth for another. They'd been the essential ingredient in the robust frontier capitalism of St. Louis, where money was scarce and the coin of several nations vied for goods.

He had departed from that when he'd taken over a few years before his father's death. At first, he'd brokered commodities as well — so many robes for so many blankets; so many hanks of beads for so many elkskins. That, at least, was something to be managed in St. Louis and Independence, a natural extension of the financial business of Straus et Fils. But the buffalo company was a radical departure, and as he sat in this historical chair, he felt the disapproval of his father. That's what he'd come to the office for — to justify himself to his stern forebears, who stared at him from their gilded frames on the walls.

8

He couldn't do it. He'd fallen into a trap. He'd plunged into a risky enterprise. In the robe trade, losers were plenty and winners were . . . just two. The Bents and the Chouteaus. At bottom, he knew, the frontier had planted something in him his Europeanized family hadn't received. He himself hungered to plunge into the wild lands, the unknown prairies and mountains out to the west on a mysterious continent. And if the bug had bitten him, it had infected his robust boys all the more, and even his daughter Clothilde. Still, he couldn't justify a great business decision on something as fragile as that — an itch to soar into the unknown world beyond the rim of civilization. No. He'd made a business decision on grounds that now eluded him as he sat in that chastening chair, beneath the hawkish Sephardic face of his father in the unseen portrait above him.

But he knew that was all there was to it. This brawling city, gateway to the unknown West, had cast its net over him and fished him in. Long hours sipping harsh coffee at the Planters House with the great men of the mountains, including his friend Robert Campbell, had infused the passion in him, until he'd lusted for his own company to extract the bonanzas of the wilderness, and for becoming a sort of lord over unseen dominions where no cartographer or surveyor had ever ventured. And in the back of his mind there had always been another private goal — he was going to go West some day and see this amazing wild for himself. He would go to the Yellowstone country, up the endless Missouri; he'd wagon out the Santa Fe trail to Mexico, across the continent.

Not much of a reason for risking the family business, he thought grimly. He'd wrestled with this so many nights that now his thoughts were merely reiterations. And yet he could find no good reason — the kind of reason he could present to the brooding presence in that oil portrait behind him — for doing what he had done. He'd done it because he'd done it.

It had become an agony of waiting. He could trust his captains or not, but he couldn't direct them, not when they'd ventured so far beyond his beck and call. Pierre Chouteau had talked much about that — about the waiting. About sending a costly outfit into the unknown and then waiting for good news and bad, much the way Yankee owners of the ships that set sail out of New England waited for days, months, and years, with their barks in the hands of trusted masters who not only had to know seas and men but the value of goods — all with nary a word of instruction from those who waited and hoped and prayed and cursed.

Well, he thought, he would cut his losses. He peered grimly into the gloom at those portraits of his father and grandfather, and knew they were right, and he'd been a fool. He would end his uneasy alliance with two mountain men whose natures were as alien to him and the Straus family as were creatures from another planet. When they returned to St. Louis for the July meeting of the company, he would have an announcement for them: the Rocky Mountain Company would be dissolved immediately. He thought if he acted swiftly, the hemorrhage would be manageable and Straus et Fils would survive, barely. He instantly felt relief, as if some impossible weight had been lifted from him.

He turned to the portrait behind him. "Papa," he muttered, "you were right. I'll salvage what I can and return to the business of Straus et Fils while I still can."

CHAPTER 2

July, 1841

By the time they reached Council Grove, Jamie Dance had a good idea who the troublemakers would be. There were always one or two in any outfit wagoning out the Santa Fe Trail, and the sooner he dealt with them, the safer the trip would be. This outfit was a small one, a vulnerable one, so it was plumb vital to get it hunkered down and rolling smooth.

He had a dozen teamsters, each responsible for a big Conestoga made by Joseph Murphy in St. Louis, along with six yoke of oxen. In addition, he had a light wagon full of food and camp gear and bedding, drawn by three span of mules. That was the empire of the black cook, Rodriguez, who spoke not a word of English—or professed not to. Jamie had a pair of camp tenders and herders too, men who herded the loose stock—spare horses, mules, and oxen—and did camp chores. Fifteen men, not counting young David Straus, the greenhorn son of his partner in the Rocky Mountain Company. And of course Teresa María, his wife. Or more precisely, Teresa María Antonia Juanita Obregón of Taos, who thought she ruled him. He smiled about that.

That was one of the things he was keeping track of. Fifteen hired men, a partner's son, and a woman. He admitted that Teresa María didn't help matters any. In fact, she added to his tribulations. The pretty little thing with the jet hair, brown eyes, golden flesh, and curvy figure knew exactly how

11

she affected men. If she knew nothing else about herself, she knew that. And exploited it. She plumb drove men dizzy, and made them all—including him—want to fulfill her every whim, especially when she favored them with her scornful smile.

At Council Grove, an oasis of towering trees on a brookside flat a hundred sixty miles from Independence, they were completing their shakeout. Soon they would get down to the business of hauling tons of trade goods across a scorching prairie, through buffalo country—and lands where Cheyenne, Pawnee, Kiowa, Comanche, and Jicarilla Apaches roamed. The shade, cool air, sweet water, and abundant game there made the impending journey seem easy; the green-bellied flies, mosquitoes, and all the other bugs that crawled and stung reminded them it wouldn't be.

This evening, the second one at the grove, he'd have to deal with at least a pair of men. Most of the teamsters had fifty or eighty pounds on him, but that didn't worry Jamie. He'd always been a scarecrow, and he'd always slouched, standing or sitting, as if he didn't have a vertebra in him, and was incapable of erect posture. But the seasoned men—those who knew Jamie or had heard of him—understood that his slouchy frame deceived the unwary. Indeed, he'd learned to use it, learned to be disarming and to conceal his lethal ways until dire moments occurred.

Now was one of those times. He wandered out to the herd, where one of the camp tenders, Phineas Boggs, stood guard, an old fowling piece nestled in the crook of his arm. Boggs had turned out to be a loner, steering clear of the others around the evening fires, a dour presence who had a rank smell about him, as if from decaying feet. Jamie had spotted a malicious stare and an unusual curiosity about the contents of the Conestogas, which Boggs hovered around too much, peering in, studying whatever lay under the Osnaburg wagonsheets stretched over the hickory bows.

One of old Pierre Chouteau's men—or one of William Bent's men—smuggled into the crew. Jamie had expected that. The giant fur-trading outfits never bridled at a little spying and sabotage. He laughed softly, tickled by it all. That

12

sort of stuff was going fullbore back in the beaver days, when it was old Gabe Bridger, Tom Fitzpatrick, and the Sublette boys against Vanderburgh, Drips, and the rest of them working for Astor.

"Well, if I ain't a deaf coyote. It's old Boggs watching the stock," he said.

Phineas Boggs nodded and spat.

"I been watching, Boggs. You're some camp tender. Some herder, too. I think maybe I'll promote you."

"Promote? What's that?"

"Run you up the ladder. Give you new duties."

Boggs peered narrowly at him. "You gonna pay me more?"

"I reckon you'll have your reward when we get there."

"I don't do nothin' free."

Jamie nodded. "You got a lot of experience, Boggs. I got a greenhorn I want to teach the ropes. You know, how to picket the animals on good grass so the stock gets fed and the picket pin stays put, how to herd loose stock, hobble an animal. Make camp comfortable. Keep track, see nothing's left behind. All that. I want you to teach young David Straus the whole thing. He's never been out in the wild and woolies—"

"Straus, him that's the son of the partner?"

"The same."

"Me teach that pilgrim clerk?"

"Yup."

Boggs hawked and spat. "Reckon I could teach that smart-talk overeddycated whelp a thing or two."

"Wish you would. Teach him everything. Make him do it right. Like checking the stock for galls, sore feet. Like getting firewood whenever we find it out on the plains. You know."

"That's the trouble with them rich ones. They don't know how ta work. They don't have a ounce of common sense. Them types are helpless around hyar."

Jamie grinned.

"All right, if you pay me. I hate all the extry work. Can't say as I welcome the company."

"I'll tell David to stick to you like glue, Boggs."

Boggs scratched his belly. "Can't say as I like that much," he muttered. "You better pay me good. I could teach that

13

Abel Cannon a thing or two—punk kid."

Cannon was the other camp tender. Jamie nodded. He did, indeed, want David Straus to learn everything. He also wanted David to keep an eye on Boggs and prevent any minor sabotage, such as losing supplies and tools day after day. He'd talk to David about it shortly.

Council Grove was the jumping-off place, and he had his men hard at work here. Several were cutting spare wagon tongues and axles. Others were chopping kindling and stacking it in canvas slings under the bellies of the Conestogas, making them all look pregnant. One crew was casting balls of various sizes for every rifle in the camp. Hunters out looking for deer. They were a long way from buffalo country, and needed all the meat they could shoot.

Abel Cannon, a runaway apprentice blacksmith with a hankering for the West, was shoeing oxen and resetting horseshoes. Pony Gantt, a teamster good with horses, was helping him. Emilio Rodriguez was sawing deer loin into steaks. Jamie had to be careful about who he put to work with Rodriguez. Wilbert Ames, for instance. The big teamster from Macon, Georgia, from a dirt-poor tenant-farm family, hated blacks and got violent when he drank. Jamie had Ames mauling limbs into firewood.

Two of his teamsters were hunting. Labor Jonas, one of the youngest in the outfit, had been born on a frontier farm near Galena, and was a crack shot. And so was Lyle Black, a Missourian. Black had downed a doe yesterday evening, just an hour after they'd pulled in.

He found Boar Blunt cutting spare wagon tongues, along with Mazappa Oliphant and Philpot Launes. Boar was going to be trouble, and he had to be dealt with *now*. The teamster had always been called Boar—and took no other name—perhaps because he looked like one. Wagon outfits often had a man like this one, sowing trouble. These men never responded to reason; only force.

"Boar."

The man stood up, hefting his double-bitted axe. "How come you got me workin' like this, and that rich pansy doin' nothin'?"

Jamie didn't answer. "You can quit, Boar, if you aren't happy."

"Hell no. I'm stickin' just to see the Injuns scalp you big-shots. Especially the greenhorn." He swung his axe loosely, menacingly.

Jamie slouched closer. Blunt had fifty pounds on him, and a longer reach, but Jamie wanted to stay inside the reach of that hickory axe handle. The others stopped adzing the tongue and watched.

"Boar . . . what do you want?"

"Huh?" The man looked bewildered, and then crafty.

"Boar. You want to see me make mistakes? Bad mistakes, so you and your pals can laugh?"

"You'll make 'em, Dance. By gawd, you don't know so much."

"Hey, Boar. Maybe you want to pound on me. Stomp me into the dirt."

Boar grinned. "I can do that any time, and every man here knows it."

"Boar. Maybe you want to stomp on David Straus. Stomp him and see him go back to St. Louis. You want that?"

Boar snorted. "I give him a day or two more. Then home to mommy."

"Well?"

"Whatdoya mean?"

"That what you want, Boar?"

"You got a big mouth or something?"

Jamie watched the glowering man sort it all out, and then lower the hickory axe handle slightly.

"Any time, Boar. You get busy cutting tongues until you decide what you want. Then come to me and see if I'll give it to you."

Jamie left the big teamster, knowing it all would come to blows sooner or later. Later, he hoped, mostly for David's sake.

For David Straus, the prairie trail west of Council Grove was a new world, one harder to master than English, Span-

15

ish, Latin, or Hebrew. This world, so far from the muddy streets of St. Louis, was full of brutish, hostile men who dismissed him with a glance or made sport of him. Jamie Dance treated him kindly, but the rest didn't, not even Mrs. Dance. It made him feel all alone, desperately alone, out on these endless prairies without a tree in sight and puffball clouds rolling up from hazy horizons.

He'd wanted to come West, dreamed of it, listened alertly as men who'd seen the far shining mountains came to his father's offices or stopped at the Straus home to spin magical tales of black buffalo, sacred albino buffalo, wild Indians and freedom, an aching freedom where anyone could do anything he pleased because there was no one to stop him.

But it wasn't like that on the Santa Fe Trail. He felt his burdens. He was the Straus family eyes and ears, guardian of a mountain of costly trading goods. He was the son of the principal partner, and they all knew it and treated him worse for it. Some of the mountain men called him a porkeater, a mountain term for pilgrim, and in other circumstances he might have been amused by the inappropriateness of it. But it actually rankled. He discovered, too, it wasn't enough to be a quick study. A lot of the lore of the trail had to be absorbed from experience with men, horses, oxen, and wagons. And his usefulness didn't depend on what he could cram into his head, like the languages he'd mastered, but by the skills of his hands and the employment of his aching muscles—and the seasoning that gave a man judgment.

He learned things he never wanted to know, such as camp cookery from a black man who scolded him in whispery Spanish. It got so that he wondered if the hazing was because he wasn't one of them, a gentile. He had no way of knowing. But his father had charged him with a great task: helping the Rocky Mountain Company succeed, at all costs. If it failed, his father warned, so would Straus et Fils. He desperately wanted it to earn great profits. But with each passing day—passing hour almost—he wanted something even more, to prove himself to them. To be a man in their eyes. To show them that he wasn't just a privileged rich boy on a lark, but a hardened trailsman and leader of this outfit.

He didn't know whether he could ever earn that kind of respect, but he reasoned that he would begin by mastering the entire business. Jamie Dance must have thought the same way, and had assigned him, day by day, to experienced men like Pony Gantt to learn everything. How to yoke and unyoke wily oxen. How to watch for sores in their flesh, to check their feet. How to back a yoke into the tugs and chain up the wagon tongue between them.

Once Dance had stepped in to prevent a big blowhard teamster named Boar Blunt from pounding on David. That had humiliated David all the more. He almost wished he'd been allowed to take his licking rather than have the captain protect him. But then, at Council Grove, Dance had told him to learn about herding and camp-tending from a foul-smelling old fool named Phineas Boggs. And he had also given David a mission, the first real responsibility David had acquired.

"Watch the old goat, David. Check every camp tool. Check every wagon. When we leave a place, poke around the bushes for things. Watch him around rivers. He'll think he's teaching you and won't know you're keeping an eye peeled," Jamie had said in a quiet moment.

And that was how it had been since Council Grove. Boggs had spat and piled up the indignities, but in the middle of all that were lessons David could use.

"Now see that cloud thar. The one looks like an anvil. I suppose you dumb city boys never took a notion to look into the sky. That thar's a thunderhead brewin' up, and if she comes thisaway, we got to get this loose stock tied down. She starts flashing lightning and booming on these grasslands, and first thing you know, all the loose stock bolts off. Especially mules. Mules are plumb lightning-mad. Horses can be worse. Oxen, they run a while, but quit. Mules and horses, they start running and they're over the horizon afore you city slicks collect your wits. So here's how you do. You see a storm coming, you git some horses tied down. I mean tied to wagons, not to some picketpin they can pull up. Tie 'em up. If'n all the horses git run off, then we got a hell of a time collecting all our stock on foot. You got that in your haid, city boy? Git horses tied down and hobbled if a storm rises. I guess you're too dumb to know how to hobble a horse. We got a dozen thar, in the light wagon. You'd probably hobble their rear legs and git yourself kicked for it, green as ye be."

David nodded. The old man scattered contempt, but it didn't matter. He'd listened to the man drone on for several days, and when he couldn't bear him anymore, he had befriended the other herder and camp tender, Abel Cannon, who was David's age and was shy rather than hostile. Together, they drove the spare oxen for the Conestogas, the spare mules for the light wagon, and a dozen saddle horses.

Ahead, a teamster walked beside each ox team, cursing the slavering creatures with language David had never heard uttered, his mighty growls and oaths, punctuated by the crack of a tasseled whip. David swore that any teamster could make a prayer sound profane, the way the curses snarled over the oxen. The cook, Rodriguez drove the light wagon, and Mrs. Dance often sat beside him, though she sometimes walked or hiked her skirts and rode, baring golden calves that drew darting gazes from the men.

They rolled into Cottonwood Grove late that afternoon. This grove, like the famous one to the east, had a gravel-bottomed creek running through it, shaded by majestic trees. But David sensed that this place was hotter and dryer, and soon there'd be no trees at all, only the carpets of thin grass rolling toward some omega beyond knowing.

Old Boggs left David to care for the stock alone—a heavy task at the end of each haul. The sweat-soaked oxen slurped water from the crick, and then were turned out upon the lush grasses of the bottoms, under David's careful eye. David picketed horses and mules on good grass, while trying to keep an eye on Boggs, who drifted toward the swaybacked Conestogas and out of sight. David realized suddenly that Boggs had successfully ditched him; he couldn't leave the herd and keep an eye on the snooping old man at the same time. Abel Cannon was tending camp and couldn't relieve him.

Occasionally, through trees and brush, he spotted Boggs poking his head through the puckerhole of a wagonsheet, and examining whatever lay within. It alarmed David. As soon as he could get to Jamie Dance, he planned to say something. Maybe this was the place where the old man would start wrecking the outfit, piece by tiny piece. But Dance was nowhere in sight—probably hunting or scouting ahead to see who was around. And David knew better than to ask a teamster to watch the stock.

David thought he might at least get some sort of look at Boggs in the soft light of the dying day if he busied himself around the wagons. He selected a good saddler and tugged it through the grassy parks to the line of freighters, tied it to one, keeping an eye out for Boggs. He spotted the man at last, crawling out of the farthest wagon. Boggs peered around sharply, saw David, and ambled straight toward him.

"Har now. Ye shouldn't be tying up a nag afore it eats, ye know."

"I . . . I'm sorry. Guess I've got things to learn."

"Say, boy, how comes the company to have a bundle of long sticks in the last wagon. I reckon firewood can be slung underneath."

David thought swiftly and decided to take the risk.

"That's bow wood."

"Huh? Bow wood?"

"Yes. Mr. Dance thought he might do a good robe trade for Osage orange bow wood. There's not a tribe in the West that doesn't prize it. Osage Indians do a trade with it. Osage orange bows, they—"

"You don't need to tell me nothin'. I know about Osage orange. Knew it afore you was born. If Dance's so smart how come the other outfits don't trade with it?"

David shrugged. "They never thought of it, I guess."

"Don't know as how some Injun'd trade a robe for a stick."

"Maybe they won't. But Jamie Dance is guessing they'll snap them up and it'll be a great item—dirt cheap—for us."

"Dirt cheap, eh?"

David nodded.

"Don't make sense to me. Another dumb idear, I reckon. Just thought I'd ask," said Boggs. "You git that horse back on grass if'n you don't intend to starve the brute."

19

"I guess I will. I can tie one or two up later."

"Don't know why. Ain't any storm brewing."

"Mr. Dance said this is where we begin looking out for Indians, Mr. Boggs. I just thought—"

"You let me figger it. You're supposed to larn from me."

David nodded and untied the horse. As soon as he could, he'd find Jamie Dance and tell him. He had an idea, and if it worked, he'd catch old Boggs red-handed.

He picked up a camp axe from the light wagon and headed back to his herd, planning to cut some saplings while he tended the animals. Maybe if he used his wits . . .

CHAPTER 3

They rode past sand hills on the sixteenth day, watching cloud shadows riding the bucking earth. They hit Cow Creek and fought mud and mosquitoes and a muck bottom. That was the eastern edge of the buffalo country, and from there westward, Jamie dreamt of boudins and tongue and hump-meat. They pushed past Round Mound, a hillock bristling with plum trees, and headed for Walnut Creek. And there, resting beside that cold flow, were a thousand times a thousand buffalo.

Jamie, scouting ahead, saw them first, a mass so black it looked, from his distance, as if a grassfire had blackened the bottoms. He reined in his gelding, grateful for their poor eyes and for the hot southwest wind sluicing the stink of his sweated body away. His mouth, unsatiated for all the months in St. Louis, watered with the memory of the mountain man's joy, raw liver sliced hot from the carcass, followed by a drink from the boudins, and then the ambrosia of tongue and hump, the tenderest parts, the portions that put beef to shame.

He studied the country, knowing that where buffalo roamed, so did Indians, whose whole universe had been built upon buffalo meat and hide and bone and horn. He saw none, but that meant little. Puffball clouds spun gloomy shadows across the endless grass, making hills leap. Breezes shook the tall grasses until the whole panorama writhed like a thing alive, hiding the movement he really was seeking. He

21

turned his sweat-soaked horse east to catch the wagons before they hove over the crest of the prairie and sent the giant herd thundering off, like a rumbling storm.

"Buffler," he said to his lead teamster, Lyle Black. "Over the hill. Stop below."

Swiftly, word flew back among the wagons. "Buffler! Tongue and hump tonight!"

Jamie wanted only seasoned men for the hunt, men skilled with horses and rifles; men who wouldn't do fool things around a herd of lumbering monsters. Men who knew enough to shoot the cows and let the leathery bulls go. They'd need only one or two for meat before the carcasses rotted; but buffalo were sport. Countless numbers roamed the short-grass country, an inexhaustible army of them.

"Lyle," he said, "saddle up."

The teamster grinned, and ran toward the loose stock to catch a horse.

Jamie picked Pony Gantt, Mazappa Oliphant, and Eggy Willis to run the buffalo. All seasoned men; all men who knew horses and buffalo.

"How come I ain't going?" asked Boar Blunt. "You got something against me?"

"We need good men to hold the teams and defend the wagons. You're a good man with a rifle," Jamie said.

"Bull," Boar retorted.

Jamie ignored him. "Better let your stock graze," he said. "There won't be any grass left at Walnut Creek." He turned to Blake Goodin, the one-armed teamster who had made a few journeys to hell and back. "You're in charge," he said. "Bring on the wagons as soon as we leave. We'll camp on Walnut Creek, if there's grass."

Goodin nodded. He was a man of few words.

But Boar Blunt hadn't finished complaining. "Why didn't you pick Straus for the hunt?" he asked.

Jamie ignored him. This had been going on since West-port, and the best way to deal with it was to ignore it. David was actually coming along fine, working hard, blotting up this new world as fast as any mortal could.

His hunters checked their loads. They held cumbersome

22

mountain rifles, heavy percussion-lock pieces that would be hard to reload on a running horse. Jamie envied the Indian warriors who could drop powder and ball down their trade muskets and seat the charges with a blow of the butt on the pommel without slowing down. He'd never known a white-man who could do it. These horses weren't buffalo-runners, either, trained to veer close to the side of a lumbering cow and then duck away from her deadly horns.

They topped the grassy rise, and before them the prairie swept away toward the coiling bottoms where the buffalos lumbered under a brass sun.

"Jumpin' Jehoshaphat," said Mazappa. "I ain't ever seen the like."

"Must be a million," said Eggy.

"Aw, a few thousand anyway," said Pony Gantt.

"Impossible to know. More'n I can count," said Lyle.

Jamie nodded, and they edged toward the herd. It stretched as far as they could see, south toward the Arkansas River and north around a bend. They were black, except for a few whose summer hair, back of the shaggy muffs around their necks, glinted coppery or tan.

His seasoned men needed no instruction. They spread out and rode slowly, edging as close as they could before the herd's sentinels bawled their alarms and the black regiments rose up, rump first, and thundered away. The furnace wind blistered the hunters' faces and raised sweat in their calico shirts, but sucked their scent away.

At a half a mile, a sentinel cow on the edge of the herd began muttering, and then another snorted, so gently that it seemed no alarm at all, and yet those massive heads pivoted toward them, and a few beasts rolled up on their haunches. Jamie's horse sawed the air with its head, its lips laid back. It had been in a buffalo run before.

They closed to a third of a mile, and the herd took off as if some magical signal had activated each beast. One instant they rested and watched; the next, they bolted into two herds, the main one heading northwesterly up Walnut Creek; the rest southeasterly toward the Arkansas. Every hunter swung south, following the smaller herd. One moment there had been silence; the next, the earth shook beneath them, and a golden haze rose over the fleeing animals, obscuring them.

Jamie kicked the horse, and felt it leap under him and settle into a smooth gallop as it closed on the fringe of the herd. They passed several limping bulls, and some blatting calves, and then Jamie spotted a fine young cow and edged the horse toward her. The cow sensed his pursuit and slid behind a cluster of young bulls. Off somewhere he heard a shot racketing over the roar, and he thought he heard another. He couldn't see any of his men through the boiling dust that stung his face.

The cow veered left, sliding between young stuff, and Jamie kneed his sweating horse toward her, feeling the animal pull hard to close in. It always amazed him that a buffalo cow could outrun most horses. Then, suddenly, he had his shot as the cow slowed momentarily; he lowered his heavy Hawken until the barrel waved at that hat-sized spot just back of the shoulder that would drop an animal. The cow hooked toward the horse just as he shot. A pop. A slight jolt. Misfire. Still, he'd hit her. Blood leaked onto her brown hair, catching dust. Cursing, he kneed his horse toward her, hoping she'd drop. But she didn't. Around him, animals raced, spraying him with dirt and prairie grass and the green flecks of manure which rivered from most of the beasts.

She limped, and he stayed with her for a mile or so, heading somewhere or other And then she seemed to gain strength, as if a shock had passed, and spurted ahead. He reined in his horse and let it blow, feeling it suck air, feeling its ribs expand and contract while he reloaded. Its whole neck had turned black with sweat, and foam soaked its withers.

Sighing, he retraced his way back to the Santa Fe trail, hunting the others, looking for the dark hulks on the ground that marked a successful hunt. He saw none. He let the weary animal walk. The grass had been pounded to nothing, and the earth lay torn and naked under him. Ahead, coming out of a shallow draw, he spotted Lyle Black, and steered toward him.

24

"Shot one in the lights," Black said. "But danged if I can find her."

"You know where."

Black laughed and shook his head.

"Let's go look. I had a misfire. Hit her but she kept on a-going."

"A million buffler and we miss," said Black.

They walked their mounts to a ridge where they could study the whole country, as much as the layering dust permitted. A solemn silence settled over them. Far off, they made out Gantt and Willis, paired up. And not a black carcass in sight.

The four of them connected down in the bottoms.

"You got yours, I reckon," Jamie said to Gantt.

"I did."

"Well, let's go butcher."

"Can't find her."

"We'll look."

"Already did. Same for Eggy here. His horse dodged just as he squeezed, and the shot plowed up his cow's shoulder."

"And none of us stopped to reload and get another, I suppose."

"I figgered I had mine; just had to follow her a piece," Gantt said.

Jamie turned his horse southward, in the general direction of where the herd had splintered into innumerable fragments. They walked their horses quietly, not wanting to tire them more, especially if there were Indians about. Gantt reloaded, not a hard thing at a quiet walk. An hour later, after studying every dark lump on the ruined prairie, they turned back to the trail, chagrined.

"Ten thousand buffler," said Lyle.

"Slow bulls, limping critters, calves, the whole works," said Gantt. "I coulda clubbed a dozen."

"I can taste that tongue," muttered Willis. "It wets my craw, thinkin' on it."

"They ain't far. We'll get some tomorrah," Jamie said.

"Haw!" said Black.

Ahead, the line of sagging wagons snaked down into the

25

bottoms, and Jamie didn't like what he'd be saying to all those buffler-starved men.

Or what Boar Blunt was going to say to him.

Teresa María had mastered English fast, the better to scold Jamie, for he pretended not to understand when she berated him in her own tongue. She spoke English with the staccato throb of Spanish, making the words erupt like rifle volleys. Jamie Dance needed reform, and she had dedicated her life to his improvement. Not until he spoke softly and addressed others politely, like any good charro, would she be content. The only trouble was, he just grinned through every barrage—*Madre de Dios*, he didn't take her seriously!—and always reduced her to a fit of the giggles.

And there he came, across some bottoms where the dust of a thousand times a thousand buffalo still hung in the air, and he had no meat! Oh! She'd married a burro! A *yanqui barrachin! Madre de Dios*, this time he wasn't going to make her giggle.

"Some provider you are!" she cried. "Some *cibolero!* I'm doomed to poverty all my life. Rags. That's what I get for marrying a freckled *yanqui!*"

"Pore thing," he said.

"Don't make a joke of it, you . . . burro. I'm sorry I ever set eyes on you."

He was smiling. The other hunters were trying not to. "I reckon we're stuck with beans again. We plumb got skunked."

"Skunked? What is skunked?"

"That's beans for supper. I suppose I oughter tell old Emilio."

But the Haitian cook had observed it all from his seat on the light wagon. He began clicking. He rarely spoke, but expressed his displeasure startlingly, by clicking his teeth in a way that sounded exactly like dry-firing a rifle, the very sound of a hammer clapping a nipple. This was also his all-purpose horse command, and on hearing it, his mules pushed into their collars and Emilio headed for the river.

"Emilio!" yelled Jamie. "No grass hyar. Git water and

wood, water the mules, and keep a-goin' to grass."

Somehow the cook always understood, even if he never spoke. Teresa María didn't blame him. English was a despicable language. She'd suffered great hardship and pain learning it, but it was one of those things that had to be done, since she'd married a *yanqui*. She sighed, thinking of Estaban Porfirio Dominguez, so fiery and cool, with silky black eyelashes . . . and what she'd missed. She cursed her impetuosity, running off with this burro of a *muchacho*. Too bad the Church didn't allow her two husbands. Or three. Or none. This Jamie was twice too much husband, and a cross to bear. Well, if she bore her suffering bravely, she might become a saint. Saint Teresa María de Taos. If she ever got back to Taos she would tell the padre about her patient, holy suffering. Too bad she would have to wait until after she died to find out if she'd been canonized. If only she could find out beforehand . . . Maybe the pope would grant her a decree while she lived, some parchment she could clutch to her black-clad bosom as she sank away from the world on her bed. Ah, there was something! Teresa María of Taos, beloved patroness of suffering wives, especially ones married to heretics. She sighed. That was not possible. She'd run off with the *yanqui*, and had disgraced herself and her family. *Madre de Dios*, she might never see her father and mother and sisters again!

She spotted that *puerco*, Boar Blunt, approaching, driving his oxen and wagon. Ah, this would be good! The teamster was looking smirky, and was ready to say words to Jamie.

"Water your stock and cross the creek, Boar. We'll camp on grass yonder a mile or two," Jamie said.

Boar stopped his team instead, looking cocky. "Great hunter," he said. "Buncha great hunters. A man needs his meat. Walks all day whippin' ox, gettin' a hole in his belly. Man thinks on buffler, good strong buffler meat. And the head o' the outfit, he don't give a teamster no meat."

"Reckon we'll make meat tomorrah, Boar."

"Tomorrow's not soon enough. This here's a no-good outfit."

"Reckon you could quit, Boar."

27

She knew Boar wouldn't do that. A teamster hired on for the trip, and if he quit no outfit would want him. But his answer surprised her.

"Oh, I could do that. Quit the outfit. Take about half the boys with me. You got cash to pay wages?"

"Oh, no," Jamie said softly. "A man quits halfway, he don't get nothing. You know that."

"Maybe we'll just take it, Dance." The teamster's *cochino* eyes glowed brightly.

Her man unwound his lanky frame, stepped off his horse. He looked fifty pounds lighter than the teamster. She feared for him, knowing what Boar could do. But Jamie just smiled easily, as if this were nothing, and pulled the Arkansas toothpick from its battered sheath at his waist. He drew a line through the dirt before him. Then he stood behind it.

"Care to cross it, Boar?" he asked lightly.

The teamster hesitated. Tackling the captain of the outfit was a serious thing.

"Ever been up in the mountains trapping, Boar? Go to them rendezvous? They're some fun. Trappers, they get to brawlin' like nothing you ever seen. Man, they like to pull each other's ears off. Makin' beaver all year in cold streams does that; turns them into grizzlies."

She knew Boar had been out the Santa Fe trail a few times, but never up in the mountains with those trappers.

"Step acrost, Boar, step lively."

"This don't mean spit," Boar said. "You ain't bluffin' me."

Jamie grinned. She had to admit that grin was infectious. When he grinned the whole world grinned with him. Now he grinned at Boar, his eyes dancing, his slender body loose and poised like a coyote's. He laughed, and the teamsters beside him laughed, caught up in Jamie's strange merriment. Oh that *diablo!*

Something in Boar Blunt wilted, though the man tried to cover it. "I'm sick o' beans. Rotten cook, too. Damn furriners, can't speak nothing. You get buffler tomorrow, Dance, or maybe you'll be—"

"Water 'em and keep on a-goin', Boar."

It always amazed her. Jamie Dance had the devil's eye, it

was true. She swiftly bleooed herself, her small dark hand fly-ing from forehead to breast and across, ending on her heart. She'd married a *diablo* who could do this to a brute—walk on water almost. She blessed herself again, staring at Jamie fearfully. A heretic!

They pressed on for a while more, until they reached grass that hadn't been molested by the giant herd, and there they made a dry camp in a swale out of the ceaseless wind that chapped her face and hands all day, every day. That strange hump called Pawnee Rock loomed to the west, like a beached whale in the middle of the continental steppes.

Emilio clicked and spat and produced a meal of pinto beans, which the men ate silently under his yellow-eyed glare that dared them to complain. He had the unnerving habit of carrying an unsheathed butcher knife in his belt—why he never pricked himself was a topic of endless conversation among the men—and not a few teamsters were certain he'd stick that wicked thing into them if they groused about his cookery.

Jamie had brought a small pyramid tent for their use. She was the only woman in the party and needed her privacy. But she cursed the center pole which wrecked her favorite sleep-ing arrangement, which was to mold herself into his back. Oh, how she loved that part of marriage, and how much she puzzled that they had no *niños*. Jamie was a crazy man at night, and she secretly admitted that at times mad *yanquis* were better than polite caballeros, even if her mad *yanqui* scratched her with the unruly stubble of his face. Ah, the sor-rows of being married to a heretic. Any polite hidalgo would have shaved, with a great lathering of his jaw, the scrape of a blade over blue-black beard.

She waited in the blackness for Jamie to finish his watch at midnight. They'd pierced deep into Indian country, and Ja-mie kept a two-man watch, which changed every two hours by the ticking clock hanging from the camp wagon. She gig-gled. Had Jamie been of nobler mind, he would have rotated the watches with his men, taking the sleep-robbing ones from midnight to two, and two to four, and four to six. But he never did. He just grinned, and took the early watch and gave the harder ones to the rest. He rarely clambered into his bedroll before midnight anyway, because he was too delighted with being alive.

Ah, Jamie! What sins of omission and commission! Or anyway, what privilege! Jamie had never been one to do work he could fob off on others with that wry smile of his. At least he did something to keep *los Indios* at bay. How they'd love to steal the horses and mules! Or a fat ox to eat! Or the things in the heavy wagons! She shivered a little. They were nearing Pawnee Rock, the site of a great battle between the Pawnee and Comanche. That name, Comanche, filled her with dread. No tribe, not even the Apache, had terrorized frontier Mexico more, stolen more burros and horses and women, killed more hombres, tortured more innocent people along this very trail. The Comanche were great torturers. They would bury a man to his neck in sand, then sew his eyelids open so he had to stare at the sun until he died of thirst and blindness and craziness. Or they would stake him down over an anthill and let fire ants drive him mad. Or tie a woman, spread-eagled, to posts set in the ground, and do everything *el diablo* told them to do. And soon the Rocky Mountain Company—and her Jamie—was going to trade with them! *Madre de Dios!*

He pierced the tent opening, and his arrival startled her because she had Comanches on her mind.

"Caramba! Can't you be more careful?" she cried.

He said nothing, but she knew he was unlacing his boots, and soon the tent would reek of his feet. Then he would crawl into his bedroll over on the other side of that pole. She had her own name for the pole. She called it Padre Martinez. Padre Martinez was always making homilies about marriage, and everyone in Taos laughed at him behind his back. Padre had a concubine, but no wife. What did priests know about such things? She thought that was a splendid name for the tent pole. Padre Martinez.

"You should have stood up to that Boar," she said, by way of letting him know of her amorous intentions. "You let them get away with everything."

He laughed softly. "You fixin' to come over here?"

30

"Not until you wash your feet."

"I reckon you'll come anyway and lick 'em clean."

What an insolent thing for him to say. Just like a *yanqui*.

Outside, a coyote yelped off to the north, letting out a sly bark at the North Star. Then another yelped off to the west.

"Well, damn!" he said.

It startled her. Jamie Dance was never profane.

She heard him pull his boots on again, lace them.

"You better git on over to one of them big wagons and lie low, betwixt barrels and crates and stuff," he said.

With that, he picked up his Hawken and slid out into the night again, and she felt chilled.

31

CHAPTER 4

They were out there. Jamie could feel it. That feeling had saved his life more than once in the mountains. He studied the dark, hearing nothing, seeing phantasms in the moonless void. Horse-stealing party probably. Plains Indians rarely got into pitched battles at night — too many spirits of the dead roaming around. But that didn't apply to snatching horses, an enterprise they'd perfected in the cover of darkness.

The wagons had been left in a string, and it was too late to pull them into a corral. Whoever was out there would go for the horses and mules, and let the oxen — the white man's buffalo — go. The oxen were too slow; their flesh too soft for the Indian palate. He didn't know who was on night guard — two of his teamsters, at any rate. He had to find them and start bringing in the picketed horses and mules.

He edged through the grass, nerves taut, wondering when some lithe form would leap out of the night and club him to earth. He didn't know for sure whether he was doing the right thing: he had only to shout and shoot to awaken them all, and maybe frighten the thieves off. And yet he didn't. His experience with men awakened by a shot or shout wasn't reassuring.

"Night guard," he said softly, in a voice that didn't carry.

"Here," came a response.

That was David, and it dismayed him. A greenhorn kid. "Who's the other?"

"Boggs."

He winced. "Pull the picketlines, get the horses and mules

close to the wagons. Tie the lines to the wagons. We got visitors."

"How do you know?"

"Do it!"

He found his own two horses and pulled the pins. He found four mules—he was pretty sure they were mules—on one long picket, and pulled that, too. That was enough. Swiftly he tugged the resisting animals toward the wagons, and tied the lines securely to the wheels.

A coyote yelped—closer then before.

David showed up with two horses.

"Tie them and wake up the rest, quiet-like, a hand on each man. Tell 'em to hurry!"

"Are we going to be—".

"Just do it, and watch your topknot."

The teamsters sprawled in their bedrolls near the wagons, and he watched for a moment as David slid among them, bringing them to life with a clamped hand. Jamie feared that one or another would leap up and slit David's throat, but none did.

Jamie hurried back out again, something crabbing at him. "Boggs!" he hissed, and got no response. It worried him.

A horse snorted, and Jamie knew it was too late to worry about Boggs. Another horse neighed. He ran toward the animals, grabbed one picketline, saw dark forms darting toward him, and retreated toward the wagons, mules thundering and jerking behind him. Something whirred by, silky in the night. An arrow, he thought.

"Coming in," he yelled, just in case one of his men got itchy-fingered. Men stirred around the wagons, fetching rifles, taking cover under boxes.

Horse-stealing parties rarely came on horseback. They stalked their prey on foot, and rode their prey away, herding what they couldn't ride. His experienced men knew that. He reached the wagons and tied the mules to one. He'd brought in most of the mules at any rate.

He found Lyle Black up and armed. "Where's Boggs?" he asked.

"Ain't seen 'im. You got any notion about this?"

33

"Nope. Don't even know where they're comin' from. Tell 'em to git around the wagons and watch both sides."

"Who—"

"Don't rightly know. Git!"

He found David. "You remember where Boggs was last time you saw him?"

"Out there. That's all I know. He called over a couple of times, down the gully a ways, over toward the oxen."

"Okay. You sit here quiet by this wheel and watch these mules. Injun comes in, he won't untie a line, he'll cut it or try to panic the stock. Shoot if you have to, but be careful. And roll after you shoot. They'll pop arrers at the place the gunflash come from."

He wished he'd taken time to instruct David. But he had other duties now. He glanced at his tent, hoping Teresa María had buried herself in a wagon box. He crept toward his men, feeling his stomach churn. No moon caught him, but the night sky vaulted over him, open and starry, and made its own subtle light. Most of them sprawled on the earth, their rifles making a small perimeter on both sides of the line of wagons.

"Who they be?" asked a voice.

"Don't rightly know," he whispered. "They ain't comin' in, not for horse-stealin'. But if they do, don't all shoot at once."

They knew that. He just felt like reminding them. Someone snorted, and it sounded like Boar Blunt.

"Who was guardin'?"

Jamie addressed the unknown questioner. "Phin Boggs and David Straus. Boggs is out there, unless he's here. David's watching the stock we got in."

"How much stock?"

"Eight mules, four horses."

Out upon the grasses, they heard horses whinny and snort, and the delicate pulse of hoofbeats. The lowing of oxen followed, punctuated by bellowing, and the growl of motion.

"There they go," someone said.

He saw shadowy men leap out of the earth and onto freed horses. He tracked one, and shot. Around him, he felt the bark and pulse of other shots. He poured unmeasured pow-

34

der down the warm barrel and rammed a patched ball home, slid a cap over the nipple and aimed again—and saw nothing.

"Let's see what we hit," he said, already knowing the answer. No one was eager to follow, not into that deadly maw. He nerved himself, leaped upward, and trotted out to the pasture, his rifle at the ready. Nothing. These thieves had ghosted in, made off with stock, and rampaged out unhurt. He couldn't spot blood, not on a moonless night. No animal remained. His men trotted up, making him whirl his Hawken around. They stared.

"We got horses to round up the oxen in the morning," Jamie said.

"Less'n they cut the throats of them oxes. They ain't likin' traffic on the Santy Fe trail no more." That was Pony Gantt.

"Will youse shut your mouths? The devils may be around, waitin' to put an arrer in us." That was Boar.

No one spoke. The tautness slowly drained from Jamie, like a departing fever. Only now, in the silence, did he realize how cramped he'd been, his stomach rebelling and ready to chuck his supper. This is the way it always is with a bunch of horse-stealers, he thought, a quick foray and then they vanish. Not even the whisper of the breeze disturbed the black silence.

He pulled his hand off his rifle and stretched his fingers, limbering them. It amazed him how hard he'd clamped the Hawken. Maybe they'd made it without losing a man—if Boggs made it. Boggs . . . The thought of the man crabbed at him. Maybe Boggs was a part of it, paid from Chouteau or Bent coffers. But even as he thought it, a faint rasping rose out of the grass yonder.

"Don't shoot. It's me."

Jamie felt men ease off on their triggers. A moment later the shabby old camp tender crawled in fearfully, while teamsters stared.

"Saw them divils and got me into a ditch and lay flat as a dirt beetle," he said. "Ten, twelve, I saw, glidin' around."

No one spoke. Jamie knew what they were thinking. He was thinking the same thing. Boggs might have tried a little harder to warn the rest, catch some stock and get back to the wagons.

He sighed. Horses and mules lost. They'd probably get the oxen in the morning. Could have been much worse. No man lost.

He reckoned by the dipper it was three, and they would have plenty of waiting to do before dawn. He debated putting them all to forting up, pulling wagons around, putting the picketed mules inside a makeshift corral, digging rifle pits. But he let it go. It was over. This horse raid was like every other he'd experienced, snatch and run. It was almost a game among plains tribes. Well, he'd sit up because he had to. Not a man could sleep anyway. They'd sit up, watch the sun pry away the night, and get rolling in the morning, not too much the worse for it. The loss of the saddle horses hurt the most; it'd cut into their hunting.

Even though the night slid by peaceably, men started at terrors of the mind. Out in the darkness he heard one man cry out and then start cursing softly. Another kept sniffing and blowing his nose. Visions of scalping knives and tomahawks and sizzling arrows and Comanche torture tormented them all. Comanche. They didn't know that, but they'd all assumed the worst. It could have been any of them—Kiowa, Cheyenne, Pawnee. Maybe even Lipans. But he knew every man of them thought of Comanche.

That'll go away with the rising sun, he thought. Let a man see grass and empty horizons, and the ghosts inside him settle down. They'll stretch stiff limbs, gulp down some of the cook's coffee—if there was still water in this dry camp—and slowly lay to rest all the ghosts of the night. He'd put together an outfit of seasoned men, and he knew how trail-wise men would greet the pale light.

Except that's not what happened. When the misty dawn finally gave them vision they saw not empty prairie, but more mounted warriors, than they could count, naked and painted for war, sitting their painted ponies just beyond rifle shot.

* * *

The sight of countless painted warriors surrounding the small caravan made David so tense he could barely breathe. He felt as if bands of steel had clamped his chest. He might die! It was one thing to hear trappers and mountain men talk of narrow escapes, sitting beside his father at the Planters House in St. Louis, the rendezvous of all Western men, quite another to be here on a lonely prairie with fifteen other men and a fortune in trade goods, facing an overwhelming force of Indian warriors.

The seasoned teamsters weren't wasting a second. Two were digging shallow rifle pits with the two camp spades; others were building barriers with saddles, bedrolls, and casks and boxes of trade goods—anything to hide behind, to stop an arrow or ball. Still others were loading a couple of spare company rifles, or making sure all had balls and caps and wads and powder. The Conestogas were too heavy to move by hand, but four men wrestled the lighter camp wagon forward, parallel the others, to protect the stock tied to the big freighters. They weren't defending the long line of wagons, but making their perimeter around the last two and the camp wagon.

Paralyzed, David watched, not knowing what to do.

"Barricade yourself, boy. Front and back and sides. You got no protection from the rear," said Jamie.

The command jolted David into action. He eyed a heavy wagon, and knew at once what he'd do. He swiftly loosened the wagonsheet and rolled it up a foot and tied it, giving him a view in all directions. Then he burrowed into the mountain of goods near the center, and settled there in a wooden fortress, the carbine he scarcely knew how to use resting on the top of crates, his powderhorn beside him, caps and balls in his possibles bag.

And still they didn't come. He watched them with dread, waiting for the terrible moment when these bronzed horsemen would race toward him, their bloodcurdling cries rending the peace. He didn't want to die. So young! But how could sixteen men and a woman repel so many? A hundred. More than a hundred! Last night they'd all thought it had been a horse raid and they'd recover the oxen in the morning.

But not this! They hadn't any water—at least no more than Emilio had eked out for coffee for breakfast—and they were two miles from Walnut Creek. How long could they last before the sun parched them?

"Who are they?" he cried.

No one answered. No one knew.

"Why don't they come?"

Boar Blunt turned back from his barricade, stared at David, hawked and spat. "Seems like porkeaters got to talk all the time," he said.

But Jamie answered. "They haven't got their minds made up, David," he said quietly. "Hyar, take a look." Over the wagon transom, he handed David a brass, field telescope.

Fascinated, David swung the device from warrior to warrior, the bobbing images filling the lens and vanishing again. Some of the warriors lifted their arms skyward making medicine. Others sat their ponies and stared. These were stocky men, wearing very little, scarcely even a feather in their hair, which was more often loose than braided.

"What'm I supposed to see?"

"They got maybe twenty pieces among 'em, David. Trade muskets is all I make out. The rest got to get in awful close to be effective with those bows and arrers."

"But there's so many—"

"Injuns don't much like fightin' if any big number get killed. They like to tempt fate, be brave and all, steal a mess of horseflesh. And they don't much come in a bunch. It's sorta personal bravery that counts. And that's not all. They're probably thinkin' maybe to get them some gifts, make us pay a price to cross their country. They got us hogtied here—they know that. But it's maybe cheaper to get themselves some stuff from us than get a big bunch kilt."

"I'll kill me a few of them red devils," said Boar, who was listening nearby.

Jamie smiled. "Reckon we'll wait and see. I don't want a shot wasted. No sense fighting if we can trade our way out."

"Yellerbelly. I'll shoot the red devils if I can. This here piece can reach a couple hunnert yards farther than their arrers."

38

"You heard me, Boar. We're here to trade for robes if we can, not get into fights."

"Y'always was some coward, Dance."

Jamie Dance ignored him. Some sort of commotion was building off to the south. It looked like an argument. Dance took the spyglass from David and studied it. "Looks like they got a little tiff o' their own, Boar, like us."

David resented Boar's goading, and wondered why Jamie didn't deal with it. A captain needed to impose discipline. An unruly Boar Blunt could put them in even worse trouble. Acidly, he resolved that if he survived this, he would tell his father about Boar, about Jamie Dance's lax ways.

Just then, one of the warriors to the south howled something bloodcurdling into the dawn, and kicked his pony on a slanting run toward the wagons.

"Let him go, boys, and watch for his arrer. I don't want no one shooting. And, David, you watch the other side. We got 'em all around us. They start crowding, let us know."

The pony, a dappled gray mustang, had settled into a hard gallop on a vector that would cut across the rear of the wagon train. The man's howl sang through the quiet air, terrifying in its intensity.

"He's a brave divil," said someone.

"You remember now," Jamie warned.

David desperately wanted to watch the oncoming warrior, who was now being cheered along by howls and bloodcurdling shrieks from all sides. But he could afford only glimpses, and kept his eyes on the warriors to the north as Jamie wanted.

The horseman raced into easy range now, but no one shot, though Boár followed the Indian with his gun barrel. Then, astonishingly, the warrior vanished. David thought he'd fallen off until he spotted an incredible thing: the warrior had somehow gotten down on the far side of the racing pony, and was aiming his bow from under its neck. But that was impossible!

The arrow streaked harmlessly by. Boar's piece boomed, and the horse stumbled, a red streak blooming across its chest. But it kept onward. The shot galvanized the tribesmen, who howled and milled about, nerving themselves for battle.

Jamie was on Boar before the beefy man knew what hit him, and wrested the rifle away. "I told you," he snarled. Boar rolled over to throw Dance off, but Dance leaped off him, Boar's rifle in hand. "Like to get us all killed," he snapped.

Boar bulled to his feet like a sore-toothed bear and started after Jamie, who stood stock-still.

"Git down and reload," Jamie growled in a flat voice so terrible that it halted the man. David had never heard Jamie use a voice like that; indeed, in all his life he'd never heard a voice so laden with repressed fury and death.

"I'll fix you later," Boar said, grabbing his piece.

The limping pony and its rider made it to the northern lines, amid wild howling. The warrior jumped off the pony, and onto a spare. That spare looked familiar, a solid-colored sorrel, and David realized it was one of their own.

But then a dozen came at once, from all directions, warriors riding in to deal death, to shoot their arrows — at him. But he couldn't watch them all at once!

"Lay low, don't shoot," Jamie yelled.

"What ya mean, don't shoot!"

"You heard me, Gantt. Lay low."

"You're crazy, Dance!" yelled Ames.

"Save your powder for real trouble."

The dozen converged on the beleaguered men, and every one of them vanished behind horseflesh. Riding like monkeys somehow, they loosed their arrows — sometimes two or three apiece — at the teamsters. One whacked into the planking of David's wagon, startling him.

"Jaysas!" yelled Gantt. An arrow had splintered a crate inches from his head. "You crazy, Dance?"

"Hold 'er in," Dance replied. "Next one'll be worse. One after that plumb awful. But that'll be four, the sacred number, and if they ain't got an arrer into our meat, they'll git plumb unhappy."

"We'll all be meat. I'm shootin'."

"If it comes to that, we'll all shoot. But hold it now."

"Jaysas."

Every one of the howling attackers had reached safety, beyond the range of the teamsters' pieces.

David made out the headman now, sitting a white medicine pony to the south on a slight knoll. He wore no bonnet, but had white feathers woven into the ends of his two braids. At a languid wave of his hand, the whole southern side of the war party broke for the wagons, and howling hideously.

Teresa María shrieked from the wagon just ahead. David watched nervously, but kept his eye on the line of warriors to the north.

"They're Comanche," said Lyle Black. "That shooting under the neck, that a Comanche stunt."

"Or Kiowa," muttered someone else.

"Same difference."

"Lay low—unless they try to steal the wagons up front." Jamie snapped his voice, carrying despite the howling cries.

Once again, the warriors slid behind their racing ponies, making themselves difficult targets. This time a musket barked from under the neck of a galloping horse, and the ball slapped David's wagon. David ducked, his heart racing. He lifted his head just in time to see one warrior running straight into the line of wagons, the pony steered by the man's knees, leaving him free to pump long gray-feathered arrows at targets of choice. This one's gaze burned briefly into David and then slid toward Jamie, who watched him alertly. Just as the warrior loosed an arrow, Dance plunged straight toward him, using his rifle as a club and slamming it down across the pony's withers. The horse shrieked and reared, spilling its rider. Jamie landed on the man even before the warrior had stopped rolling. The horse bolted off, squealing.

Jamie cracked the man over the head with his rifle, and the warrior shuddered and went limp. But now arrows were sizzling past everywhere, and David slid deep into his hole, scarcely daring to peer over the edge of the box.

"Watch him," muttered Jamie to the others, as he plucked the man's quiver and belt knife and war club from him. "He comes around, hit him again. We got us a bargaining chip."

Boar Blunt swung his rifle around to shoot the warrior.

"Boar. You kill him, I kill you." The deadly lash of

Jamie's voice was unmistakable, even to Boar Blunt.

"I'll get him later," Boar said. "Why waste a shot." The warriors had ridden close at will, without drawing a shot, and now they raced back toward safety. Miraculously, no arrow had found a teamster, although dozens of them protruded from boxes and bedrolls and the roiled earth.

"You trying to run 'em outa arrers, Dance?" yelled Mazappa, across the way. Men laughed hysterically.

But it was much too late. The whole war party, encouraged by the lack of resistance, shouted and whooped and nerved itself for the coup de grace. They didn't even bother to stay out of rifle range, but worked up their medicine, shouting and singing and readying themselves and their snorting ponies for a certain victory. They wouldn't even wait for the hand of the chief, who himself had withdrawn a gleaming rifle and was edging his pony into range. He'd join the rush. Only a shaman wearing a horned headdress still stood his pony on the distant rise as the sun broke over the horizon and bathed them in orange light.

"I don't care what you say, Dance. I'm gonna shoot," yelled Gantt.

How could anyone not shoot? David rested his piece on the box and snugged the butt to his shoulder and prepared to die.

CHAPTER 5

Jamie Dance knew he couldn't keep his men from defending themselves in the next rush. And if it came to that, he wanted them to fight hard. He'd risked everything doing it this way, and doubts gnawed at him. Maybe he had cost them all their lives. A steady drumbeat of deadly shots might have kept the warriors well away. The death of two or three warriors would have put an end to it. In his experience, Indians of the plains tribes cut and run when the costs began to mount up.

But he'd chosen this daring course for another crucial reason: he had come to trade, not to make war. And if he could somehow keep from taking lives, he might yet win the day and form an alliance with this tribe — Kiowa, he guessed, though it could be Comanche — that would yield a fortune in robes. The way the Bents had forged an alliance with the Southern Cheyenne. Boar Blunt had almost ruined his chances, but still, since that first brave warrior had defied death, the guns of his teamsters had been silent. And that amazing silence was what all those warriors were shouting about now, some of them worried about it, some of them taking it for a sign of weakness.

Still, he could hear the battle lust building out there. The warriors barely bothered to stay out of range. Most of them were only two hundred yards off. But others, the graying ones especially, looked fearfully at the wagons and the entrenched teamsters, and wondered at the silence.

Jamie made up his mind, feeling his stomach knot up, knowing he might be making the dumbest decision of his young life. Hastily, he dug a bridle from the light wagon and slid it onto one of his horses. The other was injured. He freed the animal from its picket line, slid over its bare back, rifle in hand, and rode out from the protection of the light wagon. Let them all see him out there. He lifted his Hawken until its barrel poked the sky and its butt rested on his knee, and fired. That blast, the first from his side since Boar's, caught the Indians' attention. Warriors paused, stopped arguing, stopped making their medicine, stopped singing battle songs, and stared.

Good. A discharged rifle was a sign they all knew. He heeled the horse forward, rifle still resting vertically, and rode straight toward the chief. No day is a good day to die, he thought. He wanted to live, and he feared he might not last out the next minutes. All he really wanted was a little howdying, lots of trading, and a little gambling.

Several of the nearer warriors lifted their bows, but a small gesture, a slightly raised hand from the headman, stayed them. Still, as Jamie Dance rode forward, he wondered how much authority the chief had. As little as he had over Boar Blunt? He could almost feel an arrow pierce his breast, but one didn't. As he rode; he somehow transmitted his fear to the horse under him so that the animal minced its way forward, ears back, snorting and wild-eyed.

His terrible clock-tick transit across the no man's land became the cynosure of all eyes. He only hoped his own seasoned men used the brains they had and held their fire. From the knoll, the shaman with the horned headdress turned his spotted pony down the slope and toward the headman, wanting to participate in the parley.

Still, two of the warriors near the chief held drawn bows, their arrows tipped with hoop-iron points and aimed just a hair away from Jamie's vulnerable flesh. They'd shoot him with no more compunction than they shot a doe, he knew, if the slightest thing went wrong. He began sweating, feeling more and more stupid. They should have resisted from the beginning until these Kiowa got tired of their sport.

He pulled up at last a few yards from the headman, and recognized him at once, from reputation. Only Santan of the Kiowa had lost the right side of his nose; a bullet or arrow had clipped away the nostril. The stocky chief gazed at Jamie from eyes as expressionless as a rattler's. Santan studied Jamie's face, finding no

44

one he knew; studied the discharged Hawken and the Green River belt knife in its sheath, and Jamie's fringed soft-tanned elkskin leggins.

Santan. Nothing could be worse. The man, still in his thirties, was a predator chief, his soul restless except during times of war when he found his calling. He'd gradually transformed his whole band — men, women, children — into a war society that viewed outsiders, even other Kiowa at times, as enemies or prey. He radiated power. And that was good, as far as Jamie was concerned. Those headmen in the policing societies would obey this chief. With a languid, almost invisible wave of a hand, Santan signaled Jamie to talk.

Slowly, Jamie slid his Hawken across his lap, a difficult feat when his legs were not supported by stirrups. Then he made sign talk — crude language indeed, but serviceable. He made the peace sign, told Santan he was a trader, that they were headed for the Purgatoire — Jamie said the name aloud, and then gave the river's Spanish name as well, Río de las Ánimas, River of Souls — to build a trading house to compete against the Bents.

The chief eyed him without the slightest alteration of expression, waiting for more. The shaman beside the chief was reading Jamie's hands too.

Trade with Kiowa people. Trade with Comanche people. He let that sink in. The Bents traded somewhat with both tribes, but really preferred the Cheyenne, who had the run of the fort. There'd been many a clash between Southern Cheyenne and the alliance of Kiowa and Comanches and Lipan Apaches. Jamie knew the Comanche had never been happy about their status with the Bents, but could do nothing about it.

Then came the hard part. Sign talk was a crude way of putting messages across, but the only way. He wanted to say, We haven't fired on you or taken life because we want to trade with you. But we are very strong, and have many good men with rifles. The carrot and stick, he thought. Yet his stock of finger signs would be taxed to its limit with that. Still, he let his hands fly: trade, peace, no death, friends, gifts you. Strong, many guns.

Then at last the chief replied, his languid hands encompassing such a small space that Jamie had to watch carefully.

Trade with Cheyenne?

No, trade with you. Robes for good things.

Guns and powder and balls?

A few.

Knives and awls?

Plenty.

The chief lifted his gaze toward the wagons. We will take everything, he signed.

No. You can't. Who would trade with you again?

Santan considered. Then, You cross our land. You must make big gifts.

Relief flooded Jamie. He'd won. No gifts for you, he signed.

A thundercloud gathered on Santan's face.

You have my horses and mules and oxen.

Santan smiled.

Return them and I will give gifts. A knife for you.

Guns and powder and ball.

One gun and sixty loads.

One gun for each horse and mule.

None for what you stole. But gifts for friends. After you bring our stock back to us.

I can take you prisoner.

You will die. The rifles reach here.

Santan eyed the teamsters who were peering from behind their barricades, rifles ready. He nodded.

He then languidly eyed the forces arrayed on both sides and turned to his shaman. They talked swiftly in a tongue Jamie had rarely heard. He knew it was close to the tongue of the Comanche, which made the alliance work well.

They talked for an eternity, then stopped. And nothing happened. The sun, gathering its summer power in the morning skies, blistered in, cooking the men back at the wagons. Jamie waited patiently on his restless horse, while the animal slapped at flies on its rump with its tail. The delay stretched onward, one of those odd Indian things white men couldn't understand. Meanwhile the shaman studied Jamie arrogantly. Jamie let himself be studied and returned the gaze steadily. He sweat.

The delay seemed almost to be a statement. *We have you in our power, and you have no water.* Santan sat his horse and watched Jamie, faintly amused. Jamie sat his gelding and waited, not letting

46

the fleshy chief get to him. He lost track of time. The sun hiked. Jamie felt a thirst began to crawl up his parched throat.

Then a tiny lift of the chief's hand started time again. The two guardian warriors turned their ponies and trotted off and beyond the brow of the distant rise. Jamie let himself hope. Had he done it? Had he turned a raiding band into trading partners? Would he ever see his livestock again?

A while later, the bawling of the oxen told him what he needed to know. Kiowa herders drove the oxen, mules, and horses toward the wagons. Teamsters cheered and whistled.

Santan watched Jamie quizzically, and Jamie knew it was time to fetch the promised gifts. It'd be a task, because he didn't know which wagon the knives and the trade rifles were in.

Jamie nodded, and turned to ride toward the wagons, with the chief and shaman following, along with several headmen. He saw Boar swing the barrel of his rifle around until it aimed straight at Santan. Jamie stopped them all and turned his horse to the side, placing himself squarely in front of the chief.

"Lyle . . . Mazappa—get him," he yelled.

Boar swung around, too late. Two catlike teamsters landed on him. The rifle discharged, shattering the peace. Swiftly they lifted Boar to his feet, pinioning him. Boar didn't struggle.

"I'll get me a chief next time," he yelled.

Santan watched sharply and waited. Finally, when it was plain that Boar was subdued, they proceeded again.

"David, get the case of Green River knives," Jamie shouted. "And one trade rifle. We got to give a few little things to our trading partners hyar."

David knew where everything was. As clerk, he had kept track of what items were in each wagon. He needed to reach the front wagons, far from the teamsters, and it terrified him. But he willed himself out of his nest and walked forward, under the scrutiny of scores of hostile Indians, and clambered into the second wagon, where kegs of Green River knives rested. He found a cask containing ten dozen. In the very first wagon, he dug out a Leman trade rifle from an opened wooden crate, and then carried his booty toward the place where Jamie and the headmen waited.

"Hyar now, David. Fetch a couple of pigs of lead, some caps, a

47

fifty-two caliber mold, and a pound of powder. I promised 'em that, too. Sixty loads, actually, but this'll do."

David stared, uneasily.

"I got these hyar gents turned around. Kioways, they are. Santan here's a big chief. This here'll tie some tradin' knots. We'll give them some leverage against the Bents. They don't like tradin' with the Bents none, not the way they're treated there."

It dawned on David that trading was a lot more than taking in robes and handing out trade items. He hastened to the wagon where lead and powder were stored. Behind him he heard Jamie begin to present the gifts, talking in English for the benefit of his own men, while his hands sang the words to the Kiowas.

"Santan, my friend, this hyar rifle is for you to shoot the buffler. It's a little gift from the Rocky Mountain Company to the mighty Kioway. It's a payment for crossing your land hyar."

David looked back. The chief was holding the shining Leman, looking pleased. It had cost twelve and a half dollars, plus shipping from Pennsylvania. It had a percussion lock, and a forty-inch barrel, and was actually a fine weapon. Jamie was giving away the value of twenty-five robes.

David clambered into the wagon and dug around for the lead and caps and the mold, having to lift cartons and barrels. But eventually he got what he wanted, and emerged into the white light again. Jamie Dance still droned on, something about trading partners, robes, alliances.

"Give the stuff to old Santan there," Jamie directed.

David handed the chief two heavy bars of lead, the mold, and the powder, a brick encased in heavily waxed paper.

"Ah! Aeii!" the chief said, looking pleased.

"Now git more knives, boy. We're gonna give 'em a knife. Hand 'em out."

"But they cost —"

"Do 'er."

This is too much, David thought. His father's capital draining away and not a robe for it. But he dug into a wooden cask of Russell and Company Green River knives, a favorite in the mountains, and hesitantly began handing them to the Kiowa warriors, who had pressed in close. They terrified him, studying him arrogantly from their ponies, reaching down to take the gift with a

48

roughness that spoke to him of contempt. But a few smiled, ran a finger along the keen edge, and said things he couldn't fathom.

In the end, the chief had a new rifle and loads, each headman had two butcher knives, and every warrior had a knife as well. But no man had died, no stock had been lost, and an alliance had been cemented—or so it seemed.

David knew, suddenly, he'd gotten an important lesson in plains diplomacy, and resolved to emulate it if Jamie Dance ever put him in charge. They'd come to trade, and Dance had never forgotten it. All those tales of fights, horse raids, ambushes, battles he'd heard back in St. Louis had riveted him when told, but now something larger and more sober had replaced them in his mind—a sudden grasp of the way a great robe-trading empire was *really* built. His father wouldn't mind the loss of thirty dollars worth of trade items if they brought the whole Kiowa people, rich with robes, to the new post.

Santan stared at them all, one by one, memorizing their faces. The scrutiny sent a chill through David, and he wondered whether the whole thing had been a cruel Indian joke that would end with their butchery. A terror rose in his chest again. The teamsters stared back silently, clutching their rifles. Then, with that imperious demeanor that stamped him, the chief turned his powerful stallion southward and trotted off, his back deliberately exposed to the white men. The rest of the warriors followed, some reluctantly, after swarming around both sides of the line of wagons. They didn't seem grateful, but David wasn't sure whether gratitude was an Indian trait.

"Goddam red vermin," muttered Wilbert Ames.

"Kiowa. Stinkin' butchers. You see that Santan?" growled Price Agee. "Right outa hell."

Here and there teamsters stood up and watched. Others, fearful of treachery, remained hunkered behind their makeshift barricades. One headed for the coffeepot which contained the only water they had. Others followed. They hadn't even had breakfast. At last, as the crowd of bronzed warriors vanished over the crest of a low hill, ease came upon them all.

Emilio began clacking his teeth. The young camp tender, Abel Cannon, wandered around muttering. "Didja see that? Didja see that?" he asked. Lyle Black stood and stretched. Labor Jonas, the other youth in the company, grinned.

"Still got my ugly hair," Mazappa announced. They all had their hair and lives, but none wanted to say it for fear that would bring them bad luck.

'Madre de Dios!' said Teresa María, who emerged from somewhere. "I think I am dead."

"Yoke 'em up," said Jamie. "We'll eat when we get to Ash Creek yonder."

Emilio clacked his teeth harder and began dismantling his kitchen, slamming pots into the light wagon with loud thumps.

Men too shaken to say much began their chores, herding and yoking unruly heated oxen, throwing collars and britching over braying mules, all of them eyeing the horizon fearfully for the smallest sign of perfidy. But they saw only shimmering grass bending under a whipping westwind.

David, as clerk and camp tender, began toting crates and barrels, the bones of the barricades, back to the freighters, trying to put them all in the wagons they had been wrested from.

"All right, Boar," said Jamie.

David turned, feeling the chill in the words.

Jamie Dance had set his Hawken on the ground and stood opposite Boar Blunt, who stood grinning.

"You think you can do something about it, Dance?"

David turned to watch. Others paused and waited, a dread slithering into them again.

"Almost got us killed, Boar."

"You're yeller bellied, Dance. Givin' them filthy red niggers stuff. We coulda shown 'em what white men are made of."

"You disobeyed."

Boar laughed. "You gonna do something about it?"

"Whenever you're ready, Boar."

David wished desperately it wouldn't come to that. Boar Blunt stood six inches taller and weighed more, a lot of his bulk in massive shoulders. And his arms were sledgehammers. He'd pulverize the slender captain. But David intuitively knew that was only part of it: Boar Blunt would stop at nothing, including murder. And what would this battle prove? Only who had more muscle and ferocity. Why, why, why was Jamie provoking this? He could have let it ride. Boar Blunt had simply done what all the teamsters, in their fear, desperately wanted to do—shoot and fight.

But there slouched the captain, lithe and loose limbed, waiting, his eyes unblinking, his face as solemn as David had ever seen it.

"Have it your way, Dance." Boar simply walked in, not in a rush but like a bull swinging its horns, his massive hands open and ready to tear Jamie Dance to pieces.

Dance didn't budge. Boar's hands went straight for Jamie's throat, but Jamie brought a knee up and twisted sideways, staggering Boar. The teamster laughed.

Jamie slid a leg around, tripping Boar, who dropped like a wagon tongue, only to bound to his feet again. But Jamie's fist caught him behind an ear, and his other fist caught him in a kidney and again in the small of the back before Boar recovered and swung around, his mauls of hands hammering Jamie across the head and chest and then the gut, which jackknifed Jamie. Even as he folded, a fist caught his chin, jerking his head back and sending him flying, toppling. Blood sprayed from Jamie's mouth and slid down his chin, onto his shirt.

Everything happened so slowly. Jamie hit the ground hard, and David heard the whoosh of air from his lungs. Jamie rolled left, but Boar landed on him with a thud that had the sound of cracking bones in it. Jamie kicked and writhed, but Boar Blunt rode him down. Boar's giant fingers found Jamie's neck and clamped on it. Jamie panted once and stopped panting, his sucking coming in fearful gasps. He clawed at Boar's deadly hands, but couldn't dislodge them.

Teresa María screamed.

David cried out and ran toward Boar.

Jamie stopped gasping, and every twist of his writhing body was weaker than the previous one.

"Boar!" Lyle Black yelled. The teamster held the muzzle of his rifle to Boar's head. "Let go or I'll shoot."

Boar laughed, something maniacal in him.

Black didn't wait. He brought the octagonal barrel down hard over Boar's head, which bounced sideways. But Boar's hands never relaxed their grip.

Black hit him again harder, but Boar only grunted. Mazappa Oliphant leaped on Boar, clamped his own giant hand around

51

Boar's neck, and yanked him backward; but Boar didn't let go of Jamie.

Blake Goodin, the one-armed master of the whip, lashed its lead-weighted tassel over Boar's forearms, a crack that sent a jolt of terror through David. Boar screamed. Bright blood welled. Goodin cracked the whip again, and at last those hands spasmed free. But Jamie, who'd turned gray, didn't move.

All three teamsters wrested Boar away, and David leaped toward Jamie, a scream building in him.

Then at last Jamie sucked in air, with a fearsome coughing and gasping, with lungs that couldn't pump fast enough. It took eternities for his breathing to settle, and another eternity passed before he opened his eyes and peered around him through a veil of pain.

And the first thing he saw and heard was Boar, sitting nearby, bloody-armed, laughing.

CHAPTER 6

They fashioned a stuffed-tick pallet for Jamie Dance in the light wagon, and he lay there day after day under the cover of a blanket because he couldn't bear light. His headaches maddened him, and his crushed windpipe radiated pain through his neck.

Command fell to the senior teamsters, Lyle Black and Mazappa Oliphant, or would have were it not for the mocking presence of Boar Blunt. The bully and his two sycophantic friends, Mario Petti and Lewis Dusseldorf, did what they chose, and no one dared to challenge them. David, who was closest to holding company authority, tried, but their response was to rag the young man mercilessly. He hadn't the prowess to deal with his tormentors, and learned that the best response was to ignore them.

So the headless wagon train toiled westward. At Ash Creek, Boar shot a buffalo cow—and spent the rest of the day rubbing it in, reminding Gantt and Black and Willis and Oliphant of their failure, poking his head into the light wagon to ride Jamie about it too. But the meat tasted good, and for two days, before the carcass went bad, they devoured hump rib, tongue, and juicy loin, which lay comfortably in their bellies. After that they found buffalo frequently and rarely wanted for meat.

They crossed Pawnee Fork with difficulty because of high water and muddy banks, and camped in abundant timber on the far side, beneath high bluffs. The place was a favorite resort of Indians because of the wood, water, and game to be found, and because the bluffs afforded a way to observe the surrounding country. But no village camped there now. That night Boar tapped a cask of two hundred-proof trade spirits, added some creekwater, and began to drink, along with his two cronies. The other teamsters, wary of the future wrath of Dance, or at least respectful of the company's property, declined, even in the face of Boar's mockery. They finally got one recruit, old Phineas Boggs, who allowed as how he'd sip a while to cure his aches.

David watched warily, knowing that spirits would loosen what few inhibitions lingered in Boar Blunt, and knowing as well that he or Jamie would be Boar's first victims. Or maybe Teresa María, who watched these events in smoldering silence.

Lyle and Mazappa fumed, not really wanting to tangle with Boar, and David began to realize that it would be up to him to stop what was about to occur. David against Goliath, he thought wryly. And yet he was the namesake of a king who, as a young man had triumphed over Goliath with a stone and a sling and expert skill. But this was different. Boar remained an essential man to the company: a workhorse, a skilled teamster, at least when he was under discipline. David knew he could simply discharge Boar, but he bridled at that, even though Boar had come within a hair of murdering Jamie. He knew also that if he tried to discipline the man, Boar would thrash him at best, kill him at worst, or leave him maimed.

Still, a voice within begged him to try. Something had to be done before the caravan fell apart. Jamie was helpless, at least for now. It was up to David to act. And his only weapons would be his thoughts and his words.

The camp lay quiet in summer twilight. Emilio clacked his teeth and cleaned pots, angry because one of his camp tenders, Boggs, had ditched him. Teamsters hunkered near the wagons, uneasy and morose, questions in their eyes. No one said much. They watched the drinkers huddled at the side of Boar's wagon dip tin cups into a pot swiped from Emilio, laugh and whisper loud insults intended to be overheard. David eyed the loyal teamsters quietly, noting the hunger in some eyes for a good drunk, the disgust in others, and the indifference of the rest. The company was falling apart. A day or two more would see others at the liquor pot, enjoying Boar's rebel hospitality. He could see the probable end of it: the theft of much of the Rocky Mountain Company's stock and the ruin of the enterprise.

Fearing for his life — a familiar terror he'd encountered more than once on this trail — he approached the revelers and stood over them, his heart pounding.

"Go 'way," said Boar.

"Looks like a good scalp. Not as good as some ol' Kioway chief's though," said Petti.

The others laughed.

"Have some spirits," said Phin Boggs. "Courtesy your ol' man."

David felt his pulse begin to race. "Put the spirits away," he said, meaning to speak with authority. But it came out as an adolescent squeak.

"Put the spirits away he says. Are you going to stop me, Straus?" Boar peered up at him, radiating menace. One lithe jump and he'd catch David and beat him mercilessly.

"Plug the cask and put it back now, Boar. This is the only time I'll say it."

Boar laughed easily, then pitched a cupful of liquor into David's face. The spirits stung his eyes and swiftly drew tears. He sputtered and wiped his cheeks with his sleeve.

"The company doesn't need you, Mr. Blunt. I'll give you a draft for your wages in the morning, and you'll leave."

"You gonna make me?"

"Whatcha cryin' for, li'l sweet potato?" said Dusseldorf, joining the fun. "You got no rich pappy to run to out here?"

David sighed. Around him, teamsters had gathered, and off in the dusk, even Emilio had stopped clanging pots to watch. David drew comfort from Lyle and Mazappa, who'd drifted close to watch.

"Boar," he said, "you've neglected your watch for two nights. So have you," he said, eyeing Dusseldorf and Petti. "You've forced other men to do it, to keep the stock safe. To keep us all safe while we sleep."

That, David knew, had a sharp effect on those who remained loyal.

"I like my sleep," Boar said. He dipped his tin cup into the pot, but this time David was ready, and dodged the spray.

"Lookit him cry!" said Petti.

"You would too, with spirits dashed into your eyes," said Lyle Black, from out in the darkness.

Boar laughed. "This one ain't cryin' for that. He's cryin' because he's scairt."

There was truth in that, David knew. "The first watch starts now, from ten to midnight. Boar, you're up on the bluff. Dusseldorf, you're with the stock. The second watch, Petti, you're on the bluff; Phin, you're with the stock."

"Beat it before I turn you to pulp."

"Gonna get mah beauty sleep," said Petti.

"You've been forcing other men to do your work. It'll stop now," said David.

"You're gettin' pretty cocky for your kind," said Boar. "Guess I'll have tuh teach ya a few things." The man clambered to his feet, grinning.

"You heard him, Boar," said Mazappa.

Boar hooted, and closed in. David froze.

The snap of a cocking hammer clapped the dark. "You want to go under, Boar?" That was Pony Gantt's voice. "We don't like you cheatin' on the watch."

Boar froze. The moment stretched.

"Reckon me and the bunch can do the watch," he said, slowly picking up the kettle.

"Leave that," said Gantt.

Boar peered into the darkness. Every man in camp had gathered there and had witnessed the scrape. David realized he'd achieved something. The abandoned watch had been a sore point among them.

"Them chickenheads can't even shoot a buffler," Boar said. "Who got the first buffler?"

No one replied. Other men had shot buffalo since Boar got the first one.

David felt the strength coalesce behind him. It had taken only a little leadership to isolate Boar's bunch. He realized

56

suddenly that most men want to be loyal, want to follow legit-imate authority when it is properly employed.

"Think I'll go to sleep," said Boar, not yielding.

In a way, that relieved David. No one really wanted half-drunk men guarding them through the night.

"Is that your decision?"

Boar laughed again, defiance building.

"Very well. I'll give you a draft for wages in the morning, and we'll leave you here."

"Try it, chickenhead. I'll get you. I'll be comin' for you. I'll be comin' when you don't have all these chickenheads here backin' you. You keep lookin' behind you, Straus, because I'm back there. You're dead. You better count your hours and say your prayers, 'cause you just run outa time."

David was hearing a threat on his life, but he choked down the panic within him. "If I'm out of time," he whispered, "so are you."

For some reason, that evoked a cheerful laugh or two out in the crowd. When it came to David and Goliath, they were rooting for David.

"Mr. Straus," said Lyle Black easily. "These men aren't fit to keep watch. Not a man here would sleep knowing these drunks are all that stands between them and trouble. With your permission, we'll post the men I've asked."

"Chickenheads," said Boar.

David nodded, then warily picked up the pot and dashed its contents into the clay. From the perimeter of the night, men groaned and laughed.

That's how it wound down, some shabby semblance of a victory, a death threat, a failure—except that the loyal ones had gathered around him. But David feared for his life—and would every second of every day in the near future. The crowd disintegrated, the revelers whispering and snickering beside Boar's wagon; the rest going to sleep or to stand guard on this soft summer night.

David didn't sleep at all. And the next morning, owly and tired as he was, he almost failed to make his inventory check. But while the others were breaking camp, he did look around, and found camp gear—kitchen pots, knives, spoons, tin cups, and a bale of Witney trade blankets—lying out in the brush a hundred yards from the wagons.

David's whispered news brought Jamie out of his blankets in a rush. He'd suffered blinding headaches for days, along with a sore neck, but he'd decided to ignore them. His wagon train was falling apart. He sat up, shook away his weakness, and stretched in the morning sun, noting that the oxen stood yoked and hitched and the train was about to take off.

He walked forward unsteadily, past the smoldering eyes of Boar, and found Lyle at the head wagon, eyeing his progress quizzically.

"Lyle, we'll wait a few minutes. There's parties in the outfit like to be sabotaging us."

Briefly, he described David's discoveries.

Lyle Black nodded. "I'll put some of the ones I trust to lookin' around. Then we'll have us a little push and shove."

Solemnly Jamie watched, feeling his head throb and his gut rebel, while some of the teamsters swept both sides of the camp, deep into surrounding timber, and returned with the items David had discovered. The cooking and mess gear went back into the light wagon, to the accompaniment of Emilio's angry tooth-clacking, and the trade blankets were restored to the third freight wagon.

"Send the four up here—Boar, Boggs, and who else? Dusseldorf and Petti."

Boar Blunt refused to come, and stood beside his oxen, mockingly. Jamie was not up to confrontations, and simply walked down to Blunt, the rest following. It really didn't matter if he walked to Blunt or Blunt came to him. Some men might find something weak in all that, but Jamie didn't care. It was just cussedness. Cussed men were going to be cussed no matter what. Other teamsters gathered around.

"Boggs, whose payroll are you on?" he began, abruptly. His head throbbed.

"Yars I reckon."

"Ours—plus either Bent or Chouteau or both. I'm calculating the cost of these items you dumped out there and deducting it from your pay."

58

"Ya cain't do that; ain't fair. Ya got it back anahow. No proof. Why you accusing me?"

"Because you've been observed. Is that good enough?"

"Yoah pickin' on a ol' cuss."

"You can leave if you want. We can do without you. Same for you, Blunt. I'll give you a draft you can cash somewhere."

"You gonna make me, Dance?" Blunt's eyes gleamed.

"I might," said Jamie.

"It's your windpipe," said Blunt.

Jamie ignored that. The best way to deal with cussed men was not to respond to their taunts. His task was to cement the loyalties of the rest. "Tonight you'll take the first and second watches, you four, and you'll watch carefully. The rest of us are depending on you. You'll each be docked a day's wage for each watch you've missed. And I'm docking you for the trade whiskey. We've a long way to go: keep it up and you'll not have a cent for it." Then, with inspired afterthought, he turned to the others. "Those of you that did extra watches, see me. I'm giving you the day's wages they lost."

That instantly won approval. In fact, in a few moments, Jamie had achieved what he'd set out to do—isolate the bad 'uns. The malefactors stood sullenly, and Jamie knew he'd better watch his back.

They rolled out of the Pawnee Fork flats a few moments later, Jamie on his horse and wearing a headache. He had no more trouble, but knew the Blunt crowd was simply biding its time, and would strike again. Things had changed, though. The rest kept a sharp eye on them, preventing sabotage. David redoubled his efforts to check inventory. Even Emilio got to counting pots and spoons every morning. And they routinely scoured the whole country around each camp, especially creek bottoms. But the thing lay there. Boar knew Jamie was no match for him. Boggs and the rest knew they were disgraced and had lost wages. They were ripe for revenge, and Jamie could only hope that the loyalties of the rest would curb the trouble.

In the Coon Creeks country, usually dry watercourses running through barren grasslands, fierce storms pinned them down—giant thunderheads that built through the after-

59

noons, presenting a solid gray wall and a black bottom that grew until the sky exploded. They usually struck ahead or to the side, but when they hit the train, they drenched men and oxen with ice water and pummeling hail, chilling a man to the bone in moments. But the half-hour drenchings weren't as bad as the gumbo. The deluges turned the clay into such gum that not even the five-inch iron tires of the Conestogas buoyed the wagons. Teamsters burrowed into wagons at night, or sat up, rather than unroll their bedding in sopping muck. One night a bolt of lightning set the skittish mules running. It took half a day to round them up, but it wasn't time wasted because the wagons were mired anyway. And they lacked firewood—not a stick could they find on the relentless grasslands. The buffalo chips had been soaked and were useless, so they starved and cursed and dreamed of thick hot coffee while they devoured Emilio's raisins and dried apples and some raw dough he concocted from flour, grease, and water. The cold damp triggered Blake Goodin's ague again, and he lay feverish in the wagon.

When the sun finally baked the clay enough to travel, they found the going treacherous, with cavernous mudholes hidden under a surface crust. But they sweated and heaved, double-teamed the gaunted oxen, and pushed ever westward, out upon a land so forlorn and empty it filled them with foreboding and unloosed ghosts and phantasms and morbid dreams among them. The hundred-degree heat forced them to take long noonings, and to eat their main meal then. When the worst of each day's inferno had passed, they rolled on into the western twilight, always making sure they crossed any creek they came upon late in the day, lest it rise and trap them in the night.

They swung down into the Arkansas valley, and approached the river crossing at the Cimarron Cutoff that would take most Santa Fe traffic across arid wastes infested with hostile Comanche and Kiowa, but shorten the route. Here they encountered an eastbound Mexican trading party, a score or so of large carts laden with tanned hides stinking of urine—and probably bullion, the Mexican stock in trade with the Americans. These were drawn by yoked mules, burros, or oxen, gaily caparisoned, lashed along by wiry men who looked like they'd never had enough to eat. David took the opportunity to scribble a note to his father, entrusting it to the *jefe*, Juan Bustamente Díaz, who smiled cheerfully, baring startling white teeth, and promised to deliver it personally to Don Guy Straus. Jamie supposed David wrote about the brush with the Kiowa and maybe the troubles with Boar Blunt, but he didn't know, wouldn't ask, and couldn't read anyway. That power of David's, to read and write and send messages on paper, troubled Jamie. It gave David a mysterious upper hand.

There'd been news, which Díaz had shared, some malice bubbling from his heated gossip. A filibuster expedition out of the Republic of Texas was even then wending its way west to war upon New Mexico, and His Excellency, Governor Armijo, had stirred up the country and had dispatched his troops to guard his borders against the Texas rabble. "Even now, *señores*, blue-clad *soldados* patrol the south bank of the Arkansas, the Río Nepeste," Díaz said.

Jamie frowned. Probably nothing. And yet Armijo, a trader himself, had often picked on foreigners, using one perfidy after another, ranging from confiscation to enormous imposts of five hundred dollars per wagon. Still, Teresa María was scarcely a foreigner, and if necessary, the wagons, the trade goods, and even Fort Dance, could all be put in her name. It made a man wonder about trading in Mexico. The whole plan had been for the Rocky Mountain Company to take wagons south and trade in the Comanche and Kiowa villages, gather the robes of the southern tribes deep in Mexico if they could. And that would take a Mexican license and a visit to Santa Fe.

The Dance company stayed on the north bank of the Arkansas, following the alternative route that ran past Fort William, named after William Bent, and down Timpas creek, to pick up the main trail again far south in Mexico, near the Sangre de Cristo mountains. It had always been the safer, better-watered way, and offered the succor of the Bent post.

They passed corrugated sand dunes on the Mexican side

of the Arkansas, blinding white with a skiff of whipped sand blowing off their crests. The sun beat brutally on man and beast, dehydrating the oxen, turning sweat to white rime on their hides. The furnace blast dried the wagon wheels, shrank the hubs and spokes and felloes until the iron tires rattled loose and threatened to ride off. One evening they pulled the worst wheels, soaked them overnight in the river, and drove hoop iron between the felloes and tires to anchor the tires again, hoping they'd hold a little while more.

They cut through shortgrass country, spare grasses sprouting in low bunches dried tan. The oxen gaunted down on it, though the mules prospered. They hugged the broad trench of the Arkansas, often lacking firewood because periodic grassfires had kept timber from growing even on the banks of the river. But they didn't lack for game, which thrived on grass and saltbush along the languid stream. They found plenty of antelope and mule deer but fewer buffalo as the plains grew more arid.

When Teresa María beheld her native land across the river, her face softened, and her eyes lit with mysterious fires. Jamie knew she could barely contain her eagerness to set foot upon it, and chatter in her native tongue, which she spoke like an angry squirrel. She took to rattling at Emilio in staccato Spanish, and never noticed that he fled when she approached. When she insisted on riding in the wagon beside him, the cook hunkered down inside of himself. But for Jamie, the land across the river was brooding, menacing. A foreign trader could never know when its corrupt officials and tax collectors, from Governor Manuel Armijo on down to the lowliest soldier, might discover new rules, new violations, forgotten taxes, and confiscate not only trade goods but wagons and livestock as well. Or, at the least, demand a *don*, a gift, to arrange for the proper *guías*, or passports for merchandise. He had only to cross that river—or not cross it at all—to run into troubles that could impoverish him and his company, even put him into a Mexican dungeon on the whim of some tax man or prefect.

They arrived at the Big Timbers, a heavily forested stretch of the Arkansas that was a favorite resort of the Indians, especially the Southern Cheyenne, and found abundant signs of recent occupation, including a scarcity of game. But no Indians. For two days they pushed through somber cottonwooded flats, enjoying the trees' cool shade, and then emerged upon a featureless plain.

Just ahead was the confluence of the Purgatoire — Río de las Ánimas, Teresa María insisted on calling it — and the place where the Rocky Mountain Company would build its post . . . if the officials in Santa Fe agreed.

CHAPTER 7

Mexico shimmered across the dark Arkansas, beckoning and repelling Jamie. From his vantage on the north bank, he could see the Purgatoire burst free of its green girdle of salt-bush and debouch into the border river. To the southwest rose dense timber, a needful staple for any trading post: wood for beams, construction, and above all, cooking and heating fires. More forest, dense cottonwoods, lay just to the east in the Big Timbers. Beyond the woods, the shallow valley of the Purgatoire stubbornly stayed green, even in this brown season, affording pasture for the company stock, as well as for that of visiting tribes.

Nothing here seduced the eye or spirit. The land lay flat and featureless, without a single landmark. One couldn't see the Rockies though they rose not far away; from the bastions of Bent's Fort eighteen miles upriver one could discern their hazy bulk. No, there was nothing exhilarating to lift the spirit here, and summers especially would be oppressive. Jamie thought for a moment that Brokenleg Fitzhugh, his partner, had the better of it up on the Yellowstone. But Brokenleg had no Taos or Santa Fe to repair to, so maybe he wasn't so well off after all.

"Madre de Dios! Why do we wait?" his wife snapped at him.

He grinned. Across that Rubicon was her native land. Still, if he hesitated it was not because of any concern about geography or worry about planting his post in the right spot. It was because of the way that land yonder was governed. Governor Armijo, who bulged out of his *pantalones,* lacked scruples, especially when it came to rivals. And most of the rest of the officials, tax collectors, and officers were leaner versions of Armijo.

He motioned his weary caravan forward. They'd need to cross before dark, which meant finding a ford in the quick-sand-filled stream. He peered upriver and down, seeing no one. In times past he'd seen Arapaho, Comanche, and once even a Gros Ventre village down from the north, right where his post would stand. Behind him he heard the lash of whips, the snort of mules, and the squeak of dry hubs chattering around dry axles. He looked for a widening of the river, full of those ripples that suggested a high bottom, and found a likely spot just upstream. There he spurred his weary horse into the water, letting it mince forward. They scared up ducks, sent reptiles scurrying and slithering into the brush, but the ginger horse pawed at good gravelly bottom and ar-rived at the Mexican shore without wetting its knees or hocks. He ran the horse back and forth again, until the ford took shape in his mind.

Two hours later they gathered on a low grassy bench above the floodplain, and Jamie knew they were camping on the site of Fort Dance. Here lay every advantage they had calcu-lated so carefully back in St. Louis. This post would be miles closer to the homelands of the southern tribes than Bent's Fort. It lay on two rivers, the vital arteries of travel. It would have better wood and pasture than the rival post. Travelers on the northern branch of the Santa Fe Trail would reach it first.

That evening he gathered his men about him. "We're hyar!" he began. "We'll put up the post about where we set. You brought the wagons through, and we'll celebrate in a little bit. I reckon a safe trip's worth a little celebrating."

Teamsters laughed. Tonight they'd get a gill of spirits.

"Tomorrah we'll get to work." He paused, staring at them. "Most of you indentured for a year, but I've a mind to let anyone who ain't happy have his freedom. I'll be hirin' Mexi-can adobe makers, fast as I can find 'em. Anyone want to leave now?"

He directed that at his tormentors, Boar Blunt in particular. They had proved to be men of little value because their loyalties weren't certain.

"You invitin' or tellin', Dance?" asked Blunt, firelight dancing in his eyes.

"Inviting. I can use ever' loyal hand I can get my mitts on. Only I think the time's come for a reckoning. I don't really want a feller who takes his coin from the Bents. How about it, Phin? You ready to head up the river and tell ol' William that we're hyar?"

"You never knew how ta treat a man proper," said Phin Boggs, scratching his whiskers.

"Maybe you never learnt to treat a company proper, Boggs. I'd just as soon you packed your kit and got out right now."

"You payin' me?"

"Did you earn it, Phin?"

"You ain't payin' me."

"I reckon you've been paid. No sense my payin' you twice."

"It be all lies," Boggs snarled. "All right. I'll git. I got took. I git nothin'. Did a mighty heap of work all this time."

"Worked hard for the Bents."

The whole exchange embarrassed the men, and they fell silent. Jamie knew this wasn't exactly the kind of celebration they were looking for.

"That warn't me!"

"Who was it?"

Boar Blunt grinned maliciously. Boggs swallowed and said nothing.

"Boar, you stayin' and helpin'? You gonna do your share, keep watch and all?"

The rest waited somberly for Boar's answer.

"Watch your backside, Dance," he said.

Jamie sucked in his breath. "Boar. You can whip me. You got the weight. You can whip David Straus, too. But you can't whip the outfit. These hyar men, why, they're friends o' me and David. They looked after us and themselves, and didn't skip watches. By and by, I'll be leavin' for Santy Fe to get the license and pay the imposts. Me and Mrs. Dance. I'm leavin' David hyar in charge, and Lyle Black and Mazappa

Oliphant to put up the post. I reckon the rest won't like it none if you cause trouble, fail to guard. We got fifteen thousand of merchandise in the wagons, and nothin' betwixt that stuff and a lot of Injuns wantin' it. Maybe you're wantin' it too, Boar."

Jamie was rewarded by a slight jerk of Boar Blunt's body. The man didn't answer, and Jamie let it go. This harsh business had disturbed the camp too much.

He watched Boggs scramble to his feet, peer around slyly, and make for the light wagon and his bedroll. Boggs collected his goods under the silent watch of the whole camp, and then slid into the night. He vanished, and Jamie sensed that the company was not lessened by the man's absence. But he wished he could know what was passing through the mind of each silent observer. He hadn't paid Boggs for work done.

"Hyar, now," he said to David. "Let's roll out that cask."

The pair dug into the last of the wagons, and wrestled a thirty-gallon cask out upon a tailgate. It was a quarter empty, the result of Boar's escapades. Jamie thought briefly of denying Boar his gill, and thought better of it. The man might settle down and prove useful. By the time the cask was readied with a brass bung faucet, the men stood in line, tin mess cups in hand, and Jamie splashed a gill of the pure spirits into each cup. Men added water, sipped cheerfully, but didn't head for their bedrolls, and Jamie knew what they were waiting for.

He filled Boar's cup to the halfway mark—a full gill—while Boar stared brightly.

"You'll do third watch, Blunt," he said.

Blunt laughed.

"Reckon these hyar men, they won't like it if they git scalped because you didn't watch. Reckon you want to keep your topknot too."

Boar peered into the faces of the teamsters. "Hidin' behind their skirts, are you, Dance?"

Jamie shrugged.

Boar chortled, downed the entire gill with quick hot gulps, and wiped his beard. "I'll be ready," he said.

"I'm taking the fourth watch, Boar," Jamie said. It was a

warning.

Boar hiccoughed, and meandered toward his wagon.

David, who never touched spirits, had volunteered to take the first watches, and now he slid out into the fearsome dark to walk among the stock. They'd be lightly guarded this night, and it worried Jamie. Usually there were two on watch, but the men had truly earned their gill and a rest.

He found Teresa María in the rear of the light wagon, which she'd turned into her boudoir now that the staples brought from Independence were gone.

"That *cochinillo* watching alone? We'll have our throats cut!" she hissed.

"Well, I reckon that's right," he said.

"Oh! You would say that."

Jamie laughed. She kissed him, but he didn't feel much like kissing.

"You don't love me," she accused.

"We're in Mexico, that's why."

"In Mexico? What does that—? And anyway . . . I'm very passionate in Mexico. What is it?" she asked urgently.

Jamie yawned. "It don't signify nothing." He just wanted all the shuteye he could get, and mystifying her was one way to get it. The last he knew, she was mumbling and muttering and invoking the saints, especially Santa Teresa.

Blunt awakened him with a sharp rap on the wagonbox, and he uncoiled like a clockspring.

"Your watch," Blunt said.

Jamie slid out into a chill night, shivering from the sudden awakening, and then trudged off toward the herd, with little to guide him through the darkness. But he found the stock standing quietly. He wandered among them finding nothing amiss, and then settled against a shaggy cottonwood on the far side of the herd.

A while later—he never was much good at telling time—the night lifted perceptibly, and he rose. These gray moments were always the most dangerous, the time of the pouncing. He lifted his Hawken and found it dry, the percussion cap nestled over its nipple inside the little basket. He let his eyes focus through the gloom, examining the ominous woods beyond the meadow, and saw no movement.

When the night blue had faded near the end of his watch, he saw them riding down the Purgatoire and knew at once they weren't Indians, weren't using stealth. Mexicans. He made out the leader, dressed in military blue, gold lanyard glinting against his azure tunic. Behind, forming into a broad line, were dragoons, thirty or so, also in blue. And behind them, twenty *campesinos* armed with lances and an old musket or two.

The officer was well mounted. He forked a sleek bay with an arched neck and a wild eye. Most of the civilians tugged at burros laden with packs.

Around Jamie, teamsters leaped from their bedrolls and grabbed for their rifles.

"No," bellowed Dance. His men reluctantly lowered the muzzles, but none of them set his weapon down.

The lean officer rode forward, his soft brown eyes surveying the camp, the wagons, the half-awakened teamsters. The dragoons, each carrying a carbine, spread swiftly into a skirmish line and raised their pieces lazily.

"*Tejanos*," the officer said softly.

"Yankees," said Jamie.

The man sighed, burped, and eyed the burdened wagons a little too long. "*Tejanos*. We will take you now."

"Yankees. And you ain't taking us nowhere."

The baggy-eyed officer smiled blandly, raising the points of his waxed mustachio.

"Pardon," he said softly. "I am Coronel Agustino Cortez. They call me Zorro." He smiled. "The fox."

"Zorra," said Jamie, putting an insulting feminine inflection on the word that changed the meaning entirely. The colonel laughed and wiped his mouth.

"We will detain you," he murmured. "Coming into Méjico without authority."

Jamie guffawed. "Have some coffee. Emilio'll have a pot quick enough."

"We will have coffee. And inspect the *carretas*."

A head crowned with jet hair poked through the pucker-hole of the light wagon, and Teresa María began yelling in staccato Spanish so fast that even Jamie couldn't pick it all out. It sounded like a string of Chinese firecrackers, but he got the gist of it: lay off, or her daddy, the alcalde of Taos, would flay *el coronel's* hide off. The words rattled out like volleys, scarifying the songbirds of morning. A crow flapped mournfully away and then cackled back at Teresa María from a limb. She forgot she wore very little, and inch by inch her bare shoulders emerged as she yelled at the colonel. Then, as suddenly as she'd started her tirade, she yanked herself back inside, leaving visions of lush honeyed flesh in the minds of her observers.

"She is very beautiful, *sí?*" said El Zorro.

Coronel Cortez, or The Fox as he styled himself, studied the cargo manifests amiably. *Yanqui* wealth, twelve wagons of it. From Missouri. It filled his breast with joy. To be sure, these weren't *tejanos* invading his country. They all carried the *yanqui* passports that were essential in the Santa Fe trade. But it didn't matter. They were blood kin of the *tejano* invaders, and that would be . . . convenient. Ah, there was so much to exult about here! But he kept his exulting to himself, deeply hidden behind his soft and doleful eyes.

Just as exhilarating was the total power he held over these gringos, the power in the carbines of his thirty-two *soldados,* in the ball and powder packed down in their barrels. But he was careful not to let them sense his joy. Their *capitán,* Dance, was a great cat with fangs and claws. Cortez could see that. And married to *la doña,* too. It required care and indirection. Still, what was the army for, if not to improve one's condition? Surely no one in all Mexico believed an officer could live on the pittance he received from the government. But being behind the muzzles was the little gift, the little bite—the *mordida*—that made service to the new republic bearable for a man of sensitivity.

Their cook, one called Emilio, a Spanish-speaking Santo Domingan, had started coffee brewing. The gringos would provide the morning meal as well; such things were required. El Zorro, the Fox, pried open a few barrels, examined a few bales, just to make sure the cargo manifest reported things truthfully. It did, much to his regret. Ah, the pleasures of discrepancies! He found, of course, a certain discrepancy, and it amused him. The casks of spirits. The *yanquis* prohibited spirits in their Indian Territories. But transporting them was no crime in Mexico, although he might make it one. His men thirsted.

"You satisfied, Coronel?"

"Ah, Señor Dance. I am distressed to report that the manifests fail to record all your cargo. The spirits. You are smuggling spirits."

The gringo grinned.

"There is a great impost on spirits," El Zorro continued. "But tell me: why are you here, in my country, instead of on the Santa Fe trail across the river?"

"Wal," said the man, "we're setting up a trading operation here. Mrs. Dance and me, we're heading for Santy Fe today with the manifests to get us a tradin' license from your governor—Señor Armijo—and to settle up the taxes. I reckon we'll owe the wagon tax—and all the rest. My wife, she's acquainted with your governor, and I reckon he'll take his bite and license us and let us be. If not, we'll pull across the river and trade from there. I'm a partner in a new company, Rocky Mountain Company, trading for robes both hyar and up yonder on the Yellowstone."

Abominable English, El Zorro thought. But the man's plans excited and worried him. This would require great delicacy. It would not do to kill the milch cow. Let them build their post here, in Méjico, where one could fasten to its teats. Ah, indeed, it would not do to destroy an annuity, a competence for life.

"Señor, we must deal with small matters before I can permit you to travel. You are here illegally, without the license which you should have procured from His Excellency beforehand, you know. You have discrepancies in your cargo manifests, a grave offense. If you were going to Santa Fe with the wagons, we'd escort you to make sure the imposts are paid. But you aren't. You are staying here. You will need, at the least, my sworn statement assuring His Excellency that what you profess to carry is truly what you do carry. A most complicated matter. Ah, yes."

The gringo grinned insolently, and El Zorro smiled back.
"Zorra," Dance said. The feminine ending made the colonel's name a euphemism for a lady who sold herself. An insult. El Zorro enjoyed insults. He felt a growing affection for
Dance. They would see eye to eye. He would give the man a
great *abrazo* later.

That mad cook, Emilio, clacked his teeth, the sound, like
the dry-firing of fusils, making El Zorro nervous. But the
man handed the *coronel* a steaming cup of New Orleans coffee
before anyone else was served, indicating he had a refined
sense of the ordering of the universe. That pleased Agustino
Cortez. None of these gringos was a bit confused by having
carabinas pointed at them. But then, it would have been a
great sadness if they had been.

He eyed his forces amiably. His dragoons had formed a
line that pinned the *yanquis* to the riverbank. His *peóns*, with
their mules and burros, waited patiently beyond. The *yanqui*
teamsters stood about unarmed, half-dressed, harmless. The
scene suffused him with joy. Cortez felt like a surgeon, ready
to begin the cutting.

The light wagon creaked, and *la señora* emerged, clambering to earth with fire in her eye. Entrancing! He eyed her
comely shape, her jet hair, her apricot flesh, her wild brown
irises, and found himself in love, smitten, clapped to earth.
She wore a scooped white *blusa*, which revealed more than it
hid, and full red skirts, and she had done her silky black hair
in braids.

"*Ah, Señor Bandido!*" she exclaimed in her native tongue. "I
know your ways. And I'll cut your *cajones*, just you wait!"

She entranced him with the fire of her tongue. Ah, the
great prize, he thought. He remembered her name now — *la*
Señorita Teresa María Antonia Juanita Obregón. She had
run away from her esteemed parents and married the *yanqui*.
The very one! An, what a delicious bit of gossip that had
been in all of Nuevo Méjico! How silly of her to waste her
wild affections on a ruffian *yanqui!* But perhaps that could be
remedied. The very thought exhilarated him. It would take
time and care, yes. *Poco a poco.* Yet another reason not to let

these *traficantes* escape across the river. He felt love percolate through him.

He smiled, lifting the waxed tips of his mustachio and letting them quiver slightly, a little mannerism that conveyed his excitement to a worthy lady. La Doña Dance.

"Ah, little poppy," he said in Spanish, "we will arrive at a satisfactory accommodation shortly, even though there are grave transgressions of Mexican law here."

She snorted. "I'll have you strung up for the buzzards," she declared sharply. "Wait until I see Manuel."

She alluded to *el gobernador*. It delighted him. What attractive people, these Dances.

An odd young man stood close, absorbing all this, obviously understanding Spanish as well as English. A Spaniard by the looks of him, dark-haired and acquiline, with fevered eyes. More Spanish than El Zorro himself, who was mostly Indian with just enough Spanish to leaven his blood. "And who is this one?" he asked Dance, ignoring the young man himself.

"David Straus, son of my partner."

"Ah, the *socio gerente o gestor*, the managing partner. The Straus of Straus et Fils, St. Louis financiers." It delighted the *coronel*. A prize, a pawn, a valuable asset. And by the soft, innocent look of him, an easy one to deal with. A pity. Plucking roosters was more to his taste.

"He'll be directing the building while we're in Santy Fe."

El Zorro smiled. "A pleasure, *señor*." He offered a limp hand, which the youth grasped briefly. "Welcome to Méjico. We'll take good care of you here."

"Ha!" snapped La Doña Dance.

"I believe you'll find the freight manifests in proper order," said young Straus politely.

"Ah, ah. It is a pity you neglected to record the four casks of spirits. It offends the government of the Republic. It offends the state of Nuevo Méjico."

"Well, we'll pay the impost, then."

"Ah, not so simple! There is the matter of, ah, fraud, you see. And the little matter of erecting a post here without a trading license. And bringing all these goods here without

73

intending to take them to Santa Fe to be properly inspected and taxed. I fear, young man, and Señor Dance, that you might lose everything. After those vultures are done, nothing. *Nada!* But there are ways, eh? Fortunately, I am a man with influence." He smiled, waving a hand broadly toward his ready *soldados*.

"The bite." Dance still smiled, and that was good.

"A fee for services, Señor Dance. A twelfth. One wagonload, the contents of which I will select myself, making sure that you are suitably equipped to trade with the rest."

"Plus Armijo's taxes, running forty percent of the value of the goods."

He shrugged. "It could be worse, *señor*. Your papers are faulty, you know."

"That's extortion," said David. He looked indignant. Ah, the innocence of the young.

"A small price for protection. I am at your service, *señores*."

"No," said Señor Dance. "Sorry, pal."

"No? No? Have you no sense? We're at war! I could string you up for *tejanos*. Spies! False papers!"

"We ain't. I reckon you'd better march us to Santy Fe. The whole outfit."

"Santa Fe? There's no need at all. I'm here to protect you from the greed of the officials, *mi amigo*. El Zorro is your safe conduct, your passport, your license to trade here, in Méjico."

"Reckon we'll git along to Santy Fe. Likely my lady hyar, Teresa María, she's gonna start squawkin' mighty fast. She's got some papa, too. He got up a whole militia to chase us after I run off with her."

El Zorro laughed. The *yanqui* was defying him. Thirty-two *carbinas* pointed at the *yanqui*, but he didn't budge an inch.

"I will eat," said the *coronel*. "I think better on a full stomach, eh?"

"Emilio cooks with strychnine," Señora Dance spat out.

El Zorro laughed, heartily, and had his *cabo*, Ortiz, take the first bite of venison.

CHAPTER 8

David eyed the colonel unhappily. The Mexican officer ate daintily, masticating tough venison cut from a doe they'd shot the day before and swilling it down with great drafts of black coffee. Now and then the man eyed the wagons thoughtfully, with soft, wounded eyes, as if the wagons carried all the woes of the world inside them. He alone, among the Mexicans, partook of the Yankee chow. The rest, the wooden soldiers, lounged around outside the camp and seemed not at all hungry. They'd probably eaten before dawn, fed by those women among the *campesinos*.

David wondered what Mexican armies traveled on — perhaps tortillas, parched corn, rice, and whatever meat they could hunt or commandeer en route. But mostly commandeer. He knew intuitively that many a peon along the way had traded sheep for a fancy piece of scrip that wouldn't even buy a cornhusk.

The chance arrival of these troops had happened at the worst possible moment, he thought. They'd planned, back in St. Louis, to remain concealed on the remote river while Jamie and Teresa María negotiated the necessary licenses and paid the imposts either with trade goods or a draft on the company accounts in St. Louis. Colonel Agustino Cortez was right — they were in big trouble. They needed, for one thing, *guías*, or merchandise passports, stating exactly where the goods were to be transported. Any goods not directly en route to named destinations were subject to confiscation. The Rocky Mountain Company, at that

75

point, had no papers.

That was only the beginning. They'd wrestled with all of this back in St. Louis. His father understood the Santa Fe trade. They all knew what to expect. The government of Mexico imposed a brutal tariff, known as the *derechos de aran-celarios*, equal to a hundred percent of the value of the merchandise. In addition, there were the *derechos de consumación*, or consumption duties. Nor was that the end of it. Governor Armijo imposed his own duties on incoming goods, originally five hundred dollars per wagon until traders began using larger wagons and importing only the costliest goods. After that, the governor imposed an ad valorem tax on top of Mexican federal taxes.

The only thing that kept all these taxes from breaking the backs of traders was that they were negotiable. For little gifts, or little bites as they were called, the venal officials rendered the tariffs livable. Jamie had intended to settle all that while his men quietly built Fort Dance, far from Santa Fe eyes.

They'd debated it back there, around his father's beeswaxed conference table. Why trade in Mexico at all? Why not just build a post well east of the Bents on the north bank of the Arkansas, safely in the United States? The more they had talked, the more they'd understood the answer. Any hope that the new company had of going against the powerful Bents lay in the Mexican trade. Actually the Bents had a Mexican trading license, and were powers to be reckoned with in Santa Fe. But William Bent rarely sent trading wagons out among the dangerous Comanche and Kiowa and Apache residing south of the Arkansas. Instead, the Bents traded with the Cheyenne and Arapaho, tribes that usually roamed to the north. The new Buffalo Company had no chance at all against the Bents if it could not trade freely in Mexico and develop its own means to operate there.

David corrected himself. Operate here. Now that they were in Mexico and surrounded by Mexican troops with carbines, he doubted the wisdom of any of it. Most agonizing was the possibility that the entire cargo, wagons and oxen and all, could be confiscated, and the Rocky Mountain Company doomed from the start. They'd made a terrible mistake! They should have stopped back at the Big Timbers, on the other side!

Odd, though, how Jamie Dance had simply defied the man. Did Jamie understand something about the Mexicans that had eluded David? Would they all suffer for it, be marched off to some Mexican dungeon, such as the terrible Acordada in Mexico City, to rot away their lives? It had happened, and could happen again at the whim of any official. The thought of being in a Mexican *cárcel* appalled David and turned his innards taut. He had a wild instinct to give the colonel anything! Anything! to settle the matter on any terms that preserved their liberty. How could Jamie Dance be so calm, smile, talk with Teresa María, instruct Lyle Black, begin a day's routine, while this gorgeously attired officer wolfed food and pondered and eyed the wagons dolefully, plotting theft and imprisonment — and maybe worse. An execution of Texian spies?

Choking back his terror, David approached Jamie. "Why aren't you doing anything!" he whispered. "We could be planning. We could be making a defense! We could slip our rifles—"

"Aw, David, in old Mexico you gotta wait. They aren't on Yankee time."

"Wait! For what? To be killed? Marched south in chains? To have everything we own stolen?"

"Old Zorro, he isn't going to do that, David. They operate plum different. He's sittin' there figurin' how he can make the most *dinero* from it."

"And you're doing nothing!"

Jamie eyed him, grinned, and nodded. "I suppose we could force the issue — some." He wheeled off and spoke quietly to the teamsters. They began at once to collect halters and to trudge toward the oxen picketed beyond the glinting carbines of the soldiers.

A word from the colonel and the line of troops coalesced, carbines raised, into a wall between the teamsters and the stock. The short, bronzed men in blue camisas looked to be experienced cavalrymen who knew how to shoot in volleys. The teamsters halted well away from the deadly muzzles, unable to reach the stock. Boar Blunt began hurling insults at the soldiers. He called them greasers, toy soldiers, spics, sonsofbitches. The colonel listened, and smiled gently.

"An, Señor Dance, you wouldn't be thinking of abandoning the hospitality of Méjico, would you?"

"Reckon I would, Zorra. I got it in me to build my post yonder." He waved carelessly at the United States side of the Arkansas.

"A rash idea. Someone could get hurt, *señor*. Carbines shoot, do they not?" The colonel beamed. "Excellent troops. My veterans. See the *cabo* there — a mankiller trained like a dog." The colonel wiped his fat mouth with the sleeve of his tunic, and stood.

"I guess we'll build across the river," Jamie persisted. "Leave you a little sweetener. You got any notion of what tickles your fancy? I got me a bolt of blue twill that'd cut up into a few more outfits like you got on."

El Zorro laughed bashfully. "That would be splendid, to seal the partnership. That and a few more little things."

Dance chuckled. "I knew we'd come to some understandin'."

"Ah, *señor*, that is only the tip, *sí?* We are going to be partners, Señor Dance. The Rocky Mountain Company and El Zorro, *sí?* But not on paper. We will not seal this on paper. But in blood. Ah yes, blood. *Rojo sangre*. My little troop, it needs succor; it needs a base. Fort Dance, rising here on the very border of Méjico, it will be the base. From here, we will protect the whole border. Here will my fine *soldados* get powder and ball, knives, rifles, boots, good bolts of twill to make light blue and dark blue uniforms."

David's mind raced. A partner? A rogue officer of Mexico supported by the Rocky Mountain Company? "No!" he cried.

The colonel eyed him sadly, the bags under his eyes now more pronounced. "Ah, *señores*, a partnership requires give and take, *sí?* El Zorro, he will do his part. These *campesinos*, they will make adobes, and the women will cook. My *soldados*, they will lay up walls, guard the stock" — he chortled — "and hunt. It takes *soldados* to guard the trading goods too, against the fierce Comanche, the bloodthirsty Kiowa, *sí?* Useful, indeed. Free labor. Many days of free labor from my *campesinos* and *soldados.* In a few weeks you have a fort. And after your adobe fort is built, and the flags fly over it—one of Méjico, one your company ensign—then we will depart, and you will trade with the Indians. I will return now and then for a little reward, *sí?* Just a little. Some powder, a little lead. You know. Nothing much. Just a little, to help me protect you. A little for the silent partner, *sí?"*

"How little is little, Zorra?" asked Dance, mockery in his eye.

"Ah, trust Zorro. If you don't trust Zorro, trust la *zorra!"* The colonel laughed politely.

"It's not on paper! It's not even an agreement!" protested David.

"It's not the United States, David," said Jamie.

"In honor of this agreement, I'll take that bolt, *señor.* And another dark blue one. And powder. *Sí,* we make war against the *tejanos.* Powder and balls are the muscles of war. But that's all. Just a trifle. The smallest part of all that wealth."

"We got licenses and imposts to think about, Cortez. I reckon me and Teresa María better git along to Santy Fe."

"Ah, *señor,* I will accompany you. I and a small detail, to see to your protection. And of course to ease the task. A word here, a word there, and you'll have the *guías,* pay the *derechos,* have a license to trade with Indians—all it requires is a little murmur from me in the proper ears. And a few little *dons,* gifts, in the right fingers." He laughed gently. "You have all this ready, I trust?"

In fact, Jamie did. David carried drafts on Straus et Fils, good anywhere in Mexico because the integrity of the St. Louis house was well known. Those and a bag of gold pieces to make things happen. In Mexico coin made things happen.

"What if we don't want your partnership?" David asked, a truculent tone in his voice.

The colonel shrugged.

It was maddening, this amorphous agreement, the amorphous threats backed with steel. No way to do business. He'd write his father. His father could apply all sorts of pressure,

79

using the U.S. Consul in Santa Fe, Manuel Alvarez, a Spaniard who was an American citizen.

"Ah, Señor Dance, let's gather the few trinkets, just to seal our contract, and then we'll all start our day, eh?"

David went with Dance and Cortez, watching unhappily while Jamie deposited a bolt of fine twill in the officer's arms, and then a few wax-papered bricks of powder and several one-pound bars of lead.

"Hyar ya be," said Jamie.

"It is a happy beginning, *señor*," said El Zorro.

David fumed, but he kept his mouth shut and resolved to have a long hot talk with Jamie Dance the moment he was out of earshot of that pirate. But the chance never came. The colonel instructed his troops in their duties; Jamie had a little talk with his teamsters. Then Jamie saddled two horses for himself and Teresa María, and loaded two packmules with their gear. El Zorro picked six soldiers who looked tougher than alligators for an escort, and the whole party rode up the Purgatoire. David watched until they vanished from sight. Suddenly he was in charge. Except for the moronic-looking *cabo*, or corporal, with killer eyes and an expressionless face. David would begin a fort, where no Yankee fort should be.

Guy Straus scarcely knew which was worse: the news or the rumors. For days, the gossip he heard over the aromatic coffee at the Planters House had been about the filibuster, Texas expansion, and war. Everyone in the mountain trade had dissected the rumors feverishly, trying to separate fact from fiction and somehow making it all worse than it probably was. But some things had filtered through from the Republic of Texas. An expedition of around three hundred volunteers — Texas couldn't afford a paid army — along with numerous merchants hauling trade items westward, had set off to conquer New Mexico. Or trade with New Mexico. No one was sure about that. The volunteers were too few to fight wars of conquest, especially when so ill equipped and with only a small brass cannon for a field piece. Yet off they'd gone, apparently with the blessing or connivance of President Mirabeau Lamar.

Guy Straus's thoughts turned not to the Texians bumbling westward on a mad quest fueled by their conceits, but upon that sinister man who governed New Mexico while enriching himself in the Santa Fe trade through taxes and confiscation. Manuel Armijo was capable of anything. Through the years, a hundred stories had drifted into the offices of Straus et Fils about this tall, handsome, sensuous, thick-lipped man who scrupled at nothing. He'd stolen, murdered, taxed, connived and betrayed to reach his present eminence. Yankees had joked about his cowardice and his chameleon ways, but they had underestimated that man. A Texas filibuster was all *el gobernador* needed to round up all gringos and heretics, no matter whether they carried Republic of Texas passports or those of the United States. Gringos and heretics like Guy Straus's son David and Jamie Dance and the fifteen employees of the new company.

Straus realized that he was resorting to euphemisms. Manuel Armijo would do more than round them up; he would either shoot them as Texas spies or send them marching south in chains. And he would surely grab the real prize, twelve wagonloads of trade goods with a St. Louis value of approximately twelve hundred dollars per wagon, plus the Conestogas and Pittsburghs and the livestock.

In the somber quiet of his gilded office on Chestnut Street, Guy weighed the matter restlessly. It was approaching the eve of the sabbath, and he wished to accomplish what he could before his day of rest. He had means and the will to employ them. Some businessmen might bridle at sending a messenger a thousand miles through dangerous wilds, but not Guy Straus. There was too much at stake; the lives and liberty of his son, his partner, and his employees—and much of the wealth of Straus et Fils. A dispatch rider traveling across the aching reaches of the plains would cost much—and be cheap at a hundred times the price.

He reviewed what he knew: the Texas filibuster had been confirmed in the press. His people, quietly building the post on the Arkansas, would know nothing of it. He intended to warn them, and his message would be simple: stay north of the river on United States soil. If they'd started the post in Mexico, abandon it and build at the place they'd decided would be second best, the Big Timbers of the Arkansas.

Frowning, he reviewed the choices they'd carefully worked out right there in the salon a few weeks earlier. Their opposition, the Bents, were powers to reckon with on the north bank, but less powerful in Mexico, even though Charles lived in Taos and Ceran St. Vrain lived in Santa Fe and had the ear of the officials. At Bent's Fort, the company traded eagerly with the Cheyenne and Arapaho—but not the Comanche or Kiowa. That was the opening Guy Straus and the Rocky Mountain Company intended to exploit.

It had sounded fine in the waxed offices of Straus et Fils. It had seemed the best policy. Even though Mexico had always been an uncertain place to do business and its officials could impose draconian imposts, in his experience it had never worked out that way. The Mexicans never imposed all the taxes they could. That would have demolished the lucrative trade. Instead, the taxes had amounted to ten or twelve percent ad valorem, a burden that was bearable, given the advantage of operating from Mexico against Bent, St. Vrain, and Co. Dance would go to the places the Bent traders were afraid to go.

Yes, Guy thought. Send an express. Tell them about the winds of war. Tell them to pull back. He stood, intending to take one further step before he acted. Even as he reached the massive walnut door that let out onto Chestnut, one of his three slaves, Gregoire, handed him his gold-headed walking stick and swung the door open. Guy nodded, and walked briskly eastward toward the steep hill that led down to the Mississippi levee. St. Louis steamed, and Guy's brisk pace wilted under the ferocity of the August sun. He pushed through the wet air as if into a wall, hoping he wasn't too late; hoping David Mitchell had not abandoned his lair in the red brick building that was the seat of American empire, on the midafternoon of a Friday.

He had been there many times. How often the strands of frontier commerce and finance had intertwined with the affairs of the Republic, or the policies of Washington City regarding Indian matters, or the whole business of protecting the Santa Fe trade with military escorts. Until 1838, it had been the dominion of General William Clark, he who'd traveled to the Pacific and back with Meriwether Lewis. And then the general died. Now it was in the hands of a veteran of the borders, the old fur man David Mitchell, the new Superintendent of Indian Affairs, and a power to be reckoned with.

He found Mitchell in his shirtsleeves in spite of government priggishness, with his boots poking across his desk and his gaze directed toward the arched dome of the ceiling. Those feet, Guy knew, had trod the farthest reaches of Indian Country, had walked into fur posts from here to Oregon. Those eyes, buried in crow's-feet, had seen the entire West and all its rough denizens.

"Well, Guy. Back up your cart and pile it on," he said.

Guy laughed. They'd done business, or sipped coffee or liquors at the Planters House many times. He got down to business at once, as he always did, saving the amenities for later.

"What's this Texas filibuster about? What's Washington City doing about it?"

David Mitchell raised a brow, and pierced him with a wise eye. "Lamar's sent a cockeyed outfit west—traders, they say; pirates, actually. Blowhards, the whole lot. Armijo's roaring in Santa Fe, putting all foreigners under house arrest—even Charles Bent; inciting mobs, inflaming the whole thing."

The news filled Guy with dread. "My company's walking into the middle of it."

Mitchell nodded. "We're trying to keep out of it, protect United States people and property." He nodded at a worn leather pouch on his desk. "That's a dispatch from Washington City. It's going on the *Assiniboine* to Leavenworth at dawn. From Leavenworth, a military dispatch'll take it to our consul there, Alvarez. I've been instructed to keep the tribes out of it if I can; Alvarez is instructed to assert our neutrality, protect our nationals, threaten retaliation. The cavalry at Leavenworth's going to guard our nationals on the Santa Fe trail—show their presence enough to keep Manuel Armijo from acting rashly." He grimaced. "Damned fire-eatin' Texians."

A dispatch. "Is it going via Bent's Fort?" Guy asked.

Mitchell grinned. "There's stuff for the Bents in it. Here." He pushed a sheet of foolscap across the wide desk, and dug at the inkpot and nib pen. "Right past the Purgatoire."

Guy dipped the nib into the India ink, and paused. Discretion was paramount in his mind. Then he scratched at the soft paper:

Messrs. Dance and Straus: Withdraw to north bank, even if building has progressed at southern site. Build at alternative site. Southern climate not hospitable. Trade north of river for time being or until further word.

He paused, wondering whether to say more, and decided against it. He signed his name and the date, blotted the document, and folded it. Mitchell shoved an envelope toward him, and he slid the note inside, sealing it with gum. He addressed it simply to James Dance and David Straus, Arkansas River at the Purgatoire.

Mitchell smiled and dropped it into the pouch. "I reckon your outfit'll butt against the Bents now," he said. "Better'n butting against Armijo. I hope old Jamie's smart enough not to sail into Santa Fe looking for a Mex trading license now."

"I hope so too. He's got Teresa María, of course, but that won't help much. I worry about David—and the rest."

"Ah, Guy, if you didn't like risk, you'd try an easier business."

Straus smiled. Fur men were a fraternity.

"Tell you what, Guy. If I hear anything that affects your outfit, I'll get ahold of you."

That was old Davy Mitchell, Guy thought. For years, a top man in Chouteau's company, but weathered and square, playing no favorites now.

Moments later he stood on the rise of land back from the Mississippi, studying the packets at the levee, one of which would turn up the Missouri, carrying his fragile message to his son and partner. St. Louis pulsed with energy, even in the blistering heat of August. Mitchell was right, he thought; he didn't enjoy tame enterprises, not when a wilderness, unknown and unpredictable, stretched westward to challenge a man, test him, harden him. His wife, Yvonne, had never understood the wild yearnings that infused him, that fueled the men who plunged into the fur trade. Someday soon he'd go West himself, out across the virgin continent, and see his posts with his own eyes. But now he'd return to Chestnut Street and comfort Yvonne, whose mind was steeped in the doom of war.

CHAPTER 9

South they rode, up the Purgatoire, across a flat plain as empty as a desert. They passed ruined *placitas*, tumbles of decaying adobe built by families that had suffered and died at the hands of Comanche or Jicarilla Apaches, whose land this was. Jamie was glad, in such moments, that the *coronel* rode beside him along with six sun-blacked dragoons. They were some small protection against the most ferocious plains tribe of all.

They slept through the noons, when the sun sucked sweat and spit out of man and beast, finding shade wherever it was available, dozing through the oppressive white hours when nothing stirred. They rarely talked. Not even voluble Teresa María, whose smooth calves caught the eye of El Zorro whenever she climbed aboard her Santa Fe saddle and hiked her cotton skirts.

Jamie wished to travel faster, push hard into the cool evenings when the earth radiated heat it had swallowed by day. But the Mexican hussars would not be hurried. Rarely did sweat ever darken the armpits of El Zorro's gaudy blue tunic, with its glinting gold lanyards and braid, and he viewed the glaring white world serenely, from under the vast shade of his high-peaked broad-brimmed sombrero.

"Cortez," Jamie said, deliberately being impolite, "me and Teresa, we got to git ahead, get me a *permiso* and git back thar to build us a post. You reckon we could push along—"

"Aaaah," El Zorro said, dismissing Dance with a languid wave of his coppery hand and a wounded look in his eyes. "We must protect you. The people are aroused—indignant—about

86

the army of Texas coming. They would surely . . . molest, *sí*, molest you."

But Jamie sensed he was more prisoner than protected. It didn't matter much, except that it ate time. Did Mexicans ever exert themselves?

"Not with Teresa María around, Cortez."

El Zorro smiled slowly. "She is beautiful company, *sí?* I go slow so maybe I can enjoy *la doña.*"

Teresa María blushed prettily, the red staining her olive cheeks. She plainly enjoyed being back in her own country.

On they rode, a vedette to either side hunting and keeping a weather eye out for the dreaded Comanche. Rarely did they return with meat, though, and Jamie himself often ended up, evenings, chasing through the saltbush beside the warm creek, hunting anything that made meat.

Gradually the Purgatoire slid into an arid canyon as the land tilted upward toward highlands sometimes visible in the heat haze, but still they saw no one in this obscure corner of Mexico—and that was good. A party of Comanches could mean death, after some of the most diabolical torture ever devised by the human imagination. The thought of it raised Jamie's hackles.

They joined the mountain branch of the Santa Fe trail near the little pueblo of Trinidad, where the arid slopes lifted high around them and occasional eddies of coolness filtered past. In the bright village, surrounded by orchards and greenery and sweet air, they found life at last: swine and cattle, chickens, mangy dogs, bronzed children, sun-ravaged old women wrapping rebozos around them against the stares of the soldiers and the morose colonel. Most of the villagers fled, Jamie noted, and more than once he saw mothers dragging daughters out of sight of the smiling dragoons.

They rested, stole peaches and plums and *cerveza* that tasted like turpentine, shot a ewe for supper, let their saddle horses fatten on grasses, swilled mescal, and started up Ratón Pass, skirting chaparral and red rock. They rested again at the village on the south slope, Ratón, a white cluster of *jacals* and an adobe fortress where its denizens could hide during the times of the Comanche. A den of Comancheros, Jamie had heard,

87

trafficking in guns and human flesh. A mountain pass and a city named Mouse. From there they traversed an empty plain, frightening somehow, with dry mountains compassing it and towering columns of cloud building along the horizons like vengeful armies of ghosts.

"Ah, Señor Dance, Méjico, it is the place of the dead, yes? We always think of death. While we live, we take all we can of life, because soon we will be bones, and the circling vultures will pick us clean. The vulture, he is our national bird. He shows us how to live in a barren land."

"That ain't my bird, Zorro."

The officer laughed softly. "The *yanquis,* they take to the eagle. The eagle kills and eats. The vulture, he eats what others have killed."

"You'd like to feast on them twelve wagons o'stuff, I reckon. You fixin' to pick my bones?"

"Mary, Joseph, and Jesus, how you talk. No, Señor Dance. I am going to protect you. *Los indios,* they are savage there. Surely, for the protection of my *soldados,* you can spare a leetle powder now and then. You are my partner, *amigo!* We will make good things together, *si?* Think what I can do. I can keep the tax collectors, the vultures, off your back, *si?* I can say, *señores,* you will not disturb Jamie Dance. You will not clean the bones of the Rocky Mountain Company. Even *el gobernador.* I will tell him, no — this excellent company is good for Méjico. The Bents, they are right on our border, making bad designs on Méjico. But now comes the Rocky Mountain Company against the Bents. Ah! So we'll be partners, Señor Jamie Dance. You and me, and the grand one in St. Louis, Señor Straus. I am a partner, and then no one in Méjico can say, Don't do business here, strangers; go away. You will not be strangers if I am in the company!"

Jamie laughed. It was about what he'd figured. Mexico had its ways.

"How much you reckon your partnership's worth, Cortez?"

"Ah, *señor,* we must nourish this little company, *si? Nada.* I take nothing for a while. Just maybe a few rifles, a little powder. Then, maybe you make good trade, get lots of robes, you think of your *compañero,* your secret partner, and you set something aside for me. Maybe you thank me because I keep the tax collectors happy. We give them a few gifts. We tell them you have brought nothing much. Very little."

"I reckon I'd like to declare the whole lot, Cortez."

"Ah, Señor Dance, but who comes so far to see? Me, I have many dragoons. Four troops. These, they are just a few. I am *coronel, sí?* I am strong!"

Jamie said nothing. He sensed that a false word could send him in chains into the twilight of a southern dungeon. The colonel wanted a piece. Or at least an open account, a place where he could snatch private goods for his private army. A tax, actually, in addition to whatever taxes would be paid in Santa Fe. That was how the federal army worked: any handy cow or pig made a meal. And if a poor peon protested, a sheep or two was taken as well.

"You say nothing, *compañero.*"

Dance shrugged. "What's there to say?"

The colonel lifted his broad sombrero, and smiled sadly, pain in his liquid eyes. "Welcome to Méjico," he said.

Dance laughed. Colonel Agustino Cortez probably didn't want to kill the milch cow. But Jamie figured the man would ride up now and then with a company or two of crack dragoons and lancers, and levy his own little tax on the trading firm of Dance, Fitzhugh, and Straus. That is, if Manuel Armijo didn't get there first.

El Zorro touched heels to his sweated horse and trotted it forward, alongside Teresa María, who smiled at him. A little gold, a little sky blue, a quivering waxed mustache, and she would blush and sigh. A man with quivering mustachios, Dance thought dourly, could melt the soul of a Mexican lady.

The well-worn trail took them along the Rio Canadian a way, and then cut southwest, with the brooding Sangre de Cristos looming darkly in the west, lost in afternoon storms. They forded the Vermejo, camped one night on Royado Creek, hid from a large party of horsemen between Royado and Ocate Creek, and rejoined the main branch of the Santa Fe Trail near Río Mora.

From then on, they were never far from adobe villages watered by small creeks out of the mountains, or springs. Wherever they rode, Santa Ana, Tecolote, Bernal, San José, the villagers fled from the blue-clad soldiers, almost as if they, rather than Texians or Comanche, were the enemies of all the humble ones. Bold children stood their ground and stared at Jamie.

"*Tejano!*" one cried.

"Yankee!" he cried back.

Teresa María scolded them volubly, until the little ones grinned and shrugged.

"Padre Martinez, that firebrand in Taos, he tells them the *tejanos* come to steal and kill and molest," said El Zorro. "He is a born hater of all *yanquis*."

They pierced through arid canyons, gold and red rock vaulting upward, scabbed with bright cedar, dark piñon high above, and finally rode out upon a great broken plain after rounding the southern rampart of the mountains. They wound their way through chaparral and into the capital city of the province, old Santa Fe, a golden town built of dried mud. There, suddenly, Jamie beheld Mexicans in better dress; women in bright skirts and white *blusas;* men in dark *pantalones* sometimes flared at the boot, white collarless shirts, vests. Handsome people, lean and olive fleshed and happy. Civilization. Teresa María fell into some kind of ecstasy, and felt compelled to greet every soul they rode by.

They clattered through twisted streets, smelling dung, passing burro-drawn *carretas,* pushing aside old women with rebozos, and burst at last into the dusty plaza. There, across its barren earth, stood the long, low seat of government, the Palace of the Governors. And standing at the giant double doors lounged a man Jamie recognized at once from portraits: the great height, the thick sensuous lips, the predatory brown eyes, the dazzling blue uniform blazoned with the ensigns of high office, the sheathed sword, the pair of bodyguards close by, the shining boots, and the widening smile—he beheld, he knew, *el gobernador,* Manuel Armijo, who held Jamie's fate in his thick brown fingers.

A man in dirty buckskins and a gray flat-crowned hat sat his horse on the north bank of the river. He had a spare mount on a tether behind him. His signal shot had alerted David and all the rest at the rising Fort Dance, including the Mexican *cabo* in charge of the dragoons, whom David now knew as Juan Ortiz.

Several of the blue-shirted federals had followed David across the loosely wooded flat to the river.

"I got a dispatch for Dance or Straus," the man shouted across the water. "But I ain't crossin'. Got orders not to. I mighta anyway, if'n I didn't see all them federals."

"Who are you?" David called back.

"They speak English?" the man yelled.

"I don't think so."

"I'm outa Leavenworth. Got diplomatic papers. Got a letter for you in the pouch."

News from his father! "There's a ford up a bit. I'll saddle and meet you there."

The man waved, and turned his bay upstream.

David turned to the *cabo* and addressed him in Spanish. "There's a letter for me from my company."

Ortiz eyed him sullenly, but said nothing while David raced back, saddled a horse, and rode toward the ford.

There were times, young Straus thought, when he wasn't sure but what they were all prisoners in Mexico. He worried about the message. Bad news probably. No one sent dispatches with good news. He eyed the building site, satisfied that the work was going on. The Mexican *campesinos* were pouring adobes into forms they'd made, while the federal soldiers were laying up walls; and his teamsters were cutting beams, sawing plank, and hunting. A thousand times he'd wondered about all that free labor provided by Colonel Cortez. There'd be a price; he only hoped it would be a price the company could bear.

He trotted the mount to the ford and found the dispatch rider waiting on the north bank. David eased the horse into the slow current, and let it pick its way across. The man eyed him with piercing blue eyes set in weathered flesh.

"Here y'are," he said, handing David the letter. "I was instructed not to enter Mexico; got instructions hyar for the consul—Alvarez, in Santa Fe. Bent's gonna smuggle it in. They're all under house arrest, you know. Every furriner in the province. Mex all heated up about the Texians."

David didn't know. It chilled him. Jamie riding into that. "Any fighting yet?" he asked.

"None as I heard about. I'da rode acrost the river anyways, except for all them federals you got there. How come the whole Mex army's right thar?"

"They say they're protecting us."

The soldier grinned, and slid a plug under his tongue. "Some protection. Leastwise it'll keep the Comanches off ye. You got anything I should be passing along to someone?"

David thought of saying a lot, and opted to say little. "Nothing."

"What Mexican outfit's campin' there?"

"A dragoon company led by a Colonel Agustino Cortez."

"Where's old Cortez?"

"Off to Santa Fe with an escort—with one of my company's partners."

The man spat a brown streak into the river. "I don't feature building a tradin' outfit over there. Not now. Well, I got to git. I'm Overstreet. Sergeant Buford Overstreet, but not wearin' any blues. I'll pass by hyar agin, few days. You got something to go east, you stick it on this rock hyar, and I'll fetch it."

The man wheeled his horse—it wasn't a cavalry horse, David noted—and rode back to the river road. Over on the south bank, the *cabo,* Ortiz, watched the transaction thoughtfully.

David broke the wax seal and withdrew his father's thick stationery, and read the familiar hand, a guarded instruction to pull out of Mexico, abandon whatever had been built, and start fresh at the alternate site they'd discussed, east at the Big Timbers—on the United States side. His father had hinted that the Texas invasion posed acute problems.

David sighed, and slid the message back into its envelope. He steered his horse out into the ford again, wondering what to do. The instruction chafed at him. Surely the Texas business would blow over, and then they'd be stuck on a site that offered no advantage over the Bents. The *cabo* was waiting for him on the Mexican bank, and together they rode back to the rising post, David lost in wild, conflicting thoughts.

The work here had gone astonishingly well, thanks to the

92

unexpected help. What's more, even though David was young and green, he'd faced no discipline problems from his teamsters. Perhaps that was because the men really heeded Lyle and Mazappa. He'd expected trouble from Boar Blunt, but had resolved it his own way by making Blunt a hunter. Each day, Blunt and three others rode out looking for buffalo. It took incredible amounts of meat to feed over a dozen Yankees, another fifteen or so *campesinos*, and two dozen Mexican federal soldiers. Blunt had simply been too busy, too tired, to pick on David, although the mockery in Boar's eye never departed.

David himself knew little about building an adobe post, but everyone else seemed to. The peons had built forms from hewn cottonwood, and each day they mixed vast amounts of mud with wild hay and poured it into the forms to bake in the sun. Even before the heavy bricks were wholly dry, the sweating soldiers, mostly working without shirts in the broiling heat, laid them up, using a mortar made from the same mud. The teamsters hewed crooked cottonwood limbs into beams and lintels, and slowly sawed thick planks for doors and shutters. All this they did while caring for horses and oxen, guarding the wagons, and keeping a weather eye out for predators ranging from Comanche to Texians, mountain lions to wolves. Jamie's post would be a small one, not even half the area of the Bents' great fortress upstream, but it ate manpower. David doubted he could have built it without the help of the federals.

And that's what made his mind crawl now.

He eyed the rising adobe walls, three feet thick and now chest high; he walked among the thousands of adobes slowly curing under a hot sun. He stared at the great mud puddle where brown men stirred grass into a mire, and bucketed the thick slop over to the wooden forms. He peered at the naked beams, axed and adzed, sawed and hewn, lying in orderly rows—the sweat of his teamsters in each one. He saw the hanging quarters of buffalo and deer, red and fly-specked, meat hauled from distant dangerous swales with mules and carts. He saw the four cooking women, weary and bronzed, and the heaps of firewood they'd gathered, and the pile of tin cups and plates they were rinsing.

He wandered to the rising fort, and looked for the stakes set at corners, stakes that demarked the site of interior walls that would create barracks, offices, a fur warehouse, the trading room, a kitchen, guest quarters. He stood in the middle of it all, choked and unhappy, his father's message a sudden torment. This was a good place! A wild impulse boiled through him to ignore the instruction. His father wasn't here! He couldn't see how well it all was going! But then he steadied himself, remembering his responsibilities, remembering that his father would have good reason, and remembering the conservatism with which Straus et Fils had always been run. With that, resignation flooded through him.

Sadly, he summoned Lyle Black and Mazappa Oliphant and told them the news. Neither could read, so he read the message from his father to them.

"Well, now we'll see," said Lyle.

David knew what he alluded to.

He figured they may as well be about it. Quietly, he wandered from teamster to teamster, catching each one's ear. Men grimaced and swore, lashing angrily at the half-hewn logs.

"They're not lost!" he cried. "We can float them down to the Big Timbers."

All the while he was informing his men, he wrestled with a way to tell the federal troops, the *campesinos*, his hosts in this land. He dreaded that; dreaded the response. His own men had stopped their labor in that midafternoon, and had begun listlessly to collect halters. They'd have to fetch the oxen and mules and horses first, and begin yoking them.

David approached Ortiz, and faltered through the news in Spanish. "The company has instructed us to leave here and build on the north side of the river," he began. "I've told my men to yoke the oxen. We'll be crossing in an hour. I . . . the company fears that the invasion from Texas will bring trouble; that—"

The *cabo* grunted. "No, *señor*," he said. "It will not be. Here you come; here you stay."

"Look, Corporal, we've a right to leave if we want—"

But Ortiz snapped out staccato commands, not listening to David. At every hand, federal troops abandoned their sweaty labor and ran for their arms, which had been stacked neatly. It took only moments. A skirmish line of hard-muscled bare-chested men materialized between the Americans and the rivers, their deadly carbines leveled.

David turned to find Ortiz himself holding a leveled rifle on him. One with a bayonet. He peered about wildly, seeing those carbines pointed at every teamster, and each of his men standing frozen, peering into death.

Ortiz smiled. "Welcome to Méjico, Señor Straus. El Zorro, he told me to make you welcome, to give the *yanquis* the *abrazo*. We need traders here; we need a good fort. He gives you labor, lots of sweat. He would not be happy if you go away. We will wait."

CHAPTER 10

Something kindled in the governor's eyes and vanished. He wore his character perfectly, Teresa María thought; in his sensual face, calculating gaze, and garish uniform, sky blue and gaudy gold. He studied her, then Jamie, and finally the colonel and his six dragoons sitting dusty horses before the palace of the governors.

"Welcome, *señores*. Welcome, Señorita Obregón."

Hadn't he heard? "I'm Señora Dance," she replied.

He sighed, softly, an odd smile building on his thick lips.

"You'll wait here," he said. "We have business with Señor Dance."

She smiled sweetly, knowing she'd ignore him. She slid off her dusty horse and adjusted her skirts, aware she'd revealed too much calf. They marched inside, all except the dragoons, and she noted the cool gloom of the interior. Its thick walls sealed out the heat of the day.

El gobernador ushered them into a parlor, a salon glinting with gilt, and waited.

"Excellency," began El Zorro, "I found them on the south side of Río Nepeste, with a wagon or two. Several men, about to build a post. I held them there. They all had United States passports — but one could wonder about it. Señor Dance professes to be on his way here to obtain a trading license and pay his imposts. I searched the wagons, Excellency. Goods for the Indian trade, not the Santa Fe trade. I feared perhaps he would arm the Comanche and stir them against us; that he would profiteer and foment trouble. He's an agent of the Texas insurrectionists, I think. So I brought them."

Teresa María sniffed. The colonel was weaving his little plots and schemes. "You are a liar," she said sweetly.

El gobernador smiled slightly. "You will not interfere, *señorita.*"

"*Señora!*"

Armijo studied her. "There is no record of marriage at Ranchos de Taos. Padre Martinez says there are names inscribed in the book but not the signature of a true priest. One Padre Tomás, known to no one."

She gasped. Jamie's eyes darted away. "But he married us! He was from the City of Mexico! Jamie found him!"

Jamie smiled crookedly.

Armijo smiled. "*Señorita*, we will deal with this later. I may send you back to your fine father, the alcalde. . . ."

She couldn't grasp it all. Memories of that night flooded back to her: the hour after midnight when she slipped from the *casa* of her parents on the plaza, into Jamie's arms; their swift ride southward to the adobe church where the strange padre waited amid the guttering candles at the altar, ready to begin the rite and sacrament of matrimony. Ah, she remembered him, with his gold-rimmed spectacles, reading the Mass in sonorous Latin; the strange priest, Padre Tomás, pronouncing her a married woman and giving them his blessing. Father Martinez, her parish priest, wouldn't do it— he hated heretics and *yanquis*. But the traveling one, the one Jamie found . . . the one who said the rites and solemnly inscribed their names in the parish record book, that chill night . . .

She sighed, shakily, and glared at Jamie Dance, who peered back at her sheepishly. She'd get to the bottom of this! She was Señora Dance! The shame of not being Señora Dance flooded her. Ah! She would be *señora*— not *señorita!*— even if she had to be the *esposa* of the heretic.

"We've been waiting for your delightful presence a long time, Señor Dance," *el gobernador* was saying softly. "There are certain things, certain old accounts. The matter dating back to eighteen and thirty-six, when you were discovered trapping beaver in Nuevo Méjico without a license; and not paying the taxes on the pelts. You departed hastily, but came back to woo Señorita Obregón after a year or two, quite unknown to us. Ah, it has been hanging, *señor;* the imposts grow with time, and now are large. And this matter of the *señorita.* We'll delve into that later. For now we have government matters to attend to."

Teresa María noticed that soldiers barred the door. It occurred to her suddenly that they might take Jamie from her. A dread filled her, and an anger about the way things were done in this province. She was perfectly familiar with these procedures, having seen them all as the daughter of the Taos alcalde. She peered anxiously at Jamie, loving his lanky slouchy body, his *yanqui* drawl, wild humor, and slow grin. If they hurt him—if they took Jamie from her . . . She glared fiercely at *el gobernador,* knowing she'd stop at nothing.

"I reckon we can come to a little understandin'," Jamie said. "Me, I'm a partner in a new trading company, goin' up against the Bents." He paused, letting that sink in. Armijo brimmed with resentments toward the Bents and their adobe fort on the border of Mexico. "I'm partnered up with ol' Brokenleg Fitzhugh, and back in St. Louis, Guy Straus. He's runnin' it."

"Ah!" Armijo seemed delighted, though Teresa María, suspected he knew all this. "Straus. Straus et Fils. I've done business, *sí,* much business with Straus." Something contemplative filled *el gobernador's* eyes. "A full partner, Dance?"

"Me and Fitzhugh, we each got a sixth; Straus, he's got two-thirds."

"I remember this Fitzhugh. I believe he was with you when you were—"

"Him, he's up on the Yellerstone, makin' out against the Chouteaus."

"A new company. And you've entered Mexico. And our esteemed *coronel* here, always alert when our borders are threatened by bandits, he found you." Armijo turned to Cortez. "How many wagons did you say?"

But before El Zorro could speak, Jamie plunged in. "We brought in twelve, and a light wagon. Twelve freight loads. I got the cargo manifests out on my hoss thar—"

Agustino Cortez looked mildly pained. Armijo snapped an order to an aide, and a moment later a soldier dragged in Jamie's entire saddle.

"In the bags thar, guv. Mind if I call ya guv?"

Teresa María thought it was shockingly familiar and impolite. Some things about gringos she found barbaric.

Armijo pawed at the saddlebags, licking his thick lips, and withdrew the long list written in David's copperplate hand. "Ah, ah," he said, happily. "All this. All this! Fifteen thousand. A value of one thousand two hundred fifty United States dollars per wagon on the average, St. Louis prices."

"It does not cover everything, Excellency," said El Zorro softly. "There is the matter of the casks. The four casks of spirits; one half-empty."

"Not here? Not on the manifests? Ah, Señor Dance." Manuel Armijo shook his head sadly.

"Couldn't rightly put her on," Jamie began.

Armijo smiled. *"Verdad.* It is so. It is forbidden by the government of your people to bring spirits into the Indian country. We forbid it too, eh? A pity. Smuggling. It is very costly, is smuggling."

"Well, I reckon we can dicker. . . . Say, guv, I got me a leetle present from the company. Rocky Mountain Company, we're callin' it, but some of us call it the Buffalo Company, because it's the robe trade we're after. Anyway, this here certificate—if I can git to the papers thar—this here certificate is a leetle token of old Guy's esteem for his old client, Manuel Armijo."

But the governor had already spotted the certificate among the papers. Teresa María knew what it was: a draft on Straus et Fils for a hundred dollars, United States, made personally to the bulky man who dominated the salon.

Armijo smiled. "A thousand thanks to your noble partner, Señor Dance. I will remember him when I pray."

"Now me and Teresa, we were coming on over hyar to get us a license and pay up the taxes."

"A license? Ah, Dance. It is not possible. License a society to trade with the Comanche, the Kiowa, the Apache—rifles

99

and shot and powder for buffalo robes?"

"I reckon you'd rather have us tradin' and keepin' an eye out—me and Teresa María, hyar, a Mex citizen—than the Bents. Them Comanch don't trade with the Bents. They trade with any Comancheros you got ridin' out. And I never heerd of the Mexican governmint gittin' any taxes out of a Comanchero."

"It is not so simple. We're at war. A great army, thousands of *tejanos*, marches toward us. Their spies are everywhere. Their agents subvert us."

Dance sighed. "Wall, we're all United States. Old Cortez hyar, he'll tell you. Looked at every passport."

Armijo laughed softly. "Which proves nothing. You are all *yanquis*, heretics. All one. This Rocky Mountain Company, who knows where its roots run. Maybe south, south to Austin, *sí?*"

"It is not so!" snapped Teresa María. "You are saying this for reasons."

"What a beautiful lady. A *señorita* with a reputation! Truly, how I love to see you with your black eyes flashing!"

She glared back at him. Everyone knew how he dishonored Señora Armijo, poor woman, as round as a beehive oven.

"My *compadre*, El Zorro, we've heard so little from you. Pray, why did you not escort the wagons here to be taxed, as is the custom? As the law requires?"

El Zorro smiled blandly. "A company of dragoons guards them carefully, Excellency. Keeps the Comanche away, while the *yanquis* build their post."

"Ah! Build a post? On whose land? On my land!"

El Zorro blinked.

One of those thick smiles of Armijo's lifted the corners of his sensuous lips, and Teresa María felt dread. "We must think about things, Colonel Cortez and I. Señor Dance, you will enjoy the hospitality of the Palace of the Governors. *Señorita*, we will escort you to a room in my quarters."

An aide emerged from somewhere, and began tugging her away. Looking back, she saw the guards prod Jamie with their bayoneted rifles.

100

Prisoners.

Jamie Dance was not a man given to remorse, but now the stain of it crept through him, along with a dread of what his follies might have wrought. He peered about his *cárcel*, which was located at the west end of the palace of the governors, along with a guard barracks. It was lit by a small, glassless window, heavy iron bars trisecting it, that opened onto an alley which reeked of urine. Around him earthen walls, three feet thick, closed in. There was not so much as a bunk to lie on; just one stinking pail in a corner. A massive door of rough-sawn plank barred his way out. He found a hip-hollowed place in the dirt floor against the west wall where others had lain; some before him had even scooped the earth a bit to accommodate their bones.

Now Teresa María *knew*. That, rather than the difficulties about the taxes and licenses, sobered his lighthearted spirit. She knew. They'd tell her—and take wicked delight in it. He thought back to the times, three years earlier, when he and Brokenleg had slid into Taos for a spell, living quietly, avoiding the *funcionarios*. He'd risked returning to Mexico for one reason—Teresa María, cruel eyed, honey fleshed, raven haired, a laugh limning her lips at the slightest provocation. She was slender but had the build that would grow lush over the years. She seemed different from the other girls, bolder. She'd stare at him; the rest would avert their eyes. She'd returned the affection of the lanky gringo, but hadn't taken him seriously. He was, after all, a Yankee heretic, and she the daughter of the alcalde, of a prominent family. Still . . . They'd met in secret places, held hands, touched lips to lips, which set their hearts racing and wild hunger boiling through him. But always she'd said it was not possible, it was a doomed affair of the heart.

And looming over their little tragedy was that fanatic Padre Antonio José Martinez, who hated Yankees even more than he hated heretics, if that were possible. The thickheaded priest had agitated all along to throw them all out of Santa Fe, of Taos, of New Mexico. Even more did he despise the trappers, the Yankee mountain men who secretly caught beaver in the northern mountains and brought their pelts to traders in Taos—men like Jamie Dance. Even if she assented; even if her dignified father and mother assented—the priest wouldn't dream of marrying the flower of Taos to a barbarian.

Desperate circumstances required desperate measures. Jamie began first by asking if she'd elope with him—if he found a priest to marry them. That had brought tears to her eyes. Something had changed in her. She'd been thinking about it.

"Do you know what it means? Running away with you? I could not come back here. My *madre* and *padre* would never open their doors to me. I would never see my sisters. I could never walk this plaza."

"I'd give you a new life, Teresa."

"Would you? Or would you take me like a prize, and then ignore me? Would you put me in a little *casa* in some lonely place and then go back to the mountains with your *yanqui* friends, and trap? And stay away, except now and then when you'd come to visit me? It's not enough!"

In truth, he hadn't thought about it, hadn't thought about abandoning the free-roaming life in the mountains at all. She'd pierced to something important to her—and to him.

"It's not enough!" she whispered. "I'm giving up everything for you. If I say yes, you must promise me something: I want to be with you everywhere. In the mountains, trapping. In the *cantinas* where you go. You are asking me to give up everything I know for you. You must give me a new life in return—not just put me in some little *casa* somewhere and go away, roving."

He realized, suddenly, that he'd intended to do just that. He'd never dreamed of taking her along while he roamed the wild lands. But she was making it a condition of her marriage.

"I go to rough places, Teresa María—places not right for a purty woman like you."

"I will go everywhere with you—or I will say no. You ask me to give up all that I know. I will ask you to share your whole life—everything! Promise me!"

"Teresa . . ." he began, and faltered. Her sweet fragrance

intoxicated him—her burning eyes and thick lips, the crue.
beauty of her flesh which lay hidden under her *blusa* anc
skirts. "I'll do it," he croaked. A promise.

And she'd do it. He'd read an eagerness in her eyes. She'c
do it; she'd risk everything: reputation, life, wealth . . . for
Jamie Dance. He needed a priest, then, and invented one.
Down Santy Fe way was an old *compañero* of the mountain:
and beaver streams, Tomás Villanova—who'd been a seminarian in Durango before his unruly soul betrayed him anc
he fled for the high, free lands. A half-made priest. A mar
who could rattle through Latin. Ah, Jamie had thought, ɛ
man for the marrying.

But Tomás Villanova hadn't been so easily persuaded.
He'd settled in Santa Fe after his time in the mountains, and
had become a successful fur and hide dealer when Jamie
found him.

"I don't know," he said solemnly. "It might be a real mar-
riage. It's an odd sacrament, really performed by the couple.
The church is only a witness. But I would not wish to offend
God."

"You're my only hope!" Jamie replied.

"If it's not a real marriage, you'd do her dishonor, *amigo*."

Jamie hadn't thought of that.

"I'd enter it in the parish records. But then what?"

"Teresa María'll understand. She loves me. We just got to
git around all this stuff—the church."

Tomás stared into his steaming tea while minutes ticked
by. At last he looked up. "I do stupid things," he said softly.
Jamie whooped, and rode hard for Taos to lay plans.

Now, in the coolness of the cell, he wondered if Teresa
María would forgive him. Had he lost her? Desperate solu-
tions, bad results. An ache built in him, choked him. He
swung to his feet, pacing wildly, wanting to talk with her,
plumb her feelings, beg her to love him—but he couldn't,
and only the silent walls answered the pleadings of his heart.

Savagely, he forced his thoughts away from something that
had become too painful to dwell on. He had other matters to
worry about. The old charges—a minor thing, actually, but a
weapon in Armijo's grasping hands. The company. The li-

103

censes. El Zorro, hovering about, his fingers as eager and sticky as the governor's. He cursed Mexican law and Mexican officials who could ruin whatever they chose. And then he smiled ruefully. He'd scarcely met a Yank trapper who'd paid any attention to Mexican law. Mean as bear in April, whole gangs of them had wintered in Taos over the years, swilling aguardiente, brawling with local hidalgos over the ladies, smuggling beaver pelts out, with only the mildest rebukes from the amiable Mexican prefect, Juan Andrés Archuleta. Gringos had an awful reputation, even before Padre Martinez and other zealots had stirred the hatreds. Let a Yank trapper wander through Santy Fe, and mothers promptly hid their daughters, hidalgos turned their backs.

The earthen floor, rank with odors of fear, and the unyielding walls did nothing for Jamie's comfort. Neither did the terrible silence. It made him feel he was in a tomb, forgotten by the world. It was all he could do to choke back panic; he, a man born free, who'd roamed wild mountains unchecked by man or God, he was here, in an earthen mausoleum barely ten feet square. A great helplessness engulfed him. How utterly at the mercy of others—who bore him varying degrees of malice—he was. Nothing, nothing, prevented his captors from doing what they would to his weak body. He dizzied himself with visions of torture and lash, of leg irons and manacles, of weary treks deep into the darkness of one of the dungeons. The Acordada came to mind, but he admitted that was the only name he knew. Knowing the name of just one Mexican hellhole was bad enough.

Still, it was not in Jamie Dance to dwell too long on dark possibilities. His buoyant mind ran in other directions. He was a born trader; he had things to trade. Wealth for . . . freedom. He had allies, too. Guy Straus. Straus et Fils, an indispensable factor in the Santa Fe trade, as much for traders like Armijo who vied with the gringos as for the Yanks who came to Guy in St. Louis wanting capital.

Time toiled onward. Light faded. Faintly, through the window, he could hear the staccato of spoken Spanish, but couldn't make out the words. It was the hour of the *paseo*, the walk around the plaza, a time for young men to eye pretty girls; a time for pretty girls to smile shyly at young men. Darkness settled, and the scent of piñon pines drifted in. Santa Fe was perfumed by the incense given off by piñon crackling in beehive fireplaces.

He grew aware of an awful hunger and a parching thirst, but still no one came. He sprang up, hammered on the great pine-plank door, but it did not open. The smells of food drifted through his tiny window, famishing him—meat, *carne,* sizzling; chiles; the acrid scent of tortillas made of lye-treated corn flour, *masa harina,* browning on a hot griddle.

That's when muffled voices sifted through the door. It creaked open, spraying light across the black room, and Jamie made out the lean presence of El Zorro—who carried a basket.

"Ah, Señor Dance. It is The Fox, *sí?* I've brought you some food. I had to bully the guards, but your *compadre* cares for you. Here!"

Jamie took the basket eagerly. Nothing ever smelled so good. He found spiced meat of some sort wrapped in a tortilla, and wolfed it. He found an amber bottle of *cerveza,* and pulled its cork, letting the warm beer slake his thirst.

"Ah, Dance. Never say your partner doesn't help, eh? His Excellency, he was not going to feed you. Gringos, they live by their stomachs, he says. If you want to humble a gringo, starve him. If you want to make a gringo crawl, empty his belly. That's how His Excellency sees it. He wasn't going to feed you until dawn, or maybe tomorrow night if he felt like it."

Jamie fell upon a half a loaf of hard bread and ate gustily, then turned to a peach and sank his tooth in it. Meanwhile he swilled great drafts of the warm *cerveza,* letting it fizz down his dry throat.

"He's a man to reckon with, Señor Dance. Ah! He has plans for you! His blood is heated up because of the *tejanos* coming."

"I want to see our consul—Manuel Alvarez."

"Ah, Señor Dance, he's under house arrest. For his own good, of course. The people of Santa Fe, they are ready to string up gringos."

"I'd like to see Bent. Or St. Vrain."

"Kept in their houses, Jamie. The governor looks after their safety." El Zorro laughed softly.

Dance thought wildly, and chose another tack. "I got a Mexican friend here. I'd like you to get word to him."

"And who would that be?"

"Tomás Villanova. Peltry dealer. He trapped with the brigades a while — few years ago."

El Zorro smiled and said nothing. Jamie swilled the last of the beer, and belched.

"Ah, Dance, now we can talk. Trust your partner, eh? Now tell me, how did the Rocky Mountain Company propose to pay the imposts?"

Jamie hesitated. "Usual way. Part of the merchandise." Few Santa Fe traders carried gold, but David had some hidden.

"Merchandise for the license, too, I suppose."

"That's how we reckoned it in St. Louis."

"Have you no way to raise . . . cash? *Plata y oro?* Could you draft a note against Straus et Fils?"

Jamie was about to say he couldn't even sign his own name, much less draft a note, but he remained silent. In fact, David could. A note drafted by David Straus would be honored. But some intuition led Jamie to forget about that. "Nope. We just reckoned we'd pay the usual way — percent of goods, ad valorem."

"Ah, a pity. His Excellency wants gold, *oro*. Gold to pay soldiers and buy bullets to fight *tejanos*."

Dance shrugged.

"A pity," said El Zorro. "But trust in your partner. The governor . . . he has problems. The Bents know you want a trading license. So do the Comancheros, who make a living doing what you're going to do. Armijo needs them both, the Bents and the Comancheros, just now. But I have ways, eh?"

"Where's Señora Dance?" Jamie asked abruptly.

El Zorro peered at him through the golden lantern light. "She enjoys the hospitality of the governor and his lady. But she weeps, Dance. . . . Ah, she weeps to learn she is a concubine."

"Think we're married," Dance replied doggedly. "We said

106

the vows proper."

"With an impostor priest officiating. Ah, Señor Dance. Such a one. You toy with a beautiful woman's virtue. You make a scandal. Father Martinez—he hears of the elopement, he sees the parish records . . . this Tomás. And he knows at once. Another gringo trick, scoffing at the laws of the holy church. Heretics! And soon the whole world knows, and the whole world wonders who Tomás is. 'Tomás, as in Tomás Villanova." The colonel laughed softly. "I know Villanova. He loves to talk in Latin."

Jamie suddenly was sorry he'd mentioned the name.

"It can be arranged, *señor*. A marriage is a trifle. Trust El Zorro. I will wipe away her tears."

"What's your price, Cortez?"

"*Nada*," said the lean colonel. "Nothing at all for a friend."

CHAPTER 11

Warily, eyeing those carbines with respect, the teamsters retreated toward the light wagon and threw their halters and ropes back in. They milled uncertainly, afraid to do anything with those carbines aimed straight at them.

"We'll be butchered," muttered Pony Gantt.

None of the Mexican dragoons wavered. The corporal, Ortiz, stood solemnly, letting terror seep through the Yankees. The *campesinos* abandoned their mud-making to watch this thing.

A few of the teamsters edged toward their bedrolls, where they kept their rifles. Others sat down on the ground, conspicuously offering no resistance.

Time ticked by. In a few moments, everything had changed. David felt only bewilderment.

"I guess we should go back to work," he said, not at all sure of that.

"Tell them to work," said Ortiz in Spanish.

"I just did."

But his men simply stared at him. It dawned on him that something had been shattered. He couldn't simply command men to go back to work—not on a post they would abandon. How could men engage in futile labor? He knew, suddenly, that he had destroyed their morale. Once he'd told them they would abandon this half-built post, futility had corroded away their eagerness. He had reduced their striving to nothing. In one ill-considered stroke he'd ruined everything.

It flooded over him then: he had no ability to command men. He was still green, eighteen, just learning to deal with hard things in this hard world. He wished desperately that Jamie Dance were there. What would Jamie have done upon receiving his father's instructions? Nothing, probably—at least not right away. He'd have kept it in his head, mulled it over, thought about what all those Mexican dragoons would do. Nothing at first.

A bitter self-loathing struck David. "We've got to work!" he cried.

"Bull," said Labor Jonas.

"For what?" yelled someone else.

The *cabo* followed all this with interest, but David couldn't tell whether he understood. Ortiz got the drift of it, though, even without knowing English.

"Make the fort," said Ortiz in Spanish.

"He says go back to work," David translated.

But no one moved. Finally Mazappa wandered over to David and addressed him quietly. "Look, Straus, it ain't the same now. And no one's going to work with them carbines pointed at them. Let them dragoons git back to work, and maybe we'll git back to work. Me, I'm sittin' here. They want to start poking bayonets into us, nothing much I can do about it."

Ortiz watched, and then gestured violently at David.

David translated. "He says, let your dragoons put down their carbines and start back to work first. My teamsters don't want to work with those weapons aimed at them."

Ortiz grinned, enjoying himself. But he barked several commands. Twenty of his men lowered their weapons, carried them over to the soldier camp, and stacked them neatly there. The remaining four dragoons remained armed, and spread themselves loosely into an observant line. The Mexican soldiers meandered toward the half-built exterior walls of the post and began work again, but so listlessly that little would get done. The *campesinos* took their cue and wandered back to their adobe-brick forms.

But the teamsters just stared.

"We've got to put up the post," David said.

"Why?" asked one. He spoke for them all. "Seems like it's all for nothing."

"Maybe we'll stay here," David said, helplessly.

"I think maybe I'll quit. Go work for Bent," said young Abel Cannon.

Men laughed. But most of them simply settled to the earth, not doing anything.

David felt utterly chagrined, and too green to be commanding these seasoned veterans of the Santa Fe trade. He stared helplessly at Lyle Black, who stood frowning. "I don't know what do do," he confessed miserably.

"You ain't gonna get 'em to work now."

"Could you try?"

"They'll likely quit. Slide outa here. Head for Bent's Fort. Lay off. They don't much cotton to workin' for nothing. This here outfit . . . it's just ripe for pluckin'."

"I shouldn't have told them."

Black nodded. "A man's got to make his own decisions, not just follow along doin' as he's told. A man's got to know how the ones workin' for him'll feel. What they'll likely do. You tell 'em your daddy says they got to pack up, quit a half-built post, and they ain't going to feel so good, not after whacking down trees, whipping ox-butts to drag 'em hyar, skinning poles, squaring up the logs, sweating like hogs all day for weeks. Naw, son, you can't be sayin' that without they get mighty sore."

David nodded. He wished he were back in St. Louis. He wished Dance had never left him in charge. He wished he could be the clerk he intended to be, not some half-grown boy echoing his father's wishes. He wished Jamie Dance had had sense enough not to put him in charge but to have told Black or Oliphant to run things.

"Look, Straus," said Black, sympathetically, "it don't do no good to stand there lookin' like you want to shoot yourself. I'll go talk to them fellers. Maybe ol' Dance'll want to build the post hyar anyway, just like he planned. Maybe this Texas war'll all blow by, come to nothin', and it'd be foolish to throw it all away here. Maybe them Mex, they ain't meanin' no harm, except dippin' into your pockets some — like they do.

Like all you bigwigs in the company figgered anyway. Least you can do is sorta take charge. If I was you, Straus, I'd say we're gonna stay, we're gonna build Fort Dance. I'd go on over to them and tell 'em. Take the day off, I'd say. Tomorrah we'll start in again. Tomorrah we'll all work and git this post put up and start tradin' with all them Injuns wanting this stuff."

David agreed. He needed to act. He needed to put aside all the self-recriminations swarming in his head. He needed to deal with that *cabo*, Ortiz, who watched with a malevolent smirk.

"Thank you," he said.

For a response, Black pounded him on the back, jarring him, and laughed.

He found the *cabo* lounging, waiting. "Señor Ortiz," he began, "I've decided that we'll build our post here. Even if the company wants us to leave. They're afraid the troubles you have with Texas would . . . well . . . hurt the company. These men of mine, I've given them today off. They've worked hard for months." It sounded hollow, even as he said it. He hadn't decided anything.

The *cabo* eyed him cynically. "And what will your *hombres* do today?"

"Rest. Hunt. Wash clothing."

Ortiz frowned. "Not hunt. You have hunters out now."

David did have four men out, including Boar Blunt. He dreaded Blunt's mockery when the man found out about all this.

Ortiz yelled a command at one of his dragoons, and the wiry man trotted over to the light wagon and began collecting halters and ropes.

David's anger rose, but he choked it back.

"Your men, maybe they ride away and never come back," Ortiz explained. "Now I'll give my *hombres* a day off too. But not the *campesinos*. Let them make adobes. We never have enough adobes." He grinned, revealing a gap in his upper teeth.

David turned solemnly, nerving himself to address teamsters who'd lost what little respect for him he may have garnered on the trail. He found six of them, Cannon, Gantt, Goodin, Launes, Jonas, and the cook, Emilio, sitting in a circle, saying nothing.

"We'll build here."

"You mean you ain't daddy's boy?" asked Gantt, insolently.

"We'll build here," David repeated. "You have today off. Tomorrow we'll begin again."

"Seems like we took today off anyway," Cannon said. "Maybe we'll take tomorrow too. Maybe we won't even be here."

David ignored him and walked toward the rest of his men and gave them the message. At the rising tan walls of the post, the dragoons laid up adobes desultorily. The *cabo* addressed them, and they walked off, pulling on their blue shirts.

David needed to be alone. He wrestled with more feelings than he'd ever known were inside of him. He'd stepped into a man's world and played the boy. He hadn't a friend in camp, or even a sympathizer. He'd brought it on himself, the whole thing. What would Jamie say? *Ye blew 'er, boy. I got us this license. I got us all set hyar, dealin' with these Mexicanos. I got 'em off our backs. I got us fixed to whup the Bents, and the Mexicanos happy about it, too. But I come back hyar, and . . .*

And David had demolished the outfit, lost his men—maybe lost a fortune as well.

That was when Blunt and the other hunters rode in, carrying two bloody quarters of buffalo on two packmules that tolerated bleeding meat. David watched them unload over at the cook fire; watched them hang the meat; watched several of the men sidle over to Blunt, whisper, point, guffaw. Watched Blunt meander toward him. David braced for whatever would come. He hadn't a friend here. Not even Lyle and Mazappa would defend him.

The man had ballooned. Boar Blunt somehow had puffed up larger than ever. David wondered if he'd even survive if Blunt got to pounding on him.

"Work us for nothin'."

David didn't say anything.

"Your daddy's little boy. Me, I'm gonna have me a drunk."

112

Boar deliberately strolled toward the last of the freighters, where that opened cask of two hundred-proof spirits rested. They watched him—the teamsters, the *cabo*, the dragoons, the peons still making 'dobies. Blunt lifted the keg easily, gathered a pot from Emilio's kitchen, filled it half-full of river water, and the rest of the way with pure grain spirits, grinning evilly.

"Have us a party," he yelled.

Time had slid past the supper hour but no one much cared, and neither the Mexican women nor Emilio had started cooking meat. It didn't matter. Men hunted for tin cups. Mexican dragoons dug for theirs, grinning. Teamsters lifted them from the mess. The 'dobe-makers found clay pots, and all of them, even the *cabo* Ortiz, dipped into the pot. Everyone except David, who watched helplessly, an outcast.

But just then a knot of riders appeared off to the south, wending their way along the Purgatoire toward them. A dozen riders, along with a dozen burros burdened with coarse-woven cloth sacks. David could see they were not Indians. The riders wore peaked sombreros, fringed leggins, sweat-blackened shirts of unbleached muslin. They carried gleaming rifles; great knives in waist sheaths; big percussion-lock pistols, some of them two-barreled, holstered or hanging from their saddle horns. They rode into the camp with hooded eyes that missed nothing—especially the freight wagons; eyes that measured the soldiers and teamsters for burying. David had never seen a rougher lot. They sent a chill through him.

One rider, built like a barrel, appeared to be the leader. He grinned, baring startlingly white teeth in a shoeleather face, and approached the *cabo*.

"*Hola, muchachos!*" this one said in Spanish. "We are in time for the party, I see."

"Straus, what's the sonabitch say?" demanded Boar Blunt.

David nerved himself, and addressed the leader. "What is your business?" he asked, abruptly.

The heavy one turned, noticing David for the first time, and smiled lazily. "We have no business, *señor*. I am Benito, and who are you?"

113

"David Straus." We are traders from St. Louis. Building a post here."

"Traders. A post. And twelve *carros grandes* full of things. We will have a party."

"You didn't tell me what you do," David managed.

The man studied David, menace building in him like heat lightning along a horizon. "We are traders also. With the Comanche, *sí?* We will trade with you. We always have things others want."

Comancheros! No wonder these men looked like demons out of hell. David peered at all of them, alarmed by what he saw. One by one the intruders slid off their galled and bloody-flanked mustangs and stretched their legs, all the while studying the camp with predatory eyes that knew instantly where the dragoons' rifles were stacked, what arms the teamsters had nearby. Their gazes lingered on the four dragoons who stood at the perimeter, not drinking, still obeying the *cabo's* command to guard everything. David's own gaze followed the Comancheros as they walked through the camp like lords of the earth, possessing everything by their mere presence. The *campesinos* looked fearful, and the women slipped off into the night. Benito watched them, and laughed.

"Una fiesta," he said.

David remembered what he could of Comancheros. Traders and fur men gossiped about this strange breed over chicoried coffee at the Planters House. They trafficked in anything, riding out to the dreaded Comanche with guns and powder, taking buffalo robes and captives — Indian children or women from other tribes, who would become slaves at Mexican ranchos. They did a lively slave trade with the Comanche and, in return, kept that fiercest of tribes well armed and deadly. They could sell him, David Straus of Straus et Fils, as easily as they could sell a Ute squaw or a Cheyenne child. Send him south to labor in the fields. Trade him to the Comanche for ritual torture.

The teamsters watched them contemplatively, watched Benito drink and laugh, watched the rest, including a cock-eyed one-armed one, dip cups into the great kettle

114

and guzzle lustily, saying little to anyone.

Benito strolled out to the dragoon guards and whispered something. The Mexican soldiers hesitated, looked fearfully at their *cabo*, Ortiz, saw him laugh, and followed Benito back in, like whipped dogs. Now not a soul guarded this camp. It chilled David. He resolved to do so himself.

But Benito approached him then, carrying a tin cup. "You will drink too," he said, veiled menace in his voice.

"I never drink."

"Ah, it shows in your face, all twisted up. You will drink."

"I'll watch for trouble."

"You will drink, *amigo*. We will celebrate. We are *compadres, sí?* All traders here. Traders and soldiers. We make an honest living. But no one likes an hombre who doesn't drink. Such a man is not to be trusted."

David didn't like the drift of that.

"I am not used to it. It makes me sick," he said, desperately. "Someone must watch."

"Ah! Sick! Like a dog vomiting! We all must get sick the first time, *sí?*" The man jabbed the tin cup at him, spraying the spirits over his shirt. "Now."

David shook his head. Benito splashed the cup into his eyes, spraying him with fire, stinging him, drawing tears instantly. He gasped.

Benito laughed easily, rocking back on his well-worn heels. Over where men knotted close around the liquor pot in the thickening dark, spectators cackled and wheezed. The *muchacho* was learning. Daddy's boy had gotten a lesson.

Through tear-blurred eyes, David saw Boar Blunt stand, stretch, and wander toward him, like a bear who'd found honey.

"Whatsa matter, little boy, don't you like likker?"

David said nothing. Boar Blunt with a cup in hand was more menace than Boar Blunt sober. He felt helpless and terribly alone. From the corner of his eye, he saw Comancheros wander purposefully toward the freight wagons, poke their heads through the puckerholes at the rear, exclaim, debate what was in crates and barrels within.

"Looks like we'll hafta initiate you, little boy," said Blunt.

Benito understood, even without translation. The pair of them guffawed.

"I'll have a drink in a minute," David said, trying to sound calm, but knowing his voice squeaked from terror. He repeated the words in Spanish for the Comanchero.

Blunt chortled, and grabbed David by an arm, dragging him toward the men knotted around the kettle of trade whiskey. "He's joinin' us for a toddy," Boar roared. "We got us some fancy company, son of Godalmighty Straus."

Someone thrust a cup in his hands, and they all waited eagerly.

David peered at them wildly, barely making them out in the thickening night. "Black. Oliphant. I want someone to guard the wagons."

Teamsters laughed. Mazappa lifted his cup and saluted. The Mexicans smiled blandly.

"Comanches might come!" he cried.

Benito's arm slid around David, clamping him in a powerful vise. With his free hand, the Comanchero lifted a tin cup to David's lips, pried open David's mouth with a scaly finger, and poured. David sputtered, spat the liquor out.

"No, no," Benito mumbled. He spun David around, found an arm, twisted it upward until pain shrieked through David.

"Ah!" said Benito, holding the cup to David's lips. David drank, slowly, feeling the vile spirits-and-river water trickle down his throat.

"*Ah, una fiesta, sí?*" The Comanchero let go of David's arm. David swallowed again. The fiery stuff brought tears to his eyes. And pain. David gasped, coughed, gulped, half in terror, half in response to the fluid.

Boar and Benito laughed uproariously, cackled and wheezed.

David wiped his mouth and grinned, though he didn't feel like grinning. Maybe he could pretend. . . . But suddenly Benito yelled at him, a crash of a cymbal in his ears. "*Muchacho!*"

David paused. He felt an odd prick in his stomach, and stared down in horror. Benito had drawn a murderous knife

116

and poked it hard into David's belly, bringing a tiny, spreading spot of blood.

"Beberé," David cried, "I'll drink!" And he swallowed again, sobbing. He felt the first rush of dizziness as the powerful grain spirits found his brain.

He steadied himself. "Benito. Let's trade. You got robes? We'll trade. I've got things—"

Benito laughed easily. "No, no robes. No Comanche. Not twenty leagues from here. No, little Straus . . . you will drink."

"Viva la República!" yelled a soldier.

David peered about him wildly. His own men were sliding into oblivion. The *campesinos* squatted on bare feet and lifted their clay pots rhythmically. The dragoons sprawled, weapons stacked and unguarded. The Comancheros drank and explored and waited.

"Nene!" screamed Benito.

David drank dizzily.

"Otra vez!"

David swallowed more, feeling nausea boil up his throat.

"Otra vez!" That knife pricked him again.

He drank again, tears mixing with the spirits.

He vomited then, in great heaving convulsions, and more tears came while he clutched the spinning earth on his hands and knees. He was upside down. Gut-wrenching waves boiled up in his belly. Some vast distance away, vultures laughed. He felt a sharp pain in his ribs. A boot. Eagles swooped. Bile, vile and green, trickled down his chin, burning his flesh. He stank.

Papa, I failed you, he thought, and then stopped thinking.

CHAPTER 12

Teresa María wanted to scratch Jamie with her nails. Infuriating questions bubbled up in her mind. Was she married? Who was this Father Tomás? Had her slouchy gringo tricked her? Where was he? Where had they taken him? Would he ever be free? Why was he in trouble? What had he done? Oh! How could this be?

She peered about her. A single candle lit the governor's apartments, its amber light caught by the gilded portraits on the walls, and by the gilded halo of the *santo* in its niche. This *sala* was like many others in Santa Fe, with a packed earthen floor, irregular whitewashed walls, and heavy vigas supporting a hatchwork of slender crosspoles. If the governor was as wealthy as he was rumored to be, it did not show in this official residence. Perhaps he keeps his wealth in gold, she thought.

She didn't wish to stay here. Through a grilled window she could see strollers on the dusty plaza, enjoying their evening *paseo*, laughing and free. She headed for a door. They couldn't keep her here! She, a citizen of the Republic, and accused of nothing! The governor was nowhere in sight, and she hunted for him, intending to get answers.

She whirled through a second room, this one containing a pianoforte carted some vast distance, and then encountered Señora Armijo, who'd materialized from nowhere. Pitiful woman, so vast she could only wobble about in her perpetually black dresses, her jowly face peering up from a high, lacy collar like a cork in a fat bottle.

"*Señora,* I wish to see the governor."

118

The woman sighed pitifully. "He is not here. He's never here."

"I wish to see my husband. Take me to him."

"I can't do that, Señorita Obregón."

"I am Señora Dance," Teresa María retorted acidly. Why this? Why did they call her this?

The woman smiled absently. "It is said thee were married by a false priest. A thousand pardons for saying it. I only know what is whispered to me. Manuel . . . sometimes he tells me about the world, sometimes he doesn't."

"You will kindly address me as a married woman."

Señora Armijo nodded. "It was a great scandal, the occasion of much gossip. The daughter of the alcalde running away with the gringo trapper. And then Father Martinez, roaring and ranting up at Taos, writing the bishop to ask who this Father Tomás was, and then writing long letters to Manuel, telling him to drive the heretic *yanquis* out of Mexico."

"The bishop knew of no Father Tomás?"

The woman sighed. "None. But the *coronel*—Cortez—he told us this very evening he knows who the impostor was—one Tomás Villanova, an old *compadre* of your . . . husband. A peltry dealer here. I do not know him. I do not know many people here."

Something cold bit through Teresa María. "I will talk to Señor Dance."

"They won't let you, ah, *señora*."

"Where is he?"

"I imagine he is being held. Across the palace of the governors. The guard barracks are there, and a small *cárcel*. You cannot go there."

"I will."

"It is not a place for a . . . respectable woman to go. Ah . . . perhaps not even you would go there. Not even you."

"Not even me! What if you are wrong? What if I have said my vows before God? At the altar of the church? Not even me—indeed! I will not suffer such abuse!"

The woman cowered. "It was not proper," she mumbled.

But Teresa María stormed past the poor woman, out into a central foyer that divided the private apartments from

119

the military and administrative side.

A soft voice rose out of the darkness. "What brings you . . . *señora?*"

She found a uniformed guard standing there in deep shadow. "I wish to know where they have taken my husband. And I wish to see him. Take me to him."

"I can not do that. He is detained. Many charges against him, I understand."

"Such as what?"

The man shrugged. "I do not know these things. The *yanquis* are invading Mexico."

"The *tejanos!* He is not a *tejano.*"

"It is all the same."

"Where is the governor?"

"I do not know these things. Out. He spends his evenings in the cantinas. In the salons. Often he is at the *taberna* of La Tules. You would not go there."

No, Teresa María wouldn't go to such a place where men gambled and drank. "Where is the *coronel?* Agustino Cortez?"

The man shrugged again. "Ah, he is somewhere."

"I will find him," she said, starting toward a high, heavy double door. But a lance fell across her path.

"A thousand pardons, ah, *señora.*"

"Bring him to me!"

The man shrugged again.

The other doors in this dark foyer opened on the plaza. She considered, and bolted toward them.

"No, it is forbidden. You are a guest of the governor."

"I'm not a prisoner!"

"It's not proper—a woman without escort."

"Ha! They tell me I am a . . . a concubine, and you worry about that!"

The man shrugged. Was that all he could do, shrug? She glared at him in the dirty dark, and swung open the door. "Am I a free citizen of Mexico or not?"

He glanced around fearfully. "Take your *paseo* quickly," he muttered. "I will let you in."

She stalked past him into the soft night air of the plaza, boiling with fear and rage. The massive door creaked shut on its iron hinges behind her. She felt the sweetness of liberty; and rejoiced. All about her gaily dressed people walked, but not in a hurry. Unlike the driven *yanquis,* no one of her people was ever in a hurry. She smelled the incense of piñon smoke on the eddying air and, with it, the smell of food, reminding her she was famished.

She realized suddenly she had nothing but her clothing. The governor had taken away her horse; her few traveling things had been taken into his apartments, keeping her hostage there. Who did she know in this great capital city? Were friends of her father here? Where could she get help?

She needed to think—but had no place to do it. Jamie. Jamie! Had he tricked her? Was she little better than . . . Her mind refused to access the word for such a woman. A rage boiled through her and evaporated again at the thought of Jamie laughing, his easy grace catching her soul.

Then she wept, remembering her wedding, the vows, Jamie's smile, the priest's blessing. Tomás. Padre Tomás. Tomás Villanova . . . She turned abruptly, wiping away her tears. A man approached, silver-haired, an hidalgo, finely dressed.

"Señor, a thousand pardons. Could you direct me to the house of the hide merchant, Tomás Villanova?"

The man shook his head, eyeing her as men eyed unescorted women. He smiled. "We will find the house together," he said.

She fled, seeing something in his brown eyes.

On the south side of the plaza she spotted a young man, humbly dressed, the stains of work on his baggy *pantalones.* "Señor, por favor, could you direct me to the house of the hide merchant, Tomás Villanova?"

The man eyed her, and nodded. "Calle Delgado. That way. The narrow house with the iron gate, *señora.* The third one, I think."

She smiled and fled, while he stood watching her, puzzled. It wasn't far, then. Just off the plaza. She found it easily, the darkened low building frowning at her, telling her not to trespass there. She stood before it, bewildered. A friend of Jamie's, perhaps. A false priest, an impostor, perhaps. What would she say to this man? *Tell me I am a respectable woman. Tell me my yanqui Jamie did not trick me. Tell me you are a real priest, not a fraud.*

121

It would be a wicked thing, an unescorted woman on the street, knocking on the door of this man's house. What if a woman answered? The Señora Villanova. What would she say to this man's wife? Light raked dimly from a shuttered window. He would be at home, then. No one burned costly candles for no purpose. She peered at the shabby house, trying to fathom the man. The narrow building stretched back a long way, and she supposed the rear was the place he kept his furs and hides. Except for the iron gate, she found no decoration, no pretension.

It wasn't late. The northern skies still glowed blue. People were about. The time for the supper, the *cena,* had not yet arrived. Many shops remained open. It was not the hour for scandal. She braved her way to the calcimined plank door, and knocked. Someone stirred, and then the door creaked open. She peered into the face of Tomás Villanova, and froze. Padre Tomás, but without the spectacles. In the golden light of the lamp he held in his hand, he looked exactly as he had at the candle-lit altar of the church. She had seen enough, and turned away. She didn't need to know anything else. She was not a respectable woman. Oh, Jamie . . .

"Señora Dance."

"I am no *señora!*" she snapped, retreating into the darkness.

"Wait. Señora Dance. Come in. Where is Jamie?"

She peered back at the false priest, wavering. Maybe at least she could ask questions—and then accuse the worm. She whirled, and walked proudly into the man's house, scarcely bothering to peer around at the humble room where rough furniture wobbled in the candlelight.

"So!" she said angrily.

He motioned her toward a high-backed chair that would force her to sit bolt upright. She took it, glaring at him.

"Where is Jamie Dance?" he asked softly. He had a gentle voice.

"The governor holds him in the palace. For many past crimes against Mexico."

The false priest smiled. "My crimes, too," he said. "We took beaver together, without a license, far from the authorities. I went with them—six *yanquis,* all trappers. I didn't trap; my soul

122

is too tender. The beaver are caught by the jaws of the trap under water. They struggle and drown when their lungs burst. It is too much for a seminarian like me. I was camp-keeper for the rest. I cooked, chopped wood, kept watch — for a seventh share."

"A seminarian!" she hissed. "A seminarian!" She rose. Now she knew everything!

He waved her down, languidly, a soft laugh rising in his slender throat. How could he laugh? How could they plot such a thing, to bring her to shame?

"*Señora* — "

"Don't call me *señora!*"

"I think you are. In the eyes of God you are married. The sacrament lies in the vows you and Jamie Dance repeated. The church is only a witness, Señora Dance."

"You are making things up."

"I truly believe you are married. I told Jamie that."

"You told him?"

He laughed that soft laugh again. How could she be angry at such a one? "Ah, Teresa María, how he burned for you. How he raved! How many times he told me he had to have you, to use a *yanqui* phrase, come hell or high water!"

"*Madre de Dios*. Hell?"

"It is an expression of theirs that means no matter what. Flood or perdition. But how could he have you? Padre Martinez was dead against it. Your father and mother, high-born, would have nothing of such rabble. Jamie was a heretic, a protestant, a *yanqui*. Desperate circumstances call for desperate measures, *sí?*"

She sighed, remembering that wild time when he sent messages to her through tradesmen, when they trysted in strange places including Charles Bent's parlor under the eye of Ignacia Bent, when she used the *paseo* around the plaza of Taos each evening to find him and slip away to a dark corner. And when her mother suspected, finally caught them, and all the grief ever bestowed on lovers came to them. She blushed, remembering his forbidden kiss, a wild sweetness in it that made her heart trip, and the pained, desperate look in his face which she'd never seen there before.

"He dishonored me," she said. "So did you."

Tomás stared at the open window that let night breezes eddy through the chill room. "He asked me if I would. I asked him if he'd considered that . . . that he might dishonor you. He said he hadn't thought of it; he'd only thought of you, wanting you. He burned, burned for you, Señora Dance. I told him perhaps the marriage would be valid anyway — a promise before God, yes? He said, Come to Taos; I will tell me when."

Tomás stopped, as if he had no more to say.

"I don't know these things," she said. "Maybe we are married before God but not the Church. It is a scandal."

He laughed again, that infectious laugh that seemed to gloss over her anger. "Do you suppose the sacrament came from Saint Peter? From God Himself? Ah, no. It came in the ninth century, a thousand years ago, when couples came to the church door to have a priest bless their marriage." He smiled. "That is not something they teach in seminary."

She realized then that they were surrounded by books; beautiful morocco-bound books alongside shabby ones, at least a hundred of them scattered everywhere. She dreaded being among people who could read. Maybe this one was reading forbidden things — devil things. She didn't like him.

"Don't confuse me. If the church says it's wrong, then it's wrong. I won't listen to you."

"Who says it's wrong? Everywhere priests remarry the country people, the peasants who married themselves when there was no priest nearby. Does the church condemn them for not waiting? No. Why should it? Why don't you get married, then?"

That struck her as almost blasphemous. "But —"

"I will find a priest. I have many friends among the priests. I was almost one. I will make my own confession . . . and bring a priest to you and Jamie."

"How dare you! I'm Señora Dance."

He chuckled softly, like a gentle accordion wheezing out its air. She laughed with him, infected by this devil of a Tomás.

"I'm not married," she said, a sudden tear welling up. "Now I know why all these years I've been barren. No babies. It is because I was never married! Because Jesucristo punishes me!"

"Let's go talk to Jamie."

She gaped at him. "What! He is in the *cárcel* at the palace."

"Come," he said, helping her to her feet. Suddenly she felt weary and hungry. It had been a desperately long day. But she followed him into the street, full of unaccustomed meekness. She should be scolding him, scorching his ear, this . . . devil. But she permitted herself to be escorted back to the dark plaza, quiet now as the evening faded into night, and then straight in front of the Palace of the Governors.

"Where are you taking me?"

"To Jamie."

"But he's . . ."

He held a finger to his lips. He turned into a smelly little alley just west of the adobe building. A cat — or maybe a rat — skittered off. Then he pointed upward. She peered up at something, a small opening high above her, a dark rectangle. "Say something," he whispered.

"There?"

"Yes. Everyone in Santa Fe knows to come here to talk to one that Manuel Armijo has his claws upon."

She found herself weeping, and it made her snippy. "Jamie Dance, you are a burro, a beast, a pig!" she yelled.

"Worse'n that," came a faint voice from within.

"Oh! You deserve it. May you rot there forever!"

"You're the sweetest little hellcat I ever did see."

"Hellcat, am I? You don't deserve to be married to me."

"Some folks hyar don't think I am," Jamie said in English.

"Why did you do it, dishonor me?"

"So I could kiss you all night."

She blushed, and hoped Tomás didn't hear it.

"I know who Father Tomás is!"

"So do I."

He was driving her into a temper. "He says we should get married. But maybe I won't."

Jamie didn't answer. She wanted him to answer. She wondered what it was like on the other side of that thick wall, looking up at a tiny window high above.

"*Compañero*," said Tomás Villanova.

"You! How'd that little lady latch on — I mean . . . Aw,

125

Tomás, get me outa here."

"Not until you agree to get married."

"What? You told me—"

"The bishop doesn't seem to agree with my notions. Neither does Father Martinez. But we can fix these things in an hour. If you'll let yourself be baptized."

"You got everything butt-end backwards, Villanova. Git me outa here. Now! Buy out old Armijo. I'm good for it. You know, the *mordida*."

"He's off playing. Probably at La Tules. No, *compadre*, it is time for you to get married."

"Now how you gonna do that, with me in here?"

"You'll see, *yanqui*. And they say Mexicans are hot-blooded. I never saw such hot blood as yours. Boils in your veins."

"Tomás . . . seriously. I'm in trouble. Help me."

But Tomás was dragging Teresa María off through darkened streets, avoiding the ruffians who populated them after night settled. She knew where he was leading her and was too tired to care. San Miguel, the parish church, off to the south.

He steered her through the heavy doors into near darkness. Only the tabernacle candle, wavering at the altar, lit the cavernous place. She blessed herself and curtsied, and slid onto a bench that did for a pew.

"Wait, *señora*," he whispered, and vanished into a dark sacristy. It led, she knew, to the rectory. Married tonight? She rebelled at it. Married to Jamie Dance, who'd tricked her? Probably it'd be another trick! Probably this priest would refuse. Any sensible priest would! She fumed, and curled up on the bench until she felt a gentle hand shake her.

"*Señora?*"

She peered up and found Tomás hovering over her, and a yawning priest wearing a stole.

"Señora Dance," the padre said, "let us right something that is wrong. Are you willing?"

She didn't know what to say, so she sobbed. Another secret midnight wedding, with no one to wish her joy.

CHAPTER 13

David awoke to the sound of shouting. Beneath him the earth bucked and heaved, as if he were riding the swells of the sea. His stomach pushed upon his throat, and he felt parched. He rose and felt the world whirl, fell back again. But the shouting persisted, hammering into his throbbing skull.

Groaning, he stood up. The sun lanced his eyeballs and he knew it wasn't early. Around him men swirled toward the wagons, ignoring him. He was glad they ignored him. He stood, flooded with nausea, and bent over to spasm up whatever remained in his belly, but the moment passed. No one else seemed to be having any trouble; the others were inured to spirits.

The dragoons clustered around something near the wagons, a knot of blue, and his own teamsters crowded close. He walked toward the commotion, lurching uneasily but gaining strength, passing the *campesinos,* who stared at him from fright-filled eyes. Something bad had happened.

Near the lead wagon he found himself staring at a prone figure, one of his own men, lying inert with flies buzzing about, and crawling into, an awful gash in his back that had bled and then crusted brown in the night. Slowly, recognition came: Abel Cannon, camp tender, blacksmith—a youth of eighteen, David's own age. The youngest one they'd hired. Dead. Stabbed in the back. Murdered. Sprawled belly-down across the stained grass. The awful sight jolted David, froze the nausea out of him, restored his senses like a slap. He pushed through, a question in his mind.

"He musta caught 'em at it," said Lyle Black. "Musta found

'em, and they knifed him. Lad never had a chance. Big old stabber stuck in him like that." The wound was high on Cannon's left side: the knife had slid between ribs and reached the heart. From the rear.

David choked back hot rushing vomit. He'd never seen a murdered man before — had seen only one other dead man, his grandfather, lying in a bed. The *cabo,* Ortiz, slowly turned the body over, so Abel Cannon stared at the sun from sightless eyes.

"Well, little Straus, whatcha going to do about it?" That was Boar Blunt, mockery twisting his heavy features.

"About what?" David mumbled.

"About them. Those Comancheros. Are you scairt of them? Buncha slimy greaser bandits."

David realized, slowly, that their unwanted visitors were not present.

"Abel caught 'em looting whiles we was all gittin' our beauty sleep," said Mazappa Oliphant.

Looting. David stepped to the end of the wagon and peered in, finding disarray. Barrels pried open. Bales cut apart. Crates with their tops askew. Rocky Mountain Company trade goods stolen. He couldn't tell just what . . . everything had been pulled apart. Probably each Comanchero had snatched whatever his thieving heart desired.

He turned to Lyle. "The other wagons?"

"Three. Four in all. The rest . . . maybe they got scairt off by Abel."

"Whatcha gonna do, little Straus? Weep a little?" Boar Blunt started riding him, as usual. "You scairt of a few Comancheros, little Straus? Two, three Yanks could lick the whole lot."

David doubted that. Benito had been one of the most lethal-looking men he'd ever seen. The *cabo* stared at him, and he wondered if the dragoon corporal understood English. David didn't know what to do. He wished Jamie were . . . He shuddered and set that aside. He was still, nominally, in charge, and men waited quietly, sobered by the corpse at their feet. Each one was thinking how easily it could have been him.

"All right, Boar. Pick some men and go get them."

"You scairt to go, baby Straus?"

128

"Yes."

Boar's eyes gleamed. "I need three. Gimme three Yanks and I'll wipe their brown butts."

"You'd better hurry. I don't suppose they're sitting under some tree. I trust you know where they went."

Something that looked like doubt crossed Boar's face. "I'll take a tracker. Hey, Willis. You comin'?"

Eggy Willis was a good choice, David thought. He'd grown up in the hills of Arkansas and could follow any trail.

Willis nodded, hesitantly.

David turned to the *cabo* and addressed him in Spanish. "You want to send men after the *bandidos?* We're sending a few."

Ortiz smiled and shrugged. "I am ordered to stay here and guard against *los indios* and *los tejanos.*"

And not chase after Mexican nationals, David thought dourly.

Boar Blunt talked his own little clique, Mario Petti and Lewis Dusseldorf, into going after the Comancheros with him, and the four saddled listlessly, without stopping for breakfast.

"Recover what you can, Blunt. That's important. More important than revenge."

Blunt snorted. "We're going for scalps, baby Straus."

Eggy Willis had already crossed the Purgatoire, and was waiting for them on the east side. Silently, teamsters and dragoons watched the foursome ride southeast along some trail or other until they vanished behind a slight rise.

"Ol' Boar, he bit off more'n he can chaw," said Mazappa thoughtfully. "Like to get them four turned into buzzard bait."

"If you'd been watching—if we'd had a guard, as I wanted—it wouldn't have happened!" David snapped, wild anger building in him. "But no. Every last one of you went on a drunk."

Mazappa Oliphant peered back thoughtfully, measuring his words. "Oh, I reckon there's ought to that," he said. "But Mr. Straus, the boys was some put out. All that whackin' and cuttin' and sweatin' and haulin' we done, we found out it warn't worth nothin'—all that sweatin' under the hot sun until we plumb dropped into our bedrolls at night. Maybe a man has earned himself a drink, he gets word like that from the boss."

David felt stricken and couldn't reply.

Lyle Black rescued him. "I reckon you want us to git the trade goods in order and figure out what got took. Isn't that what you want, Mr. Straus?"

David nodded, gratefully.

"And I guess maybe ol' Emilio better start some chow—I'm plumb starved. Coffee. A man needs coffee after tying one on."

David nodded. Emilio had understood, and he wandered toward his kitchen, teeth clacking again.

"And I guess we got some things to do about him." Black pointed at the remains at his feet. "Reckon you want me to put some men on diggin' a proper hole and collectin' his stuff to send back to his folks. And maybe Philpot can do some talkin' at the buryin'; he's got a Bible in his pack, and reads like a perfesser."

David nodded numbly. "Who will volunteer?"

Surprisingly, every teamster responded. They had all liked the young camp tender and 'smith. Some of them drifted to the light wagon to extract the two spades from it. The dragoons watched them silently.

"And if you got other instructions, we ought to be hearin' them. Otherwise we'll just set until Mr. Dance comes back."

This was the thing he dreaded. He could go against his father now, tell them to keep on building. Or he could obey. They could tarry, doing nothing, waiting for Jamie. They could wait for the dragoons to pull out and then sneak away. The Mexican soldiers couldn't stay here long, not with a war going on. But if he told these men to build, there'd be no turning back. He couldn't ask them to abandon everything again. He wrestled angrily with the decision and then snapped out, "We'll stay here."

The men eyed him skeptically. "Ye mean for now . . . until Dance gits back?" asked Gantt.

"No, I mean permanently."

"Ye mean till them Mex dragoons pull out. Then we folla yer daddy's orders."

These things stung, but David set them aside. "No. My father was worried about the Texas trouble. He's far from here. I'm making my own decision. We're staying. We're building. We'll do what we started out to do—trade from Mexico, go against the Bents from here."

The men stared quietly at David Straus, and he withered under their gaze. He'd failed; he'd never been one to command. But their gazes weren't hostile; in fact, he saw something else in them, something he couldn't fathom. Maybe that was only because Boar Blunt wasn't around to rub his nose in manure.

The teamsters broke up silently, some of them to dig a grave at the edge of the timber, the beginnings of a cemetery for the new post, a cemetery that was bound to grow. David's lieutenants, Black and Oliphant, took charge, as if no great lapse in discipline had ever happened. Black found sheeting and wrapped the murdered youth in it, lovingly carried the heavy burden out to the edge of their world. Oliphant set to work in the wagons, putting things back in order. David watched, trying to fathom what was missing; trying not to think about Abel Cannon, a life snuffed out so early.

David didn't have the cargo manifests; Jamie had them for the Mexican tax collectors. Even so, he had become so familiar with the wagon loads that he could pretty well list the stolen goods. Knives. The Comancheros had taken a fancy to some good Wilson knives made in Sheffield, England, and had made off with two dozen of varying sizes. Leman rifles. A long crate had been pried open, and three were missing. The Comancheros were well armed with new-looking carbines; these Lemans were heavy buffalo-hunting rifles. Even so, they had disappeared. Along with a bale of good Witney blankets, some bolts of flannel and one or two of calico. A wooden box of awls, highly prized among the tribes, was gone. The rest was guesswork: he thought some hawk bells were missing; several hanks of trade beads, a burlap bag of roasted coffee beans. A lot. Worth a lot of robes. A great anger broiled through him. It might have been prevented!

"I reckon that does it," said Mazappa, sweat dripping from his brow. The insides of those canvas-covered furnaces dehydrated the men rummaging in them. "You got some handle on the loss?"

"Between two and three hundred dollars," David said shortly.

131

"Coulda been worse if'n they wasn't interrupted. Mighta stole some of our horses and made off with lots more. Stole a wagon, even. You owe that lad somethin'. His folks too."

David swallowed back things that needed saying.

They collected at the far edge of the meadow, solemn men on a sun-baked flat. Mexican dragoons, too, a sea of blue around the raw hole in the tan clay. They were all waiting for him. David didn't know why. He wouldn't conduct this service; he was not of their faith. But he realized he was still in command. It wouldn't proceed without him. Launes stood with Bible in hand, waiting for David to begin this solemn ceremony.

David Straus shrank from it. Why him? Still the men waited. He swallowed back fear. At least Boar wasn't present to mock him. He pulled off his wide-brimmed beaver, and felt the breeze cool his dampened forehead.

"Abel Cannon was my age. That's too young to die. He died for this company. He caught them stealing, and they killed him — murdered him, and fled. Because of Abel, we didn't lose a lot. A few hundred dollars' worth. Because he cared about me" — David's voice cracked — "about our common enterprise . . . about us all . . ." He felt himself faltering, and pulled himself together. "Because he wanted the Rocky Mountain Company to succeed, and because he was loyal, he lost his life. What greater sacrifice can there be? He'll not see the sun, or feel these breezes . . . May he be with the Divine Father forever."

He felt he'd failed, but the men had liked what he'd said. Plainly, they thought he'd fulfilled some duty they had in mind, and gradually David settled back, at ease, while Philpot Launes read from the Scripture, some of which David knew; and then they-prayed, every one of these rough blasphemous men who could blister oxen with their foul tongues. The Mexican dragoons, most of them bareheaded, blessed themselves at the end of the prayer, and the boys slowly shoveled clay over that solemn cylinder of canvas below.

David didn't quite know what had happened, but order had been restored and his world had turned better. Out of death and chaos, a man had been born inside him. But one who'd experienced hatred, buried like yeast in his soul, for the first time.

* * *

Wearily Teresa María followed Tomás and Pedro—Padre Pedro, she'd learned—through the inky streets of Santa Fe, all of them wary of the ruffians who owned the night. Had this been a wedding? What woman would ever want such a wedding as this? They had gathered beneath that barred window high above them, in a gloomy alley that reeked of urine; her Jamie on the other side of a thick wall and barely able to hear the priest. And there they had said the vows again. What woman wanted to be married in such a fashion, alone, without flowers, without a wedding dress, without a feast and the blessings of family and friends? Without a *baile?*

They slid through the creaking door of San Miguel, bowed or curtsied, and wound their way to the sacristy, where Padre Pedro kindled a lamp and set it beside a large, morocco-bound volume. Then he plucked out a quill pen and some stoppered ink, and scratched in a ledger. Teresa María could not read, so Tomás told her what was written: " 'The sacrament of matrimony; James Dance and Teresa María Obregón' "—he paused when she flinched at her maiden name—" 'Seven September, Eighteen-Forty-One. Pedro Olivares.' " That was all. The church had witnessed.

"I am truly married now?" she asked suspiciously.

"For as long as you both shall live," replied the padre.

"There is no more scandal?"

"There never was scandal. Only an irregularity."

"The church recognizes Jamie?"

The priest chose his words carefully. "It would be helpful, when he's freed, for him to come to me to be baptized."

"Will I have babies now?"

"God willing."

"Will the officials punish us—Jamie and me—for anything?"

The padre hesitated. "Your parish priest in Taos has the ear of the governor."

Tomás said, softly, "The Republic of Mexico recognizes civil marriage."

Something restless passed between the men in that wavering

133

lamplight. The Republic of Mexico had weakened the church's grip on the lives of its citizens.

The priest stood silently, plainly wanting to be freed of his guests. Tomás thanked him and steered Teresa María through the close gloom of the nave to the creaking doors and out into a starlit night.

"Have you a place to go?" he asked.

"I am the guest of the governor and his wife."

"I'll take you there. It's not proper for a respectable woman to be out alone. And not safe, either."

"Am I respectable?" she asked, bitterly.

"You always were, *señora.*"

"I don't know that I want to go there—to the palace."

"I cannot take you to a *posada,* not you alone. I could take you to my *casa,* but it would cause a scandal—and I am semi-honorable."

She didn't laugh at his small joke. Something ahead moved, a person of the night, and they froze in star-shadow. Then, after the night ticked by, they walked again, this time silently, through crooked streets to the plaza.

She didn't know whether she hated him, the impostor, or not. She was rather taken with him, actually, but could not forgive that charade at Taos. For that matter, she didn't know whether she was angry with Jamie or not. Something in her turned rosy with the thought that her lover had gone to such drastic lengths to marry her—stopping at nothing. Nothing! But her reckless *yanqui* had caused a scandal, too, had destroyed her reputation. She didn't know whether to adore him or scold him. Maybe both. She adored him actually, but she wouldn't let this go. She was going to use it again and again. She'd never let him forget it!

They reached the plaza, a rectangle of open night surrounded by dark walls that still radiated the day's heat. Tomás steered her across the dusty ground, straight toward the massive door, and there they halted.

"Go now," she said. "I don't want you seen here. I live with scandal enough."

"Will you be—?"

"A guard stands inside."

134

He nodded and slipped softly eastward toward his *casa*, swallowed by the dark.

She knocked, an odd loudness to the hammering of her small fist in the deep quiet. The door swung open, revealing a gaunt night guard, one she'd never seen.

"I am Señora Dance; a guest of the governor and lady."

He peered at her sharply, noting her lack of escort. He coughed. *"Barracha!"* he muttered, and swung the great door shut.

"No! Wait!" she cried, but the door thumped shut. Drunk, he had said. He had judged her for a sporting woman.

A terrible weariness overtook her. It had been an endless day, full of fears and anguish. She felt herself sagging, hardly able to take a step anywhere. Alone, but so close to Jamie, behind those thick walls. She hadn't a peso. She couldn't enter a respectable *posada* anyway. Frightened, she wondered what to do. She'd never been alone like this. Always, there'd been someone—her family, Jamie, someone. This night, Tomás. She could go to his home. She could go back to San Miguel and—She didn't want to do that, didn't want to stare all night at the altar of God, or have the altar of God stare back at her.

She turned toward Calle Delgado, wondering angrily what Tomás had meant, calling himself semihonorable. He played jokes on her.

When she knocked, fearful he would misread her intentions, he opened at once, still dressed and awake.

"I waited," he said.

"The guard didn't know me."

Tomás laughed. How could he laugh at a time like this? "Now it is a scandal. A married woman coming to another man on her wedding night."

"Oh!" She turned to leave, swept with weariness.

But his laughter was infectious. "I have only this room. It is yours. I will sleep on the pile of buffalo robes in back, in my warehouse, and hope the fleas don't eat me."

She was mollified, and too tired to argue. "A thousand thanks," she said, fighting back a sudden tear. Then she couldn't fight the tears any more. They bubbled up unbidden, slid down her cheeks.

"Ah, *señora*, I would hold you if I could, and wipe each tear away. Tears that my own rash conduct—and loyalty to my *amigo* Jamie—caused you. Sleep, *señora*. Sleep the sleep of the innocent. And tomorrow, I will help you. Maybe we can get Jamie out."

"I don't think anyone can get Jamie out."

He cocked an eyebrow. "To deal with the devil, you lead the devil into temptation," he said.

But she was too tired for his conundrums, and sank wearily onto a small bed, an adobe bench projecting from the wall, as he slid through a back door. If there was more heartache tomorrow, she thought, she'd scratch Manuel Armijo's eyes out. The thought satisfied her.

CHAPTER 14

They came for Jamie midmorning, sometime after a church bell had tolled the tenth hour, two mestizo guards in spotless blue uniforms. They marched him past clerks in claw-hammer frock coats, and waited at a burnished door until his legs ached. When at last he was admitted, he found himself in Armijo's office, a long, narrow affair with vigas overhead. At the far end the floor was raised a step; and on that rise stood a dais. Resting on that, like a coffin, was Armijo's desk, an elaborate table carved of some tropical wood. And behind it, in a high-backed ornate throne sat the governor, gorgeously adorned in his sky blue cutaway tunic with gold-corded epaulets at the shoulders and spanking white *pantalones*. From his lofty height, he eyed Jamie through hooded eyes, and Jamie grew conscious of the stubble on his face and the dirt on his fringed buckskins. He was forced to look up — far up — at Manuel Armijo; but Armijo merely looked down like the Archangel Michael, as upon a worm.

A functionary laid a pasteboard portfolio before the governor and then tiptoed through a side door, leaving Armijo and Dance quite alone in the gloomy room. It was lit only by a small window at the rear, behind Armijo, which illumined his head and gave him a halo if Jamie squinted from just the right angle.

"Ah, Señor Dance. I trust you enjoyed our hospitality."

"I got married."

Armijo laughed politely, his thick lips pursing, and turned to the portfolio, nodding as he read. At least Jamie thought he read. Armijo's thick finger traced the paper, and he silently formed words one by one. Time stretched again. No seat had been provided for those attending the governor. One stood in his august presence. Jamie thought of settling his lanky frame on the hard clay floor, but decided it would offend the man. Jamie hated to stand, especially upright, and chose to slouch against any convenient post or wall if he could. Standing upright had always been an ordeal.

"The prefect of Taos reports, *amigo*, that in eighteen thirty-six, you and five other *yanquis* trapped beaver in the mountains a few leagues to the north — and without a license. Further, that one hundred seventy-three beaver pelts, skinned and dried, were discovered in your possession in Taos! Ah, untaxed wealth. Contraband! The pelts, of course, were confiscated by authorities. But there remain the taxes, fines, and penalties, which come, all told, to three pesos per pelt, times one hundred seventy-three pelts. There were several of you, but Mexican law says the fines and penalties fall entirely on all, and since you're the only one we have in custody, they fall on you."

Armijo smiled blandly, something almost joyous in his liquid brown eyes. "It comes to five hundred and nineteen pesos."

"That's a heap, guv, a peso bein' like a dollar. Reckon a beaver pelt brung about two, three dollars in the trade."

"It's a trifle. You'll have to pay it. I can't release you until . . . the amount is paid. *Todo, todo.*"

"Reckon you'll just have ter lock me up and throw away the key, guv. Never had such a bucket of money in my life, and I don't reckon I can lay my mitts on it."

Armijo frowned. He closed the portfolio and peered down upon Jamie, who didn't like the melted-wax look in the man's eyes. Jamie slouched his way to the left wall, and leaned into it comfortably. He could slouch that way for hours on end.

"Are you ill?"

"Just gettin' comfortable, guv."

"Are you not a partner of the *yanqui* financier, Guy Straus?"

"Yup."

"Then the fines and taxes will be available to you."

"Aw, Straus, he won't ante up for some old fine. Fact is, he finds out about this and he's likely to let me rot hyar. That sort,

138

they don't get rich bailin' out pore boys like me."

"You brought twelve wagons of goods for the Indian trade. But you didn't bring them here to the capital, along the proper routes, to be taxed as required. Instead you hid them." Armijo arched a brow. "You planned to build a post! Without our knowledge, without a license—without even owning one hectare of land under it. Ah, Dance. It's a pity. So many laws. So many imposts. Our excellent Colonel Cortez found you at once, on his alert patrol of our borders, looking for those miserable *tejanos,* and of course you were caught at once—red-handed."

"Reckon it didn't make sense to haul all them wagons couple hundred miles to Santy Fe and couple hundred miles back thar again. Me and Teresa, we were fixin' to ride in with our cargo manifests and ante up, get us a license and all."

Armijo smiled. "An honest merchant."

That miffed Jamie, but he just smiled.

"An honest *yanqui* merchant. With bills of lading that neglected to mention . . . all the cargo—such as barrels of spirits."

"All right, guv, git to the charges. We ain't got all day. What do we owe to get set up?"

Armijo seemed disappointed. He hadn't even gotten to elaborate on the infractions yet: the unpaid wagon tax, the lack of *guías,* the improper this and that. The licenses. But that suited Jamie fine. Best to let the thick-lipped buzzard know he was wasting time.

"I might confiscate everything, Señor Dance. The penalties and taxes run twice the value of your merchandise."

"Reckon you don't want to kill the trade betwixt hyar and Saint Louis," Dance replied. "Reckon you want to stay on the good side o' old Guy Straus. Straus et Fils underwrites the trade, including yours, I hear. You got dealin's with him."

Armijo smiled blandly. "Señor Dance, it isn't polite to threaten the government of New Mexico." The light haloed his head. He looked like a carved Santo.

Jamie shrugged.

The governor pouted some, the frown lines thickening on his brow. "We think you are agents of the *tejanos.* You have no proof against it."

"You got no proof for it."

"We've put all foreigners under house arrest for the time being. For their own protection, of course, as well as to prevent certain, ah, plots and subversions."

"Even our consul, I hear, which ain't very social."

"Ah, Dance, it is to keep our enraged citizens from tearing Señor Alvarez to pieces."

Dance shrugged again. Let the governor fish. The man wanted money, lots of it, for his own coffers, for his ragtag army. And the longer Jamie delayed coming to some sort of agreement, the better he figured the terms would be—if he could wait out the endless hours in that grim hole. "Reckon you'd better slap irons on me and march me down south to old Mexico City if that's the way she be. Take a squad of these hyar guards, just to keep me from busting loose—or them Texians from busting me free."

Armijo yawned. Jamie wasn't getting anywhere with him. Time ticked by.

"You done with me, guv?"

"Ah, Dance. I wish . . . I have no choice but to send you back to the *cárcel*. I fear you will not enjoy the company of, ah, your lady."

"I reckon she'll get along."

"For a small favor, the guards might let her visit. She declined our hospitality, Dance. We are looking for her. I've sent word to her father—he has dominion over her, of course. He will have his ways of dealing with the rebellious girl. So will Padre Martinez."

"Like I say, guv, we got married last night."

Armijo laughed pleasantly. "Perhaps you know where she is. Tell me, Dance."

Jamie shrugged.

"I fear you will go hungry until you let us know."

"Reckon I lived through pore meat before. You ain't gonna starve a partner of ol' Straus for long."

"I haven't time for this nonsense. You need further humbling, *amigo*. Maybe it'll take a few days, or weeks. Or will it be months and years? An, how it must feel to rot away one's only

140

life, sleep away one's only days."

He stood, barked an order, and guards materialized.

"You send a man to look at the parish record over to San Miguel, guv."

Armijo froze, then swiftly smiled. "You *yanquis.*"

The guards poked Jamie ahead, their bayonets never far from his back. He stared at the governor, wondering if he'd gotten himself into a worse jam, or whether Armijo might soften a bit.

But back in that cool gloomy cell, where the walls pressed down and suffocated him, he regretted his cocky ways. He didn't know how long he could endure in a hole like that, all alone. He'd been born free; he'd spent a lifetime wandering over unfenced, unowned land, trespassing nowhere because it was all just there, and grand, and belonged to no one. That's how they all had felt, the beaver men, like lords of the wilds, exempt from all the designs of ambitious politicians who loved to tax and enslave and who regarded their fellow mortals as property.

Boar Blunt and his friends rode southeast, across open grasslands that had burnt brown. Ahead, Eggy Willis picked out the faint trail, not so much from hoofprints in the baked clay as from the occasional bits of darkening manure he found.

Boar exulted. They made good time, and he knew they were gaining on the Comancheros, who were slowed by their pack burros. He'd show them what four Yank teamsters could do to a dozen greasers, half of them buckets of lard, and the other half skin and bones. He smiled happily at Petti and Dusseldorf, who smiled back, anticipating the fun ahead. They'd catch that big cheese Benito and prick him a few times with their Bowie knives, just to teach him respect. Maybe they'd string up a few—them greaser thieves needed stringing up. But mostly Boar intended to show them dinky Mex who was chief bull round about those parts.

The plains lay as flat as a billiard table, stretching out to a hazy horizon. Somewhere up ahead, they'd see those high-peaked sombreros and dust and a dun-colored mass of burro flesh and horses hurrying away. And then the fun would begin.

"Me, I want that big pig Benito. Then maybe I'll teach a few more greasers some manners."

Mario laughed. "Got to put the stickers to 'em first. I figger I'll get tired out if'n I got to wallop more'n six."

"You ever cut a finger off? I'm gonna cut one of them greaser's fingers off," said Dusseldorf.

Ahead, Eggy Willis waited for them. He had never been a part of their cabal, and Boar half-resented having him along. It was like having a ghost of Jamie Dance among them.

"What you waitin' for?" Boar demanded, as they pulled up.

"Sign's fresh. Maybe we should be watching more, talking less," Eggy said, half-apologetically. He pointed at some bright green manure.

Boar smirked at the man's timid advice. "Willis, do you see any of them greasers?"

The tracker shook his head. "But they're around. This here country has some surprises."

"When I see their pointy sombreros, I'll start worrying," Boar said. "But not very much."

"They're twelve, and they're armed with good rifles," Willis persisted.

Boar cackled. "You ever seen a greaser could hit anything or load fast?"

Willis didn't reply, but reined his little mustang and continued forward. Boar thought they'd ridden eight or nine miles.

They sweated ahead another mile, through blinding light, and then the shots came from nowhere, utterly nowhere, a ragged volley from unseen places, the balls thumping into their horses. Boar felt his own sweated horse shudder and sink. Petti's squealed and bucked, but another shot from nowhere caught it in the chest, and it caved to earth. Willis's horse bleated and began running, then slowed, stumbled, and died, just as Willis slid off. Dusseldorf's horse dropped, poleaxed by a ball in its brain. It hit the earth before Dusseldorf could pull free, and rolled onto his leg. The teamster screamed when bone snapped.

Boar hit the ground on both feet, carbine in hand. Where were they? He peered wildly around, hunting the cowardly

142

greasers, and couldn't spot any. Willis, the Ozark boy, had lithely dropped behind his fallen horse, but his heavy plains rifle was pinned under the beast's weight. Petti's rifle was free, and in hand, but he tugged violently at a saddlebag that contained his spare balls and powder, caught under his horse.

From somewhere Boar heard laughter, and knew the voice. Benito. He'd heard that soft nasal sound long enough around the whiskey pot. He'd kill the greaser; that's what he'd do—if he could just find him.

"Señor Yankee. It is good to live, *sí?* Better than to die, *sí?*"

To the left. That voice rose from the left. Boar squinted through the blinding light toward the place of the voice, and saw the subtle suggestion of an edge of some kind, something that interrupted the vast sweep of prairie.

"I tell you once. I will not tell you twice."

Boar peered about wildly—he had no help from any of his men. But he'd show that greaser a thing or two. He laughed, raucously. "Benito, nice day!"

The shot slapped his rifle stock, shattering wood, driving splinters into his ribs. His hand stung. He winced, stunned. Where had it come from? Somewhere else! Surrounded by ghosts.

From somewhere, men laughed, and droned among themselves in Spanish. He knew he'd kill the suckers; it'd just take a little doing. But not now.

"*Yanqui!* You are slow to learn about Méjico."

"Better lay it down, Boar," whispered Willis, behind him.

Just like Willis, he thought. No guts. But involuntarily he set his rifle down. Beside him, Petti lowered his. From nowhere, men laughed. Cowards. Petti and Dusseldorf didn't have the balls of an ant, and Willis didn't have none at all.

To the left and ahead, Comancheros rose, as if climbing out of badger holes. Eight of them anyway, including Benito. None of them wore a sombrero. Boar peered around, astonished, an awareness rising in him that these Mex had been lying in the curve of a hidden waterway, elusive even from fifty yards.

The barrel-shaped leader wandered toward him, while the others kept their gleaming carbines lowered and ready. Benito stared at each man; Boar first, then Willis, then Petti, and finally Dusseldorf, who sweated out his anguish. Dusseldorf's leg remained under the belly of the dun he'd ridden.

Benito issued some staccato command. Three of the Comancheros caught up the hooves of the dun and pulled. Dusseldorf screamed, but the horse came clear. The man's leg projected off at a grotesque angle.

Benito sighed, lowered his carbine to Dusseldorf's temple. The shot jolted Boar. He stared wildly at Dusseldorf, and found nothing much to recognize. Benito shrugged apologetically, then began reloading. "In Méjico, a mule breaks a leg, we put it out of pain, *sí?*"

Boar wanted to vomit. Petti looked ashen. Willis had shut his eyes tight, not wanting to see what he had seen.

The Comancheros stripped gear from dead horses, collected weapons, and prodded the three survivors down a slope into a grassy watercourse that dished subtly in the prairie. There, below the level of the surrounding flats, were a dozen more bandits the teamsters had never seen before, their burros and horses laden with loot—bright bolts of tradecloth, shining metal objects—carelessly mounded upon the backs of the beasts.

"Now you will walk," said Benito.

Boar wasn't inclined to argue. It had struck him like a fist to the gut that he might die at any moment.

The little caravan proceeded straight up the grassy watercourse as it wandered southeast. No one seemed to be in a hurry, and no one pressed the Yankee teamsters. Boar was used to walking; he made his living walking beside yokes of oxen. The travel wasn't unpleasant, except that Boar's thirst raged in his throat and terror lurked at every pause.

"Where you takin' us?" he asked Benito, as the leathery man eyed him silently.

"You are slaves."

"Slaves?"

"We'll trade you to the Comanche for robes. They like slaves. Lots of slaves to do the chores."

"You'd trade us to Injuns?"

Benito shrugged. "Maybe four, five robes for each of you."

"You'd turn us over to Comanch?"

Benito shrugged. "It's a living, *sí?*"

144

Boar knew the Comancheros trafficked in human flesh. The Comanche traded captive women and children, and the Comancheros sold them to help-hungry *hacendados* for field workers. White women and children, too. The Comanche sold white captives as well as Indian ones, always for a good price — powder and ball, knives, hatchets, blankets.

"What do them Comanch want with white men?"

Benito shrugged, his gaze wandering off toward the horizon.

For three boiling days they wandered southeast, always in the shallow watercourse that allowed them to progress just under the surface of the prairie. They always enjoyed a noon siesta when the heat was whitest.

Whenever Boar tried to talk to Willis or Petti, the Comancheros prodded them apart, but otherwise they were treated well enough. He wondered what his pals thought, but both Petti and Willis kept their silence, afraid that a loose knife might separate them from life if they spoke. But they didn't suffer. Neither did all those horses and burros.

The dry watercourse opened out upon a dished basin fed by a lazy spring. A few trees clustered where their roots could soak up water. Here the Comancheros stopped, and for four days they did nothing except hunt and play monte with ancient cards.

Boar suspected this was the rendezvous place and they'd be seeing wild Comanche soon. The thought brought sweat up on him. The other two captives looked plenty worried, too.

Mario Petti managed to whisper something to him at last. Just two words: Tonight. Run.

"Willis too?" Boar whispered.

"Yeah."

But when they turned, they found Benito's gaze upon them. The man smiled under the brim of his sombrero.

"Ah, ah, it is not good," he said. "You don' like the hospitality of Méjico."

He summoned men in that nasal Spanish of his, a score of them, until they surrounded Boar and Mario. Languidly, he waved a finger. And they jumped them, all those Mex, several on each man, and subdued Boar swiftly.

Then Benito pulled a wicked knife from his belt sheath, and Boar saw his own doom in Benito's amused gaze.

But it wasn't to be final. The Comancheros wrestled off his tattered boot, and Benito drew his knife swiftly across the narrow place above the heel, severing Boar's Achilles tendon. And then he performed the surgery on the other heel. Hamstrung!

Boar struggled, aghast, feeling the bite of pain — and the bite of knowing he'd never walk again.

CHAPTER 15

The Fox, Coronel Agustino Cortez y Jaramillo had one great ambition — to be important. Nothing in all of life could be as satisfying as to be a man of renown, a man whom all citizens must deal with sooner or later. And how better to be important than in the army of the republic? It was the key to everything: wealth, power, the adoration of women. Ah, women! Let him but enter a *sala* in his dazzling blue uniform with all its gold braid, and how the dark eyes flashed, how the *señoritas* clustered about him, laughing and purring!

But women were merely the froth, the foam on the *cerveza* of life. A *coronel* had great avenues and opportunities to importance; to being an indispensable man. It was simple enough in theory, but hard to achieve in practice. One way to be important was to be an obstacle. If one was truly an obstacle, then the world could do nothing except with one's cooperation. The idea, then, was to discover what others wanted and to be the obstacle to their achieving those goals. Ah! The secret of power and success in Mexico! He prided himself on having figured it all out rationally, where most ambitious men never grasped the underlying principle of success. Little did they know, or understand, how to be an obstacle — or how to avoid the obstacles others set up.

It was simple, really. One first had to acquire informants to help one learn what others desired. Informants were deliciously easy to collect. A little *don* here and there; a cigarrito for a soldier; a flagon of aguardiente for a man of some substance, like that fop Trujillo, the governor's aide. For that tri-

147

fle, the *coronel* had learned precisely what had happened between *el gobernador* and Jamie Dance. Ah, that Dance. Offering nothing at all to Armijo! Telling Armijo to send him to Ciudad Mexico! All Armijo wanted, really, was money—money to fight the *tejanos,* money to gamble at La Tules' *taberna*. The man obviously didn't want to bleed the Rocky Mountain Company to death; just bleed it white, so he could bleed it again in a while. The *coronel* understood the sentiment perfectly.

Oh, he knew a lot of things. He knew that a priest from San Miguel had married the *señorita* to Dance last night. A guard had listened from the barracks window down the alley. One *cigarro* for information so precious! He knew she'd gone off with Tomás Villanova—no doubt to stay with him. It would seem a scandal, but wasn't really.

Now take Dance, he thought. He knew exactly what Dance wanted, too. It was simple. People were transparent. The partner in the *yanqui* company wanted to get out of the *cárcel*. He wanted to settle the old trapping imposts. He wanted to license his company and trade with the Indians. He wanted to pay as little tariff as possible on the trade goods he'd brought into Mexico. He wanted to make a good profit, take robes back to St. Louis. He wanted to settle the little matter of those casks of spirits smuggled into Mexico. Ah, it was all so plain.

Therefore, Cortez thought. It was the task of El Zorro, the Fox, to be an obstacle. Only that way would he be forever important to all concerned. Thus, he must be an obstacle to Armijo—without the army, *el gobernador* could do little—and thus he must be an obstacle to Dance. Without the cooperation of El Zorro, Dance would lose everything. And indeed, he must be an obstacle to the *señora*, who wanted her husband freed; only then might she reward him with her favors. And maybe he ought to be an obstacle to that Tomás Villanova, too; the almost-priest, the fur trader who managed to evade the attention of the authorities. Who knows what heretical books one might find in that room on Delgado?

It was perfectly clear. But he scarcely knew where to start

on this afternoon at the time of the siesta, when no one stirred in the dense September sunlight. He sighed, thinking perhaps the place to be the greatest obstacle, the place to become most important—as important as a rich hidalgo—would be the chamber of Manuel Armijo, who was no doubt slumbering after a light lunch of fruit. The man rarely stirred until late in the day.

La señora gorda admitted him, wearing this day a blue tent with white lace about her jowls.

"Ah, *Coronel,* he is enjoying his slumber."

That pleased El Zorro. "I will awaken him. It's a matter of state."

"*Tejanos!*" she cried, her chubby hand flying to her mouth.

"Worse!" said Cortez. "The *tejanos* I don't worry about. We'll string them up by their heels. No, this is worse!"

"Oh, go right in," she cried.

Armijo filled the entire fourposter bed imported from St. Louis, and that raised an interesting question in El Zorro's mind about the repose of the *señora. El gobernador* wore only his white *pantalones.* He cocked open an eye, yawned, and opened the other.

"*Coronel,* I do not speak before coffee and a *cigarro.*"

El Zorro shrugged. "Very well, then." He turned to leave.

"*Coronel! Alto!*"

"I don't wish to disturb Your Excellency. . . ."

"You have something to tell me. I will listen before my coffee and *cigarro.*"

"Your Excellency, I am leaving for the *frontera.*"

"*Tejanos?*"

"It is time. I cannot stay away from my dragoons and my duties. The *tejanos* may be upon us."

"Have you news of them?"

El Zorro shrugged. "None. But President Santa Anna would cut off my *cajones*"—he ran a finger across his gut for emphasis—"if I let the *tejanos* take Santa Fe. Is your militia ready?"

Armijo grunted. "Fifty *peons* with broomsticks."

"The question I came about, Your Excellency—how do

149

you wish to deal with the *yanquis?* Señor Dance and the wagons. My dragoons will leave them now. We will fight the *tejanos.*"

"You can't leave them! Guard them! They'll steal away!" His Excellency bolted upright. The bed groaned under his corpulence.

El Zorro shrugged apologetically. "You could send your militia, Excellency."

Manuel Armijo grunted. "I command you to guard them."

"Por favor, understand, Excellency, I am at your service, but also at the service of *el presidente.*"

"But they're right on the Río Nepeste! They'll slink away — twelve wagons of goods for, ah, our army."

"Excellency, I have more important duties given to me by our esteemed Santa Anna. We are being invaded."

"Tell them to bring the wagons here for the taxing."

Cortez shook his head. "Excellency, it is a long wagon trip — maybe a fortnight each way — and the only wagon road is the one past Bent's Fort — in *yanqui* territory. These *yanquis* are in Mejico, but there's no road from there to here within our borders. *Comprende?* I had long talks with Dance. He said the company would pull back across the Nepeste — the Arkansas — if Méjico is not, ah, hospitable. Ah, Excellency, the federal dragoons cannot keep them there forever. You have a decision to make. Either license them or lose them."

Armijo scowled. "I don't intend to license them. I don't want another nest of *yanquis* on our border. The Bents are enough. . . . Of course, if they took in a mejicano partner — myself, for example — I would welcome them. Padre Martinez, that calf, howls about the foreigners. Yes, yes, give me a third of the profits and I would welcome *yanquis.* But Dance . . . ah, the stubborn burro. Maybe a few days in the *cárcel* will change his mind."

"He wishes to make a profit, Excellency. Not see it all lost to imposts."

The governor smiled. "Why so do I . . . if Dance and I can come to a little agreement."

Agustino Cortez smiled. He knew his man. "A sound idea,

Excellency. A partnership—and then a license to trade and forgiveness of a few trifles that hang over him. But of course they may flee across the river when we leave them."

Armijo scowled. "*Coronel,* you desert me?"

"I am bound by the instructions of *el presidente.* You are a bright man with many resources, and the government of a whole province is at your beck and call. You'll think of something. You have a giant brain. Why not give Dance what he wants—for now? For a third? Better to keep them there, happy, than to see them escape across the river, *sí?*"

Armijo stared. "We have to collect some imposts."

Cortez shrugged. "Of course. Dance expected to pay. He told me he wanted the tax collectors to come there; it would save driving the wagons four hundred miles to Santa Fe and then back. Come yourself, Excellency—or send a tax man."

Armijo frowned. "I can't leave here, not with an army of *tejanos* coming." He brightened. "But I can make things easy for Dance. Welcome to Méjico, Señor Dance. Welcome, Rocky Mountain Company, eh?"

"You'll offend the Bents, Excellency."

"So? That nest of *yanqui* spies on our border needs offending. Charles Bent always remembers my natal day, as if a few sweets will buy a governor. It takes more! Ah! We will have our own company in Méjico now, to keep the Bents humble. If, of course, Señor Dance will accept a silent partner."

"Silent, Excellency? There must be a public partner, or the people will be inflamed. They're ready to hang every foreign heretic in the province."

"Why, *Coronel,* perhaps I will have Dance put your name on. You'll be the Méjicano partner. I'll give you some sweeteners now and then, just for the use of your name."

"I am honored, Excellency. I'm sure Señor Dance will agree. A trifle."

Armijo bawled happily, slapped Cortez on the back, and gave him a great *abrazo.*

El Zorro left the governor to his siesta, and cheerfully considered other arrangements.

* * *

Teresa María awoke ravenous. She peered about Tomás's room, and saw at once that Jamie's friend didn't take his meals in his quarters. Like most bachelors, he did not eat at home. She studied Calle Delgado, and found it empty. She could slide out and not be seen if she chose. But what then? She didn't have a *centavo,* and all her things were in the governor's suite. She could go there, of course—except she feared his grasping hospitality. She might not escape again.

There was no option but to wait for Tomás, the book-reading false priest. She sat indignantly, waiting for him to emerge from his smelly warehouse. When he eventually did, politely knocking at the door first, the morning was half-spent, and she was more famished than ever.

She started to rail at him, but he spoke first. "You are hungry. We will eat. Do you want to brave the gossips of Delgado Street, or shall we slip out the warehouse to the alley?"

"You could have got up sooner. Some wedding night. *Madre de Dios!* I'm humiliated!"

He shrugged. "You could try the floor at San Miguel tonight, *señora.*"

He opened the heavy front door, admitting a swirl of piñon-scented air.

"Let them all cluck," she said, and whirled out into the busy crowd. She wished she had fresh clothing, and a place to wash, but those luxuries were available only if she surrendered to the governor's snares. No. She had business on this fine golden morning. She would talk. Today her tongue would wag. Today she would blister ears, mortify officials, condemn tax collectors to *infierno.* Today she would tell them what she thought of them, these officials who put her husband in the *cárcel. Madre de Dios!* She would wear them down! She had only a woman's weapons, which consisted mostly of her tongue, but it was used to constant exercise, well honed to speak in staccato bursts so fast that no one could get a word in, least of all her Jamie, who drawled his slow English and whose tortured Spanish sounded like peyote talking. Poor Jamie! He always said she talked too much. She would find the *coronel* first and talk his ear off. She would try to visit Jamie. Maybe she would talk to the secretary of state, Don Guadalupe Miranda, who always liked *yanquis*.

But now Tomás steered her toward the *panaderia* of one Barcellona, and into a gloomy haze. A sweet smell hit her, and she decided to devour a meal before warming up her tongue on Tomás, who deserved what he had coming.

He brought her a mountain of glazed pastries, butter-drenched and fragile, and hot coffee thickened with cream, and she ate lustily, as if to make up for the sort of wedding night she had endured. Tomás watched, blinking, from behind his thick gold-rimmed spectacles.

She determined not to thank him. To thank him would be to admit she owed this heretic, criminal, this false priest, something.

"What are you going to do?" he asked, choosing a moment when she was licking her fingers and wondering whether to tackle the last pastry.

"No business of yours."

"I thought I might help you get Jamie out."

"There's nothing you can do."

"I can say a mass."

She stared at him, outraged, and then laughed. "You are impossible."

"You can see Jamie."

"I don't think I want to see him. He didn't sound very happy last night reciting the vows. Maybe he didn't want to get married—again. Maybe I didn't either."

He scowled owlishly. "*Señora*, you need a plan. I will suggest one. Otherwise, you will waste words on deaf officials."

His soft insistent voice captured her, and she settled back to listen to Tomás, the false priest.

"Go see Jamie first. He will have things to say, things to ask of you. He needs your help, *señora*."

"But how . . ."

He smiled. "Pastries. I'll buy you a stack of them. The guards—they welcome the wife of a prisoner. And you'll have a sweet or two to persuade them if they need persuading." He

153

blinked, and she sensed his mind working. "You will learn what he is charged with, what he needs. Maybe how much money it will take to free him. That's first, *sí?* The information?"

"I was going to give the officials a piece of my mind."

He laughed silently, and she felt insulted. How could he laugh at her distress? "Go to him first. He might want me to do something. I will if I can, but I have no money. I earn enough for the cantina and a few candles. And once in a while a book from Ciudad Méjico. But I can talk to people, *sí?*"

Something in his quiet tone calmed her, and she found herself agreeing. She would start with Jamie.

"I spoke to Padre Pedro, *señora*. You have a friend there. Maybe he can get word where it is needed. And if you stop there, at San Miguel, light a candle." He stood, apologetically. "I have *ciboleros* coming to sell me hides, and tanners coming to buy hides for shoes and chairs and vests and *chapaderos* . . . but I'll be there if you need me."

She nodded, not wanting to like him. He negotiated for more pastries, a dozen of them, and brought them to her wrapped in a cone of St. Louis newspaper. "Let me know," he said, blinking like an owl again.

She crossed the bright plaza, stirring dust, and presented herself, *esposa* of the prisoner Jamie Dance, to the guard. She had no trouble. He peered into her cone of sweets, nodded, and took her back through a barracks room, empty now, and into a gloomy corridor. There he took a black iron key from a wall peg, and opened the creaking wooden door. Jamie stared at her from the clay floor, his face stubbled with brown hair. The guard locked her in. "Pound when you are ready, *señora*," he said.

"Jamie . . ."

He leapt up, his lanky frame uncoiling like a clockspring, and gazed into her face. She saw pain in his, the pain of an eagle trapped. She set the sweets on the clay and hugged him, feeling a fierce hunger in him, not lust but something more profound that reached into her like holy communion as

154

his hands slid down her back, caressing, finding, sending her messages of need and love.

"*Querido,*" she whispered, melting into him, "*querido.*"

They clung desperately, succoring each other, and she felt secure in his arms, the waspish anger melting away. Then he ate, appreciating the Mexican sweets, his eyes gleaming.

"They do not feed you?"

"Not that my belly knows."

"Tomás said I should come."

"Tomás. You and him got acquainted."

"He is a heretic—reading those books. No wonder he . . . made a lie of the wedding."

"I did what I had to. He thought it'd be a proper weddin' leastwise as God in heaven reckoned it. We talked about that. He blinked at me and said he could do it without botherin' his soul none. He understands love, Tomás does."

"He said he will help you, but he has no money."

"Reckon he would. People that read them books never have no money. Books don't ride along with money."

"He said I should ask you what you need."

"Money."

They had had a few pesos with them for the trip, but she had no idea what the officials had done with them—or whether they'd stolen them. "How much?"

"Much as ol' Armijo can dig outa me."

"Why, Jamie? What did you do?"

"Caught a few beaver. Without, ah, a license."

"It's nothing!"

Jamie shrugged. "Two, three pesos times one hunnert seventy-three, he says."

A lot of money. She listened solemnly.

"And then they've got the rest cooked up—comin' into Mexico the wrong way, them casks of spirits in the wagon, all that. All I wanted to do was fetch a tax man out there and pay the imposts. But that's not how they see it. Armijo says the taxes and penalties, they're about worth the goods in the wagons. He's fixin' to take the whole lot—unless you got some way to get us out."

"We've got to get help from David. From his father."

Jamie looked weary. "I don't reckon Guy Straus'll pay for any fines like mine. But maybe you can git word out. Maybe Tomás can hire someone—he's got *ciboleros* ridin' in and out."

"Maybe Coronel Cortez—"

Jamie laughed harshly. "El Zorro, he just wants a finger in the pot."

"I can talk to him, Jamie. I can try. . . ."

He eyed her dourly. "I don't want you talkin' with him. I know the type."

She sensed what he meant, and felt indignant at him for defaming a federal army officer.

The door creaked open, and the colonel himself appeared in it, smiling gently. "What type am I, Señor Dance? Have you a pastry for me?"

CHAPTER 16

A stranger rode in on a good saddler one day, a man with a flat-crowned hat, trimmed beard, and intelligent eyes. He studied the rising post, noting the Mexican federal soldiers working on the scaffolds, took in the twelve freighters nearby, and the Mexican peasants operating the adobe brickworks along the Purgatoire.

David watched him curiously, and waited. The young man seemed in no hurry, and rode around the rising tan walls and finally toward one of the teamsters, who pointed at David. The man turned the big chestnut toward David.

"You're Guy Straus's boy," he said. "Is Jamie Dance here?"

"I'm David Straus," David said, nettled at the boy part of it. "And you, sir?"

"William Bent."

So this was the man. The rival. One of the brothers who had built an adobe empire here, with connections in Santa Fe and St. Louis. This was the man who had married Owl Woman, daughter of Gray Thunder, the Cheyenne medicine man, and thus cemented trading relations with the Cheyenne nation. William Bent, whose fort stood on the mountain branch of the Santa Fe trail, a haven for travelers, a resupply source, manned by a small army of engagés, all of them fierce. William Bent, the very one that the struggling new company, Dance, Fitzhugh, and Straus, would clash with for every buffalo robe on the southern plains.

157

"Mr. Bent, you've come to see the competition."

William Bent smiled. "Yours is the first we're worrying about. Anything Guy Straus puts a hand to, a man takes notice."

That's how my father impresses men, David thought. "Jamie Dance and Mrs. Dance went to Santa Fe to settle the licenses and taxes. He left me to see to the building."

Bent surveyed David so long that David wondered about it. He had a feeling he was being read. "Build it strong. You never know about Comanches. And better bring in the stock at night."

"I'll leave that to Mr. Dance."

"Who's your Mexican partner, Mr. Straus?"

"We have none, sir."

"Odd. Federal soldiers laying up adobe."

"Colonel Agustino Cortez came by with these dragoons, looking for Texans. He took the Dances to Santa Fe, and put his men to helping out. I thought it was kind of him."

Bent laughed. "You got a partner. The Mexicans always make sure they have a Mexican in any foreign outfit operating on their soil." He dug a bootheel into the clay. "This land here—several Yanks applied for it, got turned down. I hear Manuel Armijo's interested in it . . . but the application's down in Mexico City. If he gets it, you got the governor for a partner."

"I hope not," said David. "We'd just as soon pay the imposts and operate without—"

"It never works that way, son. I can guess why you're here, though, and not on the north bank." He looked amused.

"I imagine you're right. We're going for the trade that you don't get easily."

"We don't let a Comanche into the post. Cheyenne, yes. We trade a little with the Comanches when they come in, but we don't like it none. Keeps the rest away. Well, its your scalps, son."

"We'll risk that," muttered David.

"Has Cortez helped himself to anything? They got a war going."

"A few things. Some Comancheros stole some more."

Bent laughed easily. "Welcome to Mexico," he said. "Mexican cavalry building you a post, all for free, goodwill. Comancheros taking their first tax, sort of compensation for you showin' up. I'd love to know what Armijo says to Jamie Dance."

David blinked, not wanting to say anything.

"Come on over and share a cup. That's how we do it out here, Mr. Straus. We may compete, but we enjoy each other. And call on me if you got any problems. Ceran, in Santa Fe, he can untie Mexican knots. They got him under house arrest—they think we're all Texas agents. But St. Vrain, he has his ways."

"I'm indebted, Mr. Bent."

"You want to sell your stuff and get out, you come talk to me. I'll pay a fair mountain price for it. Same way with robes. We'll buy robes at the going price, carry 'em east for you, too, if you need. I reckon if you get in too deep, we could buy you out and salvage Guy Straus's investment."

They always offer to buy out, David thought. "I guess we'll bloody our noses trying, Mr. Bent."

William Bent clapped David on the back, and mounted his saddler. "You come visit," he said, and rode north.

David turned, and found the *cabo*, Ortiz, staring.

The talk of partners disturbed David. It was hard enough establishing a robe-trading outfit, without diluting the profits. And yet . . . here were Cortez's troops, sweating away at this the rising walls of Fort Dance. David gazed at them, as if seeing them for the first time. Not free labor after all.

Things had gone well after the Comancheros fled. All the men, his and the Mexicans, settled down to work. The only worry was that Boar Blunt's party hadn't returned. David had started to fear that they'd deserted, taking company horses and saddles with them. At least Boar and the other two troublemakers. Still, Boar was a determined man, and probably was hellbent after the Comancheros. David had had to recruit new hunters, and he'd asked them to look for the missing men. Beyond that, there wasn't much he could do but wait. The days rolled by with no news.

And what was taking Jamie Dance so long? Was it so hard to get a trading license and bring a tax collector here? He pushed the worries aside. His task was to build a post, following the plans Jamie had drawn for him. The adobe walls would rise to fourteen feet, narrowing from three feet at their base to two feet at the parapets; they would form a perfect square, a hundred feet on either side, much smaller than the Bents' post, Fort William, upriver. Inside, low rooms would line the walls, their roofs forming a gallery, a walkway for riflemen if the fort were besieged. Maybe some day they'd add bastions at opposite corners, but not now. The gates would lie under a high watchtower with vertical slits for windows. There'd be two, the inner one admitting entry into the yard, the outer one permitting entry to the trading window where the tribesmen could bring their robes and collect their trade goods from the trading room.

That afternoon, about when the men were ready to quit for the day, one of the Mexican dragoons up on the half-finished north wall cried out. *"Indios!"* he yelled, pointing north. Arrayed on the north bank of the Arkansas were knots of horsemen, their almost naked bodies coppery in the low sun. The Indians stared across the water, pointing at the rising post, and then began snaking down a soft grade, intending to ford.

"Who are they?" David asked Mazappa.

"Durned if I know."

Lyle Black couldn't say either.

David turned to the *cabo,* Ortiz, who was snapping directions at his dragoons. Everywhere, the soldiers were racing for the stacked muskets, gathering up haversacks, and arraying themselves inside the fort, up on the scaffolds.

"Who are they?"

"Indios."

"Comanche?"

Ortiz shrugged, and returned to his command. The *campesinos* raced from the brickyard into the compound.

Suddenly David remembered the twelve freighters groaning with trade goods. "Mazappa, the wagons!"

"Too late," the teamster replied. "Oxen half a mile away."

But at least his remaining teamsters didn't race into the shelter of the post; they grabbed rifles and formed a thin line around the wagons. The cook joined them.

The Indians didn't hunt down a ford, but plunged into the Arkansas, swimming their wild-eyed horses across a deep but narrow channel, many of them holding bows high in the air to keep the sinew bowstrings out of the water. David watched them, ready himself to flee into the fort, where the dragoons had efficiently organized a defense. But these tribesmen weren't painted. Not even bonneted. Most wore a headband, anchoring loose straight hair. Scarcely even a feather decorated them.

"I know what they ain't," said Lyle, beside him. "They ain't Cheyenne and they ain't Comanche. Comanche are shorter and meaner lookin'. Maybe Arapaho. But I don't know. Dance, he'd know in a glance."

"Keep them from the wagons, Lyle!"

Lyle laughed shortly. "Whiles they steal the stock up the Purgatoire. I don't see no wimmin or travois, so I guess they're up to some sort o' mischief."

One of the Indians, on a spotted white horse, pushed ahead a little, his arm high, his palm forward.

"Means he wants to parley, David. That's a good sign. But the rest ain't. I count maybe hunnert fifty. You got to go out there."

"But I can't speak. I don't know the signs. And I'm . . ."

The *cabo* approached and nodded at David. Nothing in David's life had prepared him to walk out into a no man's land and parley with unknown Indians. But the corporal led him along, and David dragged behind, his heart in his

161

mouth.

They stood at last before the loose-haired man on the white horse. His agate eyes bored into the corporal, and then into David. For the second time that day, someone was reading him.

The headman said something. David couldn't reply. The headman's powerful arms and fingers flashed. David couldn't read the sign language either.

"Do . . . do you speak English?" he stammered. He got no response. "*Parlez-vous français?*" Nothing. Then the *cabo* asked, in Spanish, and the headman lifted up slightly. "*Sí,*" he said. "I am Uno. We are Utes. Maybe we will trade. We want gifts. We want spirit water first."

"But . . . we're not ready. Come in a moon. Two moons," David said in Spanish. He was no trader. Jamie was the trader.

Uno surveyed the wagons thoughtfully, and the handful of men guarding them. He studied the rising post and the muskets bristling from its walls. He peered up the Purgatoire, seeing not a single animal.

"We will trade," he said. "You will bring us gifts. We will smoke. We will make peace first."

Peace with mountain Utes—out here from their western homelands to hunt buffalo probably—would be a tricky thing, David knew. He'd heard about the Utes—about harassment, stock theft, slave trading, and treachery. And he didn't like the prospect before him at all.

Pain lanced up Boar Blunt's legs, tormenting him. The muscles in his ankle drew his foot upward grotesquely, and he could do nothing about it. He could barely move his feet with the Achilles tendon severed. Waves of pain radiated through him, drawing sweat from his brow. Beside him, Mario wept, experiencing the same torment with feet pulled in grotesque directions. In the flash of knives, their lives had been ruined—if they lived. Over against a tree,

Willis watched grayly, saying nothing.

"I'll get you, Benito. I'll get you somehow, some way," Boar growled, between waves of hurt.

"Very funny, *sí?*"

"I ain't done yet."

"Now you're not worth even a *peso*. Maybe a few *centavos*. I can't get robes for you. Maybe for him." Benito jerked a thumb at Willis. "But Comanches enjoy you anyway. They like *blancos*, especially hombres like you."

Benito squatted nearby sweating and stinking, great patches of wet in the armpits of his coarse muslin shirt. Boar clambered to his knees somehow, fully intending to strangle Benito, but a Comanchero shoved him back. Boar rolled helplessly in the dust.

Boar had always been a walker. That's what teamsters did—walk beside the teams, applying the whip. He stared at his hamstrung feet and knew only murder. He'd die, but he'd take Benito with him. His thick fingers itched for a throat. He got up on his knees again, lanced by the pain in his legs, and awkwardly made for Benito. This time, when one of the Comancheros jumped at him, he was ready. He pulled the man down and clamped his thick arm around the man's neck and squeezed. The Comanchero writhed, and Boar squeezed harder, feeling things crack in the man's neck. Then something hard slammed his head, and he saw white and let go, fading fast.

He shook his head, clearing the dizziness, feeling a new wave of pain. His ears squealed. He saw double. Beside him, Benito chuckled and sweat and stank. Comancheros bound Boar's hands behind his back with a thong that bit deeply into his flesh. Mario Petti stared vacantly, muttering prayers to the Virgin.

Boar lay quietly for the next hours, grateful for the shade of the cottonwoods. But he knew he would die. He knew there were good ways to die . . . and bad. He desperately wanted to die fast. He lay there, wanting to die fast, wondering how.

"Benito—finish me. Finish me!" he demanded.

Benito smiled, baring his gapped teeth, and licked his lips. "Then you be worth nothing. I still get something. Maybe even a robe, big *cochinillo* like you."

"Eggy! Do it!" he rasped.

Eggy Willis stared and did nothing. Then, slowly, Eggy lifted his hands, bound tightly together. Eggy's eyes said no.

Benito belched and stank.

The Comanche arrived a while later, materializing on the rim of the grassy horizon and then flowing down the slope and into the basin like a cataract. They rode barebacked on small ponies of all hues, and steered them so easily with no visible motion it seemed they'd been born on horses. They wore nothing in their hair, not even coup feathers. Most of these short, wiry riders had quivers slung over their coppery backs, and carried bows. A few pinned their loose hair with a headband, but apart from small breechclouts and simple moccasins, they were naked. He guessed there were seventy or eighty—a lot, anyway. And without their squaws or travois. A war party, then, or maybe buffalo hunters. They slid off their disciplined ponies and studied the Comancheros. At every hand, Comanche boys held horses or watered pairs of them at the tepid pond below the spring while the older warriors stretched, urinated, and gossiped. A vedette remained up on the brow of the basin.

Boar watched them with dread. Mario Petti began praying, a bee-drone of Hail Marys interspersed with sobs. Eggy stared, ashen. These were the most accomplished torturers on the plains, diabolical in their inventiveness. Boar had heard all the stories. About men with eyelids sewn open, buried in sand up to their necks, staring at the sun; about men smeared with sweets and then staked spreadeagled over a fire-ant hill in the blistering sun and left there for eternity while the biting ants discovered their nostrils, eyes, mouths, and private parts. Boar trembled, and watched the muscular Comanches gather in the shade and gaze at him and Petti and Willis with flat agate eyes.

164

But nothing happened to him—not yet, anyway. The Comanches were pulling their own prisoners off ponies—several Indian boys and one girl, all of them looking gaunt and frightened. The boys were not yet in their teens; the girl looked to be nine or ten, and peered about her with hard, frightened eyes.

Benito clambered to his feet, muttering happily. The Comancheros welcomed the Comanches with *abrazos* and a lot of shouting, and then began looking over the prisoners, poking and pinching and making the children walk.

They jabbered in Spanish, the lingua franca of the southern plains and Mexican possessions, and Boar could grasp little of it. They seemed to be haggling. Benito snapped a command, and the Comancheros pulled trade items from the panniers resting on the ground. The notorious Comanches didn't look so deadly in the flesh, but even so, Boar's stomach flopped with dread. He sweat on the hard clay, itching to kill just one, just one. . . .

They haggled for an endless time, and finally the Comanches collected bolts of gingham—stolen from the Rocky Mountain wagons—numerous knives, some awls, some ready-made iron arrow points, and the stolen Leman trade rifles, fifty-two-caliber percussion locks, along with powder in waxed paper bricks, caps, lead, and a bullet mold.

Benito clacked happily, and burped. He steered the Indian prisoners toward the spring, where they fell to their knees and drank, a few feet from Boar.

"They are worth a lot. The *hacendados* buy them to work the fields, *sí?* The *muchacha*, she's a Pawnee. She will be a good domestic slave for some *hacendada*. The *muchachos*, they are Arapaho. Miserable tribe, *sí?* But these will sell for five silver *pesos*. We sell all we can get. There is never enough labor."

The Comanches had brought soft-tanned buffalo robes as well, and around the array of trade goods the individual warriors haggled with Comancheros, then hauled off twists of dark tobacco, hanks of trade beads, hawk bells, vermilion wrapped in waxed paper, yards of calico, needles and thread, and roughly smithed iron knives with bare metal hafts but no handles—most of the goods stolen from the Rocky Mountain Company. A few of the warriors traded for coffee beans that the Comancheros sold by the pint. But iron lance points and hatchet heads, smithed in Santa Fe, were the top items.

The whole basin had come alive. Ponies and mules squealed and brayed. The Comanches finished their trading, and filled pipes. Boys curried ponies. Evening settled, and Boar wondered if he might yet live. Huge chunks of bloody buffalo meat appeared from somewhere, enough to feed the whole mob. Lithe warriors collected dead cottonwood and built cookfires, and soon the smell of sizzling meat overpowered the odors of sweat, horse offal, and the smell of fear oozing from Boar's body.

Now and then a Comanche would peer at Boar and Mario, or gaze at Willis over at the tree, and walk away, and every time one approached, Boar's heart raced and his tormented muscles hurt all the more. The Indians and Comancheros ate haphazardly, spearing meat with their knives as blackness settled deathlike over the basin.

At last a quiet settled, except for a rhythmic whisper of gourd rattles shaken by a shaman. Some Comanches started to build a new fire, gathering tinder at a place beneath a sturdy cottonwood tree with spreading limbs, and igniting it there. They stood around silently, eagerly, watching the small fire catch and grow hot, a yellow eye in its glowing orange socket of ashes. The night thickened. The silence was filled with something, some eagerness, some lust almost unfathomable, except that the Comanches radiated its intensity.

Benito paused beside Boar. "I tell them you are *tejanos,*" he said simply. "I got good buffalo robes for you."

Texans! For generations, Comanches and Texans had warred with no quarter. Boar sweat.

They came for him, half a dozen of the wiry Comanches.

Boar went wild, writhing, kneeing, smashing them, knocking them back like tenpins, hoping they'd knife him to death, squirming, brawling, fighting—not for life but for death. But they overpowered him, pinned him to earth until the only thing that moved was his pounding heart. They spun a thong around his ankles, yanking it deep into his wounds until he swore the cord cut against bone. They tied stout braided rope to his legs, and carried him to the fire. He screamed.

They threw the cord over the thick cottonwood limb, and then half a dozen hoisted Boar up, up, until he hung by his feet, his whole body stretching, his muscles aching instantly as he swung—a pendulum—back and forth, rocking, twisting, closer and closer to the hot little fire caressing his dangling hair. He screamed, he yelled at the heavens and earth, he yelled at the trees and the devil and God, and he yelled as the flames burnt his hair and blistered his skull, yelled and yelled and yelled.

CHAPTER 17

Before the immaculate colonel in his navy blue tunic, Jamie Dance felt filthy and unshaven. He lifted himself from the odorous clay, intending to stand anyway. It never did a lick of good to have a man like Cortez look down at you. Teresa María stood too, brushing the foul litter of the *cárcel* from her begrimed skirts.

Ah, Señor Dance. I'd like a sweet," the colonel said, eyeing the paper cone. Dance lifted it, and the colonel plucked a moist pastry.

"Muy bueno," he said, chewing. "I have sweets for you."

"I reckon not. I'll just stay hyar until things are fixed up proper."

"Such a burro. I come with a carrot, not a stick. I have interceded with His Excellency for you. Call me San Agustino."

Jamie thought it'd be wisest not to say a thing, so he just lounged there, his lanky frame half-capsized. In a moment or two he'd go lean against the cool wall. He never was one to stand.

"A little difficulty, Señor Dance. Nothing serious. It is required that foreigners doing business in Mexico have a Mexican partner. A simple matter. His Excellency thought perhaps if you had a partner, everything would proceed swiftly and sweetly."

"Himself, I reckon."

"Ah, how you gringos think of us! No, that would be . . . not quite proper, eh? A little too friendly? No. I volunteered to be your partner. A simple transaction, and a few sweets for me when I stop by. It is nothing. *Nada.*"

Jamie didn't like the sound of it, and wondered about the rest. "How big a piece? What percent?"

El Zorro shrugged. "At your discretion, *señor*. A little piece. Enough to satisfy Santa Anna in Ciudad Méjico. I would do it as a favor."

"I can't go taking up partners. Guy Straus, he could maybe do it, but you'd have to git aholt of him back there."

"Ah, but Señor Dance. It is not an official partner that is required. No papers. No percentages. No fodder for vampire lawyers. Just a little whispered agreement, a handshake as you *yanquis* call it. An agreement of the handshake."

Jamie considered. "What's in it for the Rocky Mountain Company?"

"Ah, Señor Dance. A protector. A *coronel* of the federal army keeping the tax collectors away."

"What's Armijo get out of it? He told me that's his land we want to put the post on."

El Zorro shrugged. "Not exactly. He is a silent partner of the Miranda-Beaubein combine, which applied for that grant. Turned down, of course. So, he is simply the silent partner of whoever does get the grant when the federal government decides."

"My silent partner, is that it? Oh, Armijo wants a piece."

"Oh, I wouldn't say that. A few sweets now and then. For now, Señor Dance, he would settle for one percent ad valorem, one hundredth of the value of the trade goods, plus of course a small fee for each wagon and each ox or mule. After that . . ." El Zorro shrugged again.

"What about these old charges, what he tossed me into this here hole for?"

"*Nada.* His Excellency doesn't really care. I made him not care by telling him how much the province would profit from your company—competition against the Bents. But it must be a *mejicana* company. A little brown Mexican color in it, a mestizo company. He insists on that."

169

"He was fixin' to get me into trouble with . . . my private life."

"Ah! The marriage. But that is resolved, *sí?*"

"How do you figure that?"

"Trust El Zorro to know everything. To know of the nighttime visit of Padre Pedro to that alley out there."

"*Caramba!* Is nothing sacred?" snapped Teresa María. "How many informants do you pay? Do you pay Padre Pedro?"

El Zorro straightened. "I am your protector. With me, you can do everything you wish. Without me, nothing. *El gobernador* would send your husband off to Ciudad Mexico, and pack you off to Taos. But I, I see opportunities for Mexico."

"You see opportunities for ol' Cortez," Jamie retorted.

El Zorro shrugged. "I'm glad we have come to an understanding," he said.

"How long do I wait for the trading license?"

"It depends. Who favors it, who doesn't. How many little gifts. The officials have a sweet tooth."

"Any objections if we start tradin' right away?"

"It would be illegal. But we have understandings, *sí?* Trust me to smooth the path."

"My company, we reckoned if we couldn't trade hyar at a profit, we'd build across the Arkansas. Go against the Bents on the north side. Not trade in Mexico at all. We reckoned that maybe the Comanch might cross the river and bring robes to us. We reckoned that'd be a tougher row to hoe, but better'n being bled to death."

"Ah, Dance, how you sadden me. No one in Méjico wants to bleed you to death. We welcome you."

"Yeah, I know about bear hugs."

Out on the plaza, someone was shouting. Jamie heard the faint snort of horses. Beyond the door, which stood ajar, the guards stirred.

El Zorro sighed. "There are obstacles. This door to this *cárcel* is one. How will you ever go through it with so many laws broken, so many fines and taxes that must be paid?

170

And . . . it will not be possible for your company to go to the north bank after so many federal dragoons have donated their sweat to your fort."

Licked. Jamie knew it. They'd let him rot here, or down in Mexico City. And they'd make sure the wagons never crossed the Arkansas river. All right then, he thought. Live with 'em. "Reckon you got me."

El Zorro smiled graciously. *"Bienvenido a Méjico"* he said.

A guard appeared at the door. *"Por favor, Coronel . . ."*

"A little moment," said El Zorro, slipping into the dark passage beyond. He returned, looking excited.

"Tejanos. We've captured three. A Howland, a Baker, and a Rosenberg. Near Anton Chico. They are being brought in, of course. Spies and agents. I must return to my dragoons—"

"Reckon you ought to get this settled first."

El Zorro laughed. "Why? You are here in the *cárcel*, and the door is very thick. It can wait."

"What's ol' Armijo doin'?"

"You are disrespectful, you *yanquis.* Organizing the militia, of course. He will have an army of a thousand by tomorrow." He turned to leave. "Are you coming, *señora?*"

"Go with him," said Jamie. He wanted someone outside looking after him; he'd likely starve to death in the middle of all the uproar. She rose, hesitantly.

El Zorro waited impatiently, his mind already hundreds of miles away, loosing his well-trained dragoons upon the Texas rabble.

"Reckon you're going to pick up them dragoons and leave my post be," said Jamie sharply. "David Straus, he'll pick up and move north right smartly."

El Zorro's motion was arrested.

"We'll see," he said, ushering Teresa María out. Jamie watched the door slam, heard the heavy bolt drop. Alone again. He felt the cold walls close in. He swore they crept toward him, pressing, choking, until he could hardly breathe.

Faintly now, the sound fragile through the window on the

171

alley, he heard the clamor in the plaza and the toll of a church bell somewhere. The governor would commandeer the services of every able-bodied male in Santa Fe, along with countless burros and mules and provisions. What they lacked was arms. He doubted that there'd be two hundred rifles or muskets in the whole town. But they'd go, Armijo's ragtag militia, and confront the damned Texans, whoever they were. He raged at the Texas filibusters, at their Anglo conceits, at their giant Texas egos, which were all ruining his life as a fur merchant. He halfway hoped Cortez's dragoons and Armijo's militia would whip them good.

The day slid by, and no one fed him. By nightfall he was parched. No one had brought him water. He hammered steadily on the door, but no one heard. He waited for Teresa to appear at the window; maybe she could toss him something. But she didn't come. He yearned for Tomás to show up, but he knew Tomás had been conscripted along with the rest. He lay in the blackness, suffering, while outside the clamor never ceased and the smell of piñon campfires, tortillas, and roasting meat drifted into his black cell. The night turned miserable, and he huddled in the grime, trying not to think of water.

He reckoned it was not far before dawn when he heard a commotion outside the door, and then it swung open and he blinked into a blinding lantern.

"Señor Dance." The man speaking to him was one of the six federal dragoons who'd accompanied El Zorro and the Dances to Santa Fe. "Come. The *coronel* awaits you."

"I want water."

"There's a pail in the guard barracks. Come."

Jamie clambered to his feet and followed, the rush of freedom pulsing through his body.

The guard room was hollow and gloomy. "Where's Armijo?" he asked the dragoon.

"Entertaining the *tejanos*. Then they'll be put in your *cárcel*."

Jamie stopped at the bucket and ate water, clamped his teeth down on it as it slid into his throat. Ate water until he

172

burst, while the dragoon waited impatiently.

He found the plaza lit by bonfires. Around them militia-men huddled in the chill, and burros and mules were every-where. Before him, El Zorro sat his fine chestnut, looking military. His dragoons sat their mounts beside the colonel. Teresa María sat on a mangy horse, her skirts hiked, and her ankles glowing honey in the firelight. Beside her stood his saddled chestnut with all his possibles and weapons upon it.

"There's no time, Señor Dance. We must ride," said El Zorro.

Uno slid off his white horse, and gestured to another Ute, who rode forward. This one looked older, his straight black hair shot with gray. Except for a pendant medicine bundle he was as bare as the rest, but David sensed he was someone special among them. He carried a long pouch of velvet-soft leather.

"He is Orem, a *po'rat*, Uno said. "He has *powa'a*."

David and the *cabo* stared blankly.

"Medicine man. We will smoke the peace pipe."

The two Utes waited for something, and suddenly David remembered. He was the host. He turned toward Lyle, who stood back near the wagons. "Tobacco. We're going to smoke. And some extra twists, please."

Lyle Black nodded and clambered into one wagon and then another, not sure which contained the trade tobacco. The two headmen watched quietly.

Then at last Black brought the twists, three in all. The medicine man untied the thongs of the soft sack, and with-drew a pipe, and the four of them sat in the grass. The shaman tamped the pungent tobacco into the red pipestone bowl.

"Lyle, have Emilio bring us some live embers, please," David ordered.

Black retreated toward the cookfires, while the peace party waited. The teamster returned with a small kettle full

173

of gray ash with live coals glowing orangely. The shaman plucked up one with his fingers, amazing David, and soon had the pipe lit. They went through a ceremony that David had heard of many times at the Planters House, but had never seen. He knew what to do. The headman, Uno, saluted the cardinal directions, sky and earth and all the spirits therein, smoked, and passed the pipe to David. David did the same, hoping he wasn't committing some sort of offense against God.

In time, the charge of tobacco burned down, and the shaman knocked the dottle to the earth.

"We are Uncompahgre. We have come to hunt the sacred buffalo. Our village is a half-day away. We killed many buffalo, and our women make many good robes," Uno said in Spanish.

David had heard of the Uncompahgre. They were one of the eastern Ute bands, nesting in the valleys of the Rockies, but very like the plains Indians. They depended on buffalo, like plains tribes. There were other Ute bands not far from the plains; the Yanpa and Muaches. Jamie had told him once that they were not to be trusted; their hearts were often bad. They warred against the Mexicans, yet traded with them—especially slaves.

"Our trader is in Santa Fe. He will be back soon to trade."

"Many suns?"

"I don't know."

"You will not trade now?"

David had never in his life traded for a robe. A dread of it gripped him; he might blunder, give much too much. He didn't know a good robe from a bad one—except for a split, a robe made of two halves sewn together. That was worth less. Jamie had intended to train him, but that was no help now.

"We must wait for the trader, Señor Dance."

Uno sat quietly, staring so intently at David that it unnerved him. "What is this company? We do not know about you. Is this the Bent, St. Vrain Company too?"

"No. This is the Rocky Mountain Company. There are three partners. My father, Guy Straus; Señor Fitzhugh; and Señor Dance."

"You will give us more for robes than Bent? Than his trader there, Mr. Goddam Murray?"

David warmed to this. "We'll give you a better price for the robes, and we'll sell you our things for less." But as he said it, he realized he hadn't the foggiest idea what the Bent traders offered, or what their prices were for the items on their shelves. David knew he was indulging in bravado, yet it didn't hurt, he supposed.

"You will trade then. We will bring the women and the robes." Imperiously, Uno summoned one of his warriors, and with a few sibilant words sent the man off somewhere.

Suddenly David knew he was about to trade, seasoned or not. But he wanted to delay. "Señor Dance will be back soon," he said.

Uno spoke sharply. "We don't want to wait for Kiowa or Comanche to come. We don't fear them, but we don't want to wait. You told us you would trade better than Bent."

It worried David plenty. He turned to the *cabo*. "We don't have a Mexican trading license."

Ortiz smiled. "It is a risk," he said. "Perhaps the colonel will take you away to Ciudad Méjico."

That unnerved David all the more.

Uno interrupted. "We will see what you have."

"I want to see your robes first. And you will tell me what the Bents offer."

He felt utterly vulnerable. Whatever Uno said were Bents' prices, he would have to believe, and top. He didn't want this baptism into trading—not yet. Neither did he want a hundred fifty sullen Uncompahgres hanging around a half-built fort, probing into the vulnerable Conestogas, deciding to run off his oxen and mules and horses.

Uno smiled. "You don't know."

David decided that candor would be respected. He'd heard that absolute truthfulness was honored among the western tribes. "I have never traded. I do not know the

175

prices. I don't know how to grade the robes. But I will trust you, Uno, with all that. You are a great chief. Bring the robes. You will look at each one and tell me: It is a good robe; it is a bad robe. And what the Bents would give for it. And I will have my men bring here the things we have to trade, and again I will trust you: you will tell me what the Bents want for each thing, and I will do better. We have smoked the pipe. If you are a friend, then we will trade as friends, and you will want to come here again whenever you have robes and need good things."

Uno stared at him again, making some sort of assessment that unnerved David. *"Bueno."*

David felt vulnerable and alone. He wondered if he might set a bad precedent, might be so generous that Jamie would be horrified and be forced to drive harder bargains, maybe angering the tribesmen. Still . . . the Rocky Mountain Company had come to trade for robes. Here were robes. What's more, David knew the St. Louis price of every item, he knew good robes would bring four dollars in the east, and he knew mountain prices ran eight or nine times St. Louis prices. He only hoped he could do this figure fast enough . . . and that Uno would be as good as his word.

He turned to the *cabo.* "We are with friends. Perhaps you could direct your dragoons to return to work."

Ortiz hesitated, and nodded. He walked back to the walls of the post, and David saw men withdraw those angry barrels and begin to stir. Good. Some sort of tension seemed to seep away from the Ute warriors, too. Uno observed all this sharply, and with obvious satisfaction. There'd be no killing today.

David walked toward the wagons, where his teamsters waited, and instructed them to bring a few samples out to the grassy area where Uno sat. Except for the cask of spirits. There would be some trading.

"You ain't waiting for Jamie?" asked Mazappa.

David shrugged ruefully. "The Utes aren't waiting for Jamie. I'm about to trade. If any of you know anything about it, come help me—after you dig out some stuff."

But none of the teamsters volunteered.

"Can any of you grade robes?"

"I reckon I can," said Black. But the others shook their heads. Black had been out the Santa Fe trail a dozen times. Most of the rest had been out several times. The Bents and other established Santa Fe traders had commandeered the best of the westering men.

David smiled. "Join me, then."

He turned back toward Uno and the shaman, aware that he'd been making decisions again, and that he alone would be responsible for the results, good or bad. Always before, he'd been the dutiful son, learning, leaving decisions to his father or to experienced men like Jamie Dance. But necessity had thrust decisions on him. He felt his eighteen years, and wondered what sort of trouble he was making for himself. Yet at the bottom of his soul, he felt a surge of something—pride, surely, but something more. A manhood he'd only just begun to fathom. He found himself bursting with the hope that he could present Jamie Dance with twenty, fifty, a hundred good robes—the beginnings of profit!

Bit by bit, his teamsters lugged out an array of goods: awls, hatchet heads, hanks of beads, a few Witney blankets, three point, four point; hawk bells, vermilion in waxed packets, coffee beans, sugar, gunpowder and a cup to measure it; one-pound bars of lead, bullet molds. Bolts of calico and gingham in bright colors. An array of Wilson knives, all with wooden handles. Cast-iron and brass kettles.

Uno watched patiently, saying nothing. David worried about the increasing wealth arrayed before Ute eyes. They could snatch everything here, well away from the wagons and adobe walls, and be off with it before anyone could respond. Indeed, Uncompahgre warriors dismounted and crowded close, perusing the array. David knew this was a foolish act of trust on his part; at the posts, one warrior at a time was admitted to the trading window for security reasons. And yet, nothing had happened—so far.

The *cabo* returned to watch.

177

"Where are the spirits?" asked Uno.

"We can't trade for the spirits," David said. Without a license, it'd be one more mark against him. And in any case, he didn't want his wagons plundered by redmen full of whiskey.

Uno stared again, but dropped the matter.

"We are ready now," said David.

Uno nodded toward a warrior who carried a thick robe. The man laid it before David, who examined it carefully, feeling more helpless than he'd ever felt in his life.

"Is it a good robe, Uno?"

"It is the best of robes."

"What does he want for it?"

"The red cloth." Uno pointed at a bolt of flannel.

"How much do the Bents give?"

"The armlength."

David knew that much. A mountain yard was the length of cloth from the fingers of an outstretched arm to the chin. He picked up the bolt and stretched out the proper length, then added a foot or so more.

"Will this make my word true?" he asked.

Uno nodded. "It is so."

David cut it carefully and handed it to the warrior, who at least didn't look unhappy. Then he gave the robe to Lyle.

Fort Dance had acquired its first buffalo robe.

CHAPTER 18

Several things amazed Jamie Dance at once. The adobe walls were almost done on two sides, and halfway done on the north and west. Even as he rode in, dust-caked and weary, he saw the dragoons up on scaffolds, patiently cementing sun-dried bricks into place.

"Ah!" exclaimed Colonel Cortez. "See what they have done!"

But as they rode closer on their jaded horses, another sight caught their attention. Lounging about the plain were scores of Indians, all warriors, most of them on foot, wandering freely all over the dusty flat. Jamie didn't know who they were, but they seemed not to be at war.

They rode in cautiously, though, the colonel and his six dragoons, as well as Jamie and Teresa María, expecting trouble. The hordes of people—Indians, *campesinos* at the brickyards along the Purgatoire, dragoons, and teamsters—paused, watching them come. Jamie spotted no signs of trouble, but something tightened in him. Teresa looked weary and scared, as well she might after days in a crudely made saddle. He helped her off, while the other dusty travelers slid down from their mounts and stared.

The other thing that worried and astonished Jamie was the knot of activity over yonder, where David was standing—and doing a lively robe trade. Could it be? Could that young chip off ol' Guy's block be trading? Behind David lay a mountain of brown robes. And sprawled across the dusty earth lay a small collection of trade items. Trading! But who with?

179

He studied these warriors, and found clues in the angular moccasins. Utes. As tricky and touchy a tribe as lived in the far west. The wagons so vulnerable. The robes in a heap. The trade goods lying there, easy to snatch . . . it worried him. And yet . . . That was wealth heaped there. Looked to be eighty, a hundred robes. But how was David doing? Was he giving the place away? Were the Utes cheating him?

"Making trade," said El Zorro, beside him as they walked to the knotted crowd.

Sure as daylight, David was trading, with Lyle helping him; and there was a pack of Utes, a headman, and a shaman sitting there. And that *cabo*, Ortiz, was studying it all from nearby.

The colonel saw Ortiz too, and summoned him with a sharp command. "The *tejanos*. We will leave in an hour. Tell the men. Tell the camp followers. We are riding for Anton Chico."

Ortiz nodded, and trotted toward the dragoons. In moments, they would start to pack up, fetch their mounts and pack mules, load the panniers, and be off. And all those camp followers would load up their burros and depart.

"*Coronel!* Whoa up! We got maybe a hundred Utes here. A lot, anyway."

"*Tejanos*, Señor Dance. We can't stay. President Santa Anna has ordered me to repel the *tejanos* at all costs. Which reminds me: the federal impost, for now, will be satisfied with all the trade rifles you have, plus your powder and ball."

"All?"

"The *tejanos* are well armed, Señor Dance. I will have the *cabo* send men to collect them. And I will watch."

"You figurin' on leavin' us some to defend ourselves with? Hunt buffler?"

"It is a pity. You can buy more at Bent's Fort."

At the adobe walls, troopers slid down from the scaffold, pulled on blue shirts. Several ran toward the cavalry horses up the Purgatoire. Others began to break camp. The *campe-*

sinos, too, suddenly began scurrying about, gathering their braying burros.

"We got a dozen men, no way to fort up, wagons out hyar, and a mess o' Utes!"

El Zorro oozed scorn. "They are peaceful enough."

At the trading ground, David stared, and so did those Ute headmen and the rest. Jamie hurried over there, eyed the whole operation sharply.

"What the hell are you doin'?"

David looked stricken. "They wanted—they demanded we trade," he said in English. "I have eighty-seven robes."

That was a lot, but it didn't mollify Jamie a bit. The whole lot could be stolen in a trice. "We'll talk about that later. Cortez, he's leavin' with the whole troop. They got word o' Texans marching; caught a handful. We'll be naked as jaybirds hyar in about an hour."

"But, Jamie, we smoked the pipe. The headman here . . ." He switched to Spanish. "Señor Dance, this is Uno, of the Uncompahgre Utes. They've come to trade. They've sent for the rest of their village; lots more robes when the village gets here."

Uno. Jamie had never met the man, and ransacked his memory about him, coming up with little. But the Utes could make plenty of trouble if they felt like it—and Uno's outfit was a fighting outfit with a young chief.

"Chief Uno," Jamie said in Spanish, "welcome. I'm the trader, Señor Dance. I see you are making good bargains."

The man rose, tall and lithe and the color of clover honey, and assessed Jamie with a sharp unblinking stare. He nodded finally, and so did that shaman behind him. "Why do the soldiers hurry?" he asked, getting right to the point.

"They're off to fight. Mexico's in a war."

Uno peered at the dragoons as they gathered their cavalry mounts and saddled them. "All going away," he said. "This young trader has made us welcome."

A squad of men, led by Ortiz, approached the wagons and began digging into them. Teamsters looked questioningly at Jamie.

"What are they doing?" demanded David.

"They're taxin' us. Cortez is takin' the trade rifles and powder and ball for the imposts. The federal imposts, anyway."

"But . . . but the Comancheros took rifles. A few of them."

"What?"

David looked frightened. "The Comancheros came after you left."

Things were going much too fast for Jamie. He needed a powwow with the boy. But there was Uno—and a passel of Utes waving robes at David.

"Chief Uno," he heard himself saying, "we're going to shut the trading window and have a feast. We'll trade some more tomorrow. A thousand pardons. *Por favor*, tell your people we will begin again at dawn, good bargains for the robes."

"The village will be here tonight," Uno replied. "Many robes. We are in a hurry. We are close to the Comanche here."

Jamie nodded. "We'll trade. And I will have a gift for you, and your headmen, *sí?*"

Uno said nothing.

Jamie turned to Lyle. "Black. Get these hyar goods picked up and back in the wagons. And git some men to haul these robes to the wagons—no, into the post. And git some oxen yoked up to pull the wagons into the post."

Lyle Black turned on his heel. Uno spoke something in his Ute tongue to the warriors waiting to trade. Jamie waited impatiently until he saw that his commands were being carried out. The whole place throbbed with activity.

"All right, David. Me and you got some palaverin' to do," Jamie said, dragging the boy toward the adobe walls, apart from other ears.

David looked as frightened as any eighteen-year-old would as he stammered out the story. "An express came from my father," he began. "He said Mexico was at war,

182

and to pull out. Go to the north bank. By then, the walls were well along, and . . . and . . . everyone had done a lot. I told them. I told our men. I told the *cabo*. And it was like . . . everyone quit. They were all disgusted. All that work for nothing. And then the *cabo*, he ordered the federal dragoons to . . . keep us from going."

That figures, Jamie thought. Welcome to Mexico. "Anyone hurt?"

"No—not then. But the men wouldn't go back to work. I . . . I'd wrecked it. They got out a cask. Boar did."

A drunk. That figured too. "Then what?"

"The Comancheros came. More than a dozen of them. The meanest-looking men I've ever seen. Armed with new rifles, and knives. They had lots of mules and burros and horses. Big sombreros. And I couldn't make any of the teamsters guard the wagons. They all got drunk. No one cared. It was because I'd told them we would leave here . . . you know. I shouldn't have told them. I shouldn't have . . . I should have waited. I wanted to do what my father asked. I shouldn't have . . . I tried." Suddenly David was weeping. Jamie looked sharply at the boy. "They forced me to. The leader, Benito. He made me swallow the stuff. They all laughed. I got sick. So sick. That night the Comancheros tried to steal from the wagons, but Abel, he . . . he . . . They killed him when he caught them."

"Abel Cannon? The boy?"

David wept. A meanness settled in Jamie. He didn't press for more, not until David was ready.

"They took all they could carry. Lots. I tried to stop . . . but everyone was still . . . drunk. Every Mexican dragoon. The *cabo*. Lyle Black. Mazappa. No one watched. . . . I tried, God, I tried. . . ."

"I know you did, David."

"Then . . . then Boar wanted to go after the Comancheros. This was after they'd all sobered up. The next morning. He said he could lick the whole lot. He took Petti and Dusseldorf. And they needed a tracker and talked Eggy Willis into going. They . . . didn't come back."

"How long ago?" Jamie asked, his voice tight.

"Two weeks. They might just be tracking still, don't you think?"

"No." They were dead or captives. Jamie felt a chill run through him. "Who's left, David?"

"Emilio Rodriguez. Lyle Black, Pony Gantt, Wilbert Ames, Blake Goodin, Labor Jonas. Mazappa Oliphant, Philpot Launes . . . and Price Agee."

"Nine, including the cook. You'n me and Teresa. And a whole village o' them Uncompahgres comin' in."

"They're peaceful!"

Jamie grunted. "Peaceful under the eyes of a comp'ny o' dragoons."

"But Uno—he's an honorable man. I had him tell me, on his honor, what the Bents paid for robes and what the Bents charged—you know—for a pound of coffee beans. And he did. And I did a little better."

"That how you figgered it?"

"Yes. But I know what a robe goes for, Jamie. I'd been told by Papa."

"He graded the robes, too, I reckon."

"They were good robes!"

"Not as soft as Comanche. Those devils make the best around hyar. Crows do up north." The boy looked so unhappy that Jamie slapped him on the back. "I reckon they was about to trade, whether you felt like it or not, eh?"

"I told them to wait for you."

"And this ol' Uno, he wasn't one for waitin'—not with all that plunder just settin' thar, and his warriors gettin' the itch, and horses and mules to steal and all. I guess I got the idear, David. You done what you could. You made us a profit. We took in our first robes. I'da done the same. You're gettin' to be some man. We got us into a tight corner, but maybe if this hyar Uno's fixing to trade hyar some more, and beat the Bents, why . . . we'll squeeze through."

David looked relieved. But Jamie had his private doubts. They could all donate their topknots to that Ute outfit after El Zorro pulled out.

The dragoons formed a line, standing beside their mounts and pack mules. The Ute warriors watched silently, missing nothing. Over at the wagons, the colonel and a squad of the dragoons plucked casks of powder and pigs of lead and wooden crates of Leman rifles from the wagons, and loaded up packmules.

Jamie didn't wait. He found Mazappa. "I reckon you'd better keep your rifles to hand. Is there water inside them walls?"

Oliphant shook his head.

"Git some in. Who's guardin' the stock?"

"Goodin and Jonas."

Jamie sighed. "Best you fetch them in. With some oxen."

"You figuring on trouble with them Utes?"

"I'm just takin' a few precautions. Them dragoons pull out, and we'll see. Mazappa, send Jonas off to the Bents for help. Make sure he gits away secret. I reckon they'll send a posse or two."

"Maybe Jonas is the lucky one," Mazappa said tartly.

Jamie watched Oliphant trot south, pausing to tell the other teamsters to keep their weapons at hand. He headed toward the colonel, with another idea in mind.

"*Coronel*, I've got to talk. I want them civilians of yours to stick around. I'll pay—I'll give up some goods."

El Zorro peered at his camp followers, who had loaded up their burros and stood waiting beside the dragoons. "Ah, Dance. It is not possible. We need them to war on the *tejanos*. Who would cook and wash and tend the injured?"

"I'll hire the lot, *Coronel*."

"There are lots—lots." The colonel waved an arm expansively. "You can find all the *campesinos* you need, and for a few *centavos* a day. And, Dance, the Comancheros took three of the rifles, so you have not met your federal impost. We will take two bolts of blue wool for uniforms. And some kettles."

Indeed, Jamie noticed, they had already yanked the booty from the wagons and were loading it into panniers.

"How many?"

185

El Zorro shrugged. "We will tell you later when the papers are written."

With that, Cortez wheeled toward his saddled mount, a flashy chestnut, and climbed on. Then the column of dragoons trotted smartly south, two by two, its hardware clanging from the backs of mules and horses. The camp followers wheeled in behind, a bedraggled white-clad army towing little burros.

Silence settled. Uncompahgre warriors stared at the vanishing column and then at the handful of men remaining, and at Teresa María, who stared back, her chin lifted a little higher than usual. Jamie took stock. He had four men out at the herd, trying to corral some oxen. Goodin, Jonas, Oliphant, and Black. That left Gantt, Launes, Ames, and Agee plus Emilio the cook, David and himself. And Teresa María.

He grunted, knowing exactly what thoughts percolated in the heads of those Uncompahgres.

"Well, I reckon we'll get back to tradin', David. You done so good, I think I'll just have you keep right a-goin'."

He sought out Uno, who stood contemplatively. "Chief Uno," he said in Spanish. "We have time to trade some more before the sun goes down. We'll get the trade stuff out again. And I'll start the cook to making a big feast of buffalo. Your village is coming in soon. Good. We'll have a feast if we have buffalo enough. And I'm thinking of a big friendship speech, too, and some tobacco for the headmen."

"Your men walk around with rifles in their hands."

"We are pulling inside the walls. That's all."

"You have other men."

"Some out with the oxen. Some left to chase down some Comancheros who took things."

Uncompahgre warriors drifted in clusters toward the wagons, while the remaining teamsters eyed them. But none of the warriors clambered into a wagon, and Jamie took it for a good sign.

"Who is the woman?"

"My wife, Teresa María. She is the daughter of the al-

calde of Taos. An important woman to the Mexicans."
Some folderol, he thought, but he was letting Uno know a
thing or two that might help Teresa María if it came to
that.

"She is comely. She is worthy of a chief."

"She's worth better than ten chiefs and she's mine."

The warriors grew bolder. One clambered up on a wagon
tongue and peered into the belly of the third Conestoga,
ignoring the muzzle of Gantt's rifle, which poked casually
in the warrior's direction.

"Chief Uno. I think it is time to call in your warriors,
before there's trouble. You smoked the pipe, David tells
me."

Uno smiled. "We are all friends." He did nothing to deter
the warrior, who had vanished into the bowels of the
wagon, making it creak and groan. Encouraged, other warriors drifted toward other wagons.

"Well, we'll be friends then," Jamie said, feeling like a
man sitting on a powderkeg. "I just don't want that one that
crawled into the wagon to take a bullet—which he'll do if he
thinks something in there is his."

From the south the sound of bawling oxen arose, and Jamie spotted one-armed Blake Goodin whipping four of
them before him with remarkable skill, with Black and Oliphant helping.

Uno explained. "That one is not happy with the trade for
his robe and wants something more."

David looked frightened. Teresa María edged into the
walled compound. Jamie wished she'd head into the river
brush and hunker low. The light was getting bad, and she'd
be safe there.

Several more warriors had crawled into wagons from the
tongues, or over the tailgates. Jamie could wait no more. In
one fluid motion he pulled his Arkansas toothpick from its
sheath, swung around the chief, caught him from behind,
and pressed the gleaming blade to Uno's throat.

"You're first," he breathed into Uno's ear. The chief knew
better than to struggle, but he eyed the warriors milling

around the wagon. Only the shaman stood nearby, radiating menace.

"David . . . let me know if that 'un takes one step." He wasn't sure David would tell him anything.

"Red blood on the ground," said Uno. "All white men. And the *señora*."

"Not if you call them off," Jamie whispered, pricking skin for emphasis. The chief winced.

"You are soon dead," said Uno.

"We're just tradin'. You want to trade? We'll trade. You want to fight? We'll fight. And Bent's on his way with a pack of lions. You smoked the peace pipe—you goin' back on your word now?" Jamie was mixing English into his Spanish, but he didn't care. Uno understood. He understood the razor edge of a knife.

"The Umcompahgre will do what they please."

Off near the adobe walls, Black and Oliphant spotted the trouble, and were whispering heatedly, obviously wondering what to do. The Utes noticed too, and muttered to one another, circling around toward Jamie and his prisoner. Blake Goodin abandoned the oxen there at the rising post, and stalked toward the wagons, his good arm snaking the bullwhip with sharp murderous cracks. Jamie had to admire the man, bulling into a hornet's nest like that. He had one advantage, though: the warriors had not picked up their bows and quivers.

Every available teamster had armed himself. Black and Oliphant had raised their rifles, but didn't know what to do with them. Warriors slid through dusk away from the wagons, toward their own weapons.

"Well, Uno," Jamie whispered harshly, lapsing into English. "Live or die. Call 'em off or not. I ain't waitin' for them warriors of yours to reach their bows."

Then the shaman yelled.

CHAPTER 19

The voice of Orem, the *po'rat*, crackled nasally into the twilight, galvanic with authority. Uncompahgre warriors paused; the heads of several poked out from the puckerholes of the wagons.

The shaman snarled at them, ducked to the earth, plucked up powder, and spilled it onto the breeze. A few warriors furtively nocked arrows, but the medicine man snarled at them in a hoarse voice that broke into a long wail.

A moment before, David had known he was about to die, and a terror choked him. Now it ebbed, as the gnarled old shaman glowered at his own warriors and they reluctantly obeyed. David didn't understand a word of it, or even grasp the man's meaning. All he knew was that the Utes had pulled back from the brink of a slaughter.

Jamie watched sharply, and released Uno, who turned to stare at him with eyes leaking murder. A thin line of blood oozed from the chief's throat.

"You smoked the pipe, you offered peace, you betrayed the peace," Jamie snapped in Spanish. "You spoke lies. Your priest is a better man than you."

Uno said nothing, but his eyes burned like the coals of hell. Jamie wouldn't let go of it. "You came to trade. We gave you the best price. We trusted you. We gave you peace gifts. But your heart was bad. You are no chief in my eyes. You are nothing. You are less than all your warriors."

David grew alarmed. What was Jamie doing? He'd get them all killed. He winced with every lash of Jamie's tongue.

189

"Next time, when your heart is bad, come fight me," Jamie continued savagely. "Come challenge me. Bring a knife, and we will fight to the death. Next time your heart is bad, I will come after you. I will track you down. I will not honor you. I will not make peace with a bad-heart."

David feared mayhem again, but Uno stood glowering. Why was Jamie doing it? Why this lashing? It'd ruin trade with these Utes. Was Jamie mad? Did he have a temper he couldn't govern? Was he fit to run this post?

The shaman listened solemnly, and David wondered how much of the Spanish he understood. The warriors glared.

What was it about Jamie, the thin man who never stood up if he could help it, but slouched against any wall or tree, folded into a heap when he sat, viewed the world from any supine position he could arrive at? Here was a Jamie Dance unknown to David, full of a savagery that made him seem larger than he was, like an arched cat with its fur up. David knew he was seeing a man he'd never even suspected lay within that lanky, languorous frame.

The handful of teamsters got the gist of it even if they didn't understand the Spanish.

Then Jamie softened. "You have a choice, Uno. Go trade with the Bents again and never come back here. Or bring your village here in peace."

Uno slid a hand to his neck, found the blood there, and smeared his fingers with it. The chief grunted, saying nothing.

Jamie slid his knife back into its sheath, and approached the shaman, Orem, who was as craggy and ugly and sinister as any man David had ever seen. Then Jamie's hands began to work; his fingers and palms and arms cutting air, slapping against each other. David wondered if Jamie was assailing the medicine man, too, but it didn't seem like it.

Jamie turned. "David, get me two twists of tobacco."

David scurried to the wagons, hoping he'd find what he wanted after the warriors had torn so much apart. He felt afraid there among the Uncompahgre warriors, but he tried not to show it. Most of them had plunder in hand—knives, hatchet heads, lance points. He doubted that even the shaman could force them to return the stolen items. But the twists of tobacco were where he'd left them.

David supposed that one would go to Uno, and the other to Orem, but Jamie surprised him. He gave both to the shaman, accompanied by more sign language, while Uno watched sullenly.

"But aren't you going to make peace with—"

Jamie turned on him. "I told the shaman he gets both; he gets the chief's gift because he kept the peace. Uno, he don't get nothin' after what he done."

An uneasy quiet settled on the camp in the twilight. Lyle and Mazappa took it for a sign to set their rifles on the earth and yoke two of the wandering oxen. Then they hooked the yoked oxen to the first wagon, and slowly drove the creaking Conestoga into the yard of the rising fort. No one stopped them.

The Uncompahgre didn't leave; neither did they begin a feast. They simply stared, making David nervous and suspicious of treachery. Uno did nothing either.

Emilio broke the tension. The cook began heaping firewood on a bed of coals until it blazed brightly. Muttering and cussing in a tongue beyond mortal understanding, he jammed a long iron spit through a haunch of buffalo and set it over the flames. The smoke carried with it the promise of food. Blake Goodin and Wilbert Ames corralled two more loose oxen, yoked them, and began moving the freight wagons. Teresa María materialized in the yellow firelight, and began helping Emilio.

Uno stood silently, still absorbing Jamie's tongue-lashing. But some of the Indians kindled their own fire out on the flat, produced their own buffalo meat, and set it to roasting. There would be two camps that night: a handful of people with the Rocky Mountain Company, and at the other fires the whole warrior contingent of a Ute village, still uncounted by anyone, but numbering over a hundred. And separating the large army from the small one was only an uneasy truce abrasaively hammered home by a Ute shaman and Jamie Dance. David wondered if he'd see the dawn.

David caught up with Jamie, rebuke building in him. "You

treated the chief badly. Now we're in trouble!"

"Trouble? This ain't nothing compared to the trouble we had. Badly? That there Uno, he was fixin' to butcher us and steal the loot; the whole twelve wagons. And our stock just for dessert."

"You don't know that!"

"David, there comes a time out hyar, if you live long enough, when you know things without figgering them out."

"We lost their trade!"

Jamie looked at him. "No, we kept our scalps. Which appeals to you more?"

"But you insulted him!"

"That's right. That's how I deal with a bad-heart—a chief like him, that isn't keepin' his word. Makes peace and plans somethin' sneaky. I lashed him good. He took it. They got their own system, sort of. Their own way of doin' things. You make peace, smoke the pipe, then you live by it. He didn't. I just tol' him so. Same as any other chief woulda tol' him. That shaman, he didn't like it neither—he's seein' bad medicine if they did what they was edgin' up to do."

David didn't feel mollified. "You insulted Uno, giving both twists to the shaman."

"That was my purpose, all right."

"But now he'll have it in for you. He'll try to kill you. He'll take his band to trade elsewhere."

Jamie laughed, that slow, easy, drawling chuckle of his that melted arguments into a puddle of lead. "Naw. Real chief, except maybe in battle, is the shaman. They're the ones figger out if bad things are comin' or good, and whether the spirits ain't with 'em because they've been . . . sorta like bad boys, up to no good. That's what that Orem, he was yellin' about."

"But he can't keep a hundred warriors—look at them!—away. Look how they keep eyeing us."

Jamie's smile disappeared. "You're right, David. We got to sweat out the night. And tomorrah, too."

"What can we do? We don't even have gates we can close. And some walls are only chest high—they'll swarm over."

"Reckon we'll have to risk it. You got a better idea?"

David didn't.

192

"If yellin' spares us a fight, I guess I'll yell," Jamie said softly. "We can't hold out. Remember, ol' Cortez, he nabbed all our powder and lead and the last of the trade rifles. Our boys, they got the powder in their horns, and the balls in their kits—and that's it. So maybe the yellin' is what we got. Maybe it's better'n lead pills."

Slowly, the teamsters and the two yoke of oxen dragged the wagons into the yard, where they stood like galleons at anchor, crowded together.

"Blake, reckon you'll picket them oxen right in there tonight?"

"Ox meat's good as any," Goodin said.

That's how it went. The teamsters finished dragging the wagons into the compound, and then stabbed at slices of tough buffalo haunch. Jamie saw to it that the water cask on the light wagon was filled and that the light wagon was hustled inside. Over yonder, shadowy warriors clustered around their fires, awaiting the village—and either trade or war. They would enjoy both.

David couldn't sleep; couldn't even imagine sleeping, and neither could the rest. They formed a watch, two men up on the scaffolds, watching for throat-cutters in the night. The rest pretended to sleep.

Well into the chill night, a body of horsemen approached, not attempting to conceal their arrival at all. Utes stirred around their fires. Inside the compound, teamsters clambered to their feet. David climbed up the scaffold to see. About fifteen men rode up, their wide-brimmed hats announcing the presence of men from Bent's Fort.

"Be that you, Jamie Dance?" yelled one.

"Sort of," Dance yelled back.

"Ye got yer topknot?"

"Reckon I do."

"This hyar porkeater Jonas, he come fetched us."

They rode close, their horses snorting, smelling the warrior camp a hundred yards distant.

David sensed, more than saw, the Bent men. In the starlight he saw bearded ruffians alight from their horses and hooraw around. Some of them clapped Dance on the back and howled and hawed like a pack of wolves.

"Dance," yelled one, "you larned to stand up yet, or are ye still leanin' agin' every tree?"

David sidled over to them, recognizing none, but Jamie took him in hand.

"David, me boy, this hyar bunch of coons is from ol' Bent, and he'll charge us for borryin' them. This hyar runt may not look like it, but he's hell in the mountains. Name's Carson, Kit Carson. Meanest divil ever trapped a plew."

That was a name David knew. He shook hands shyly. He was meeting men whose names he'd heard again and again, at the Planters House and around St. Louis. He found himself being slapped on the back by Dick Wooton, and shaking hands with a slim, dark breed named Jean Baptiste Charbonneau, Sacajawea's son, raised by General Clark after the great expedition. And Bill Williams, the profane old preacher who knew every obscure corner of the West. Even the Bents' factor had ridden over, Lucas Goddam Murray.

But it was Kit Carson who got down to business around the wavering fire in the yard. He and Jamie hunkered into a squat. It always amazed David that mountain men could squat like that for hours and not even feel it.

"Jonas said you was about to lose your topknots," Carson said. "Looks like you held 'em off."

"I give hell to old Uno. He comes smokin' the pipe with David here, and when the Mex dragoons pull out, things change fast. So I tell the old boy he's got nothin' to be proud of."

Carson nodded. "I speak the tongue some. I can put in a few words."

"He speaks Spanish, Kit."

"I like to talk in their tongue if I can. I'll just tell him that if they get to lifting goods and topknots of traders, hyar or anywhere else, they won't be tradin' at Bents. Ol' William'll slam the doors shut. That's the only way. We got to stand together. It keeps wagon-traders out in the villages safer too."

"Except for Comanche."

Carson grinned. "They got their own ways, and they got Comancheros to trade with. I hear you're gonna risk your hides and try it."

Jamie grunted. "They tan good robes."

"We'll stick out the night and I'll talk to Uno, and then we'll git on back to the post and try to whup you good. You got guards posted?"

"Two here. None at the herd. We don't have men enough."

"Not enough men?"

"Four teamsters took off after some Comancheros led by a bandit named Benito. Long time gone."

Carson frowned. "He's a murderin' one. When he gets to smilin', watch your throat."

"He cleaned us out of some trade rifles and powder. The Mexican dragoons got the rest." Jamie turned to Murray. "You got some to sell? Want some trade goods in return?" He waved at the twelve big wagons lined up on the far side.

Goddam Murray eyed the wagons. "We're always shy of something or other. I'll send the trader over in the morning with a cask of powder and some lead and a coupla spare rifles. George Simpson's his name."

"Obliged," said Jamie.

"You gonna favor us with a gill o' mountain hospitality since we come outa warm beds to guard your topknots?" asked Williams, crouching beside them.

"Soon as I find some," said Jamie.

They laughed. "Tomorrah," said Murphy.

"I reckon I'll owe ye a party soon enough."

They accepted that. David felt relieved. Neither he nor Jamie wanted these men drinking now, not with a hundred or more Uncompahgre warriors glowering just beyond the firelight.

The teamsters and the rescue party plucked robes from the pile that had been acquired, and rolled into them under the wagons. Old Bill Williams set himself against a wagon, his Hawken rifle aimed at the yawning doorless gate, and seemed to doze. David knew, from the legends about him, that he could doze and watch at the same time.

But David barely slept.

* * *

Teresa María found herself alone. Around her, *yanqui* trappers and ruffians barked and roared in a strange twang that wasn't even English. And Jamie had joined them, become one of them, bonded in some way that left her out. She stood at the edge of the firelight, watching their strange hoorawing rituals, and then slid over toward the light wagon. Beneath its wagonsheet she would have a little privacy. After most of the food from Independence had been eaten, she and Jamie had made it their nest.

It occurred to her, as she slid out of her *falda* and her *blusa*, that something had saddened within her when Colonel Cortez and his dragoons had ridden off, along with the camp followers. They were Mexican. They spoke her tongue! They were like her! All these others, even Jamie who could speak a detestable Spanish, were as distant from her heart as the seas. She lay there alone that night, watching orange firelight flicker on the canvas walls of her home, listening to the hoorawing of these wild men. In Taos she'd loved that; loved to see the wild *yanqui* trappers ride in from the mountains, with great brown beards and murderous eyes and pinched squints, eyes that had seen things she could barely imagine. All the girls of Taos loved that, loved the wildmen more than their polite Mexican suitors; loved blue-eyed men with vicious knives in their belts and uncouth ways; men who spat and snarled and roared through the sleepy village each winter.

Now she yearned for someone, anyone, just one *hermana*, one Mexican sister to gossip with. She knew, suddenly, that her life as a lone woman, a lone Spanish-speaking Mexican, would become hell here. She waited for Jamie to crawl in beside her and hold her, but he didn't. He remained out there even as the world whirled and night faded. He had kept his marriage contract; he had taken her wherever he went. She had gone with him to far St. Louis, to the mountains, to the places of the *yanquis*. But it wasn't enough anymore. Desperately, she wanted to return to her people, hear her tongue, laugh with her sisters. She ached to see her parents again, and knew it could never be.

She conjured up a vision of her father and saw him as she

remembered him balding, baggy-eyed; peering at the world through dark windows of shrewdness and suffering. She wanted to talk to him. Tell him how sorry she was that she had caused a scandal to the alcalde of Taos, a man prominent and esteemed, and run off with a *yanqui*. She had made her father suffer, and her family endure her folly. But it was too late. If he met her now, he would walk past her, ignore her, disown her, and not speak her name. It hurt. She slept little, pierced by a loneliness that she was not prepared for at all.

She dozed, and then awoke to uproars in the yard. She dressed and hastened into a green dawn, and found the *yanquis* staring from the gate off onto empty flats. She walked to the gate so she could see, too, and discovered, out on the soft-lit flats . . . nothing.

"They lit out. Left in the night, I guess," Gantt said.

"That village ain't comin' thisaway," said a Bent man.

She saw Jamie wandering out there on the barren meadow, poking about, looking for something. Then he walked back.

"Fires cold. Must of left early. Maybe they got wind of Comanch round hyar. Maybe I just annoyed old Uno too much. Maybe that shaman—Orem's his name—maybe he took 'em off."

In a way, Teresa María was glad of it even though they'd lost some robe trade. Now she felt less threatened. She found herself walking freely outside the walls, able to slip down to the Purgatoire through its protecting wall of saltbush, and wash herself far from the prying eyes of the *yanquis*. There, beside that slender creek, she felt she was in Mexico; but in that walled compound she didn't feel that way at all.

By the time she'd refreshed herself, the Bent men were riding off with goodbye whoops and a shot or two. She was glad. They had taken Jamie from her. But even now he scarcely noticed her. He was giving out the day's commands. A gate, first. Four men sawing planks in the sawpit and bolting them together; two men herding the stock; a couple of men laying up the dried adobes left by the peons. A couple of men hunting . . .

Then he realized he didn't have a couple of men to hunt. "I reckon I'll do that myself," he said. "David, you get them robes

197

folded and in a wagon. Move stuff around; make room. Then I want an inventory—what's been took. We don't even know what we got, with all the takin'."

David looked at Jamie sullenly and wandered off.

Emilio had a fire snapping and was roasting the last of the meat, heating a black pot of coffee, and clacking his teeth at everyone, making the rattle of dry-fired rifles.

"Reckon you oughta help ol' Emilio, Teresa. We lost our camp tenders, so it's you and him."

"You're leaving to hunt?"

"I reckon."

Somehow, she sensed her own future misery in that, but she said nothing as he rode off into a sunny wilderness.

That's how it went over the next days. The *yanqui* teamsters made giant gates and hung them. They laid up a few adobes, and made a few more at the riverbank, but there weren't enough men to build a fort. Teresa María worked beside Emilio for much of each day, though they didn't speak. He was loco.

Several times travelers on the Santa Fe trail, across the Río Nepeste, splashed across the ford and visited awhile. The *yanquis* she didn't care about, but the Mexican traders brought her to life. They gossiped about the war—most of the *tejanos* had been caught and were being herded to Santa Fe by Governor Armijo. It made her feel good to talk with her *compadres*.

Jamie was often gone all day, sometimes for several days. And sometimes the post came precariously close to starving. But somehow he brought in meat. If not buffalo, then deer from the Big Timbers; if not deer, then an occasional antelope. The days grew chill, and so did the soul of Teresa María. She yearned for Taos; for her family; for the young men who'd invited her to *bailes*, who groomed their horses and single-footed past her in proud charro costume, who spoke her tongue and knew the gossip—and sometimes eyed her hungrily, barely concealing something in their brown eyes that had excited her imagination.

Odd collections of Indians, half-breeds, Mexican *ciboleros*, *campesinos* from the surrounding *placitas* in white baggy pants wandered by, staring and whispering. David, ever alert to op-

198

portunity, tried to hire them or trade with them. From some *ciboleros* he got buffalo tongues in exchange for hatchets. From some peasants, he got labor—a few thousand more adobes for a blanket or two. And so the fort grew by fits and starts, or languished without progress for days because they were short-handed. But somehow, as the days grew nippier, the outer walls reached their final height, and the first of the rooms within—the trading room and warehouse for the robes—began to rise.

But none of it pleased Teresa María. She hardly saw Jamie, who was always off somewhere, hunting, visiting Bent's Fort, or doing the nightly guard duty shared by everyone.

But then a visitor arrived, a Mexican man on a mangy yellow mule, with several pack burros. She couldn't see beneath his wide sombrero, and knew only that he was slender. A *compadre* to talk to! Someone who might know all the gossip of Santa Fe! She rushed from the cookfire, where she'd been helping Emilio, and out through the opened gates, and beheld Tomás Villanova.

"The false padre!" she exclaimed. *"Caramba!"*

"The new trader for Señor Dance," he replied, a curious light in his eyes. He sent for me.

CHAPTER 20

Tomás didn't arrive alone. The next day five *ciboleros*, Mexican buffalo hunters, showed up, each with a *carreta* and a string of burros. Jamie set them to work at once. They solved his food problem, and their good flintlocks would be welcome in a time of trouble. They also freed him for other urgent tasks.

"Ah, Tomás," he said. "With you here, we will soon be in business. You know robes and pelts. You'll be the chief trader, David the clerk. But I want you to train him, so we have two experienced traders even when I'm away."

"I didn't know my humble talents were so valued. I'm good at marrying, too."

Jamie laughed, and whacked his *amigo* on the back. Tomás had changed everything. Especially the countenance of Teresa María, who began chattering again after weeks of gloom.

Others materialized at the rising post, too—Mexicans from every rancho and *placita* in the area, many of them bringing things to sell or trade: goat cheese, eggs, chickens, maize. They walked down the Purgatoire, or down the Arkansas, their feet dusty in their huaraches, wearing baggy white cottons and bright serapes. Whole families came, the mestizo women golden-fleshed and Indian, the children ragged and bright-eyed.

He put them all to work, all who would stay and make adobes. Many did stay, wanting payment with the alluring trade items that Jamie showed them. Almost before he knew it, he had a dozen brown men mixing mud by the river and pouring it into forms. He had youths hauling adobe blocks to the post, and women cooking great kettles of meat. He found expert young herders, and put them out to keep an eye on the oxen and mules and horses, thus freeing his own teamsters. Even the smallest Mexican children helped, gathering dry sticks for fires, toting heavy buckets of water.

The sudden influx enabled him to put his teamsters to cutting wood. He needed all sorts of wood, for posts and beams, the vigas that would support roofs, planks for rude tables, split logs for benches, hewn limbs for barracks cots. As the work progressed, sawn wood for the shelves and tables in the trading room was needed, as were planks for doors. Firewood had to be gathered against the coming winter. They had no stoves with them, and would rely on fireplaces, larger ones of stone and smaller adobe ones shaped like beehives and set into the corners of a few rooms. They needed prairie hay, too, and Jamie set a couple of teamsters to scything it.

Things changed swiftly. The exterior ramparts rose to their full height of fourteen feet. The trading room and warehouse rose next, along the east wall where the gate was. The weather swiftly chilled and the days shortened through October. The Mexicans fashioned rude *jacals* along the Purgatoire—the Río de las Ánimas, they called the stream, the River of Souls.

One October day they roofed the trading room and the warehouse next to it, lifting hewn cottonwood vigas up and then covering them with the latticework of little poles that would do for a ceiling, and over that shoveling a thick layer of adobe, then greasing the top to fend off water. The teamsters moved into the warehouse, glad to get out of the frosty weather. The Mexicans came and went, and Jamie never knew how many of them he'd have at the start of each day. But always there were enough, and he employed them all for day wages. Often they'd take their pay in a new knife or kettle or coil of rope or blanket or length of flannel. And Jamie paid the Mexicans for whatever foodstuffs they brought; whatever *carreta*-loads of prairie hay or firewood. His stock of trading goods dwindled some, but they'd provided for that back in St. Louis.

They had visitors, too, for the post was visible to any traveler on the Santa Fe trail. Traders and teamsters splashed across, and sometimes Jamie was able to acquire needed things, sacks of flour, a fowling piece, powder and ball, in exchange for robes or, in one case, fresh oxen. It dawned on him that he might have a Santa Fe trail trade after all, even though he was on the wrong side of the river. Any outbound trader from St. Louis would reach Fort Dance first.

He knew few of the travelers, but once in a while one or another of the old mountain coons surprised him. Black Harris one day, Pegleg Smith another. Uncle Dick Wooton frequently, and Kit Carson now and then. He welcomed them all with a hooraw, and a gill of spirits if they stayed the night. From them, and from Mexican traders, he got wind of great events to the south and west. The Texas army had spent itself wandering across the Staked Plains, fighting its vast canyons, gradually starving to death, jettisoning everything, even rifles. When at last the Texians drifted into Mexican settlements, they were exhausted, weak, and helpless. It had been nothing at all for Manuel Armijo and his militia to round them up, shoot a few of the advance party as a terrifying lesson, and haul them off to Santa Fe to be displayed in chains to the cheering mobs. From there, Jamie learned, the Texians were being long-marched south to the dungeons of Mexico, even a journalist with a United States passport, whom Armijo refused to release.

All this had absorbed the governor and his officials, as well as El Zorro, and Jamie was glad of that. But soon, he knew, they'd remember him up here in a far corner of New Mexico. Remember him all too well. Remember that he lacked a trading license, that an impost had been levied haphazardly by federal troops; that the land upon which the post sat was unowned so far but sought by many. They'd remember that an enterprise in Mexico required a Mexican partner, and a largely Mexican staff. All that was all right with Jamie, so long as it didn't cut too deep.

By mid-November, the post was almost done. Jamie's own quarters were complete, as were the office, kitchen, dining area, barracks, quarters for three married couples, and guest quarters. The trading room had been furnished with shelves and tables, and was ready for business. Bedframes had been built for the barracks, woven strips of rawhide anchored to them for mattresses. They still had to dig a well in the yard—crucial if they were besieged—and they lacked furniture and corrals. They needed to build a big robe press to bale the robes for shipment east. They needed to construct a wooden gallery on the roofs, under the parapets, where riflemen could stand and shoot over the walls.

Still, it was time to celebrate—and time to form a permanent staff. Jamie had kept his eye on the Mexicans. He knew which ones had worked hard, and decided to employ eight or ten permanently. One by one, he drew them aside and offered employment. Some refused. They had ranchos of their own to look after. But others joined him gladly. In one of the rooms for married couples, he installed young Hector Chávez, with his Juanita and his half-grown children Rosa, Manolo, and Juan. Hector had a genius for carving unruly cottonwood into useful things. Juanita cooked the best tamales Jamie had ever tasted. To the bachelors in the barracks, he added Juan Cordova, Pepe Alvaro, Luis Soto, José María Trujillo, Ono Valdon, and Fidel Santa María. And all the *ciboleros*. A good start. Over time, he would add more. And with each additional hombre, he would make it harder for Armijo to ruin him, or that Yankee-hating priest Martinez in Taos to roar against the Rocky Mountain Company.

But even before he could announce a fiesta day to celebrate the completion of Fort Dance, an entire village of Arapaho rode in from the north, fording the low water of the Arkansas as if it presented no barrier at all.

"Who are they, Jamie?" asked David nervously, as they viewed the Indians from a parapet.

Jamie had no trouble identifying these members of a powerful plains tribe that roamed from the North Platte clear down to here, and from the front range of the Rockies well to the east. They were Southern Arapaho, close allies of the Cheyenne, and they were gorgeously attired and mounted, their ponies caparisoned with bright tradecloth and leather. A rich tribe, obviously. The squaws wore full skirts of tradecloth, and sat in high-backed saddles. The warriors wore fringed leggins, calico shirts, leather vests, eagle feathers tucked into braided jet hair, or full bonnets decorated with red flannel, ermine plumes, and conchos. And among them were ponies drawing travois loaded with mountains of things; a rich band, with abundant robes.

Trade at last! Jamie raced back to his quarters and slid into his black britches and frock coat for the ceremonies. He corraled Tomás and David, and selected some gifts for the chief and headmen; tobacco always, and some round hand mirrors, and ribbons. Then they raced out from the compound onto the barren flats, and waited. Around them Arapaho tribesmen gathered and stared. They were well armed. Most of the warriors had a carbine or musket in a leather saddle sheath. The chief himself was an old, weathered man with bowed legs and a hawk nose and black penetrating eyes. He wore a large medicine bundle at his neck and a bearclaw necklace.

"We ought to make a few hundred robes out of this," Jamie said. "Maybe more. But we got to beat the Bents. These here 'Rapahos been trading up the river now for years. And it's up to us to get the trade."

The chief stayed mounted on a fine buckskin, no doubt enjoying the subtle advantage a man on horse has over men on foot. But most of the warriors and headmen slid off their half-trained ponies, which shrieked and snorted around them. Everywhere, mutts of every description raced about. The Arapaho commissary. Other tribes called them the Dog-Eaters.

Jamie lifted his hand upward, palm forward, in the peace and welcome sign of the prairies, and the chief returned it. Jamie knew a little Cheyenne but no Arapaho, which was a similar tongue. But he intended to try English and Spanish first. If the Arapaho had traded with the Bents, one or another of them would speak in a familiar language.

"Welcome to the Rocky Mountain Company. I'm Jamie Dance. We're here to trade for robes and pelts."

The chief shook his head, and slashed the air with his hand. Jamie tried it again in Spanish, and failed, although a

204

headman seemed to understand, and listened intently.

Sign language then. Welcome, and let us smoke the pipe. And we have gifts for you. Who are you?

"Inuna-ina," the chief said. Our People. White Wolf. The village of White Wolf. He looked grand there, on his big buckskin, his seamed face owning the world around him.

Jamie knew of him but had never met him. White Wolf was a peace chief who had encouraged his people to tan robes and trade them, especially for rifles, shot, and powder. This band had more firearms than any dozen villages put together but rarely used them. The threat of all that firepower had curbed rival bands and horse-stealing parties. If Jamie could win the trade of this band he'd have a great prize. There'd be perhaps a thousand fine robes in it each season. He knew, suddenly, that he'd go to great lengths to wean this village away from the Bents. And he knew, unhappily, that the Bents would go just as far to keep the trade to themselves. Jamie felt himself being put to the test, before he was ready. This day, and this trade, could make or break the Rocky Mountain Company.

Things looked good. Jamie smoked with the chief and headmen, while all about him handsome lodges rose as squaws raised the lodgepoles and then wrestled the fine cowhide covers over the poles and laced them. He reckoned eighty lodges, and over four hundred souls in this band. Young men ran the vast herd of ponies across the Purgatoire and put them on good grass there. A good thousand ponies, including some fast war horses and buffalo runners, Jamie estimated. And everywhere among the lodges lay heaps of finely tanned buffalo robes, most with thick, curly winter hair on them. Wealth unimaginable! Jamie's mind raced, and he itched to begin the trading at once, wanting every one of those fine robes these industrious people had patiently scraped, brain-tanned, and soft-tanned by rubbing them over a tanning pole. He wanted to take this treasure back east, carefully baled, and lay it before Guy Straus's unbelieving eyes!

He wished he knew Arapaho, but he didn't. His fingers

would have to do. He brought White Wolf and his six headmen into the new trading room, and let them see the dazzling array of goods on its pristine shelves and tables. Witney blankets, mostly natural cream, but also red, green, and blue, with black bands, and anywhere from two points to four. Bright bolts of calico, gingham, flannel in every rainbow color. Bed ticking. Aromatic tobacco twists. Hanks of big, glass trade beads made in Venice. Brass hawk bells made in Leipzig. Clay pipes made in Cologne. Arrays of gleaming Wilson butcher knives made in Sheffield, England, and Green River knives made in Massachusetts. One-pound bars of lead from Missouri. Flints and English fire steels, awls, round mirrors, brass and tin kettles, iron skillets and pots, hoop iron for arrowheads, Delaware gunpowder. New Orleans molasses and sugar, coffee beans, sacks of cornmeal and flour, axe and hatchet heads, needles and thread, brass buttons, bits and bridles, gray flints. A box of abalone shells from the Pacific. German silver conchos. Brass rings and ear bobs with glass bangles. Dangling from pegs in the wall, iron traps for beaver and small game. Fishhooks. Gun worms, ramrods, spare locks. Pasteboard boxes of percussion caps. Vermilion, or cinnabar, wrapped in small papers by Chinese.

The headmen wandered among the tables and shelves, as if in a wonderland, while Jamie and David and Tomás guided them, urged them to touch and try, heft and handle. He presented White Wolf with a fine beaver tophat, a mark of authority. To the headmen he gave German silver conchos of several sizes, which would decorate the headstalls of their ponies, and a paper of vermilion as well. The headmen seemed pleased, and talked among themselves in a tongue Jamie wished he knew. A trading post needed traders who could speak each tongue.

He signaled for his guests to seat themselves, which they did, in a ring on the clay floor. Now began a crucial, serious business. If the headmen traded here, so would the village. If the headmen preferred Bent, St. Vrain, so would the village. But Jamie was good at this, and his deft fingers could talk.

I will learn to speak Arapaho, or hire a trader who speaks it, because you are valuable friends, he began, hoping that

206

these tribesmen would read the movements of his hands and interpret the often-crude ideas conveyed by sign-talk. We will give more for your good robes—your people make the best of robes—and we will charge less for trade goods. We will buy all the robes you give us—and protect your people. You can get two pounds of coffee beans for a robe from the Bents. We will give you three. You can get sixty loads of powder and shot for a robe from the Bents. We will give you seventy. You can get a yard of cloth for a robe from them, but we will give you more than a yard. We will give you four pounds of sugar for a robe—not three.

He waited, hoping all that had been understood. The headmen listened intently, weighing him, eyeing the glistening rainbows of goods lit by the low sun of October through the single window.

White Wolf stood, dignity radiating from him in his new black beaver felt tophat. He had a way of expressing himself with his hands. His movements were almost violent, a great force rippling from his fingers and palms and forearms. A willful, powerful man, Jamie thought. The chief's hands slashed through sunlight, swirling dust motes. You have many good things. You offer us much. You have made good gifts. We are friends of the Cheyenne. The Cheyenne are friends of the Bents. We have always traded with the Bents. Their prices are high. They are powerful. Maybe they will drive you away. If we trade with you, maybe the Bents will treat us badly. William Bent talks to the fathers of your people, and tells them of our needs. He is married to a Cheyenne. You are not married to a Cheyenne or Arapaho. You have some things the Bents don't have. Maybe we will trade a few robes for those. You are across the medicine line of the Mexicans. Our enemies the Comanche might come. We will think on these things.

Jamie didn't like the sound of that. His fingers flashed. Invite the people to see the trading room. Let them trade while you and the headmen think on these things. Bring your medicine chief, and let him see me, talk with me.

We will think on these things, the chief repeated. It was a dismissal. The headmen stood and filed out into the whipping air of a fall day.

Jamie followed them out, but paused at the door. "Tomás, take a box of awls out to the ladies. One awl per lodge."

Tomás Villanova grabbed a pasteboard box of the simple metal devices, pointed iron with a jag in the middle. The tribesmen would add their own hafts of bone or wood.

"Mordida," he said. The bite. An old Mexican custom. But Jamie saw it more as gifting to ensure future trade.

The headmen walked toward a large lodge, brightly painted with suns and lightning bolts and stick figures. Waiting there were two white men, beside their horses, and Jamie knew at once he had troubles. They were Goddam Murray, the Bents' chief trader, and Kit Carson, sunny and blue-eyed and smiling. *Not Carson!* he thought. Kit's first wife, Waanibe, had been Arapaho, and Kit had loved her dearly and mourned her death. His daughter, Adaline, had been born of that marriage. Kit could speak Arapaho; he was an old and honored friend of the tribe.

Jamie wanted to rush over there, promise anything, but he held his peace, and watched Tomás cheerfully wander from lodge to lodge and delight the ladies before each with his own amiable grace. An awl a lodge. A gift from the Rocky Mountain Company! But Jamie knew that not all the awls in the world would change matters if Murray and Carson had their way. Odd how they'd shown up within a few hours of the arrival of this village. Not so odd. He didn't doubt the Bents kept a sharp eye on everything here. And that sharp eye was probably wheezy old Phineas Boggs, who would be watching from across the river with a spyglass, knowing everyone, ready to report any news. Jamie cussed him out once again for the worthless whining man he was.

But all he could do was wait patiently while that meeting inside Chief White Wolf's lodge went on. Tomás finished his work. That's a lot of awls to give away, Jamie thought rancorously. Brown children eyed him curiously, and dashed away laughing. White Wolf's several wives busied themselves with a cookfire and a haunch of buffalo. A feast, too, it seemed.

A few warriors did wander to the trading room, and Jamie hoped that David would treat them well. Then he remembered that David didn't know the sign talk, and hastened back there. He let the few Arapaho who ventured to the trading window actually come in and wander through the room itself, pinching wool, rubbing fingers over steel knife edges. It was a great privilege he was granting them, a mark of unusual trust. One brought a fine robe, black and curly, and Jamie gave two yards of red flannel for it, an extraordinary amount of cloth. That exchange brought in a few more. As the day dragged on, Jamie acquired a dozen robes, trading almost double the usual amounts for them. A dozen costly robes.

But then, at last, Kit Carson wandered in, and Jamie knew the fateful conference was over.

"It's a hard game, Jamie, the robe trade," said Kit.

"You don't have to tell me."

"I want to tell you. They'll stick with Bent. Pulling out in the morning. Coming on over."

"How'd you bribe 'em?"

Kit shrugged. "How does Bent or American Fur drive out the competition? Same way. Offer 'em twice what you do — no matter what you give. That'll be the price until you're whipped. That and the alliance old William's worked out with the Cheyenne and southern Arapaho. Sorry, Jamie. I feel bad about it, but . . . Charles Bent's my in-law."

Jamie knew that. Charles had married Ignacia Jaramillo of Taos; Kit had married her younger sister, Josepha. Both of the girls had been close to Teresa María. "I imagine you speakin' the tongue and being married to Waanibe didn't hurt none," he said.

Kit grinned. "Didn't hurt at all. Ol' White Wolf, he says he don't hardly know how to trade with an outfit that don't speak his tongue."

Jamie left the trading room to David and Tomás, and wandered out onto the bustling flat, feeling the vitality of the whole village around him — a rich village whose robes he'd not collect. As he stood there, feeling the chill air eddy out of the northwest, a young man approached him, leading a fine, clean-limbed coyote dun horse. The youth stopped, and with deft signs informed Jamie that he was Chief White Wolf's oldest son, True Arrow, and that the horse was a gift from his father.

Jamie nodded and accepted the gentle animal. The horse eyed him with a peaceful gaze. Jamie always thought he could read a mean animal by his eyes. He signaled the youth that the horse was much appreciated, and the boy whirled away. At the chief's lodge, White Wolf stood watching. A horse, then. It was an Arapaho way of paying debts.

Carson and Murray rode out, their undercutting done, leaving Jamie to his own thoughts. It wasn't any different from a thousand other ploys in the fur trade. More civilized actually, he thought, remembering the bloody beaver wars.

No Arapaho trade. No Cheyenne trade. Those were reserved by the Bents. If the Rocky Mountain Company were to survive, it'd have to reach the dangerous Comanche. It would have to fight off the Comancheros, its Mexican rivals. *Comanche!* He didn't like to think about what he'd have to do.

210

CHAPTER 21

David chafed at his duties. Jamie had made him the company clerk, and his days had become a dreary round of taking inventory and recording trades and adding or subtracting sums. Jamie had made Tomás the chief trader, which stung David. What kind of reward was that for bringing in so many Ute robes—more robes than all the rest of the trading put together! It angered him. Instead of being rewarded, he had been punished. It didn't seem right, being made a clerk, condemned to sit half the day on a stool and record every transaction in a record book for an ungrateful tyrant who couldn't read or write.

Not that there'd been much trading. Mostly individuals. The villages stayed away, either because they didn't know about the new post, or because the Bents persuaded them to. Jamie didn't seem to worry about it, but David did—this huge business wasn't even beginning to pay its way. Still, in one sense it was a blessing. It freed them to complete the post. Jamie started up the brick works again, using local Mexican help, and with these adobes a corral was rising on the south side of the post, along with a wagon yard for those valuable freighters still within the fort. In the yard Jamie had another crew gouging a well—a task absolutely essential for defense—and three experienced men building a robe press of cottonwood poles. Others cut firewood, scythed prairie hay, hewed and sawed logs for furniture, and completed the wooden walkway, or gallery, under the parapets.

At Jamie's request, David kept a post journal, and all these activities were recorded, as well as the trades. One November day, a small band of Jicarilla Apaches arrived and traded forty robes, many of them light summer skins rather than the more valuable winter robes that had thicker hair and held warmth better. Prime winter robes were sought in the east for carriage travel. The army made greatcoats of them.

Angrily, David watched Tomás trade, pulling the summer robes through the small window for examination, and then signaling their worth. David realized, suddenly, that Fort Dance lacked an interpreter, and would be at a disadvantage until someone could speak the tongue of each tribe. The Bents had several such valuable men, old mountain hands or squawmen mostly. Why not himself? he thought. He had a way with languages. He knew five. But scarcely a word of any Indian tongue. He resolved to learn, somehow. The Bents paid clerks and traders who could speak the court language — the Indian tongue — anywhere from eight hundred dollars to a thousand a year. A lot more than the herders and laborers who got a hundred a year. A clerk like himself was paid five hundred dollars and a suit of broadcloth for a three-year stint. Not much more per year than a laborer. Even a craftsman such as a carpenter or smith earned two hundred fifty a year, and a hunter got four hundred. An interpreter was one of the most valuable men in a fur post. And Fort Dance didn't have any. Not even Jamie Dance. David decided to make himself valuable. He'd learn tongues — every tongue he could master! Maybe then Jamie Dance would look upon him as something more than a bookish youth fit only for scribbling in a buckram-bound ledger!

The idea excited him. What's more, he knew how he'd learn. Fort Dance had acquired its share of loafers, men who descended from nowhere, lounged around doing little except gossip and spit and waste their days. Among them were a few whites who called themselves trappers and mountain men, but mostly were lazy riffraff drifting out the Santa Fe trail. But there were breeds and squawmen too, and several Mexicans, mostly *ciboleros* going or coming from the herds out on the plains, stopping for a free feed and a few supplies they'd trade for a hide or a tongue. The breeds interested David, especially a slim one called Ramon Sanchez, son of a Mexican father and Comanche mother. David had chafed at these freeloaders, lamenting the cost of their feed, even though Jamie didn't seem to mind, and considered them a part of the life of a fur post. But now David saw some good in them.

David toyed with the possibility of hiring Sanchez as an interpreter, but the man hadn't a thing to recommend him and was distrusted as a possible thief. Instead, David sought out the ragged breed who was lounging in the barracks, and drew him aside to offer him a deal.

"I want to learn Comanche, fast as possible. You teach it for a while each afternoon, and I'll reward you with trade goods."

Sanchez yawned, probably pondering whether it was easier to filch things than to earn them, and finally nodded. From that time on, David corralled Sanchez—the breed never showed up on his own—and had him say Comanche words and phrases, then give their meaning. David patiently copied each word phonetically in his own ledger, along with its meaning. Soon he extracted conjugations and idioms and sentence structure from Sanchez, and began speaking simple sentences. It went well enough. Sanchez earned a Wilson butcher knife, and then a yard of flannel.

Obsessed with learning, David rooted out more help from the post parasites. One bearded old Missourian had once had a Kiowa woman, and knew the tongue. Pickett was his name, and he wanted a gill of spirits now and then as his reward, which David furtively supplied. From Pickett he got some Kiowa words, and began to acquire a second tribal tongue. Someday soon he'd show Jamie Dance what a Straus was made of!

He got some Arapaho words from a Mexican trader who stayed a fortnight; and more from a *cibolero* who'd had an Arapaho squaw once. Gradually, the pages of his ledger filled, the words of each tongue in an orderly column, spelled phonetically, with English or Spanish translations beside them, all in his careful copperplate. He wore out quills and had to make ink from carbon black, water and gum, but he kept at it as the weather turned cold and gusts of raw northern air ed-

213

died into the yard and through badly heated rooms whose adobe walls bled warmth.

And he felt less resentful about feeding the loungers with buffalo meat that was sometimes hard to acquire. They'd had to add two more hunters to the rolls, another *cibolero*, and a Missourian who had a knack for shooting deer. Even then they had bad days, when Emilio's angry teeth clacked at the world and the Haitian produced kettles of mush.

The post was becoming known. Most travelers on the Santa Fe trail now splashed across the Arkansas for a look and a visit, or, in the case of wagon trains, delegated one of their number to ford the river and purchase something or other. That gave David a chance to send letters to his father — and to deal with something that had gnawed at him. Somehow, he had to explain to Guy Straus why he hadn't followed the instruction to retreat from Mexico. David thought at first of blaming it on the dragoons and the *cabo*, Ortiz. But that would be a lie. After the Mexican cavalry had left, they were free to abandon the post.

He decided instead to take the nettle.

> Dear Papa,
> Your instruction for us to pull back to the north bank because of the Texas troubles came when I was alone in charge at the post. Mr. Dance had gone to Santa Fe for the licenses and imposts. I could not immediately comply because a company of Mexican dragoons prevented it, and we were effectively prisoners. But later we could have abandoned the largely completed fort. I chose not to. The fort is almost done, and we are here.

He supposed that would anger his father. What did an eighteen-year-old greenhorn know? But at least it was transparently honest, and he prided himself in that. He gave his reasons, described the progress of the post, told his father that at present they had over two hundred robes, but had suffered some losses of trade goods to Comancheros and a federal colonel, that they'd won over no tribes, and the Bents were undercutting ruthlessly to keep the Cheyenne and Arapaho trade.

The future of Fort Dance hung in balance. They would need to cement alliances with the Utes—and the dreaded Comanche. And no one yet knew how to do it without losing his scalp. Mr. Dance hadn't tried, and was hoping they'd come in. . . .

Satisfied, David blotted the letter, sealed it with wax, and sent it off with the next packtrain heading east. He missed his papa and *maman*. He knew it was a solemn letter, but he wanted his father to see he was a man now, with responsibilities. He half-expected his father to summon him East and put him to work in the gilded confines of Straus et Fils. But maybe not. Guy Straus had never been an ordinary man.

In early December word arrived that a band of Kiowa had wintered on the Cimarron, not far south. And a few days later, a trading party led by old Santan himself, three lodges, twenty warriors, and packhorses laden with robes, showed up at the post, looking as bloody and murderous as their Comanche allies.

Even as the Kiowa began raising their lodges, the northwest sky darkened, and a wall of indigo cloud stretching from horizon to horizon rolled down upon them, turning the sky white first, freezing the sun to impotence, and then exploding into a howling blue norther that whipped stinging snow horizontally and piled up granular drifts on the sturdy exposed faces of the fort.

Robes! The great question mark that hung over Fort Dance slid away, at least for the moment. Jamie Dance hastened into the biting blizzard and brought the blanket-wrapped chief in, along with two headmen, and sent firewood out to the lodges. Santan was not a man to inspire confidence, even though they'd smoked the pipe with him back on the Santa Fe trail. His scarred mouth hung in a scowl, and his glare measured white men and Mexicans for bullets and arrows and knives. All three visitors had wrapped themselves in lightweight Mexican serapes. Jamie brought them straight into the trading room, where they warmed themselves at the fireplace and stared at the glistening array of goods.

With sign language and a little Spanish, which they understood somewhat, Jamie welcomed them while David and

Tomás and a few trading assistants stood by.

"We remember you. We might trade," said Santan in Kiowa, using sign language to supplement. David was pleased that he'd understood the Kiowa. "We will talk. We might trade at Bent's Fort, even though they don't like us."

Jamie didn't grasp that. "Here's a little gift," he said in Spanish, handing each of the Kiowa a twist of aromatic tobacco.

"We welcome you. We want to trade with you and your allies, the Comanche," Jamie continued, speaking mostly with his fingers.

"We want rifles, powder, and the heavy metal," said Santan. "We brought robes."

David understood the Kiowa. But the post had no rifles, lead, or powder—at least not for trading. The Comancheros had made off with some; El Zorro and his dragoons had taken the rest. Jamie had been forced to trade robes at Bent's Fort for enough to keep themselves and their hunters armed. They'd bought a little more powder and lead from passing traders.

Jamie looked puzzled. "They want rifles and ammunition," David said.

"How do you know?"

"I've been learning Kiowa."

Jamie looked astonished. "You? Where from? . . . Tell 'em we got cleaned out, but we got lots of other stuff."

David ventured it, having to conjure up each word. Santan listened intently, never smiling. But he nodded. That was all the sign he gave that David's Kiowa words had been recorded.

"We will go to Bent for rifles," the chief said.

David translated it in English.

Jamie surprised him. "Tell ol' Santan that if they go to Bent, they won't trade hyar again."

David didn't want to say that. "Why drive the trade away—especially this large trading party from a tribe they wanted to come in? "Jamie . . . that's just throwing away—"

"Do it! Tell 'em!" Jamie roared, unwinding his lanky frame from its usual slouch.

"But . . . Jamie . . ."

Jamie's sudden glare lacerated David, and bred a swift-rising anger in him too. He turned wearily toward the chief. "Mr. Dance said that you must trade here. If you go to the Bents, you will not be welcome here." David loathed every word he spoke.

Santan stared at David, then Jamie. "Maybe we will trade with the Bents." With that, the chief and headmen stalked quietly through the door, and out the gate, into the howling blizzard.

"You lost us trade!" David snapped.

"Maybe I did."

"You let them go out to the blizzard. You didn't even invite them to shelter here."

"I reckon their lodges are warmer than inside these mud walls, David. And there's reasons not to let them stay hyar."

"You don't care about profit! You have nothing invested in this. It's my family's money."

"Reckon I'd like to succeed and earn me a piece, David."

"Then why—"

"Because they're Kiowa."

"What difference does that make? They had robes! They were willing to trade some, even if we had no weapons."

"They won't get weapons or powder from the Bents neither, David. Only from Comancheros. They're Kiowa, boy."

"That doesn't explain anything."

"I reckon it does. You don't deal with Kiowa or Comanche the way you deal with other tribes. You let them in hyar as guests, they'll likely slit our throats and loot the place. They've done it. They take a notion, and they'll do it agin. As for tradin', there's only one way—all or nothing. If they figger they can do a little with old Bent, and do a little hyar, they'd have no loyalties at all. They don't trade much with old Bent. Murray lets 'em shove a robe or two through that little trading window, and take away a blanket or two. So they won't git much there. They'll be back, David. And on our terms. Trading with Kiowa and Comanche, it's not the same. It's like gettin' into a cage with tigers. We got to learn 'em we're makin' the rules, and learn 'em right now. If we don't learn 'em, it's yore scalp and mine."

217

David had no answer to that. But out there in the snow were hundreds of robes, and he couldn't forget it.

From the penciled notations on the letter, Guy Straus knew it had been turned over to an army patrol out in Indian Territory and had been taken to Fort Leavenworth, then had come on a river packet from there to St. Louis. The address was in David's handwriting. Alive, then, at least as of six weeks ago or so. He tore at it, experiencing the eagerness and dread that he always felt when such a letter wound its way across a wild continent into his hands.

It began almost defiantly. They were staying in Mexico. The fort was almost done. The Texas troubles had passed. David had made the key decisions . . . after some difficulties—against Guy's command. . . .

The rest was a mélange of good news and bad. David himself had traded with some Utes and gotten good robes. Comancheros had pilfered over two hundred dollars of trade goods. Four teamsters who'd set out to punish them had never returned. Jamie Dance had been briefly imprisoned in Santa Fe, and had not obtained a license or paid the imposts. A Colonel Cortez had "taxed" the company by taking all its Leman trade rifles, powder, and ball—to fight the Texas invaders. But the colonel had left his dragoons there, and the federal soldiers had helped build the post, and it was now almost done. . . .

That gave Guy pause. Federal Mexican troops building his post? He well knew what it meant—the Mexicans would have their reward, many times over. It angered him. If David had only followed explicit directions, they'd all be safely on the north bank of the Arkansas, out of Mexico. Ever since Guy had seen the train off, he'd had misgivings about locating the post in Mexico, misgivings that ballooned with the news of the stupid filibustering expedition of the Texans. Mexico had always been an enigma to entrepreneurs, welcoming them warmly with an initial burst of good feeling, only to confiscate their goods and drive them out with the next spasm of feeling. Honorable merchants had taken goods to Mexico only to have them all confiscated. Some even ended up in dungeons their fates unknown.

Once a Mexican post had seemed the intelligent thing to do. A trading license was a way around the Bents—a way to draw in the southern tribes and do a fat business on the Mexican plains. And yet . . . not for nothing had William Bent built his adobe fortress on the United States side. Not for nothing had his partners, Ceran St. Vrain and Charles Bent, moved to Santa Fe and Taos to exert their powerful influence upon Manuel Armijo and all the rest. As the summer had ripened into fall, Guy had concluded that Mexico was too risky. A large part of his family fortune had ridden west into that nation, and there it would be at the mercy of officials enforcing draconian laws and relaxing them—for the *mordida*, the bite. Just like this Colonel Cortez, whose "protection" could easily cost the Rocky Mountain Company its profits.

Guy peered out of his wavery glass window into a slate gray December day, thinking about David. The young man had defied his father, and with a bit of truculence. Guy heartily wished the young whelp had obeyed. To be sure, the best thing an entrepreneur could hope for was a good man out in the field. But this was different. Something had raged in Guy to pull out of Mexico. When war rumors floated into St. Louis from down in the Republic of Texas, he knew the matter had become urgent, and he'd prayed he wasn't too late.

He hadn't been, as it turned out. But now he might be, thanks to his son's insolence. He felt helpless, eight or nine hundred miles from his son and Dance. He felt all the more helpless because winter had arrived, and travel out the trail had halted until spring. He thought, wildly, of going out there himself, braving mud and starvation and blizzards and swollen rivers—and knew that he couldn't do that. Straus et Fils demanded his attention, and such a trip would be suicidal for a sedentary man.

But he might send an express.

That would be costly, and he had nothing to spare. He ruminated about it, toyed with it, and finally rejected it. An express would reach Dance and David in January. But they couldn't begin a new post on the United States side until the weather moderated. Until then, they would stay in Mexico, and endure whatever plucking this Colonel Cortez, and the wily governor, Armijo, and the horde of impost collectors, had in mind. The thought of it made Guy's bile rise.

Angrily, he strode out of his salon and headed next door. Yvonne would welcome news of her sons. She'd never reconciled herself to their absence, and lived in daily fear that they'd be slaughtered by Indians, or die by any of the thousand snares the wild continent laid for the unwary.

He'd go share the news, and then he'd head for Planters House, and a julep with Robert Campbell, and any of the other veterans of the mountains he could find. Maybe he'd find someone, somewhere in St. Louis, who was braving the winter weather and would take a firm, unmistakeable instruction from him out to his obstinate son and his dubious partner, Dance. He'd even send the letter via a Bent rider if one was going that way. Guy was going to get the Rocky Mountain Company out of Mexico, one way or another. No matter what that eighteen-year-old said.

CHAPTER 22

Santan and his Kiowas didn't return. Jamie waited impatiently as the weather turned warm and a breeze out of Mexico scalded away the rotting drifts. The matter festered in him: had he misjudged? Lost a major trade with the Kiowas? Had Bent whipped him?

He walked out to the herd one morning, caught his shaggy chestnut horse, and saddled it. He rode up the river, his collar turned against the sharp wind, his gaze always upon horizons, studying them for menace. He forded the Arkansas, which ran low at that time, and let his horse shake off water on the United States side. Then he turned his horse into the deep ruts of the Santa Fe trail, and let it carry him the fifteen remaining miles to the great adobe fortress of the Bents.

The post looked as if it had been there forever, though it had stood only a few years. Melting snow had stained the tops of its ramparts brown. It hulked on a low bench near the river. On this day no lodges were gathered around its massive double gates, and it looked lordly and serene, its two bastions and their six-pound cannon unnecessary. But Jamie knew they were necessary. There, in the graveyard just outside the wall, was a fresh grave, its raw earth heaped up. It lacked a board or stone, but Jamie knew who was in it, and was saddened by it.

Here was a far outpost of American empire, as well as the heart of a merchant empire that had gestated in St. Louis. The outer gates stood open, giving visiting tribesmen access to the trading window, but the inner gates were closed. A watchtower stood over the pairs of gates, and no doubt his arrival had been noted. He was sure of it when the inner gates opened magically, admitting him to the yard.

He slid off his horse in the weak winter light, while the posts engagés watched amiably. The yard was enclosed by rooms, two stories of them at some points: barracks, William Bent's quarters, St. Vrain's quarters; a dining area and kitchen, trading room, warehouse, blacksmith and carpentry shops, a magazine in the far corner, guest quarters, and even a billiards room up above and to the rear.

He was looking for Lucas Murray, Goddam Murray, the chief factor. And if not Murray, then William Bent himself. He tied his horse to a hitchrail and headed for the trading room, where he'd find warmth—and coldness.

He found his man in the cold warehouse, grading robes.

"Shall we 'Dance'?" said Murray.

Jamie cut through the amenities because he felt like it. "You do some Kiowa trade? Old Santan?"

Murray grinned. "You bet. Took in four hundred—these right here."

"What'd they trade for?"

Murray cocked an eyebrow. The man was built like a Spanish fighting bull, and had a bull's way about him. "Rifles, powder, and ball mostly. They cleaned us out. We're casting ball back at the smith right now."

A tightness built in Jamie. "I thought Bents don't trade rifles to Kiowa and Comanche."

Murray hoorawed. "We don't. Except when we got to beat some competition. Long as you're thar, Dance, we'll trade anything, any price. When you quit, we'll quit."

"Those rifles could be used against your people on the trail. Against us."

Murray sobered. "Plumb right, pal. It worries us some. Especially with Robert bein' killed an' all."

Robert Bent, youngest of the four brothers, had been killed and scalped by Comanche in October on the Santa Fe trail. That was his fresh grave just outside the wall. That—and other bitter experiences with the Comanche—was why the Bents didn't trade rifles to them or the Kiowa. Until now. Jamie had been counting on that when he'd dealt with Santan.

"I figured you wouldn't trade rifles—accounta that."

Murray hawked and spat. "You reckoned wrong. William, he sees Santan come in and says, 'Give 'em what they want,' and walks off. That's because o' you. Fort Dance. That's the price the Bents pay for owning the turf."

Jamie knew he'd calculated wrong. It made him mad. The first rule of war among fur outfits was to *erase the opposition*. Up north, American Fur and old Chouteau did it by any and every means: price cutting, alcohol, bribery of chiefs, and maybe even murder, if the murder could be ascribed to Indians. Down here, Bent did it. Jamie had forgotten what he knew. "I reckon you'll undercut, too."

Goddam Murray laughed. "Any time, until you're out."

"We're stickin'."

Murray's hoorawing echoed in his ears.

Jamie wandered into the yard and watched a crew press the robes Murray had graded, working the pole lever of the press in the yard until the robes had been squeezed into a compact bale. He wandered into the trading room and found George Simpson manning it. The Bents sold a wider variety of foodstuffs than he did, much of it to the Santa Fe traders. Here were pickles and pinto beans, onions, chiles, chocolate, crackers, rice, raisins, and a lot more, including spices. It gave them an edge, he thought. A lot came up from Mexico. He'd start that too—if the post survived.

"Mr. Dance."

Jamie turned, and found William Bent behind him.

"You're checking our stores. Just as I checked yours." Bent grinned. "How's your trade?"

"What trade? You got it all."

"We've been here a while."

"You're sellin' rifles to the Kiowa." Jamie let it be an accusation.

"A painful choice. There were over four hundred robes in it. Excellent robes."

"You change your policy?"

"We do what it takes. But we're always open to an accommodation."

"What's that mean?"

"We'd be happy to guarantee you a profit. That's a fine post."

"This another buyout offer?"

"Partnership. There are advantages to us. You're closer to many bands. You're in Mexico. You've got a Mexican trading license—or you will have."

The Bents had good ears, Jamie thought. They probably had informers all over Santa Fe.

"We'd offer you half the St. Louis value of your goods and stock and wagons for a controlling interest in your southern post. Your company would be a subsidiary of ours. In return, we'd let you open trade with the Cheyenne and Arapaho, and we'd stock your trading rooms better. Guy Straus'd get half his investment back right away, and a guaranteed robe trade. He—and you—would give up fifty-one percent of the company. The profits would be distributed in the same proportion."

William Bent was a likable man, and Jamie didn't mind the dickering. An offer to merge was rare in the fur business, and it meant that the Bents were worried.

"I guess I'll let Guy know," Jamie said.

"Better hurry, Dance."

"Lots of time," said Jamie. But there wasn't. The trading season was half over, and Fort Dance had a couple of hundred robes to show for a heavy investment in trade goods, wagons, livestock, fort furnishings, and wages.

He rode home on the Mexican side, his eyes and ears alert for trouble—an old mountain habit—but with his mind on other things. He was not inclined to work for wages. He never had. He'd almost been a bound boy in Knoxville, but the day his indenture to a cabinetmaker was to begin, he'd fled—and starved. He and Brokenleg Fitzhugh had teamed up in the mountains as free trappers, selling plews to the highest bidders. It chafed now even to be a very junior partner in the Rocky Mountain Company. A sixth interest in the Company didn't give a man much say, and he was bound by Guy Straus's will. If George Bent, the brother back in St. Louis, talked Guy into the deal, then Jamie would find himself a wage man. The whole thing would be decided by powerful men, the Bent brothers, Guy Straus, and probably Robert Campbell, who'd made such a fortune in the beaver days.

Well, by God, he could quit.

That didn't make him feel any better. He'd heard the death knell of Fort Dance there, from William Bent and Goddam Murray. The Bents had corralled all the tribes, including the Kiowa, which left Jamie trade with the one tribe no one wanted to deal with—the bloody Comanches. It filled him with a bleakness even to think about it. They'd just murdered Robert Bent. A couple of years earlier, they'd killed a Bent herder and stolen fifty Bent horses. The year before, the Comanche chief Old Wolf, along with a thousand of his tribe, had come to the fort to make peace with the Cheyenne—and with the Bents. It had lasted not much more than a year, and now the youngest Bent lay in a fresh grave.

That's my sole option, Jamie thought. Trade with a tribe notorious for murder, torture, and perfidy. Trade with a tribe now supplied by cutthroat Comancheros who were as murderous as their trading partners, and were itching to butcher their new rivals.

Still . . . maybe there were things worth trying. They had a United States license to trade with several plains tribes, including Ute, Cheyenne, Arapaho, Pawnee, Kiowa, and Comanche. It was time to send trading wagons north across the river, and do some robe-trading out on the prairies far from the eyes of the Bents. The idea excited him. He'd send David out, with a teamster—Lyle Black, maybe. He'd go himself, with Mazappa Oliphant, and leave Tomás in charge. Up to the Pawnee, over to the Utes, out to the Arapaho, with wagons full of trade goods. If robes didn't come to him, he'd go to the robes!

That cheered him. He hurried his shaggy chestnut along, driven by the biting wind at his back that blistered his ears and whipped over his boots. He plunged through the great cottonwoods forest west of his post and out upon its flat, heartened by the sight of Fort Dance, standing proud. He spotted milling activity there, horses and men. And when he drew close enough to see, he made out the blue uniforms of federal Mexican dragoons.

Colonel Agustino Cortez greeted Jamie effusively. "Ah, it is grand to see you! How fine is your complexion! How healthy you look! How clear are your eyes! How beautiful is the *señora!* How splendid is your progress here—I've been admiring it all!"

"Reckon you have," Jamie said. He'd spotted ten dragoons, a squad, meandering through the post.

"The walls are up; the interior done. You have your Mexican post, Señor Dance. And you've hired *campesinos,* and our acquaintance, Tomás Villanova. You are good for Mexico!"

"If we get any trade," Jamie added, irritably.

"Why, you have two hundred robes. I looked. And many more to come."

"You looked. You bring me a license to trade?"

"Ah, a few difficulties. The application is off to Ciudad Méjico. But don't worry about that. El Zorro is here to make sure that everything goes smoothly—as smooth as a woman's cheek."

A balding bony Mexican in a black clawhammer coat wandered through the yard, surveying the building. He had emerged from the trading room. "Who's that?" Jamie asked, pointing.

"Him? He came with us from Santa Fe. He is Don Francisco . . . Archuleta."

Jamie waited, knowing there'd be more to it. Quite probably, this entire squad had escorted the man here for a purpose.

"He will take only a bit," said El Zorro. "I made sure of it." Jamie waited, dourly.

"He is the impost collector for the province. For Nuevo Mexico. He was sent by the governor. It is a small thing. Provincial taxes—they don't amount to anything. A few beans."

"Armijo's man?"

"Sí. He is adding up the value of your goods and robes and wagons and stock. I have told him, this is a struggling little enterprise. Just starting. A fine competition for those sinister Bents who plot and scheme across the river. We must be gen-

226

tle. El Zorro protected you, Señor Dance. Señor Archuleta, he will not impose much. A little bit. But you should give him a small favor, a sweet, as a way of thanking him."

"How much is a little?"

El Zorro shrugged. *"Nada.* The governor wanted two hundred robes. Two hundred. He said he didn't want to take your merchandise, your trading goods. He didn't want to hurt your trade with the Indians, so he has chosen to take the robes—to tax only the profits, the gain."

"Two hundred robes!"

Cortez lifted his hand, gently. "Ah, Señor Dance. I know how much that hurts. You have barely two hundred robes in your warehouse. I told Don Francisco, two hundred is too much. It should be one hundred fifty. And he agreed. I saved you fifty robes, Señor Dance."

Jamie didn't feel very grateful. "I thought we'd paid our imposts when you took all them rifles and powder and shot."

"Ah, Señor Dance, that was the *federal* impost. We took the arms for federal purposes of course. It is duly recorded in Ciudad Méjico that you are paid in full. I myself saw to it. As a little partner in the enterprise, I wanted to make sure the officials understood."

Under the guidance of Archuleta, dragoons were hauling two bales of robes out of the warehouse, and lashing them to the back of a big mule. They made a heavy load, and the mule shifted its feet to accept it. An anger rose in Jamie. He spotted David over at the warehouse, looking helpless, his face screwed into a scowl. Tomás had made himself scarce.

"Maybe we'd have preferred to pay with a draft on Saint Louis!"

El Zorro shrugged. "It is up to the impost collector. I have done what I could."

"You're fixin' to haul away our robes!"

"El gobernador prefers the robes. He sent instructions to collect in robes."

"That's because they're worth less hyar, and he can git more in Saint Louis."

"I am at your service, *amigo.* Come, let us examine your defenses here. You know, I am a military man and I view

227

such things with a professional eye. Now take these walls. With your twenty or thirty men — *campesinos,* your workers, your, ah, guests — how will you defend these long walls . . . and the herds? I have come to offer you a small service. I must tell you, Dance, that you can't. You could be overwhelmed. You need bastions in the corners. And a pair of six-pounders to rake the field."

Jamie glowered. "I suppose you'll build them for me, and find me the cannon too."

Cortez looked hurt. "I might. I might. I have ways. I can't do it just now. But I am a little partner, yes? Maybe I can, soon. Trust El Zorro. I will have to locate two cannon, but I know where there are many. A little gift or two, and I will have two brass cannon for you. Trust El Zorro!"

"Whoa up!" Jamie exclaimed. He didn't want any more trouble than he had. Especially in the form of a couple of cannon purloined from the federal army. "*Coronel,* no cannon."

El Zorro gazed mournfully at him. "I am here to help."

"We'll deal with trouble as it comes."

Cortez sighed. "It is a poor defense. You need more. How will you save the livestock?"

"This yard will hold them. We got a well dug now."

Archuleta approached, bearing papers. "*Por favor, Señor Dance?*"

The tax man wanted his signature. Embarrassed, Jamie summoned David. "He's my clerk," Jamie muttered. "You mind readin' and figurin' and seein' it all came out right?" he asked David.

Irritably, David studied the documents, and then stalked to the company offices. He returned a moment later and handed the papers to the tax man, being a little rude about it.

They stood there in the sunny yard, David and Jamie, Archuleta and El Zorro. The dragoons led ten loaded packmules out of the post. It grew silent.

El Zorro coughed. Jamie knew something was expected, but didn't quite know what. "Ah, Señor Dance. Don Francisco has performed a great service out of the kindness of his heart. . . ."

Then Jamie knew. The *mordida.* The sweets. He turned

abruptly toward the trading room, with his guests dogging his heels.

Inside the gloomy room, he waited, while El Zorro and Don Francisco wandered along tables, eyed burlap bags, studied shelves, examined implements hanging from pegs. Tomás watched gleefully, his eyes speaking sentences to Jamie, his lips curled into a happy smirk.

"Bienvenido a Méjico," he said, and snorted into a handkerchief.

Jamie slouched into a wall near the fireplace and waited. Eventually Don Francisco smiled, slid out the door, and returned with a dragoon, and pointed. The dragoon lifted a fifty-pound sack of coffee beans and hefted it out to the waiting packmules.

"Mil gracias, Señor Dance. You are a generous man and a true patriot," said Don Francisco, baring long, yellow, rodent teeth.

El Zorro fondled merchandise, fingered fabrics, and pointed at last to a bolt of lustrous brown taffeta. "For the ladies," he said, rubbing his mustachios. "For the beautiful girls." He laughed pleasantly, and lifted his booty from the shelves.

Tomás laughed softly. Jamie was ready to kill him.

"Hasta luego, compadres," the colonel said.

"Not soon I hope," muttered Jamie in English. He followed the colonel out. The dragoons sat smartly on their mounts in a column of twos. A moment later the armed might of Mexico trotted south, up the Río de las Ánimas, the River of Souls.

Jamie stormed back in. "What did that cost?" he snarled.

David, alarmed, pawed through papers looking for prices.

"Never mind. I know," Jamie snapped. The coffee came to fifty dollars in trade; the full bolt of taffeta came to twice that. Plus a hundred fifty robes for the governor's empty purse, at an eastern wholesale price of about four dollars apiece.

Tomás chortled. "First payment," he said.

Jamie felt a sudden chill run through him. There'd be more. And they didn't even have a license. Every robe they traded amounted to an illegal act.

He stood, surveying his colleagues. "We've got around fifty

robes out thar. We've lost a fortune. We're going under unless we pull in three thousand robes—yes, that many at least—between now and next May. Reckon four thousand'd be more like it for starters. And no one's comin' hyar. So we're going out thar. Tomorrah, I'm taking a wagon and heading across the river and north. David, tomorrah you're taking a wagon across and heading east. We'll get us some robes or lose us some scalps doin' it."

CHAPTER 23

Jamie sat his horse on a lonely swell of prairie, watching a circling column of raptors a mile away. Something had died over there. He waited for Lyle Black to bring the wagon up and have a look. A quarter of a mile back, Lyle walked beside the two yoke of oxen, cussing them along. The wagon contained a load of carefully selected trade goods, and some camping gear.

Lyle halted the slobbering oxen at the crest, and stared at the circling birds and the indistinct something on the ground.

"It sure don't look good," he said.

Jamie agreed. They turned the wagon east, and rode across a scooped dish of shortgrass prairie, brown in the winter light. The something before them gradually emerged as an abandoned *carreta*, laden with spoiling meat — and a raft of crows, hawks, and lesser birds. But it was not the cart that caught their eye. Nearby lay two human bodies.

Jamie spurred his horse ahead, and found himself staring at two of his own *ciboleros*, García and Roja. Both lay naked and spread-eagled, their limbs bound by thong and staked to the earth. Dead. Only sockets remained where their eyes had been. Coyotes had chewed on Roja's leg. But they hadn't been dead long, hadn't decomposed.

"Jesus," whispered Black.

"Comanche, maybe," said Jamie, suddenly restless and half-desperate. Their wagon was a beacon for any eye within three or four miles. He felt pity for these two, his own meat hunters, caught and murdered in this lonesome place.

"Have we a shovel?" he asked, knowing the answer.

231

Black shrugged.

"Help me," said Jamie. He cut the thongs, meaning to gather the two dead men and make some kind of grave from the *carreta*. But each man remained rigidly spread-eagled, and there was little they could do. Nothing belonging to these two remained: no clothing, weapons, or gear.

"We'd better git back," Jamie said.

"I'm ahead of you," said Black.

They turned toward the fort, with Black staying as much as possible in the hollows of the prairie to keep out of sight, while Jamie halted before each slight rise and crawled to the crest to peer into the beyond, his stomach crawling with terror. But the day remained serene and peaceful, and gave no hint of murder on its wind.

Jamie's mind worked feverishly, wondering whether he could sight the Comanches before they found him — and whether it would do the slightest good. Two men, two rifles against . . . what? After awhile they struck a dry watercourse that led southward toward the Arkansas. They slid down into it, and soon it deepened enough so they were below horizons much of the time, out of sight. It seemed scant protection.

Jamie worried about David and Mazappa in the other wagon, and cursed himself for sending them out to trade just now. But there was nothing he could do. A helplessness settled over him. Mazappa was no greenhorn. He could read whatever there was to read. Still, the foreboding snatched at him and possessed his mind. The day remained perfidiously serene under the low winter sun. He rode ahead frequently, and then crawled up slopes to survey the murderous world outside of the long draw — and found nothing. He realized once that he was sweating, though the temperature wasn't much above freezing.

At the Arkansas, about midway between Bent's Fort and Fort Dance, they stumbled upon another horror. The same thing all over again: two of his *ciboleros*, an abandoned *carreta*. These two had died more recently, as recently as a few hours ago and the carrion birds had yet to find them. They hadn't been tortured, either. They lay naked, their throats cut, their necks bloody, their tongues hanging out, their brown eyes sightless. Terror sifted through

Jamie, and then pity. Two more of his own men!

"Lyle, climb up a little and keep lookin' around. We can't bury these two, but I can pull 'em up and lay some of that stone over them."

"We don't have time, Jamie."

"I reckon we do. We're almost on the Santy Fe trail hyar. People comin' by."

"Who?" retorted Black, his gaze darting nervously from one horizon to the other.

"We'll take them. It's maybe six miles," Jamie said. He hated it; hated to lift those two sagging bodies and slide them onto the dropped tailgate. But he did. These, at least, he could bury at the post — if they ever got there. None of the four murdered *ciboleros* had been married. He had no messages to bring to widows. But he took no comfort in it. Four hunters dead. It dawned on him suddenly that there might be a method in it — starving the post. He boiled up with rage against the Bents, and then let it escape. It wasn't the work of the Bents. Starving the post. He knew, suddenly, just *knew*, what David and Mazappa were likely to find off to the east.

Lyle watched him silently, waiting for instructions. Intuitively, Jamie decided to cross the river and slip into the post from the south. These marauding Comanche — or whoever — were on the north side . . . for now. Perhaps.

"I'll look for a ford," he said.

He rode toward the river, Lyle following with the oxen and wagon, the both of them wrestling with terror every step. He found a good ford a half a mile east, a sandy bottom. They crossed without trouble and headed toward the post across a naked land that did not hide them. Jamie catfooted his horse toward every copse of brush along the riverbank, his hands sweaty over his Hawken. A crow erupted from brush ahead, and his heart exploded into a throbbing race.

Four ciboleros. Maybe the butchers weren't Comanche, even though a favorite Comanche torture had been used. His post was vulnerable. He couldn't even man the parapets properly with his twenty or so men, much less send buffalo hunting parties out for food. They could be starved out.

Nothing happened. When they reached the dense cotton-

233

woods near the confluence of the Purgatoire they swung south, avoiding the trail through the gloomy timbers. Nothing happened. They raised Fort Dance a half hour later, hulking somnolently in the winter sun. Jamie dared hope. Lyle hawed and cussed the muttering oxen into a faster walk, and the beasts strained into their yokes, whipping the lumbering Conestoga along. Half a mile more.

Movement caught Jamie's eye. Another wagon, with a rider on horseback across the Purgatoire, careening down a gentle grade toward the river. The crack of a lash echoed on the breeze. David and Mazappa! And behind them, riding them down, horsemen!

They'd never make it. And no one at the post had spotted them or could help them in time.

Jamie yelled at Lyle. "Git on in. I got ta help."

He spurred his tired chestnut into a lope toward the Purgatoire, cut through its thick bankside wall of brush using a game trail, splashed across the shallow creek into another wall of brush he couldn't penetrate, and finally slid off his horse and left it there in the riverbed.

He heard shots. He pushed through brush, crouching low, and emerged into the open valley just as the wagon careened downslope, Mazappa whipping the frothing oxen. David raced forward on horseback, clutching his rifle.

"Hyar!" Jamie roared.

David raced toward him. "Git acrost and git help. Leave me yer rifle."

David pushed his sweat-soaked mount through brush and into the creek. Riders swarmed down the slope, a dozen, fifteen, heading straight for the wagon.

Jamie lifted David's Leman rifle first, settled the sight on a rider who was aiming at Mazappa, and fired. The rider threw up his arms. His rifle catapulted away. Red blossomed across a shoulder.

Mazappa spotted Jamie and whipped the oxen toward the Purgatoire. Jamie settled his Hawken into his shoulder and let himself quiet down. Each shot mattered. He waited, feeling his pulse throb into his fingers and spoil his aim. Then he tracked a horseman—a horseman wearing a peaked sombrero—and

234

squeezed. The loping horse faltered, shivered, stumbled, and slowly collapsed, spilling the rider.

Now he had two empty rifles. He stuffed powder from his horn down the barrel, not bothering to measure, and plucked a patch and ball from his possibles and rammed them home with his hickory rod, and finally flicked off the old cap and slid a new one over the nipple. Mazappa abandoned the lumbering wagon and ran toward Jamie. Shots racketed. One skinned past Mazappa, catching clothing, spinning him.

Mazappa saw Jamie reloading, and dove down close beside him, their backs to the wall of saltbush.

"Comancheros," muttered Mazappa.

They were galloping toward the wagon. Jamie jammed his Hawken into his shoulder, peered down the octagonal barrel, taking his time, and shot. The ball pierced the withers of a horse. It shrieked and bucked, spilling its rider.

Mazappa shot while Jamie reloaded. They knew the rhythm; knew never to have two empty rifles at once. Shots plucked around them now, and Jamie crabbed back into the brush. Mazappa did too. Mazappa reloaded furiously. The oxen lumbered through brush, smashing it, while the wagon careened and scraped behind them, and then stopped squarely in the creek, the wagon tilted awkwardly, water flowing through its wheel spokes.

Good! Jamie thought. The Comancheros swarmed in now, making it too hot for Jamie and Mazappa. They slid backward into the wall of brush, hearing balls whip through it with ripping sounds, severing leaves and stalks. From the rear he heard shouting and shots — Lyle and David had gotten some help together. A horse and rider plunged through brush nearby, and into the creek water. Jamie shot him point-blank. The hombre sighed, coughed blood, and slid into the murky water, staining it red. The straw sombrero hit the current and drifted north.

Staccato Spanish. Jamie translated pieces of it. "Get out. They're coming. We can't get the wagon." He heard the clatter of hooves, the press of horses squeezing through brush, the murmur of war, and then the Comancheros dashed south, followed by shots from the rescue party.

"Hyar we are," Jamie shouted. A moment later his own men

235

swarmed into the bottoms around the wagon and oxen, while others pursued the fleeing Comancheros on foot.

Jamie and Mazappa stood warily.

"Run into trouble," Mazappa said. "Yonder a few miles. We was lookin' at a pair of our hunters, them two that usually head toward the Big Timbers. They'd got their gullets sawed in two. I sniffed trouble, and figgered we'd better git, so we gat. Left 'em there, and lucky we did. They jumped us a mile off. Reckon we owe ya."

Jamie sighed. "Same story, only we found the other four. They killed every hunter on the post, Mazappa, and they'll get any we send out. And I don't suppose we got meat enough for a day around hyar."

Jamie trudged wearily back to the post, feeling the heat of his rifle barrel scald his palm, even as fear scalded his muscles. At the gates a wagon sagged, and knotted around it was a crowd. He knew what they were staring at, dead men lying inert on the tailgate. The two *ciboleros* with their throats cut were not a pretty sight. He saw Juanita Chávez chase away Rosa and Juan. This was not for children's eyes.

Comancheros! he thought. His rivals for the Comanche trade, systematically murdering the post hunters, starving Fort Dance. These wild hombres were waging war, using surprise and assassination. Slaughtering men engaged in innocent pursuits. A fight with no quarter, waged by stalking anyone who came to or left Fort Dance. And at stake, the prize — a mountain of trade goods to barter to their Comanche friends. Jamie knew he had an enemy, and knew the Comancheros were implacable and deadly.

He veered toward David, who was also walking back to the post. "Tell me about them," he demanded.

David glanced at him sharply. "There were fourteen, led by Benito — I've told you about him. They were well armed. Sidearms, new rifles, knives. Riding fine horses — faster than any of ours. Lots of mules and burros. They're not . . . not civilized. They'd kill anyone. For sport. For a penny. I . . . thought I would die."

Jamie nodded. He didn't doubt that these brigands could whip his teamsters in any sort of pitched battle. And was certain they could influence their Comanche allies easily.

At the wagon, Juan Cordova and Pepe Alvaro were gently lifting the *ciboleros* off the tailgate and onto the hard clay. Luis Soto arranged their limbs, and folded their hands over their chests and brushed their eyes closed. Oso Valdez wept. He had been a good friend of these two. There'd be a funeral soon, not just for these two, but for six. Six! Fidel Santa María emerged from the gates carrying two shovels, and soon enough there'd be new graves beside that of Abel Cannon, at the edge of the cottonwoods.

Back at the Purgatoire, the rest of the men had freed the other freighter and were whipping the exhausted yokes of oxen toward the post. Restlessly Jamie scanned the horizons, looking for more trouble and seeing none. Winter wind sliced through them all, flapping clothing.

Jamie got hold of Pony Gantt. "Put these oxen into the post yard. The horse too. And the ones coming in."

It would cost them some precious prairie hay, but it would keep some of the stock safe, he thought.

"Por favor, Señor Dance." Jamie turned to find Hector Chávez at his elbow.

"Señor Dance . . . we are worried about Manolo."

Manolo! The twelve-year-old son of the Chávezes who herded each day. Alone out with the stock! Out a mile to the southwest, maybe more.

"I'll go look," he said, dread filling him. "Lyle—get a horse and come along."

A few moments later he and Lyle Black rode out to a hinterland of grass where the fort's oxen, horses, and mules found adequate pasture. Each day, fair weather or fierce, the smiling boy drove the stock out to good grass and lounged there, watching puffball clouds, eating a tamale for his lunch, keeping a sharp eye on predators—and two-legged thieves. Each sunset, he patiently walked the herd back to the post and corralled it. It had been a man's work, cheerfully offered.

A foreboding filled Jamie as they trotted south and west, angling away from the Purgatoire. Fifteen minutes later they still had not sighted the herd. Twenty minutes later they found where it had grazed that day; the manure still green, and even warm. And there, on a barren patch, lay Manolo.

"Oh, God," muttered Lyle as they raced toward the lump of human flesh. Little Manolo lay on his back, lifeless, his brown eyes studying the universe, his throat cut. They'd murdered a boy. And stolen the entire herd.

Jamie fought back the impulse to vomit that rolled hotly up from his bowels, and then fought back an impulse to spur his horse into a gallop and murder the murderers, one by one. They couldn't be far ahead. Instead, he forced down his gorge and slid off his weary chestnut. Lyle said nothing, his eyes studying every horizon, his rifle at the ready.

Jamie picked up Manolo, wondering at the lightness of the youth, and lowered him across the saddle on his stomach. Blood slid from the cut throat, and trickled down the boy's cheek and into the boy's hair. The chestnut shied nervously, not liking the smell of blood. Jamie walked back, leading the horse, feeling a wintery wind slash through his fringed elkskin coat, slice down his throat like a butcher knife. Lyle walked his horse beside him, his gaze restless and his mouth pressed thin.

Jamie dreaded what was to come; Hector and Juanita seeing the horse with its awful burden; the tears, the agony, the digging of yet another ditch into the hard cold clay . . . and not a priest to comfort them—except Tomás. Tomás the false priest, who would soon perform a very real office of a priest.

Seven people murdered this time . . . so far. Not by Comanche or Kiowa, but by Comancheros who traded with both tribes. War, then. Jamie would take it to them, fight it across the prairies and arroyos, along the creeks and beside the springs, from the *playas* to the mountains. He'd root them out; he'd hunt through every village and *placita;* he'd find them. He'd find this Benito, a man he'd never seen but already knew perfectly. He'd come here to trade peacefully, to earn profits, not to war. There was something about trading that he liked. It benefited both parties to the transaction. He wanted a robe; they wanted a blanket or gunpowder or vermilion. He liked that, liked the sweetness of it. But now war was forced on him, and if that was the way of it, he'd take it to them.

Hector and Juanita didn't weep. They stared solemnly at the body of their son, as silently as statues, until Jamie wished they would sob. Their grief was worse than any Jamie had experienced, made worse by their stiff, erect postures, the lift of their jaws, and their obliviousness of the brutal wind that cut through them. Jamie watched them, amazed and anguished. Fort Dance had claimed seven that day, including a sunny boy.

No, not Fort Dance, he told himself. The fort hadn't killed them. The Rocky Mountain Company hadn't killed them.

Late that afternoon they gathered around the wide grave, where all three sheet-shrouded bodies lay. Tomás did not apologize for being less than an ordained priest. Instead, he buried the dead gently, using whatever rites he chose, while Hector stood bareheaded, and Juanita, wrapped in a thick blanket, stood shrouded beside him. Then Cordova and Trujillo threw the yellow clay upon the bodies until the earth swallowed them, and the small crowd dissipated into a bitter night.

Jamie ached. The day had been long and brutal. But his restless spirit demanded more, and so he quietly saddled his unhappy chestnut in the shrouded dark of the yard, while Teresa María and David and Tomás and the rest watched him solemnly, then let himself out of the gates and into the blackness.

He turned the chestnut south, letting it walk quietly to husband its failing energies, and followed the Purgatoire, which became a black mass of brush on his left. He hadn't paused to eat, but he wasn't hungry. Nightwind out of the north sliced into him, numbing his neck. It'd be worse riding back. He let the horse pick its way along the bottoms, over gullies, around rare copses of trees, ever southward. Two hours and seven miles later he topped a gentle rise well above the riverbed, and beheld what he had come to see; what he knew he would see. Stretching along the Purgatoire were a hundred or a hundred fifty dull lights glowing dim and orange. He counted them swiftly. The night air was transparent, each glowing light distinct. Over a hundred fifty. A large village. Nearly a thousand. He couldn't see the horse herd, but knew he was dangerously close and his scent, whipped southward, might be picked up by the horses, which would alert the herders.

He knew the fort's herd would be there. He knew the Comancheros would be there too. And he knew he stared at a village of the deadly Comanche. It harbored a small band of Comancheros, also deadly, carrying with them stories of conquest; of a weakly defended post loaded with riches, a post growing hungrier by the hour.

He turned and rode home, into the wind, the air so fierce it made the ride seem uphill, like the slope of a mountain. He couldn't escape the wind, not even when he twisted sideways in his saddle and let the air quarter down. It was like life. No matter how he twisted in his saddle, life blew through him, sliced him, numbed him. He wondered what tomorrow would bring. Robes or death or neither. He and his twenty or so armed men would succumb to any serious assault on the post by a few hundred Indians. But it might not come to that. Out in those cowhide lodges were countless robes, exquisitely tanned, the very wealth the Rocky Mountain Company sought. Robes or death. Tomorrow would bring one or the other.

CHAPTER 24

That cold dawn, Jamie told them all what he'd seen. His own men took the news somberly. His teamsters each had a rifle, but of the Mexican employees, only Tomás and Hector had one. The post could muster only a dozen rifles to defend four walls.

"We're not in the war business; we're here to trade with the Comanche, and I reckon that's what we'll do," he said, to reassure them. But if the Comancheros were stirring up the Comanche, he doubted there'd be much trading. There was a possibility, of course, that the village he'd seen at night wasn't Comanche—but he discounted it.

The old Missouri squawman, Pickett, eyed Jamie and spat. "They got my hoss? They got all our hosses?"

Jamie nodded.

"I reckon I'll git me over to Bents," he said.

Ramón Sánchez and another fort loafer, a breed called Cajones, decided to join him.

"We need you," said Jamie.

Pickett spat again. "Reckon you do. Only I ain't gonna be nowhere around."

Jamie wanted to say maybe they owed some help, but clamped his mouth shut. The three loafers gathered up their kits and slipped out through the gates into a bitter dawn. Three more valuable riflemen gone, Jamie thought. He watched them cut north at a swift walk, almost a trot, and vanish into the cottonwoods.

"Glad you enjoyed our hospitality," he yelled after them.

They didn't hear him. And even if they had heard, they wouldn't register his barb. Some men lived like that; parasites who took and never gave, and never knew themselves to be losers.

David shut the heavy gates and barred them. Jamie peered around at his thoroughly frightened men. They had plenty to fear. The post had no corner bastions to defend the walls, no cannon loaded with grapeshot. Not even crenelated walls to protect riflemen. It could be overwhelmed by several hundred Comanche warriors in minutes—especially with the Comancheros egging the Indians on and picking off the post's men with their excellent rifles. Jamie didn't have much going for him. But I have a little, he thought. The Comanche weren't much for sieges. They were great horse warriors. He had a well, and he had eight oxen inside the post for meat. He had the fortified watchtower over the gates, which would help. Riflemen could shoot from the four vertical window slits.

One good thing, anyway. The loafers would notify the Bents. It would take them six or seven hours to walk there, and four hours for relief on horseback to return—assuming Bent's men wanted to tackle an entire Comanche village. The prospects chilled Jamie more than the frosty dawn did.

"All right," he said bleakly, "let's fort up."

He directed his men to build barricades in the yard to shelter men shooting at the gates; to take poles up to the roofs, where they could be used to knock away assault ladders. His men worked listlessly, sensing the futility of it.

He turned to the women and children. "Find some thin poles, your brooms maybe, and make them look like rifle barrels. Rub ash into 'em, or if that don't work, scorch or smoke 'em. Get hats from the trading room so you look like men. Make 'em think we got ten, twelve more rifles than we got. But if trouble comes, you git. You git into a storeroom and hunker thar."

He repeated it in Spanish after they stared at him blankly. "And you get buckets o' water set around the roofwalk. And you get a hospital set up, water and bandages."

He hated it. Hated warring with the tribe he needed to trade

242

with. The whole business pulled and tugged at him—wanting to befriend these dangerous people, wanting to smoke the pipe and trade for robes . . . and wanting to survive if it came to that. It was the Comancheros, he thought. Stirring up all the trouble they could. Ruthlessly planning to destroy their competition. And competition was exactly what The Rocky Mountain Company would give them. The Comancheros were poor. They had a little Santa Fe iron to trade, that and a few serapes and slaves. Nothing like the array of goods nestled in the post trading room. Jamie knew what they'd do: while the Comanches were busy torturing and slaughtering, the Comancheros would pillage the trading room and warehouse. Eventually, the Comancheros would possess the post.

He climbed up to the watchtower over the gates and peered out the slit windows restlessly. He could see in every direction from this perch. An icy lavender dawn slowly wrestled the night away. White hoarfrost covered the prairies, giving the illusion of snow. A profound silence lay upon the cold world. Nothing moved, not even a bird.

Tomás slid in beside him. "It is like the old days in the mountains, *sí*? Only we didn't have walls then, just the mountains. And a hundred Utes looking for us. We still have our scalps. Maybe I'll lose mine here, *sí*?"

"I'm thinkin' to bribe 'em if I have to."

Tomás laughed. "Not with this Benito around."

"I'm thinkin' on it," Jamie repeated shortly.

"Think hard, *amigo*. Me, I am looking for a priest to hear my deathbed confession and give me extreme unction."

Jamie didn't laugh. "Tomás, listen. Get a couple kettles from the trading room. Fill them half full, maybe three-quarters full, and pitch in a twist o' tobacca into each one, and git some red peppers and drop a few in, and tea, and mix it up till the water's yeller as piss. Then carry 'em over to the gates. Just leave 'em like that. No spirits yet."

Tomás stared and guffawed, his thick spectacles bobbing on his nose as he wheezed. "Don Jamie, maybe you'll bribe them. Maybe not. Maybe you'll make them loco, make it worse for us."

"You got any better ideas?"

Tomás didn't.

The winter sun crept coyly from its nest to the southeast and gilded the hoarfrost. Down below, Tomás was doing Jamie's bidding. Two brass kettles were filled partway with well water, the ingredients thrown in. Men watched with knowing eyes, and found hope in this. Or fear.

But nothing broke the silence. Jamie smelled coffee below, and knew Emilio had put together a breakfast. An ox bawled, wanting hay. He watched Lyle Black spear prairie hay from an emergency stack in the robe warehouse, and feed the eight beasts.

From his perch up in the watchtower, he scanned the horizons once again, and this time saw movement. Not the passage of a village, but the passage of a few horsemen on the far side of the Purgatoire. He had his Hawken and the company fowling piece with him. But these horsemen were half a mile away, and staying well out of range as they leisurely rode north.

He made out the Comancheros. This time of year they didn't wear their peaked straw sombreros but old felt hats or buffalo-hide caps. A wintry glint of metal bounced off their rifle barrels. His own rifle glinted too. These desperados had murdered six *ciboleros* and a boy. Let one — just one — come into range of his heavy, octagon-barreled Hawken!

One did, at last, bearing a white flag. Jamie respected it, although he didn't feel like doing it. Let the butcher have his say. The horseman splashed across the Purgatoire and paused hesitantly at the edge of the flats, within rifle range. Jamie's men had spotted him, and peered over the east wall of the post.

"Let him come," Jamie said quietly.

The Comanchero yelled across the silence. "*Señores.* We will talk, yes?"

"Come ahead," Jamie yelled back.

David materialized at his side. "Benito — their *capitán*," he whispered. "I'd know him anywhere."

Jamie peered down upon a short, fat man, warmly dressed, edging his shaggy black horse closer. Just beyond the river, his *compañeros* had spread out, their rifles poking upward, no doubt at the post men lining the parapets.

"*Señores*. Who do I have the honor of talking to?"

"Dance."

"Ah, Dance. *El capitán*. We will be partners, *sí?* Together we will trade with the Comanche."

Jamie didn't say anything.

"Partners. Half for us—half for you."

"*Adiós*," said Jamie.

Benito laughed nasally. "Ah, you will think about it. The Comanche are *amigos*. They don't like white men."

Jamie didn't respond. Let the butcher talk. Jamie knew up in the watchtower he was barely visible to the Comanchero chieftain. It was a small advantage.

"You have something we need—many trading goods. We have something you need. Life, *señores*, life. We will be partners."

"I hear that a lot in Mexico."

Benito laughed. "It is so, *sí?*"

"Get on with it, or get shot."

The squat man on the pony just shouting distance away turned still and eyed the riflemen along the wall.

"*Señores*. A great village of Comanche is near. Most of the Comanche nation. Two thousand. Maybe four hundred warriors, *sí?* This place—it is nothing against so many."

"Reckon we'll trade, then."

Benito chortled. "They are saying, why trade? They can climb your walls and take what they want, *sí?*"

"With your help."

"*Sí, sí*. It is so. We can help you too. We will be your partners and help defend the walls, and then we will share the trade."

"Forget it, Benito. Comanches ain't much for a siege."

"Ah, but Comancheros are. Your walls are naked. You have twelve rifles."

"More than that, and help's comin'."

Benito laughed. "Help. Why would the Bents help? How many Bents would come against four hundred warriors?"

"It ain't four hundred, Benito. I saw maybe a hundred fifty lodges."

245

Benito laughed until he seemed to shake. "You have a good eye. We have a good eye. We can count. But *señores*, this help . . . it is not coming."

Jamie said nothing, suspecting what had happened. It sickened him.

"It is a good day to die, *sí?* And for what? *Nada.*"

"Go tell the chief we'll trade, have a smoke. We want robes. They want knives and pots and blankets."

"He do not like white men. The Bents treat him bad. Insult the Comanche. The Bents won't trade rifles or powder or shot. Won't let Comanche into the fort for a smoke. But we can make a little arrangement, *sí?* For a price. We have offered our services, *señores*. Live or die."

"Your services add up to cut throats, Benito. No one's lettin' you in hyar. Not now, not ever."

The man appeared to be hurt. "Ah, Capitán Dance. You do not trust me. We came here to be partners and save your lives, and you insult us. Together, we are strong against the Comanches."

"That graveyard's all I need to know, Benito. We'll have us a smoke when them Comanche come. Talk it over a while. They're wanting to trade robes, I figure."

"You think help comes, eh?" Benito turned and untied a heavy dark-stained sack he carried behind him, its bottom black with something.

The *capitán* lifted it and then emptied it onto the frosty clay. Three heavy spheres dropped out, and bounced. Spheres with hair and bloody necks. The heads of Sánchez, Cajones, and Pickett. Benito laughed wildly, wheeled his black horse, and raced out of range before a single man in the post could tear his gaze away from that ghastly sight.

So little time. Down in the yard, barricades went up facing the gates. Every likely broomstick and pole was blackened to look like a rifle barrel. Trade hatchets and axes were fitted with handles and given to those Mexican employees who lacked firearms. It seemed pitiful to Jamie, but it was at least something.

David worried him. The youth stood in the yard, pale and paralyzed, death haunting his face. Some of the others seemed almost as frightened. Juanita Chávez went about her work with tears coursing down her brown cheeks; Manolo's death, and now this. Even the more determined had a doomsday look about them. The ones whittling handles to fit into hatchet heads went about it listlessly, as if it were all an exercise in futility. The very word, *Comanche*, brought despair into their souls.

Jamie left Lyle in the watchtower above the gates, and clambered down to the roofs lying below the parapets, then down a rough rawhide-bound ladder to the yard.

"Hyar now," he said, catching as many as he could with a loud voice. "We're not going to fight; we're going to trade for robes. But we'll put up a little show of force. Them black sticks'll give us another dozen rifles, far as they're concerned. They won't be so eager to tackle twenty-five, thirty rifles behind high walls."

That didn't seem to comfort anyone. Fear of the Comanche, blanked out reason — and hope. "They're comin' in to trade," he insisted, and got nowhere. He realized his people had lost this battle even before it began, and saw these minutes as their last.

"All right," he said. "You that got rifles, if it comes to fightin', leave them Comanch alone and aim for the Comancheros. They're the ones puttin' steel to tinder. They're the ones fillin' them Comanch with notions of looting this hyar place. That's my word, and I want it followed. Get them Comancheros. And no shootin' until I say it. Our best hope is tradin' and smokin' the pipe. If some fool fires his piece, he's likely to end up a scalp danglin' from a lance."

No one said anything, but at least they were listening.

"We ain't after the Comanche. We want to trade robes. But we're after them murderin' butcherin' Comancheros."

Again, silence. He wished someone would talk, laugh, cheer, whoop. But death loomed too close for anything like that. More than one man was making his peace with God off in some corner. Even Tomás, that mocking scholar, seemed pale and withdrawn. And David. He wondered if David might do some fool thing and start a war they didn't have to have.

They did everything they could think of to prepare, and still the wintry day lay silent. From the watchtower, though, Jamie could see shadowy Comancheros surrounding the whole post, hovering in the cottonwoods north and west; lingering up and down the Purgatoire just out of effective range. He got to planning a little sally to drive them off. He wasn't cut out for a siege, any more than the Comanches.

Then around midday, the vanguard of the village appeared in the south, a body of horsemen in blankets, warriors leading the procession. And following it, innumerable ponies dragging travois loaded with lodges and poles and the infirm; pack burros and horses laden with food and robes and parfleches full of household items. They snaked forward in an unending line—squaws, children, old people, all flanked by those powerful, stocky warriors who made the Comanche nation the most dreaded on the plains. The warriors—and the Comancheros—directed them onto the vast flat east of the Purgatoire—a bad sign. This enormous village would not camp in the peaceful shadow of the post, but far out of range of its rifles. The empty flats nearby would be either the scene of struggle, or an awful no man's land.

It took hours for the village to reach its destination. Travois after travois, by the dozen, the score, the hundred, deposited lodgepoles and smoked cowhide lodgecovers over there. The pony herd arrived, two or three thousand strong, guarded by innumerable young men in buckskin leggins and blouses. Some wore blanket capotes. The herd itself, pride of the Comanche nation, spread out for miles, as far south as Jamie could see. This tribe lived with horses, did things on horseback that were beyond the skills of any other tribe. They knew horses, loved them, counted them as wealth, and considered them war power. Any one of the young men could ride one at full gallop, with no saddle at all, and duck under the neck of the charging animal and shoot an arrow accurately, protected from rifle fire by the horse itself. The warriors could circle the post, he knew, firing steadily at his riflemen up above, and not offer much of a target, except for expendable horseflesh.

That was one reason he didn't want his riflemen wasting

shots on Comanches. One of many reasons. Kill just one, and all chance of peaceful trade would vanish. But kill a Comanchero, and the chance for peace would increase . . . he guessed. No one could know how it'd go. He confessed it was all just a notion.

They weren't in any hurry at all, almost as if they knew they had their quarry surrounded and helpless. Lodgepoles rose like a forest on the far side of the creek. First, the squaws set up a tripod of three lodgepoles bound together. The rest of the poles were fitted into the tripod. And then the lodgecovers were wrestled up by two or more women, a hard, frustrating task. That cone of leather was pinned together with green-wood wands, through holes made for the purpose, and the lodge staked to the clay. Then the women tied the inner liner in place within, pinned it down with stones they gathered from the distant outcrops, and set up the ears or smokeflaps with special poles. Finally coveys of squaws wandered toward the Arkansas to hunt firewood.

Yellow and gray curs whirled among the rising cones, barking and snarling. Warriors tied their favorite war ponies to their lodges, and idled away the time while their women slaved. All of them eyed the adobe post curiously—and the lonely fields of pounded clay and beaten grass that lay to all sides of it.

Jamie peered around and found that somehow small parties of warriors had circled the post and now sat their ponies a rifle-shot away in every direction. He sighed. No one inside the post was going anywhere. It'd all play out right here, in Fort Dance. It oppressed him. The silence within his post had turned even deeper, and had a tinge of terror to it now.

He reckoned he might cash in, but he'd make it plumb hard on whoever was doing it. Benito. He wanted the Comanchero *capitán*. That was all he wanted. Those grisly heads still lay out about fifty yards from the front gate, an obscenity that seemed to prevent trade or peace or a smoke with the headmen.

He turned to Lyle. "Cover me. I'm gonna git them heads."

Black muttered something unintelligible. Jamie clambered down to the yard, and let himself out while his men stared. The heads were out fifty yards; no warrior stood closer than two hundred. No one stopped him. He squinted at the saltbush, at the staring tribesmen beyond the river. His heartbeat lifted, as if readying for a run. He'd left his rifle at the gate. He'd need both hands. He reached the heads at last, and swallowed down his gorge. They were the heads of men he'd talked to just that morning. Dead eyes mocked him. Severed necks revealed gray windpipes. He grabbed Pickett by his greasy hair, and found the head heavy. He got Cajones next, and then Sánchez, two heavy burdens in one hand pulling him to the right. Then he walked slowly toward the gate, feeling his back prickle. He knew he'd hear a shout if trouble rose.

He made the gate and set his grisly burden down in the yard, while men slammed the giant doors behind him.

"Bury these," he said to no one in particular, and climbed up the wobbling ladders to the watchtower. He found himself trembling.

"Why?" asked Lyle Black.

"Keepin' us from trading. Too much war lying out there."

It seemed an odd thing to do, and he wondered why he'd done it. But when he peered out of the slit window onto that meadow it seemed clean again, blank as a white page.

"I don't see it," said Lyle. "But maybe you showed 'em we're tough."

"I wasn't tough. I was about to lose my vittles."

"Maybe them Comanch'll see it their way—brave."

The talk made Jamie angry.

"Was it for them? I mean, Pickett and Cajones and Sánchez? I mean . . . dammit, was you doing it for them?"

"Naw. They run out on us." But Jamie thought maybe it was for them. From the slit window peering over the yard, he could see men hastily digging a pit in the far corner. But no one wanted to carry the heads there; he could see that.

"I guess I got to do that, too," he said aloud.

But much to his astonishment, David and Tomás approached with a piece of canvas, gently settled the grisly heads on it, and dragged it quietly to the far corner. And there men blessed themselves with sweeps of brown hands from forehead to breastbone, from left to right. He noticed that Juanita had swept her children away and Teresa María had vanished inside somewhere. The two-day toll had reached ten.

CHAPTER 25

By the time the sun had slid low in the southern sky, the Comanche had their village up and lodgefires burning. Gray smoke coiled out of the lodges and drifted south, layering the lavender winter sky. Jamie wondered what had pulled this huge village out of its sheltered winter camp somewhere south and dropped it here, on a windswept flat across the Purgatoire. Big medicine of some kind. Or maybe need. The Bents had slammed their trading window shut. The Comancheros could supply them with very little, except for Santa Fe iron, and wool. Need, then. Need and greed.

Need meant opportunity. Greed meant menace. With the deepening chill, warriors slipped blankets over their shoulders. They began to gather along the riverbank, leading or riding their superb ponies to the place where they were massing. Jamie thought for a moment they might yet strike on this fading winter day, but he set it aside. They weren't painted. They weren't stripping down for battle. But they did carry their weapons: lances with iron points; battle axes and hatchets; short reflexive bows, ideal for use on horseback, and quivers bristling with arrows; warclubs of shaped stone bound by rawhide to a wooden haft; and trade muskets, mostly large-bore flintlocks.

"They fixin' to come at us? It don't look it," Lyle said, answering his own question.

"I reckon not. But I think we'd better get our broomstick brigade up hyar and marchin'. They're gonna show us what they got; we'll show 'em what we got."

Lyle slid out of the watchtower over the gate, and yelled down to the yard. Swiftly, Pony Gantt rounded up every soul in the post, including Emilio and the women, who tucked their hair into traderoom felt hats and wrapped blankets about themselves. In a couple of minutes Jamie had them all, even the children, marching behind the chest-high parapets; a dozen men with real rifles, and a dozen others with black sticks. Not bad, he thought, eyeing them in the gray light. The darkening day would help. From outside, those blackened sticks looked like barrels.

"Keep movin' " he yelled. "Makes 'em think there's more."

His people hastened along the walls, knotting together and then separating.

"Don't take notions and shoot," he warned. "They ain't attacking. I think we'll see a parade in a moment. They're just showin' off. Kill one and we all lose our topknots."

His people seemed glad to have something to do. The afternoon had gnawed at them, and they'd watched the village rise across the creek with deepening terror.

At last the warrior parade began, led by several headmen, all of them in bonnets. Most wrapped themselves in blankets. The braves were strung out loosely into an armed mass of dark horses and obscure riders, more and more impressive as knots of them forded the river, threaded the saltbush, and began slowly circling the post. On and on they came, more and more warriors, until Jamie couldn't count them. Two hundred. Two hundred fifty — walking, trotting, spinning into a great noose that slowly tightened around the post until they were well within rifleshot, deliberately provoking war and a chance for scalps.

He quit counting. They moved too fast. Just as his own people fluidly walked along the parapet, grouped, scattered. He laughed shortly. They were like a pair of cats, backs arched, tails puffed out, mincing sideways to look bigger than they were. Except for the snorting and whinnying of ponies, a swift cold silence settled over the whole crowd. Jamie wished he knew who the chiefs were. He knew a few names.

Normally, with the arrival of a whole village, he'd have

253

wrestled into a black frock coat and tophat, collected some tobacco twists, and marched out to welcome the headmen— the usual trading ritual. But not for this village, camped across the creek with a potential battlefield in between. Somehow, he had to parley with those chiefs and headmen, invite them to trade, offer a few gifts. He wasn't sure how to do it. It occurred to him then that he'd seen no Comancheros in this massed display of Comanche warriors. It was hard to tell in the tricky gloom. But these men were short and lean, unlike the Comancheros, who ran to fat, and they wore their black hair either braided or shoulder length, pinned by a headband or a winter hat. The Comancheros wore shorter hair.

"Lyle, ask the men to spot Comancheros if they can. Don't shoot. Just count. Repeat it—don't shoot. I just want to know what they're up to."

Lyle stalked along the gallery walk behind the parapet once again, and Jamie saw men squint into the murky light, examining those amassed warriors one by one.

Off in the cottonwoods, Jamie saw a few spectators he suspected were the Comancheros. He wished he had a spyglass to check, but he didn't. Somehow, though, this parade seemed as much Benito's doing as the headmen's display of naked power.

The Comanche warriors circled the post ten or twelve times, slipping the noose tighter with each loop, until they were riding only twenty or thirty yards from the walls, eliciting terror in the men within.

"They're just scarin' ya," Jamie shouted. "Save your powder. Anyone shoots, he'll start a war we don't want."

He was glad, in a way, Boar Blunt wasn't around to defy him. Boar and his friends. Jamie had a pretty good idea that they'd met the worst possible end. He didn't suppose he'd ever know, though.

"Lyle, git a few men on down to the barricades, just in case I'm wrong and they bust the gates. Hyar." He handed Lyle the double-barreled fowling piece, the most effective weapon they had to halt a rush through the gates.

He watched six of his men collect in the gloom of the yard.

An ox bawled there; The beasts hadn't been fed or watered. Eight oxen — food if they needed it. That was one thing going for the post.

Chill lowered. A night breeze bit through his elkskin coat, numbing his neck and reddening his ears and nose. The day had been mild, but these midwinter nights could be brutal here on the prairies. Then, when it became too dark for a parade, and too dark for war — the Comanche didn't fight at night and risk the wrath of the spirits — the assemblage disintegrated. Knots of warriors rode back to the village and the warmth of their lodges.

Teresa María showed up with two velvety robes from the warehouse. *"Madre de Dios,"* she muttered. "I think I will not live."

He took the robes gratefully and wrapped one around him, hair-side in, immediately feeling its warmth.

"I'm not so sure we will neither," he said. It didn't comfort her any, but he wasn't about to fool her with false hope. "How are them others? Especially the Mexicans?"

"They are digging graves in their mind. Invoking the saints. San Martín, San Juan, San Pedro, Santa María . . . Tomás is different. He has a rifle. He mocks them and calls them bad things."

"How's David doin'?"

She snorted. "He's so frightened he just huddles under a blanket and stares and blinks."

"It's his first taste of it all," Jamie said. "He's tougher than he knows."

"What are you going to do?"

"I don't rightly know. I can't figger it out. I'm gnawin' on it like a dog."

"Well, talk to them! You sit up here and they think no one cares, no one leads. I hear grumbles."

The scent of smoke drifted from below. Emilio's cook fire . . . maybe a blaze in the barracks room beehive fireplace, too.

"I'll come down in a bit. I got to think."

She laughed, unkindly. "Thinking won't save us. You're no

good at it anyway. Let Guy Straus think. You shoot, you do not think. Why did I ever leave Taos? For this? *Caramba!*"

He watched her worry her way down the rickety ladders in the dark. Night lay heavy on them, and with it a hard frost. He had to think. He didn't intend to leave the watchtower until he'd thought it through.

He turned to peer out the slits to the east, seeing almost nothing except the countless dull glows of lodge fires far away. It was the Comancheros he worried about. What would they do? He'd rejected their extortion. He'd laughed at Benito. What would that porky little devil do next? The man wanted wealth. He wanted to destroy his new rivals. He wanted those trade goods down there—a fortune. Worth thousands of robes. He'd try to snatch the fort. By gawd, *snatch* it, and then trade with his friends. He'd try to grab it *tonight,* too.

Jamie stood so suddenly he banged his head on the ceiling.

He knew, suddenly. Or at least he'd made a good guess, and had something to defend against.

He clambered down to the gallery, then down to the yard, and went into the barracks, where chilled men huddled around the cold, smoky fire, trying to extract comfort from it. It occurred to him that not a man watched up there, and he'd better appoint guard shifts fast. But first, he had some instructions.

"I'm thinkin' them Comancheros're goin' to try us tonight. If I was that *capitán,* Benito, I'd send a coupla men over the wall, a little before mornin' when we're weakest. I'd sneak 'em over and I'd have 'em open the gates and let the rest in, so they could creep around here slitting throats right and left."

He repeated it in Spanish.

"We're goin' to have to set us a double guard—no sleepin' either. It'll be plumb mean out there, colder than the devil's hind end. Any man doesn't stay alert, he's gonna git his throat cut, I think. Now I'm thinkin' we should maybe let them come over the wall, let them devils open the gates and let the rest in, and then—finish 'em."

That proposal met with total silence.

"You see any of them Comancheros in that parade?" Jamie

asked.

No one had.

"We'll be ready for 'em," he said.

"Ready to do what?" asked Philpot Launes.

"Pay 'em back."

"Murder them right in this yard, until the earth is red and our hands are too."

Jamie began a roll call of the dead. "Manolo. Cannon. Sánchez. Cajones. Pickett. García. Roja. Bustamente. Guzman. Mendoza. Zumarraga. I reckon we should add Blunt, Willis, Dusseldorf, and Petti. That comes to fifteen."

"You don't know that—about Blunt and them," said Lyle. "They coulda just took off."

"You got a better guess?"

No one did.

"You got a better plan?" Jamie's voice had an edge to it.

"I'm not up to butcherin'. But I got other ways," said Blake cracking the bullwhip in his one good hand.

Jamie knew what he meant.

David crouched in the watchtower, peering nervously into a moonless murky night. His two buffalo robes and buffalo cap didn't entirely baffle the numbing cold that eddied through the slit windows on a persistent breeze. He'd been given the first watch, the easy watch, along with Juan Cordova. Nothing would happen now. It'd be near dawn, when the post lay in drugged slumber, that they would strike—if they struck. Jamie had reserved that watch for himself and Lyle.

David had a Hawken beside him, its steel icy in the night. And also the double-barreled fowling piece charged with buckshot. He squinted through the slit to the east, seeing nothing on the black plain. He tried the other windows, compassing other meadows. Nothing. Not that he expected to see anything in the black of this night. The thought of all those Comanches camped across the Purgatoire roiled his stomach. Most of the lodges were dark now, but a faint orange glow radiated from a few. Tomorrow they might sing their battle-medicine songs.

He stared at his own mittened hands, knowing they weren't the hands of a soldier. And yet he was doing soldier's duty, and that duty might lead him to kill another mortal this very night. He didn't know whether he could do that — lift the heavy octagonal barrel of the Hawken, aim down its sights at a sensate human being, some mother's son enjoying life and breath, sun and food, and squeeze the trigger. He doubted he could. Many of the rest doubted they could too — especially if the Comancheros were penned up in the yard like cattle, shot at from the doors and windows of the surrounding rooms.

He wondered how Jamie could propose such a thing, even after that terrible roll call of those murdered. Those brutes stopped at nothing, butchering the *cibeleros,* slaughtering the others, slicing the throat of poor Manolo — a boy. But not even that grim picture primed David to shoot another mortal . . . unless he had to. If a Comanchero started up the rickety ladder to the watchtower, he'd shoot. That comforted him. In self-defense, he could pull the trigger. Otherwise . . . he knew he couldn't.

In the yard far below, Cordova paced, wrapped in a buffalo robe that made him all but invisible. Checking the gates. In a moment he'd climb the ladder and walk the parapets again, peering into the inkiness. David studied the parapets closely, looking for any sort of movement that signaled an assault.

He saw what he was looking for. A hump seemed to grow on top of the north wall and then diminish. Another followed. Men, catfooting onto the gallery over the rooms below! More humps grew on the lips of the west and south walls, more men sliding silently over the top. He stared, paralyzed. It wasn't supposed to happen now! The post had been quiet only an hour or so. And so many! They kept coming, sliding over the tops of three parapets and vanishing into blackness on the roofs. Then he understood. The moon would rise in the middle of the night. Jamie hadn't counted on that. These intruders wanted the cover of blackness.

He grew wild with indecision. The plan had been for one

or both of the watch to slip into Jamie's rooms and the barracks, and silently alert everyone. But not this! He couldn't
even clamber down the two ladders now. He hunted wildly for
Cordova, and saw him staring upward. Cordova had seen
something. And then he heard a hard thump and cough, and
the robed bulk of Cordova slid to the earth of the yard. They'd
killed him. Someone had thrown a knife! Others snaked
along the gallery toward his watchtower now. That did it. He
swung the Hawken toward one, his heartbeat catapulting,
and shot. The roar stunned the post. The intruder's arms flew
up. He toppled slowly toward the yard, landing with a heavy
smack.

Hands trembling, David found his powder horn and measured a load and poured it down the warm barrel. He fumbled in his pouch for a patch and ball, rammed them down
with the hickory rod he'd pulled free of its clips under the barrel. He fumbled off the old cap, and pressed a new one on. It
didn't seat, and tumbled away. He found another, and armed
the Hawken.

The intruders had paused, not venturing closer to the ladder to the watchtower. Below, he heard muffled shouts. Men
rising. And above, on the walk below the parapets, a wild
laughter he knew, Benito having a fine time. The nasal chor-
tle filled him with a murderous rage, and he knew then, knew
that he could pull the trigger—again and again. He swung
the Hawken toward the noise, but the phantasms on the walkway had shifted.

Someone—Cordova crawling for help probably—
coughed, and collapsed. Knives! These Comancheros were
deadly knife-throwers, delivering silent death with a whip of
the arm. Even as David watched, something whipped right
through the slit window overlooking the yard, and clattered
against the far adobe. Aimed at him! He ducked back, afraid
to peer out. He set the Hawken aside and gripped the icy
stock of the fowling piece, scarcely knowing how to poke it out
the slit and fire it. Another knife clattered against adobe just
outside.

Below, he heard Jamie's voice, calm and intense. "Hyar

259

now, we got us some visitors. On the roofs. Stay in the barracks. David—you be all right? Answer me."

David scarcely dared to, sure that his voice itself would draw deadly fire. "Yes," he croaked.

"That Juan Cordova in the yard?"

"Yes," David cried.

"You're our ace, boy. You just hold quiet. Stay loaded. Use the rifle now."

From the walkway, he heard Benito's wild chortling. Men slid along it everywhere, so many he could scarcely fathom it. More than twelve, more like twenty, always shifting, never stopping.

"Ah, Señor Dance, it is your *amigo,* Benito. Now you will be a partner, *sí?*"

David swung his Hawken at the sound, and fired. The shot startled his ears. The butt jolted hard into his shoulder. Out beyond, he heard laughter, wild and mad and joyous. He loaded, this time more confidently, even while things snicked against the adobe outside and one knife clattered through the slit.

From below, an occasional shot blasted upward toward the gallery, but no man fell. As long as the Comancheros hunkered low and didn't let themselves be silhouetted by the starlit heavens, they'd be invisible. And yet . . . several of them were descending the ladder to the yard. David could hear it. He heard men cursing in English and Spanish. And a woman's sob. Shadowy figures spread out in the yard, and shots from the doors and windows followed them. David dared a peek through the slit, and saw Comancheros gathering behind the barricades on the gate side, using them to protect themselves from shots. Others broke into the unmanned trading room, laughing there in the darkness. He heard the gates of the post creak open, letting in the whole night. The post lay naked now, he knew. They could loot the trading room at ease, and haul a fortune out the gates and into the night, protected by the very barricades that had been built to defend the gates.

Several Comancheros—he couldn't tell how many—huddled behind the barricade, using the post's own defense against itself. The fowling piece! But to use it, he would have to lean out of the narrow slit window and aim steeply down. He waited a moment, hoping for a diversion, and when it came it was too late. A tiny orange light sailed down from the roofwalk into the yard and exploded into flame. Whatever it was, rags soaked with lamp oil or tallow, a lit *cigarto*, it landed at the foot of the robe press, flared into bright flame, and lit the whole yard, leaving those above, on the gallery, in blackness. He knew rifles were trained on his slit window now, daring him to poke a barrel out.

Two bodies lay in the yard: Cordova, on his stomach, a knife glinting in his back; and the Comanchero David had shot. He looked for a third—whoever had coughed and crawled—but saw none.

David cowered in the lee of the adobe wall, knowing what would happen if he tried to fire. Then, desperately, he slid a barrel out. A barrage exploded from everywhere. Balls snapped inside, hit adobe, sent chips flying, blinding him. The racket continued, ball after ball thunking into the wall, digging pits into the mud bricks. Balls smacked the ceiling poles above; a hot one seared around and slapped his shoulder.

Outside, Benito laughed maniacally.

"David," yelled Jamie. "Answer me."

Terrified, David couldn't.

"Answer me, lad."

"I'm all right."

The flames ignited a post of the robe press, and licked upward to the crosspieces, illumining the entire yard in its wavery light.

Benito laughed, his nasal voice rising into a wild cackle. "Señor Dance. We are partners, *sí?* Come out and we will be partners."

From the cracked-open door to his rooms, Jamie fired upward. A rattle of shots hit the wooden door at once. David wondered if Jamie Dance was dead or injured and it was all over.

From the blackness above, Benito wheezed and cackled and mocked, making a great ruckus that almost hid the footpads of the men starting up the rickety ladder to David's roost.

CHAPTER 26

They were coming! David grabbed the fowling piece and aimed it at the hollow rectangle in the floor where they'd emerge. From the yard a shot racketed; below David, a man grunted and coughed and tumbled off the crude ladder. Then David understood: the Comanchero had to pass through an area illumined by the fire down in the yard. Safe! He heard Benito yelling commands, but none of the other Comancheros nerved himself to assault the watchtower.

David found himself shaking so badly he couldn't aim his rifle. He slid over to the east slit, peered out upon the flats in front of the gates, and saw motion there. Light from the fire in the yard pierced through the opened gates, limning a Comanchero laden with loot from the trading room. He was carrying it to a string of packmules and horses.

Looting! David slid the Hawken through the dark slit, aimed at the Comanchero, and squeezed. The wobbling rifle boomed, bucked into his shoulder. The Comanchero flung his loot about—blankets, it looked like in that murky light—and collapsed. David reloaded coldly and shot a second looter, seeing the man spin, lose a cask of something, and collapse. He reloaded again, coughing on the stink of powdersmoke in the watchtower, feeling the heat of the barrel as he rammed more powder and a patched ball home. This time, he spotted nothing. No Comanchero dared haul the booty into the maw of that deadly rifle above. So David aimed at the chest of a loaded packhorse, and squeezed. The horse bucked feebly, shivered, and caved to earth.

263

David coldly shot three more loaded packhorses, and then the rest of the beasts fled, maddened by the smell of blood. He'd stopped the looting cold. Exhilarated, pulse racing, he tried peering from the side windows, and spotted Comancheros hulking in shadow not twenty feet below, their gazes directed into the yard and the flames. Coldly, he shot one. The man jerked, spasmed, cried out, and died. His rifle clattered down into the yard, discharging as it hit the earth. David stared, horrified, his gorge rising.

Thou shalt not kill. He sobbed, loathing himself, his stomach rebelling, his soul screaming. And yet . . . it was kill or be killed. The keen cold of his soul calmed him again.

David realized suddenly that he'd slowed them down; he held the key — if he could last and a stray shot didn't kill him. He poked his fingers into the leather pouch, and found only a handful of balls remaining — nine. But patches and caps enough. He didn't know how much powder remained in the horn. Nine balls. He groped around for the other pouch, the one for the fowling piece, and found several waxed paper cylinders full of shot, caps, and patches. Everything depended on his powder supply. He would use light charges now.

From below, on the shadowed roofs where the Comancheros crouched, came the crackle of Spanish, and David knew they were discussing him. He heard Benito snarl, picking up a word now and then. And what he heard terrified him. The watchtower was the key to everything.

"You all right, boy?" That was Jamie's voice far below.

"Yes," David cried.

"They're gonna make a move. You hunker low."

Shots drowned the last of Jamie's talk. Balls smacked the adobe walls. Every Comanchero out on the shadowed roofs banged away at the slit overlooking the yard. Balls seared the ceiling above David. They caromed off adobe, shattering, spitting hot lead. Tiny fragments burned into him, stinging. Wood splinters drove murderously through the air, biting his ear and a hand. A terrible pounding echoed through the adobe as balls gouged pits outside, probing at him. He sobbed and sprawled on the wooden floor as shattered lead seared into him from everywhere. A hot ball cut across his calf, and he felt a sting and a wetness there—blood. He clutched the wood of the floor, pressing himself lower. It went on and on, never ceasing, murderous ball after ball, terrorizing him until his face was wet with tears. He would die. And then it stopped.

"You all right, David?" Jamie's voice drifting up again, from far below.

Jamie didn't feel like answering. If he spoke, the barrage would continue instantly.

He heard Benito laughing, cruelly. "Señor Dance. Now we will be partners, *sí?*"

"David—answer me. Are you all right?" Jamie's voice grew insistent.

David couldn't manage it. He could barely lift his head from the blood-slicked, tear-slicked, and urine-slicked floor.

From the Comancheros, wild crackling laughter. One tried to creep up the watchtower ladder again, but a shot boomed—from the barracks, David guessed—and the man plunged back into the safety of darkness.

"David . . . you thar?"

David finally nerved himself to sit up, keeping his head below the window slits. His calf wound ached. He touched it gingerly, touched the wetness of his own blood. His whole body screamed. His eyes watered from the adobe dust. A dozen fragments of ball had buried themselves in him, and every wound stung viciously.

He heard Comancheros crabbing over roofs in the darkness, and then Benito's voice, from a new place above Jamie's quarters.

"Ah, Señor Dance. I am above you. Maybe I'll dig a hole in your roof. Surrender now, and I will let you live. I will put you out of the post and you can run to the Bents, *sí?*"

"Go to hell, Benito."

"Señor Dance. How beautiful is your lady. I have looked upon her. She is without flaw, *sí?* She is full of fire. Ah, Señor Dance, I am in love. I want your delicious lady. I want to take her to my bed. Soon I will have her, *sí?* She will live. The rest will die. Everyone. *Yanqui* and *méjicano*. But not the *señora*. I have plans for her. She will like me, *sí?*"

265

Jamie didn't say anything.

"Ah, you keep silence! Women of the Indians, we sell them to *hacendados*. Women of Méjico, we sell them to the Indians. Maybe children too—little girls we sell to Comanches, and they breed more Comanches. Ah, Dance. This *señora*, Teresa María of Taos—you see, I know her name—Teresa María, is just right for me. I will rescue her from the heretic, *sí?*" He cackled. "Ah, the things we will do, this Teresa María and I, alone in the night. Ah, Dance! If she fights, all the better! Like a *diabla!*"

Someone in the barracks shot upward toward Benito's voice. But the *capitán* had shifted again, and his laughter rattled through the yard.

"Ah, *señores*, your little lead balls cannot touch one on the roof in the blackness. The angle, it is no good, *sí?*"

David didn't dare peer out the slit overlooking the yard and the post. But the light seemed dimmer. Less of it illumined the ceiling of the watchtower. He knew the fire down in the yard was dying; the charred posts of the robe press weren't sustaining the flame.

Not a shot erupted as Benito taunted Jamie, and David knew, suddenly, that every man there, the Comancheros as well as the post's men in the barracks, was following the exchange. Time to strike—if he could nerve himself. He picked up the fowling piece and snicked back both hammers, feeling his pulse climb again. This would be the hardest thing he'd ever done—madness. Still . . . that fire ebbed by the minute. He stood, trembling, his back to the icy adobe, envisioning in his mind just where the two barricades were, almost straight below.

His pulse raced now. He angled his body into the foot-wide window, leaned out, aimed at Comancheros huddled behind one barricade, and squeezed. The piece slammed into his shoulder cruelly; he hadn't seated it there. Below, men screamed. Several men. He swung the barrels to the right, and fired. More men screamed. He ducked back and threw himself to the floor just as a new barrage from the roofs blew balls into the window.

Below, men screamed and cursed in Spanish.

266

"David, you rascal," yelled Jamie. "Haw!"

Fumbling in deepening darkness, David poured powder into both barrels of the fowling piece, uncertain about a proper charge, and then jammed the waxed paper cylinders down the smooth barrels. He capped the piece and set it aside.

He thought he'd better check the slit overlooking the meadow beyond the gates. There two things greeted him. One was a lean, cold, three-quarter moon riding the eastern horizon. The other was ghostly groups of Comanches, standing a hundred yards out or so, studying the night violence—and the opened gates. Closer in, several pack animals lay dead, their burdens intact. And below him, a scatter of trade goods and two sprawled Comancheros visible in the little yardlight from the opened gates.

Men still screamed and sobbed in the yard. Somehow, he'd done a lot of damage with those two blasts. He didn't care. He'd discovered hate this night. It shocked him, this cold, murderous beast in his soul. He'd known anger before, but never this hardness that clutched his innards.

The light changed. The white moon spun upward in the east, casting a faint silvery veil over the frosty world. Shadows formed and regrouped as the white light bit into them. Except for the groaning and cursing of Comancheros sprawled behind the barricades, nothing happened. The shooting had stopped. The light intensified.

He heard, at last, a low command in Spanish, and the word *luna* whispered in the wind. He understood. As soon as the moon rose high enough, its rays would expose every Comanchero on the roofs. David heard the soft scuffle of men moving, the groans of wounded men being dragged. He ducked over to the window overlooking the flats beyond the gates and saw the Comancheros scurrying off, peering back fearfully at the watchtower. He slid his Hawken out, tracked one brightly lit Comanchero—and couldn't shoot. They were leaving. He spotted another, his arms loaded with loot from the trading room, and swung the rifle that way. He didn't feel like killing. He aimed for those running heels, and squeezed. He missed, plowed up clay, but the man tumbled to earth, lost his booty, and ran off. David reloaded quietly, watching the Comancheros, their numbers thinned, raced beyond range, out to the knots of Comanche.

He turned and yelled down to Jamie. "They're running. Some Comanches out there."

From the barracks he heard cheering.

"David. Take a peek. Check the roofs before we git ourselves shot."

Uneasily, David edged into the narrow window that had been the focus of so many shots. He studied the shadows on the roofs, against the parapets, and saw nothing. He slowly peered down over the barricades and saw nothing. Only the sprawled white body of Juan Cordova. They'd taken their dead and wounded.

"They're gone," he muttered.

"You sure?"

He checked again. "Yes."

"You did it! David, I reckon you saved us!"

He felt nothing. Below, the post's men edged out of the barracks, scanning walls and roofs and shadowed corners.

He could see Jamie below, sliding softly along wall-shadow. "Git out and pick up the loot before them Comanch git it, and then shut the gates," Jamie commanded.

Men trotted through the gates under David, and he could see them out on the flats swooping up bolts of cloth, blankets, pots, crates; dragging burlap sacks off dead mules. Then he heard the giant gates swing shut, and the bar fall across them. Out on the eerie whited plain, he saw Comanche turn and walk toward the Purgatoire and their village beyond.

He heard steps on the ladder below him, and swung the fowling piece toward the rectangle in the floor, a wildness flooding his marrow again.

"Whoa up, David!"

Lyle Black had paused just below the floor, sensing the gun on him. David melted into sobs.

"Whoa up, lad." Lyle emerged, carrying a fresh pouch and powderhorn. "You done it. You done it!"

"The moon did it."

"You fought the whole fight. They had us pinned, all except you hyar. Not a thing got stole. But pore Oso Valdez got hurt. Caught a knife in his thigh. He'll make it, seems like. But Juan Cordova, he's got a big knife stickin' in his back."

David said nothing, feeling nauseous.

"You git on down and rest. You let the fellers slap your back some."

Wearily, David stepped down to the roof-level gallery, and then let himself down the rickety ladder into the moonlit yard. Smoke lay thick there and made his eyes water. That and other things.

They whooped him and cheered and laughed, but David didn't hear them. He had killed. He dripped with blood. He'd taken lives. He ignored them all and stumbled toward the barracks and his pallet, filled with self-loathing.

Teresa María knew all about death. All Mexicans did. Death was the national pastime of Mexico, just as it was of Spain. Everything in Mexico, from bullfights to funerals, spoke of death and the tomb. Let someone die, and it was the occasion of a great celebration, a parade of padres and skulls and skeletons and wailing widows. No one lived long, so everyone got the chance to enjoy death, to see the dead, to weep and wonder. She herself had seen a hundred of the dead in her day, even in the little village of Taos. Let someone die, and everyone came to see.

She knew all the lore of death, too. All about ghosts and spirits; about the passage of souls from the living to *purgatorio* or *infierno*. Or maybe even to see the saints. But that was rare. She would never see saints, and knew they'd bore her anyway. But it frightened her to think of *el diablo* and the rattle of bones and skulls.

They had no priest here to give unction, except that imposter Tomás. Maybe he could do it. It'd be better than nothing. But she wasn't going to die. Benito promised it. She had heard his very words—she alone would live, and be his slave. The idea fascinated her—she alone alive after the butchery, she alone hauled away by the Comanchero to his bed! Was she so beautiful as that? *Caramba!* She would be famous! The

269

only one left!

She almost liked Benito, laughing in the night, treating everyone so badly. Anyone who could insult others so well, with so much laughter, she liked. She almost wished it had happened that way, she alone surviving to be his slave in his tent. But he would probably share her with others, and maybe sell her after a while to Comanche, and that didn't appeal to her quite so much, though she knew it would be exciting.

Madre de Dios! Maybe it would be better than Jamie's smelly feet and unshaven cheek! Maybe Benito was the better hombre! She cried in the darkness, enjoying the luxury of spilling tears. She hardly ever got to cry. I need to cry more, she thought. Ah!

The adobe room felt cold, but she dared not build a fire in the beehive fireplace in the corner, because its light would silhouette Jamie and they would shoot at him. *Caramba!* Bullets had flown into the room and she had hugged the cold clay floor! But now it was over. She felt sorry about that; these moments weren't as terrifying as the previous ones, when death lurked everywhere. Death came as a reptile, unblinking in its stare, peering first at the men, then at her.

A long silence stretched, and she could see the moon had cast a white glow upon the roofs and the Comancheros had fled.

"You'd better stay hyar, Teresa. Can't say as it's over."

"Your feet smell. Put your boots on."

Jamie sighed and slipped out into the yard, barefoot in the freezing air. She wanted to go outside too, and see death. She wanted to see Juan Cordova, see the knife in his back, and think about the pain when it had sliced through a lung to his heart. She liked to imagine death, pain, shock, gasping for breath. She liked to imagine death coming to her, as it had to that one—a searing pain and then blinding light and pain, and maybe San Pedro waiting there. She wanted a miracle when she died, just a little one, like a portrait of Santa María weeping real tears next to her coffin. That would be a good miracle for her. She hoped they'd lay her out on a bier, with lots of candles and lots of weeping, and black lace and the

270

groaning of all her friends. Her father especially. She wanted him to groan and weep most of all. More even than Jamie.

She found her rebozo, and decided it would not be warm enough, and besides, it would not cover her night dress. So she pulled a Witney four-point blanket from their bed, wrapped herself in it, slid her feet into silk slippers, and stepped out into the grim white yard.

Everywhere, half-dressed hombres put things in order, while Jamie directed them. The gates stood open, and nothing separated her from the entire Comanche village on the Río de las Ánimas. She shivered. The cold seemed uncanny.

"Bring the rifles. We got them out of it at least," Jamie said to the one called Gantt. The *yanqui* had collected three, left behind by the fleeing Comancheros.

Teresa María walked delicately through the icy dust to the sprawled body of Cordova and observed the knife in his back, right up to its brass hilt. Ah, what a blow. What a surprise, coming silently from behind. She stared, fascinated, and shivered. The Chávez children stared too, and whispered.

Jamie had tolled fourteen dead only hours before. Now Fort Dance claimed its fifteenth — not including the Comancheros who had died there. She peered about sharply, seeing black patches in the moonlit clay, knowing hombres had bled into the earth where they were. She peered sharply about for spirits, and thought she saw one hovering just over the barracks roof, but she wasn't sure. Surely, many spirits cried in this bloody yard.

"How many you think David got?" Gantt asked Jamie.

"I reckon four dead. Maybe more. Two outside; one or two on the roof. And a mess of injured behind the barricades."

"At least four. Not that it'll bother Benito none. He'll be at it in the mornin'."

"I don't know what's comin' at dawn," Jamie said wearily. "At least we got three more rifles. That reminds me, Pony. Them ladders are still leanin' against the walls. I guess you'd better yank 'em in."

Gantt clambered up to the gallery, where he could reach the ladders poking above the parapets.

"What're you doin' out here?" Jamie asked Teresa maría, an edge on his voice.

"I came to see Juan Cordova. To see how Benito murdered him!"

"Maybe not Benito."

"Oh, but it had to be. He is a powerful man, with death in his hands."

Jamie grunted.

At last some of the Mexican employees gathered around the body of Cordova. Luis Soto, Cordova's friend, straddled the body and tried to pull the knife out. It wouldn't come, and Soto only managed to raise the corpse. Two of the others held Cordova down, and Soto yanked again. When the knife yielded suddenly, he staggered back, almost toppling. It is murder in reverse, Teresa María thought. Maybe Soto would go to paradise for unmurdering Cordova. He waved the blackened blade in the white moonlight.

Fidel Santa María found a shroud for the body, and they wrapped Cordova in it and tied it with rawhide thong. Teresa María studied the scene, keeping a sharp eye for Cordova's spirit, but she didn't see it. Maybe San Pedro was busy judging it and it would return.

"Señor Dance . . . where should we put him?"

"I reckon you ought to bury him out in the cemetery right now, if the ground's not too froze up. Who knows what to-morrah will bring?"

"I'll say something," said Tomás. She studied Villanova. He looked weary and pale and disconsolate. "I wish I could be a real priest," he added. "Maybe I will someday. If we survive tomorrow, which I doubt."

Tomás's prophecy chilled her. Who knows indeed? with that *bandidos* outside, and a great village of bloody Comanche? Maybe tomorrow she would die like Juan Cordova. Or be taken off by Comanche for torture. She didn't want to be tortured, at least not very much. Just a little, to see what it was like.

She watched the hombres carry Cordova out onto the moonlit flat, watched Jamie send riflemen up to the roofwalk and the parapets to protect the funeral party. She didn't go

272

out. Instead, she clambered up the ladder to the roofs—the very roofs where the *bandidos* had lain and shot murder down into the yard—and peered at the burial party, limned by a high small moon. A chill settled in her, reaching down her throat, crawling through her nightdress, sliding around her blanket, biting her ears and nose. A coldness she could scarcely fathom, reaching into her belly. Then she knew! They always said only the devil made such cold! She peered around looking for him, but saw only the weary *yanqui* riflemen lining the parapet, while outside men chopped with axes and dug with spades.

But she knew. El Diablo himself was making the cold, and slipping invisible, around Fort Dance, planning something.

CHAPTER 27

Terror stalked the post, and no one slept. Each of them tossed and turned, wondering if these were their last few hours on earth. They hated the night and dreaded the dawn. The slightest noise set their hearts pounding. They bribed God with promises, and made pacts with the devil. Some in the barracks arose, cleaned rifles, counted balls and caps, topped powderhorns. Others feared the watch wasn't watching, and sidled out into the bitter night to walk the gallery and peer out upon the moon-whited flats. It exhausted them. An hour of this sort of dread cost them more energy than a day's hard toil.

Jamie joined them. He could sleep no more than the rest. His taut body cried out for rest, but he knew it'd never come—not with a thousand Comanche camped across the stream, and Benito and his Comancheros among them, plotting how to stir the warriors up at dawn. He eyed the bullet-pocked watchtower, and knew he had a strong defense there. Four riflemen, one at each window slit, could do a lot. He had three more rifles, too. He could give them to some of his Mexican help, who'd never shot one in their lives, or he could put a fifth man in the watchtower to reload.

He found Mazappa Oliphant and Pony Gantt peering owlishly off toward the sleeping village. They looked as haggard and fever-eyed as he supposed he did.

"You couldn't sleep neither."

"Ain't a soul in the post that's asleep, Jamie."

"Well, they come to trade. Reckon we'll just be tradin' to-morrow."

"Not if ol' Benito can help it. He'll try to wreck the tradin'—and wreck us agin," Mazappa said.

"How do you figger?"

Mazappa shrugged. "Lots of things he could do. He could whip 'em into a fight. Tell 'em all they got to do is beat a few men and then they get to plunder all them goods."

"Then he loses the trade—if they loot us."

"Yeah, but he knocks us out. He don't like the competition."

"There's no tellin'," Jamie said. "I want to parley with the headmen. Invite 'em in to trade and smoke. If Benito horns in, I'll have problems. He's got his own notions of what's going to happen tomorrah. Like torturin' some prisoner right before our eyes. Burn him. Behead him. They love that. They're all cats playin' with mice. Like Santa Anna at the Alamo, playin' with them Texians in there just for the hell of it. We might see things bad enough to make us sick. Take the fight out o' us."

No one spoke for a while. No one could guess what the ruthless Comanchero *capitán* had in mind.

"Reckon we should fort up," Jamie said. "Long as no one's sleepin'. We got them three rifles they left. I'm going to put my four best riflemen up yonder—you two, Lyle, and Tomás. And I'm puttin' them three new rifles up there, with a fast reloader. Who do you think?"

"I'd say Emilio. He can stuff a barrel faster'n he can stuff a turkey."

"He'll make me nervous, dry-firin' them teeth," said Pony. They laughed.

"Better get water up there, and some jerky and some spare gloves and hats and robes—spare horns and shot and all. Whatever you need from stores. I'm gonna put Jonas up there too—reload, shoot, whatever. It's the best thing we got goin'."

He watched them clamber down the ladder to the yard and start to collect what they would need. The night remained silent. The breeze had died, leaving the dark world breathless and foreboding. He hoped it wouldn't come to war. His quar-

275

rel was with the Comancheros. They'd killed fifteen of his men; they'd stolen most of his livestock; they'd stolen a lot of the trade goods, stolen whatever the *ciboleros* owned, including their mules and burros. He had to whip them so soundly they'd never bother him again. He had to recover his livestock from them — or the Comanches. And he had to do it all without riling up the headmen of the fiercest tribe that ran the plains. He confessed to himself he didn't know how.

Around him, men looked to their own defenses and comfort.

They were awake and working, except David, who'd collapsed on his barracks bunk, and Hector Cortez, who was in his quarters comforting Juanita and the two living children, just as Jamie should be inside comforting Teresa María. He thought a moment of smuggling her to Bent's Fort, and knew she'd never make it. Human wolves stalked the night. Her fate was his fate. But Benito's taunting stuck in his mind, and if worse came to worst, he might be able to spare her the violation and hell the *capitán* had in mind. The very thought of Benito's taunts, and of what he might have to do, threw Jamie into a vicious gloom.

Tomás joined him at the parapet. "I could be wearing the Roman collar and hearing unhappy women confess their flirtations," he said. "And I could be absolving them, if not absolving myself. Why am I here?"

"I reckon that trapping season with us did it. Whipped the priest plumb outa you."

"But it didn't. I am a priest, ordained or not."

"You as afraid as the rest of us?"

Tomás sighed. "Maybe more. I've sinned more."

"You? Haw. Leastwise, not unless you been thinkin' impure thoughts you ain't tellin' no one about."

"Maybe I have, Jamie."

The desperation in Tomás's voice startled his friend. The imminence of death did that to men.

"I'm a rebel," Tomás said by way of explanation.

"Aren't we all?"

"I didn't mean to be . . . Do you know I've heard five confessions this night? And I can't even give absolution? They came to me—nearest thing to a padre in the post. And I listened."

"I reckon you comforted them, Tomás. Maybe that's more valuable than anything else we're doin' hyar to get ready."

"Four men and one woman," Tomás said.

Jamie wondered if Teresa María had gone to him, but he didn't ask.

"What's a failed priest doing with a rifle in his hands?" Tomás asked.

"You aren't a failed priest."

"Do you know why I left the seminary? My flesh. I couldn't cross the line and become a man of spirit. Woman. But I haven't found one. I never will. Shyness condemns me. And worse, I'm too choosy. I live alone, eke out a living from hides. Not a very good prospect as a husband. But I burn, Jamie. Let me see a beautiful woman, and my flesh triumphs over my will."

Jamie realized that this, too, was a sort of confession. Tomás didn't seem to know it was every man's confession, and not just his own private suffering.

"I'm no good as a priest and no good as a husband."

"Tomás—"

"I've lusted. I've lusted for Teresa María."

Jamie didn't know what to say. "Reckon lots have," he muttered. "I wasn't alone."

"But I still do."

"Look hyar, Tomás. A man can't help what he thinks and feels. I sure can't. A man that's got himself by the handle, he keeps a lid on. Weak ones, they just scratch the itch and don't care none about hurting others. You care a-plenty about hurting others. That makes you a man in my book; rest are just skunks."

"Look at me. What am I? I read books. Some of the books are condemned by the church. What am I? A fool."

"A person thinks he's a fool—he usually ain't. Ones who think they ain't fools—they usually are."

Tomás stared off to the east. The faintest glow separated black sky from black earth. Soon it'd come—whatever it might be this new day.

277

"I expect to die. I dread pain. I dread it all. I can't even bear the thought of my body not working right—heart stopping, not breathing, not seeing, not hearing. Jamie, if I die . . . forgive me."

"For what?"

"For everything. I don't know. Cowardice today. How can I pull a trigger? Just forgive me and bury me decently, and get word to my . . . family."

"Tomás, *amigo*. You go on up to the watchtower and reload for the others. You don't have to shoot if you don't want. It's like the beaver days when you tended camp. You didn't like trappin' none, so you tended camp and that was just as valuable as wadin' the cold streams to see how the stick floated."

Tomás stood at the parapet silently, watching the light in the east thicken. "I admire David," he said. "He didn't have the stomach for war either. A city boy. A clerk. A bookworm. But he did what he had to—and we wouldn't be here if he hadn't somehow made himself do something he could hardly stand."

"David's a rare 'un."

"I'm no David, Jamie."

"Tomás. Each of us grows into whatever we are to be. Lots of things make a man. Including being helpful, being kind, giving people a lift. Who's to say what bein' a man is?"

Tomás said nothing. He pulled a robe tight around him against the bitterness of dawn. "You'll be digging a hole out there for me," he said softly.

A man couldn't answer that, Jamie thought.

The sky whitened and the moon faded. Around the parapets men assumed their posts without being asked. Most of them clasped a thick buffalo robe around them, against the mean cold. He could see them now in the weary light of dawn; he could see their numbness and exhaustion. He wondered if they'd fight well.

He caught the smell of coffee eddying up from below, and knew Emilio was beginning a meal. If a man has to die, it's easier on a full stomach, he thought. Hate to die hungry. There were good deaths and bad. Dying belly-full and fast was a good death. Dying warm, too. But dying at dawn was no good at all, not with the promise of a new day. Better to die at night, after a good day.

"Well, Guy," he muttered, "it's come to this hyar. We're gonna be dead or make her go."

The sun burnt the frost off the grass, and a morning breeze out of the west raked the post. Far across the Purgatoire, the breeze tore away the heavy smoke of two hundred lodgefires. No army marched across the frosted flats.

Jamie studied the village with a spyglass. He did not see warriors walking out to the herds to collect war ponies, nor did he see any painting up. He didn't see Benito and his Comancheros either. The closest lodges hid a lot behind them, though the Comancheros were there, and the village seemed to be waiting for something. Jamie tried to imagine what. Maybe they'd expected to trade with *Benito* this morning. Maybe he'd told them just that: come trade in the morning. But the Comancheros had been driven off, and now the village waited.

The sun arced south and warmed the day to mildness. Still, war did not march across that vast no man's land. Jamie peered at his men along the parapets, and found them haggard and hopeful. Each ticking minute seemed to pull them farther from war—and doom.

Well, he thought, if they won't come in for a parley, I can go to them. The thought of riding into a Comanche village chilled him plenty. But they were the same as the other plains tribes: they honored guests within their villages and usually treated them well. Usually. Unlike the other tribes, they harbored grudges and nursed ancient wrongs, and once in a while a visitor entering a Comanche village didn't find the peace of the village . . . but torture.

Jamie thought about it some. Not likely. Not when they'd come to trade with whoever held the post and its goods. But he didn't know what Benito had been telling them—or how it would affect a visit. He knew, though, as the sun crawled across the sky, that he had to do it. Indeed, they were waiting over yonder for him—or for someone.

279

He pulled a blanket and saddle over his chestnut, and then slid an icy bit into its mouth—which it dodged violently, hating cold on its tongue.

Men watched, carefully saying nothing. They didn't need to. Their watching became a kind of communication. Teresa María watched from the doorway of their quarters, and pulled her rebozo tighter. Tomás stared.

Jamie led the horse across the yard to the trading room, and tied it in front of it. Inside, he found the tobacco and pulled out several twists—the ancient signal. It occurred to him that he couldn't speak a word of Comanche and that David had been studying it. He'd take David. This hyar business required better talk than fingers could make. The boy— why did he still call David a boy, after that heroic night in the watchtower—the young man lay abed in the barracks, drugged by sheer exhaustion. Jamie hated to rouse him up; hated to take him on a terror-trip across that empty plain and into a Comanche village. But it had to be.

He slipped into the gloomy barracks and shook David, who stared back up at him wearily. "You larned some Comanch. I need you for a parley."

David peered back, frightened.

"It's not them you got to fear; it's the Comancheros. The headmen'll treat us about the way they should. They'll want to know who built this post and what we'll trade, and all the rest."

That seemed to register. "I'm just a clerk," he said.

"David . . . you want us to make a profit or not? Git into a war or not? Want to lose your scalp or not? Please your pa or not?" The roughness in Jamie's voice lacerated the quiet room.

David swung out of bed and began pulling on his boots, the only clothing he wasn't wearing.

They saddled up the other horse for David, while men watched from the gallery above and from doorways.

"Let me go instead of David," said Tomás.

"Amigo, you're in charge hyar."

Jamie stopped at the doorway and deposited his Hawken inside. It'd be worse than useless in the village. A man came unarmed—a peace sign—and they respected it. Usually.

Teresa María stared desolately at him, but said nothing. She looked drawn.

Jamie and David rode through the gates and out upon the hard earth, and heard the gates creak shut behind them. From above, his men watched. Far across the creek, observers darted into the lodges of headmen and chiefs with the news.

"You as scairt as I am, David?"

"I don't feel anything."

"I'm scairt. Never trust a Comanch."

"We should have waited."

"That tells 'em somethin'. This tells 'em somethin' else."

He scanned the village, worried more about the Comancheros than the Comanches. But wherever they were, they weren't visible. A Comanche escort was forming on the far side of the creek, though.

Jamie steered his chestnut along a path through the saltbush, and David followed. They splashed across a silvery flow of inch-deep water, and then into saltbush again. On the other side, amassed Comanche warriors met them, all of them armed with rifles or bows.

Jamie stared at them, trying to show no fear but feeling plenty of it. These were short, stocky men, wearing buckskin shirts and leggins, all of them largely devoid of the decorations and war pomps of the plains tribes. A few wore their straight black hair in braids; most wore it loose, with a headband pinning it.

He found not the slightest expression in their eyes. They crowded close, studying Jamie and David with unblinking curiosity—noting that both were unarmed. Jamie caught that, at least, the glances toward the empty saddle-sheaths. David looked frightened. Even worse, he looked exhausted.

Jamie didn't signal with his hands. Instead, he held up a tan tobacco twist. It was message enough. They were engulfed by the escort, which pushed in close, jarring them, making Jamie's chestnut half wild. Some form of Comanche disdain for someone from the outside, Jamie thought. David's horse reared and crowhopped after being crowded and bumped.

But at least they were progressing past fine cowhide lodges

that showed the mark of craftsmanship. Innumerable fall-fat ponies were tied to them. This village could mount a war party in an instant. They progressed up a slight grade, past staring women and children who made no welcome and whose silence was as wintry as the weather.

They arrived at last at a larger lodge on a slight knoll near the center of the village. This one bore the insignia of rank. Stick figures decorated its conical sides—all of them depicting battle triumphs, coups counted. A great lance speared the sky before the lodge, its tip crowned with two eagle feathers. On it hung twenty or thirty scalps.

Arrayed in a line before this council lodge were the chief and headman and shamans, nine of them in a row. The chief held his staff of office in hand, a feather-bedecked ceremonial spear. These tribal elders eyed Jamie and David as impassively as the warriors of the policing society who had escorted them.

Jamie reined up and waited to be invited in. He lifted his tobacco twist, and stretched his hand forward with it, intending to give it to the chief. But the chief, a weathered, bowlegged man who looked as though he'd rarely been off a horse's back, simply stared at it.

They were practicing some form of intimidation, Jamie knew, while they looked their visitors over, fathoming what they could.

"David, if you can say it, tell 'em we're the chiefs of the new tradin' post, come hyar to welcome them, have a smoke, and invite them over to trade."

David said it somehow, slowly grinding out the words of a hastily acquired tongue.

"Tell 'em we're honored to be hyar in the village, and ask who we got the honor of addressin'? And whether any of 'em speak Spanish, so I can foller along in this powwow."

David did that. And still nothing happened. Men with brown diamond-shaped faces stared up at their visitors; Jamie waited patiently.

At last the chief spoke, addressing David, who listened solemnly.

"He says he's Old Wolf and these headmen have come to

282

listen. He asks you to state your business."

No smoke. A bad beginning. "Tell him we'll talk after we sit down and smoke the pipe. We're here to talk about trade. We want robes, and we'll offer lots of things they'll see soon."

David repeated that, and listened to Old Wolf's response.

"He wants to know why we, and the Comancheros, fought last night with many guns. And why we drove off his friend Benito and killed his old friends who traded with his village."

Jamie sighed. "Tell him it's a long story, and we'd like to smoke the pipe and talk."

At this, Old Wolf nodded curtly, then barked something at his headmen. They made way for the guests. Jamie and David dismounted and headed for the oval door in the lodge, and just before Jamie plunged in, he spotted a stocky, smooth-faced Comanchero in a buffalo cap, looking a lot like the Comanche beside him.

"That Benito?" he asked David.

"Yes."

"Well, he's standin' thar with a shiny rifle." But then they were escorted into the lodge, according to some sort of protocol, and directed to a place to the left of the chief, who sat at the rear of the umber-lit cone.

CHAPTER 28

Jamie read the augurs well enough. He and David were seated in the place of honor to the left of Old Wolf. But no one pulled out the ceremonial pipe. The seating arrangement indicated they'd be treated well enough as guests in the village. The no-smoke meant that these Comanche didn't consider themselves at peace, that they wouldn't bind themselves to peace, that they would wait and see. Beside him, David sat quietly, oblivious of the things that Jamie had already plumbed.

A winter sun, filtering through the scraped cowhide of the large lodge, cast a soft shadowless brown light upon them all. In the center of the lodge a small fire crackled. Its smoke occasionally whirled through the lodge rather than exiting above. Old Wolf's medicine bundle hung near the chief, and his household parfleches and robes had been pushed to the perimeter and rested against the inner lining, which rose four or five feet and was tied to the lodgepoles. The chief's two wives had vanished.

A deep silence settled over them all, and David grew visibly nervous. But Jamie knew that Indians never were in a hurry and rarely began any kind of talk until they'd grown accustomed to one another, had absorbed the mood and spirit of all those present. It makes sense, he thought. They'd know even before a word was spoken whether Jamie and David were angry, hostile, afraid, arrogant, subservient, contemptuous, or whatever. Jamie used the quiet to study the two shamans, both weathered old men, for signs and to examine the war chiefs and headmen, most of them leaders of the various war and policing societies.

In the eyes of these he spotted that flat, cruel Comanche disdain for anything not of the People. A non-People was nothing; Jamie and David were nothing, and could be butchered and tortured for the good of the people. The Comanche had killed more white men than all the southern tribes put together. They'd killed Texas settlers without mercy, and the Texans killed them in kind. The Comanche routinely tortured and butchered men, women, and children of other tribes as well, considering all non-Comanches beneath contempt. Jamie knew that here he had no rights, that only the chief's seating arrangements overruled the bloodlust of these headmen. It clawed at him, but he concealed that. Old Wolf's temporary protection could dissolve in a moment. Jamie had only to say the wrong thing, and he and David would be hanging by their heels over a fire. He sweat, and wondered why he'd led himself and David into this sort of jeopardy.

Finally, Old Wolf broke the silence, scarcely waiting for David to translate. He began in a tongue Jamie didn't understand, Shoshonean in nature. Long before, the Comanche and Shoshone had been one people. But David stabbed at it, sometimes uncertainly.

"He says the Bents treat his people badly, like dogs. He says his people go to Bent's Fort for rifles and powder and balls and caps, and the Bents won't trade robes for them. He, uh, said some other words I didn't get. Trade items I guess. He says that the Bents trade rifles and powder to the other peoples, the Cheyenne and Arapaho, and now even the Kiowa. Jamie, I don't know their words for these tribes and I'm guessing them, from what I know—all right? He says the Bents let the Cheyenne into the fort and into the trading room, but they won't let his People in. Comanche must stand outside and push their robes through the trading window. I guess that's what he said. I'm guessing some, Jamie."

Actually, Jamie liked the sound of that, and nodded.

"He says that his People must have guns and powder to survive and kill the buffalo and fight their enemies. He says that no white men will trade with them, and their only friends have been the Mexicans—Comancheros—who come regularly and trade for robes and slaves. The Comancheros are the only true friends of the Comanche, and are faithful to the People, while the Bents are not. He says that now the Bents won't even trade at all; their window is closed."

"Did he say why, David?"

David shook his head. Jamie knew the reason the Bents weren't trading lay a few feet under the clay just outside Bent's Fort. Old Wolf wasn't admitting it. That was the Comanche way, though. All murder of non-Comanches was perfectly justifiable to the Comanche mind and spirit. The murder of Robert Bent was no exception. In some ways these people were admirable, but mostly they disgusted him. It would be no joy to trade with them—ever.

Old Wolf droned on, and David continued. "He says we fought the Comancheros—Benito—and killed the friends of the People. He says we take trade away from Benito. . . . I'm not sure what he said next—he talks too fast and I don't know all the words, the meanings. But I think he said, uh . . . Benito came in peace to us and wanted to share the trade with his People. Benito told him so, told him that soon the Comancheros and white men would have many things to trade with his people."

This was veering toward dangerous ground. Jamie nodded, pondering it. If he replied the wrong way, or said anything against Benito and his outfit, they'd end up as hanging meat.

"What does he want from us?"

David posed the question. Old Wolf pushed a stick into the faltering little fire and collected his thoughts.

Eventually the chief spoke again, and David followed. "The Comancheros are his friends. They buy slaves and robes. But they don't have much to offer. He wants guns and powder so he can make war against enemies. He wants to trade for all the things we have—guns and powder, knives and hatchets, cloth and all . . . but mostly guns and powder."

Jamie found himself in trouble. The Comancheros and the Mexican federals had taken his trade rifles and all the powder.

He grunted. "Tell him that we have no rifles or powder, except for ourselves. The Mexican army took them. I will show old Wolf myself. But we have many good things—all the rest that he wants. As many things as the Bents."

Old Wolf listened and growled out something.

"He says . . . he says we're hiding rifles from them too, like the Bents. White-man medicine makes rifles, and we are keeping the People from it."

"Tell him that next summer when the wagons come back from Saint Louis, we will have rifles to trade." He didn't feel comfortable about trading rifles to these bloody butchers who'd use them to kill anyone they could on the Santa Fe trail—including the company's own men. He felt plenty bad about it. But next year was next year. This year, he had to survive.

Old Wolf said nothing. He pulled his blanket around him and stared at Jamie, with a hard gaze that struck him like the hammering of mallets. Jamie met it, refusing to flinch or look away.

Then he decided maybe it was his time to talk. "All right, David. All right. Tell Old Wolf that we would like to trade. We have many goods. We would honor his people. . . .

"Tell him we will be here a long time, ready to trade, winter after winter. Tell him we are pleased to trade with the Comanche even if others—the Bents—won't. Tell him we have gifts for him and his headmen to begin the trading. . . .

"Tell him we like the fine robes his people tan. His people tan the best robes of all. We will trade for every robe in his village, and I will show him the things we have, so he can see them with his own eyes. The headmen, too."

David stammered through it, having trouble translating. Old Wolf listened alertly.

A shaman, whose name Jamie didn't know, said something to the rest of the headmen.

"I think he says that Benito has been loyal for many robe seasons . . . and these white men would not be," David explained. "Benito brings them guns; these white men make only lies."

Jamie took a risk. "Tell them some of the guns Benito traded were stolen from us."

287

David hesitated, his eyes questioning.

"Try it."

David stammered through it. "I don't know the word for *steal*," he said. "So I told them Benito had taken the guns."

The Comanches listened, and muttered among themselves, and Old Wolf pronounced judgment. "We know this. It is good. We want Benito to take guns from all white men and trade them to us."

Jamie decided to cut through all that. "I am inviting you to a celebration before the gates of the post this night. Everyone in the village is welcome. We will have a great fiesta"—he used the Spanish word deliberately, knowing they understood a lot of Spanish—"a fiesta with the spirit water that makes men laugh, and the next morning we will open our trading window and we will trade—knives, hatchets, blankets, kettles—all that for good robes, and you will be rich with our things. You are invited. We will go now and prepare for the fiesta."

David had no trouble getting that across, but there was no response among the headmen. They would debate it. They would consult Benito probably. And most likely, late in the day a thousand Comanches would camp on the doorstep of Fort Dance.

Jamie nodded to David, and they rose and left unobstructed. Outside, they blinked in the wintry sunlight. Their horses awaited them, held by police society warriors. Jamie felt a bad moment coming—wondered whether they'd be detained, become prisoners awaiting the whim of torturers. He and David mounted uneasily, and rode toward the Purgatoire, accompanied by a horde of silent warriors. Jamie wondered what temptations passed through the mind of each of these stocky men riding beside them. But at the river—the invisible boundary of the village—the Comanche police paused, letting Jamie and David ride through a narrow trail piercing the saltbush. Jamie and David crossed the shallow creek, probed through the saltbush on the other side until they emerged onto the flat before their post.

And encountered the whole hidden army of Comancheros.

Benito leveled a carbine upon Jamie. "Now we are partners, *sí?*" he said.

Tomás watched them coming. Nine Comancheros and Jamie and David. Most of the Comancheros had their carbines aimed directly at the Rocky Mountain Company partner, and at the son of the senior partner. Mother of God.

Beside him, behind the parapet, the fort's riflemen peered uncertainly at this spectacle. The advancing Comancheros drew within easy range of the post's rifles and ignored them. A single shot from the post would instantly put several deadly balls into Jamie and David. They all knew that. Even so, Tomás scanned his men, wondering what sort of folly lurked in their breasts.

The world turned quiet. Even the breeze seemed to die. His men peered down upon this little army, not believing their eyes, feeling death stalk them. Far across the Purgatoire, Comanche police warriors watched quietly.

"Tomás—you got any way outa this?" asked Lyle Black, from his post up in the watchtower

"We are in the hands of God," said Tomás, wondering if it was so.

Nine Comancheros. Their number had been greatly reduced after all, Tomás realized. David's two deadly shots with the fowling piece had wounded most of them. But there was no comfort in it. Cold reality was stalking them like the Four Horsemen of the Apocalypse, pestilence on the white horse, war on the red horse, famine on the black horse—and death on the pale horse. Benito rode a pale horse. No one rode a white. But there were reds, including Jamie's chestnut.

He wondered why his mind turned to Biblical allusions in such a moment. He was a poor *capitán*, and he'd be a poorer priest. He scolded himself for having such thoughts when he ought to be scheming, looking for any advantage.

But he saw none. As the party drew close to the gates, he knew they had no advantage. Worse the Comancheros knew it. Benito smiled blandly.

"*Señores.* I pray you will open the gates," he said.

"Don't do it, Tomás." Jamie's voice lashed up at him.

Benito laughed easily. "Ah, señores. If you do not open the gates, what will happen?"

"You heard me, Tomás."

Jamie's face had turned to granite. David looked silent and subdued. The Comancheros had caught their watchtower tormenter, after all.

"Señores, señores, we will be partners now. If you do not open the gates at once and surrender your weapons"—he chortled happily—"sad little things might happen."

"You heard me, Tomás."

"Señor Dance, you will be quiet now."

"The hell I will. Don't open them gates, Tomás. No matter what. Think of Teresa María. Think of Juanita Chávez."

The arcing stock of the carbine caught Jamie's head, knocking him out of his saddle. He tumbled to earth as his chestnut shied. Several carbines followed him down. He sat on the cold earth, shaking his head, clutching it, sobbing.

Benito laughed. "Ah, Tomás. You see how it is."

David looked terrified now.

From the earth, Jamie mumbled up at him. "Don't do it, Tomás," and then collapsed onto his stomach.

Tomás peered about desperately. No ideas came winging in out of the blue to salvage the day. "I'll think about it," he yelled.

Benito chortled again. "Ah, Tomás, there is no time. While you think, these two will discover pain."

Tomás ignored him. He peered along the parapets. He had, actually, enough riflemen to shoot the entire lot of Comancheros if each one took a target. But it would take doing, and probably would result in the deaths of Jamie and David. Still . . . Jamie and David and all the rest would die anyway if they surrendered.

Mazappa stood beside him. "Señor Oliphant," Tomás said quietly. "Go along the wall and instruct each man to pick a target, and to make sure there is no duplication. Pronto!"

"Ah, Tomás, how you plot and scheme up there. But it is too late, sí? Death, she comes. But first a little amusement."

Mazappa slipped along the gallery, instructing men. Below, Benito laughed. Then he barked a command, and two of the Comancheros slid off their horses and approached David.

"See, Tomás. We have this David here. The very one who tormented us last night. Now we will have our revenge. Our friends the Comanches taught us how to revenge ourselves."

"Benito—we have a rifle on each of you."

"Ah, Tomás. We will not kill them. These two are our passports through the gates. But if you begin to fire . . . ah, Tomás, these two are no more; the post is no more; you are no more."

Tomás felt rage and helplessness war within him.

"They all got a man picked out," Mazappa whispered. "Lyle, he's saving Benito for hisself."

The Comancheros yanked David from his saddle. He fought hard, with muscles built up from the long toil of the Santa Fe trail and the heavy work on the fort. But they overpowered him, yelling and bellowing like a bull calf, and tied his legs and arms with their rawhide reatas.

Benito peered up at Tomás. "Ah," he sighed. "Life is hard. We have sad duties. We suffer misfortunes. What a misfortune for us, Tomás. We make our small living trading with the Comanches, and along comes this company to drive us out of business. Our business is threatened, sí? This big company—you see how it affects a poor *campesino* like me. But I am kind. I would not think of killing these two—even though they have brought death to my *compadres.*" He sighed and slid off his nervous horse.

Slowly, eyeing the riflemen above, he set his carbine aside and withdrew a large, wicked-looking knife from a belt sheath. "Ah, Tomás, it is a pity."

The rest of the Comancheros kept their carbines steadily on Jamie and David; all but two, whose carbines pointed up at Tomás.

Those black bores terrified him. A small spasm of a muscle and he'd die, a ball through his head.

But Benito was about to exhibit something. He meandered over to where David lay on the earth like a trussed calf. He stooped down, plucked up David's hand, and sawed swiftly with his knife. David screamed and writhed. Blood bloomed, then gouted from his right hand. A small cylinder of flesh lay on the clay. David shrieked, his body writhing and twisting in its bonds, his hand turning bright red.

Benito laughed, then plucked David's little finger from the earth and held it up, a talisman. He waved it for all to see.

Tomás felt nausea flood him, felt his gorge rise, his will turn soft; felt surrender boil up in him.

The Comancheros laughed. David's howling never ceased, an eerie shriek that rose and fell like the wind, like something that had always been there, an elemental force.

"Tomás. You will open the gates and set down your rifles now, *sí?* We will let you all run away to the Bents. Do it now, or the next finger, it becomes separated from Señor Straus. Soon he has no fingers, *sí?* Just bloody stumps. He can hold nothing. He must be fed like a *niño, sí?* One by one. And then our friend Señor Dance. He's got ten fingers too. One by one!"

David's shrieking pierced Tomás like swords.

"Open the gates," he said to Mazappa. "Open the gates."

He peered raggedly along the parapets. One of the men, Ames, was on his knees vomiting.

Mazappa stared grayly. "I don't know. . . . If they kill Jamie, they'll git shot to bits. Maybe we should jist hang on."

But David's shrieking tore at Tomás, raked him with guilt.

Up in the watchtower, Lyle muttered something.

Time froze.

"Ah, Tomás—it is time for another finger!"

Tomás felt a great sagging within. He wasn't made for this. Mazappa clambered down the ladder to the yard, and Tomás heard the inner gates creak on their iron hinges.

"Don't do it, Tomás," Jamie muttered from the earth. "Think about the women."

Benito chuckled. "Delightful women. Ah, how I will enjoy Teresa María! Tonight will be paradise!"

Tomás peered around him. Teresa had vanished into her quarters and shut the door, making a feeble barrier.

Below him, out of sight, he heard the outer gates swing open. He heard a shot, and knew, horrified, that Mazappa Oliphant lay dead or dying. Benito laughed, his eerie howl echoing through the wintry afternoon. Tomás knew he'd made a ghastly mistake.

Benito and another Comanchero picked up Jamie, who struggled some, and held the bloody knife to Jamie's throat as they all staggered into the yard.

Others carried David along with them.

The Comancheros entered the yard cautiously, swinging carbines upward toward the gallery, swiftly spreading out, but two or three always kept Jamie and David in their gunsights, ready to deal instant death.

David moaned. Blood slid from his hand, reddening the clay.

Jamie had recovered his senses, and stared at Tomás. "Shoot them," he said. A lump, swollen and mottled red, had ballooned on his temple. Standing behind him, Benito clamped one arm tighter around Jamie's chest, and pressed the knife into his throat until a thin red line began to bleed drops of blood down Jamie's neck.

"Shoot them!" Jamie growled. He looked pain-crazed.

For once, Benito stopped chortling, and as he stopped, so did the world stop spinning on its axis; so did the sun stop. Slowly, holding Jamie in his deadly grip, he surveyed the post's riflemen one by one, studying each with an unblinking gaze that registered everything; a child's gaze, but one that somehow, diabolically, made men lower their rifles and shrink back from the edge of the abyss. Tomás watched aghast, seeing Benito's deadly stare do the work of a dozen rifles, while Jamie bled from the neck, half-dazed.

Tomás found himself staring down into the muzzle of a Comanchero's carbine. The post's riflemen wavered, one by one. A few Comancheros aimed up at them, but most aimed at David and one at Jamie, ready to finish what the knife at his throat would begin.

Benito nodded to one of the Comancheros pinning David to the clay of the yard. The hombre slid out a rusty knife.

That's when the shot boomed from the watchtower.

CHAPTER 29

Down in the yard, the Comanchero kneeling over David tumbled to earth, shot in the head. Lyle Black's ball had gone true.

A paralyzed moment passed. Jamie knew he'd die; the knife smarting at his throat would swipe deep, he'd feel his arteries pumping blood to the ground, then nothing more. But it didn't happen. Instead, Benito, behind him, froze. Jamie, still dizzy and confused, peered wildly about. Above, on the gallery, his own men aimed at Comancheros in the yard; below, outnumbered Comancheros ran for cover.

Why was he alive? Suddenly he knew. If Benito killed him, Benito would die. Tomás pointed his rifle right at Jamie and Benito; Jamie gaped into its barrel. He saw Black's reloaded rifle poke out of the watchtower window and aim—straight at him. Jamie alive was Benito's safe-conduct; Jamie dead meant the end of Benito.

It blossomed in Jamie, this startling knowledge that the *capitán* had overreached; greed had undone him. But that didn't settle the terror he felt at the knife stinging his throat; the terror of Benito's capricious ways; the terror of a suicidal impulse in the Comanchero to kill Jamie anyway. That above all, even as Benito laughed crazily behind him and that grim blade trembled upon his jugular.

He wanted to shout, but dared not. He willed himself to be quiet, his only defense against a berserk thrust of the knife across his bare throat. He had never known such helplessness.

"Ah, Dance," Benito whispered in his ear. "We must leave

294

here together. At the gates we will be safe. Under the watchtower. Then I will live and you will die."

He wrestled Jamie forward. The knife biting deeper at his throat, Jamie resisted inertly, slowing Benito yet letting himself be dragged toward the gates. He glanced up toward the galleries, watching the rifles follow them, his own men helpless to act. Benito had the edge, and was wrestling Jamie and himself away.

Benito laughed softly, and Jamie felt the man's wild humor gurgle upward and spray into his ear, which was inches from Benito's mouth. The post's men ran along the gallery; he heard shots exchanged between the Comancheros and his own men, even as Benito wrestled him through the inner gates and under the watchtower, out of range of the rifles.

Benito halted, laughing with joy, utterly fearless and enjoying the moment. Out on the flats beyond the gates, the saddled horses waited, held by a thin boy. From the watchtower above, a shot boomed, striking one horse. It squealed and bucked, and the rest bolted off.

Benito watched them go. "Ah, Dance. Now we will have to walk farther, *si?*"

They passed the body of Mazappa, sprawled between the inner and outer gates, shot in cold blood when he'd opened them to the Comancheros. Jamie writhed at the sight of it; at his friend lying there, the life gone out of him. This post had killed so many, maybe himself at any instant, and he felt sick of it, sick of the company, sick of his part in it.

Benito said, "He tried to save your life, Dance. Loyal to you. Opened the gates to save you. Loyalty. It is good, *si?*"

Jamie Dance didn't respond. A word could bring the spasm of fingers that would end his life.

Benito paused, peering out at the dead horse, the fleeing horses, and his *muchacho* trying desperately to catch them. From within the post came the crackle of rifle fire; a full battle now. Jamie wondered about David, trussed in the yard. Dead, dead.

Benito turned as silent as Jamie, knowing that he'd failed and now faced his own death. Then, his mind made up, he prodded Jamie forward, letting the knife cut more flesh. Jamie felt blood ooze down his throat. They marched slowly toward the outer gates. Benito was heading for a horse; Jamie would be his passport. Up in the watchtower, Lyle Black could not shoot. Suddenly Jamie knew what would happen. They'd reach the horses. Benito and the boy would use the horses for cover until they got out of rifle range. Then Benito would slit his throat—and ride away free.

He heard footsteps behind; Benito did too. A rush of steps; someone racing through the gates toward them. Benito turned awkwardly to see, dragging Jamie around.

Tomás! His rifle high! Benito released Jamie, who tumbled to the ground. Benito threw the knife with one deadly flick of his arm. Tomás gasped. A shot. Benito grunted—an explosion of air from his mouth—and sagged to the earth, coughing.

Jamie rolled up. Tomás stood, his rifle sagging, staring at Benito, whose skull had been blown open. The Comanchero's body quivered, spasmed, and grew still. Blood leaked from Tomás's left ribs, reddening his buckskin coat.

Tomás laughed shakily. "It isn't much. A scratch." As if to prove the point, he picked up Benito's knife from the earth.

Jamie didn't say anything. He was incapable of speaking. His throat hurt. His head throbbed. His brain ached. They stood there in their own dripping blood, gaping at each other.

"David," Jamie said at last. He could see the boy's trussed body out in the yard—and other bodies. Tears arose in him.

Tomás sagged, pressing his elbow against the side. "I will never be a priest," he said. "Not now."

"Saved my life."

Tomás shook his head, wearily.

They limped toward the inner gates and the yard, suddenly afraid to step out there and get shot by someone or other.

Jamie called from the shadow of the gates. "Lyle? Ames? Goodin?"

Someone yelled back. "Jamie?"

"Hyar at the gates. Me and Tomás."

"Benito git?"

296

"Dead."

He heard a ragged cheering from his men. But it wasn't enough. "We're comin' into the yard. Don't shoot. Tomás's hurt."

"We got 'em. Come ahead."

He walked in, Tomás limping beside him, walked straight toward David, passed three Comancheros sprawled in their own blood. It'd be bad, cutting the dead boy loose.

He got Benito's knife from Tomás, who now could barely stand, and reeled toward the barracks. Up above, men raced along the gallery toward the ladder to help.

Jamie peered into David's face—and found David peering back at him with wounded eyes. A vast but tentative relief swept through him. "You'll make 'er, boy. Got to cut you loose."

David said nothing. His hand had swollen grotesquely, but the bleeding had stopped. He seemed almost inert, as if these brutal events had knocked the breath out of him. But—if he wasn't otherwise injured—he'd spring back, with all the strength and optimism of youth.

Jamie sawed gently at the braided rawhide reata that bound David, and the cords fell free. "Come on, lad. We'll get that hand bandaged. Little finger ain't gonna hurt none."

David stood wearily, dazed. We're both dazed, Jamie thought, his head throbbing, his ears ringing, his neck smarting, his vision doubled by concussion.

Men reached them, helped them. They led David off to the barracks. Jamie refused help. Too many questions crowded him.

"Teresa María?"

That door remained shut.

"The Chávez family—Juanita? The chillun?"

Even as he spoke, that door creaked open and he saw them.

He noticed prisoners, three Comancheros herded out from the warehouse where they'd been held by Ames and Launes. They looked like men do when they're about to die. But Jamie was sick of death.

So were the rest. He could see that. The men averted their

eyes, half expecting to be ordered to shoot the Comancheros and drag them away, then cleanse Fort Dance of all the blood that had been spilled there in the yard, on the roofs, and at the gates.

Jamie swallowed. One-armed Blake Goodin stood among them. His talents would be good enough. "Blake?"

That was all it took. The Comancheros were herded to the charred robe press, stripped of their shirts, and tied by their wrists to the top crossbar. Blake snapped his tasseled bullwhip, the tool of choice for a one-armed master teamster, and cracked it into the first, the weighted tassel cutting a pock in the man's back. The man screamed, and his body jolted against its bonds. Then the whip cracked rhythmically; men screamed and sobbed and bled. Blake knew when to stop, when to let them go into the afternoon with a memory indelibly impressed on their minds.

But Jamie was sick of it. He walked across the yard and pushed on his door, found it wouldn't open. Teresa had piled their crude furniture against it.

"It's me," he said.

"Madre de Dios!"

He pushed and she tugged a chair and a bench and a table away, and then he caught her in his arms.

"Blood! They cut your throat!" She started to scream. He laughed, some macabre humor rising in him.

"Slit my throat in two. Benito done it. But I sewed 'er back up."

"Caramba!"

She began laughing, but his head hurt too much when he did. It throbbed with every spasm.

They hugged, he in pain, she with relief, but his mind wasn't in it.

"We're having us a party tonight," he said.

"A party?"

"Comanche. Whole village. Least I think so. They're invited. They had to sit and think about it."

"A party? With all this death?"

"In Mexico, that's as good an excuse as any," he muttered.

* * *

But no one wanted a party. They grieved the death of Mazappa. They ached along with David, who lay on his pallet, a thick bloody bandage over his swollen hand, groaning and sometimes sobbing. Near him in the barracks, Luis Soto and Pepe Alvaro nursed their own wounds.

The post's men rolled four dead Comancheros, including Benito, into slings and carried them out to the growing graveyard. They carried two injured ones out to the Comanchero ponies, still held by a *muchacho*. And they escorted the three that Goodin had bullwhipped out the gates. Each had received ten lashes. Their backs were red ruins. None could bear to put on a shirt, even in the freezing cold. They sobbed and stumbled across the field, and no one pitied them.

But it was Mazappa's death that drained the victory of all joy. Lyle Black, in particular, had partnered with Mazappa on a dozen trips out the Santa Fe trail, with a few trapping and hellraising excursions in between. Jamie had known him almost as well and as long, and he could barely stand the sight of that cooling body, his friend flown away. It oppressed him, made the afternoon leaden. And it depressed everyone else. Fort Dance had claimed too many lives, had inflicted too many wounds.

At least one of those wounds was to the spirit rather than the body. Tomás wandered the yard like a man who'd lost his mind, sometimes weeping, and sometimes staring at his hands, sometimes scrubbing his hands violently. He didn't help with the grim chores, and no one asked him to.

Jamie found him at the open gates, staring across the flats to the Comanche village. Over there, warriors were watching the post, curious about the gunfire. Tomás stood at the very place where he had shot and killed Benito, rooted there by something that engulfed him.

Jamie threw an amiable arm around his shoulder. "*Amigo,* you saved my life here."

"I killed a man here." Tomás wept suddenly.

Jamie waited until the sobbing subsided. "Tomás . . . we

all have different natures, I reckon. It didn't bother me, trappin' the beaver. But you're tender, and the thought of them caught underwater, drownin' in the traps—it bothered you. I didn't like it none. No one does, except a few who are plumb mean. . . . So you did other things. Tended camp. More valuable than settin' beaver traps."

Tomás said nothing. Jamie could feel him slump into himself.

"You saved my life. Benito, he was fixin' to slit my gullet in a moment. He's murdered more men than you can count on your fingers—you can be sure of that. And tortured a few with Comanche tricks. You weren't killin' anyone who didn't deserve it."

"I killed a priest," Tomás muttered.

That gave Jamie pause.

"I knew I would die. I had the foreboding in me. I told you about it."

There was nothing Jamie could say. They stood at the gates staring out across a windswept flat with no one on it. The remaining Comancheros had limped back to the village.

"I knew I'd die," Tomás continued. "The priest died. Hands that have killed another mortal cannot consecrate the Host. . . . I had always planned to finish up, overcome this . . . this little pecadillo of youth. Settle into my true calling. Now I'm dead."

"No, Tomás, not dead. I reckon maybe God picks and chooses some, steers a man this way and that. You told me once you'd left the seminary because, well, of woman. Maybe up thar, He figured you ought ter have a woman. And another vocation. Maybe bein' a trader."

Tomás sighed and said nothing. Jamie knew he couldn't comfort his old friend now. Maybe time would help.

"Come on over to the house, and Teresa'll brew up some tea."

Tomás shook his head and stared out upon the empty flat, not willing to face the future. He was weeping again, tears sliding silently down his sallow face.

Two blanket-wrapped Comanches riding ponies emerged

300

from the saltbush on the Purgatoire, and rode toward the post. Emissaries from the village no doubt.

"You come on in hyar, Tomás," Jamie said roughly. He dragged his friend back to the yard, and picked up the Hawken propped there.

"Couple Comanche comin'—just to talk. But look to our safety," he said to Lyle. As he turned back to the gates, he saw the company men bounding up toward the parapets.

Even with their blankets drawn over their heads against the steady northwind, these two looked familiar to Jamie. Headmen. The pair of them had been in Old Wolf's lodge during the council. They were not armed—at least not visibly.

He motioned them in, and they walked their ponies slowly toward the gates, observing the dead Comanchero horse outside, the shrouded body of Mazappa just inside. They peered about sharply, noting everything, especially the armed men on the roofs. They examined the line of dried blood along Jamie's throat with intense curiosity.

Jamie motioned them into the trading room, where a new fire smoked in the fireplace. It was scarcely warmer inside than out, but the fire radiated warmth and the air was still. Lyle Black followed Jamie in.

The older one, his gray hair in braids wrapped with red tradecloth, spoke in Spanish. That didn't surprise Jamie at all. "Chief Old Wolf has sent us to find out what happened."

"Benito and the Comancheros captured us when we left your village. Tried to use that to take over the post, kill us all. It didn't succeed. Benito's dead. The rest are dead or wounded. We lost one, and feel very bad about it."

The old one nodded. "I am Runs Fast, headman of the Hungry Horse Society. He is Walks at Night, and has medicine and sees things truly."

A headman and a shaman. About right, Jamie thought. Old Wolf would want the facts and the medicine.

"My chiefs, we are grieving now for the one lost to us."

Runs Fast nodded. "Old Wolf asked us to find out what happened. And to say to the traders that the People will bring robes tomorrow."

301

"No celebration tonight?"

Runs Fast explained. "Old Wolf said tonight you will have your victory dance and scalp dance, and we will not come."

"We won't be celebrating anything tonight. It's not a victory we care about. We're tired, and we have to bury our friend."

"We will bring robes tomorrow," said Runs Fast.

"You wait a minute! Over there, you've got our oxen and mules and horses that Benito took. You bring them with you, and then we'll trade. We won't trade until you do."

Runs Fast looked annoyed. The shaman's face didn't reveal anything, and Jamie doubted that he understood the Spanish they were speaking.

"I will tell Old Wolf. Maybe the People will trade elsewhere. We have many robes."

Jamie knew it was an empty threat. Other groups of Comancheros, operating from *placitas* and villages, traded with other bands of Comanches. But right now, Old Wolf's large band had no one to trade with.

"I will await you tomorrow. Bring our livestock." It sounded harsh, so Jamie dug into a cannister and removed two twists of tobacco. He handed one to each visitor. They accepted.

Moments later, he watched the pair of them ride across the flat, the cruel wind cutting into their blankets and harrying their ponies. They vanished into the saltbush, and that was the last he saw of them.

Tomorrow they would come. They'd found out what they needed to know. Even before they came, they knew a lot. The wounded Comancheros had straggled back into their village, their numbers reduced, Benito not among them. Jamie knew that nothing about the survivors had escaped Old Wolf's eye or knowledge.

The wintry afternoon was dimming. Necessity pressed down on Fort Dance.

"I guess it's time, Lyle," he said wearily.

"Ground's thawed now; won't be soon."

They posted Fidel Santa María and Hector Chávez to the watchtower. Mazappa's friends gathered around the tight-wrapped shroud, each of them wanting to bear the pall. Jamie too. Solemnly they marched into the twilight, toward the edge of the cottonwoods which poked their naked limbs into a gloomy sky. Behind came the rest of the post's men, save for those on watch; men with shovels. And the women too. Teresa María, who never let a funeral pass by unattended, wrapped tightly in a shawl and a blanket; Juanita Chávez as well, and the little ones.

They buried Mazappa Oliphant hastily, the wind numbing them all. Jamie dug furiously to keep warm as well as keep the others from freezing. He raged as he stabbed the cold clay, raged because his post, Fort Dance—his enterprise, Rocky Mountain Company—had shed so much blood into the soil of Mexico. But finally they did lower the stiff, shrouded body into a shallow scoop in the earth, alongside a growing line of graves. And then Jamie rested on his spade, panting, angry, while Lyle Black said some words and led a prayer. Numbly they shoveled the clay back in, hoping the grave was deep enough to keep coyotes and wolves at bay—and then fled to the fort and its fireplaces, even as night fell and the spirits of the dead wavered and howled through the rattling yard.

CHAPTER 30

The Comanche headmen arrived at the gates of Fort Dance shortly after sunup, an unheard-of hour for trading. But it was the dead of winter, and the sun stayed only fleetingly. A dozen of them stood before the post, wrapped in blankets or robes against the biting air. Behind them stood their wives, burdened with great dark bundles they could scarcely carry. And arrayed beyond, clear down to the Purgatoire, were hundreds more—the whole village of Old Wolf, waiting to trade.

Jamie lived in a fog mornings, and never came alive until night. But now the sight of the whole village waiting to trade galvanized him. At last!

He hastened into his black frock coat, found a silk tophat in the trading room, and gathered up gifts—still more tobacco, some ribbon, some geegaws. He wished David could translate, but the youth lay in his barracks pallet tormented by his hand. Tomás would keep the books today. He gathered his men swiftly; there were things that needed attention at once.

"Lyle, make a kettle of trade whiskey. One part spirits, five water. Red pepper and a plug of tobacco in each kettle. Add a bit of ginger—and some tea for color. We started to make some before. Throw that out and start fresh."

Others needed no instruction. They built a fire to warm the trading room and swung the shutter of the trading window, which opened on the corridor that lay between the in-

304

ner and outer gates. Finally they creaked open the outer gates.

Jamie and Tomás, suitably attired for the ceremonies, stalked out to the waiting headmen. At the northern posts this was always a great event, punctuated by speeches and gifts, and the firing of the six-pounders up in the bastions. Or at least a rifle volley or two. And always the running up of the American flag and the company ensign. But not now.

He stood before Old Wolf. "Welcome, my chief," he said in Spanish, knowing it'd be understood. "Welcome, my chiefs," he said to the rest. "We will trade now in friendship. Our windows are open to the Comanche. Our prices are good. Our supplies are plentiful. Your people tan splendid robes, and we are eager to have them. All that you wish to trade. We have many good things. Here is a token of our esteem for each of you."

He handed his gifts to Old Wolf and the headmen, even while the wintry wind whipped their blankets.

Old Wolf had a speech of his own, and the winter wasn't going to shorten it. He praised the company. He complained that no one among the whites would trade with the Comanche. He complained that the village lacked guns and powder and lead. He said his village would make Fort Dance their trading home for as long as the sun rose and set.

Jamie felt half-frozen by it all but endured. Then, at last, the trade began, the chief and headmen first. They lined up patiently before the trading window.

Jamie and Tomás slipped quickly into the trading room, which had turned into a feverishly busy place. Jamie settled on a stool at the trading window, while Tomás sat beside him, arraying his nibs and unstoppering the ink and dating the ledger. Behind them, several clerks waited.

Old Wolf himself had twenty robes to trade—and Jamie understood at once that this village had at least that many per lodge. He exulted. The Bents wouldn't trade with Old

Wolf, and the village had accumulated a fortune in fine robes.

Swiftly he spread the robes out on the counter, examined them for holes, for thickness, for softness, for mange or disease, and then announced his verdict to Tomás and Lyle Black. Old Wolf spoke in Comanche, pointed at things he wanted, and Jamie wasn't always sure of the requests. But little by little a heap of goods built on the counter, as clerks sprang to the shelves for the desired item. Other clerks waited to cart the robes away to the warehouse as soon as each transaction was completed. Old Wolf bought four-point Witney blankets, two cream and one green, all with black stripes. He bought axe heads, hatchets, hoop iron, vermilion, hawk bells, red ribbon, powder and lead—Jamie had little to spare of that, but humored the chief—coffee beans, sugar, salt, and finally he shoved a dull ceramic pot to the counter.

Old Wolf had traded for seventeen robes, and had a credit for three more. Three cups, then. Jamie took his pint-measure tin cup and dipped it into the kettle of trade whiskey, making sure it was brim-full. He showed the brimming measure to Old Wolf, and then poured it carefully into the earthen pot. He did it again, and a third time, grinning. Old Wolf grinned back.

The chief picked up the earthen pot lovingly, leaving the mountain of goods to his wife who gathered everything in her sturdy arms and staggered off toward the village.

Jamie sighed happily. It was a beginning. But they'd been slowed down by the lack of a translator. Only a few Comanches understood Spanish. He turned to Lyle. "We need David. Tell him we need him badly. All he has to do is sit hyar and translate. He don't have to write or nothin'."

Lyle ran out the door.

Jamie traded again. The next man, a headman, had an amazing thirty-two robes to trade, and once again Jamie pulled each one over the counter, examined it, offered a price for it, and then snapped instructions to clerks as the headman pointed and muttered, refused or accepted items, the pile of goods mounting before him. This one scorned the trade whiskey, and set no clay pot on the counter.

Lyle showed up with David, who looked pale and miserable. The youth said nothing, but settled himself beside the trading window. He'd rigged a sling to keep his bandaged hand high and not throbbing. After that, things went much faster.

One by one, the patient Comanches took a turn at the window, shoving fine buffalo robes in and extracting a heap of goods in return. Behind Jamie, clerks danced and supplies on the shelves dwindled, while out in the warehouse the new robes built into a mountain. Clerks kept the fire in the trading room bright, letting it cast its glow over shining metal, bright cloth, dazzling ribbons. Once an elderly man pointed at the Osage orange bow wood stacked in a corner. Jamie had quite forgotten about it. He grabbed several and let the man examine them, while David explained it was dried bow wood, the best there was.

The Comanche nodded, and rubbed his hand over the orange-colored wood. He surrendered two robes for the one he chose. After that, several warriors traded for the fine bow wood, a rarity in this area. Jamie was delighted. They'd hauled the wood clear from Missouri where it grew. And the gamble was working.

They didn't pause for a nooning. The feverish trade continued unabated. Over the counter went an array of Wilson butcher knives, Green River knives, awls, hanks of beads, blankets, yards of calico and gingham and bed ticking, packets of vermilion, axes and awls, beaver traps, kettles and skillets, and pints of coffee or sugar, wrapped in fragile paper. The robes poured in, and along with them came other peltries—doe and elkskin, wolf and fox pelts, beaver plews, otter and ermine, all of them fit to grace my lady's clothing back East.

But the item most popular was the one that did the village no good at all, other than offer an ephemeral wild time. Jamie didn't think much about it, except to worry about dealing with a whole drunken village. In the past, there had been disasters among Indian traders when the spirits had turned tribesmen sullen and murderous. He worried about that; he didn't worry about the rest. If they wanted trade whiskey, that was their choice. He was there to provide it. If he didn't, they would go somewhere else with their trade.

They paused for nothing. By midafternoon David was white with fatigue; Jamie not much better off, especially after the brutal previous day and night. But still Comanches came, dumping their treasure on the counter and taking their choices. Some of them wanted nothing but the trade whiskey, the more the better. They slapped robes down, and then their drinking pot, and waited.

The clerks manufactured another kettle of it, and another, and several more. Each kettleful was worth a hundred fifty robes or more. As the day waned, they watered it more, weakening it, as was the custom of traders.

Not even the approach of twilight slowed down the trading. Normally, a post would shut its window around four, and begin the next day's trade around ten. But not this time. Jamie wanted robes and hides and pelts, and would stay open as long as anyone came to the window. And come they did. But more and more now, the women showed up with robes they'd held out earlier. They came for needles and thread, awls, cloth, ribbons, bells, looking glasses—some had never seen an image of themselves, except in the still water of a pond—and sugar. They loved the New Orleans brown sugar.

Jamie began running low on goods. The kettles were gone, except for the two they used for the whiskey. They were low on knives. The calicoes and ginghams were half gone.

Not until full darkness did the trading stop. The very last at the window was an old woman, too weak to stand and wait in the deepening cold. She was obviously poor, and brought an old and dirty split robe. Jamie looked into her seamed face, saw the resignation and pain there, and knew he'd cap this amazing day with something good.

"Ask her what she wants for the split, David."

David listened. "She'd like a small knife."

"Ask her what else."

"She'd like a bit of sugar."

"And what else?"

David looked at Jamie, and smiled wanly. He consulted with the ancient woman. "A little coffee, a little cloth, a few ribbons . . ."

From the doorway, Teresa María said, "Give her all, Jamie: Some day we will be old too."

Surprised, he turned to her. She wasn't smiling.

"I'm fixin' to," he said. She looked as weary as the rest, drained of energy by the terror of recent hours.

In the end, the bent old woman trundled a treasure worth ten robes back across the flats. He knew she'd wade the icy Purgatoire and head for a shabby lodge, where her ancient husband was probably drinking from his pot or sleeping. It seemed a good way to end the day. He pulled the shutters tight, while the post's men swung the creaking gates shut. Across the flats, fires glowed in lodges, and if one listened hard, one could catch the whoops and howls of revelry.

Wearily, Jamie and Tomás and David wandered toward the dark warehouse, lit dimly now by a candle-lantern. They knew they'd exhausted the robes in this village, but over the next months many more would come in as the hunts continued.

They found Hector Chávez there, supervising a crew of three. The robes lay in heaps, each higher than the height of a man.

"What is the count, Hector?"

"It is a good take! We have two thousand eight hundred fifty-nine robes—most of them prime. We have a hundred and twelve deerhides; twenty-three elk hides; fifty-five of wolves and coyotes, and a few other things—thirty beaver, a few rabbit."

Something joyous built in Jamie's breast. These, plus what they'd traded for earlier, gave them a profit this year. And the season was only half over. A profit—if Colonel Agustino Cortez didn't swoop down again. Jamie knew he'd do something about that: most of these robes would be swiftly baled and carried over to the Bent warehouse and stored there for a small fee, on the other side of the boundary. That was a common enough practice, even among fierce rivals.

They'd won! For this year, anyway. He stood in the gloomy warehouse and howled, an eerie sound like a lobo wolf's cry. A mountain man's howl; a howl out of the wilds of an untamed land. David stared at him aghast. Tomás smiled. Men paused in their labors.

Emilio had started a meal. Jamie smelled coffee. They were out of meat unless they slaughtered an ox. It would be cornmeal cakes again. But it didn't matter. He'd hire more *ciboleros* soon.

"Go eat," he said to his assembled men. "Go rest. Me, I'll git on up to the watchtower. Someone's got to keep an eye on that village."

They began to disperse, reluctantly.

"Hyar now," he cried. "After that village goes, we'll have us a party. Spirits enough for that. A rare whoop-up. But not until later. Them's still Comanche out there. And we're still gonna watch."

He plucked a pair of robes from the heap and clambered up to the tower in the dark, relieving Pepe Alvaro, who huddled there in the blackness. It'd be another brutal night, with icy air eddying through those window slits. But it didn't matter. He hardly felt his weariness.

He leaned into the adobe wall until he was comfortable. It'd be a long cold watch. Below him, dimly lit by a few lanterns and the dull light leaking from shuttered windows, lay a whole trading post that hadn't existed a few months before. Within that dark warehouse lay a fortune in robes. In the trading room remained an array of goods. Out across the flats, the lodge fires of a whole village of trading partners glowed softly. They'd traded all day, and would trade again before the winter had passed, and yet again in the spring before the buffalo lost their winter hair. And other Comanche villages would come in; maybe their allies the Kiowa too.

He turned his gaze again toward the post below him and felt a wave of sadness engulf him. This place had cost lives, more lives than he wanted to think about. A terrible price. One by one he named them, conjuring up their images — Mazappa, Manolo, Juan Cordova. . . . He wept. It had been too much. But then he calmed his soul and watched through the night.

CHAPTER 31

The Osage had been sighted. Frowning, Guy grabbed his gold-headed walking stick and wove through the quiet salons of Straus et Fils. At the burnished door, Gregoire handed him his tophat. Out on Chestnut Street, his chaise stood ready, pinned to the curb with a carriage weight.

Guy sat in the chaise awaiting Yvonne, who had been summoned as well. The door to their brick home next door opened, emitting Yvonne, dressed in white gauzy cotton against the steam of late June. Dark-haired Clothilde followed eagerly. The door closed behind them. They settled silently in the plush seat beside him, and he turned the silky gray trotters toward the Mississippi levee a half a mile away.

No one spoke. They knew this would be a hard meeting, no matter the joy of seeing David again. Guy had come to his decision about the Rocky Mountain Company, and it would be painful news for some of the people arriving on the packet from Independence. The robe trade was the hardest business of all.

He'd known of the impending arrival for several days. The Rocky Mountain wagon train had traveled in tandem with the Bent one for mutual protection, and at Council Groves they had sent an express ahead. At Westport, near Independence, the year's returns from Fort Dance had been transshipped to the packet, and the teamsters given their leave, the livestock and wagons pastured and stored. Jamie

Dance, Teresa María Dance, and David continued ahead on *The Osage*, along with the Bent contingent.

A turmoil gripped the levee. Stevedore slaves awaited their tasks. Embarking passengers hovered around their valises. Chouteau's sweating clerks erupted from their fur company offices to tally bales going into the Chouteau warehouse. Both the Bents and Guy's company would store their bales there. In the bedlam Guy and his family awaited quietly on the hot carriage seat while the twin-chimney riverboat maneuvered toward the levee, its main deck teeming with restless passengers too distant to identify.

Then he saw them. His gaze lingered on David, who looked browned, lean, and more muscular through the shoulders. Dance and his wife were beside him, unaware of the coming unpleasantness.

"I see him!" cried Yvonne. "Oh!"

That part of it was fine. Having David home safely, after his year in the wilds. The rest—tallying the losses, ending the company—wouldn't be.

The packet seemed to sag into the water as it glided in, its duckbill prow poking ever closer. Deckhands tossed hawsers to sweat-streaked slaves on the levee. A sudden violent shrill of the steam whistle announced the arrival, jolting Guy's senses. Then the stage clattered down, lowered by harried deckmen, and the passengers surged forth.

Yvonne and Clothilde ran ahead of him. David, first off the boat, laughed and caught them. And then shook hands with his father. Guy scarcely knew the boy. Was this hard, tanned man his son?

"You look . . . so healthy! So strong!" exclaimed Clothilde. And so he did.

"Papa! We made it! With all the robes!"

Guy smiled and said nothing about that. This was the son who'd defied his express instruction, and it would be dealt with shortly. Still, he gripped his son's hand gladly—and discovered something odd.

"David . . ."

The youth held up his hand. The little finger was missing. "I donated it to the company," he quipped.

Yvonne gasped. "You were hurt!"

David peered at her. "That's for later. We've much to celebrate now."

Guy stared, amazed. His son had never addressed his mother just like that. He studied the youth while David and his sister jabbered and Yvonne touched and patted and cooed.

And then Dance and his wife bloomed into the reunion, both of them looking fine. Guy shook hands amiably with each of them, not letting the emotions of the moment override the stern realities that would darken this day later.

"I don't suppose Brokenleg's down from the Yellerstone yet," Jamie said.

"Not for another two or three weeks, Mr. Dance."

Jamie looked at Guy, an odd expression in his face.

"Let's ride back to my chambers. I'm sure the ladies will excuse us while we do business."

They all squeezed into the two seats of the chaise, and Guy set the trotters to laboring up the steep river bluff. An odd silence had settled upon them all. Good, he thought. It'd make the decision easier for them to swallow.

A few minutes later they drew up before Straus et Fils, the women heading toward the brick house, pulling sticky skirts loose as they alighted; the men into the salons of the company and then into Guy's office. He closed the door while they settled themselves.

The portraits of his father and grandfather comforted him as he swung around his desk and awaited the news. "Tell me first the figures. I want the dollars and cents first," he said.

Jamie looked to David to do that.

The young man pulled papers from his frock coat, peered at them. "Papa, is something wrong?" he asked.

"Give me the report."

Both Dance and David stared at him bewildered. Let them.

"Of buffalo robes, we traded four thousand eight hundred ninety. A hundred seventy-six splits; another fifty-seven poor or summer robes. In addition we traded a thousand fifty-seven pelts, mostly deer, elk, and beaver—with some wolf and one bearskin."

It was Guy's turn to stare.

"The May one inventory of shelved trade goods came to one thousand seven hundred in Saint Louis prices, nine or ten thousand mountain prices. We are out of many items, which I have noted here."

Guy's mind swept into the calculations. Almost five thousand robes at a wholesale price of four dollars and more; a thousand pelts . . .

"Imposts and taxes . . . a hundred fifty robes, worth six to seven hundred dollars; rifles, powder and ball, bolts of cloth and other items, including gifts to officials, probably five hundred in Saint Louis prices. We aren't sure."

"Not sure?"

"A lot was confiscated by the federal dragoons, Papa."

Guy frowned restlessly. Now his son was getting to the nub of it.

"Theft, about three hundred dollars Saint Louis."

"Theft? Theft?"

"By Comancheros. Rivals. We'll discuss that later, Papa. Do you want the rest? Storage charges, shipping charges paid the Bents? Salaries? Purchases . . . powder and ball especially? Wagons and livestock?"

"Yes, that," Guy said.

"All wagons are intact and in working condition. We left half there, returned with half. We lacked manpower and oxen or mules to bring them all. Some of our robes came here in Bent, St. Vrain wagons."

"You lost oxen?"

"Some. We've added mules. We might have brought all the wagons back, but lacked teamsters. We lost

315

several, and needed others to man the post."

"Who is manning it, David?"

"Tomás. Tomás Villanova, a trapping friend of Jamie's."

Guy frowned. Still, something in all this excited him. He began scratching figures on the foolscap, calculating, muttering. Twenty thousand for the robes; three thousand for the rest of the pelts. Against trade goods with a St. Louis price of under fifteen thousand . . . Salaries under two . . . Imposts, purchases, theft, storage, shipping by Bent, about two . . . Wagons and livestock—well, he'd planned to amortize them over several seasons. . . .

A ball of disbelief grew in him. A profit. A handsome profit—for the southern post.

"Let me see your figures, David."

Wordlessly David handed him the battered foolscap. Jamie Dance remained silent as stone, his eyes squinting hard.

Guy checked and rechecked, somehow angry because these neat columns of numbers in David's hand undermined everything, all the anguish he'd invested in his decision. These figures ruined the wisdom of his father and grandfather. These figures made him, Guy Straus, the family rebel, the winner. They demolished all the hard-won wisdom he'd mastered. Everything.

He checked his anger. "All right, Jamie. Tell me the whole story."

His partner eased a bit, something in him relaxing with Guy's softened tone of voice.

Jamie Dance talked. "Well now, we had us a time of it," he began, and droned onward through the sticky afternoon. Armijo, imprisonment, the Texas war, Colonel Cortez, Comancheros, Kiowa, Utes, *ciboleros,* murder . . . Then it was David's turn, and Guy learned, one by one, about his son's harrowing experiences. The Ute trades, the drunken Comancheros, the unruly employees who stopped work when David said they'd move the whole operation across the Arkansas, the learning of Indian tongues, the dragoons, the *cabo* Ortiz. The battle with the Comancheros for possession of Guy Straus's fortune . . .

Jamie Dance broke in. "I reckon this hyar fella saved us all," he began, and a few minutes later Guy had learned of David's one-man stand in the watchtower. And about the last horror, their capture and the mutilation of David's hand. He stared now at that hand and at the lean frame it was connected to, and his gaze slid up to the face of a man, a seasoned veteran of the robe trade. An adult capable of making sound decisions far from the counsel of his father . . . A stranger he would get to know and love and enjoy, a stranger to delight a father's heart in the brief weeks they would share now. He had a son and a partner who'd nearly laid down their lives for the company, who had lived and breathed for it, made it work somehow, beaten away predators—and triumphed.

Guy Straus found a large white handkerchief and honked into it, honked again, and left the offices a while.

It took him a few minutes to settle himself and undo the ravages that stained his cheeks. Then he returned.

"We'll plan next season's campaign now, while we wait for Brokenleg," he said. "And be thinking how you'll be squandering your bonuses."

AUTHOR'S NOTE

This story is pure fiction, as are its central characters. But it is set against real events. The Texas filibuster and Governor Armijo's response to it are history. Among the real characters in the story are Old Wolf, William Bent, Lucas Murray, Kit Carson, Uncle Dick Wooton, Bill Williams, David Mitchell, Pierre Chouteau, and Manuel Armijo.

Western Adventures
From F.M. Parker